Little Eagle

Awaken
and
Sleep

John A. Maddux

Little Eagle

John A. Maddux

BITINGDUCK PRESS
ALTADENA, CA

PUBLISHED BY BOSON BOOKS
AN IMPRINT OF BITINGDUCK PRESS
ISBN 978-1-938463-34-1
EISBN 978-1-68553-008-2
© 2022 JOHN MADDUX
ALL RIGHTS RESERVED
FOR INFORMATION CONTACT
BITINGDUCK PRESS, LLC
ALTADENA, CALIFORNIA
NOTIFICATIONS@BITINGDUCKPRESS.COM
HTTP://WWW.BITINGDUCKPRESS.COM

This novel is a fictionalized account of the working relationship between Canadian Ojibwa artist, Norval Morrisseau, and a young man he hired to be his traveling companion for six months in 1979.

The novel is loosely based on interviews conducted with the young man in the spring of 1994. I thank him for the information provided; however, the novel has veered in a different direction than the original intent which was to focus on forgery and art fraud. When I was commissioned by my then agent, Mrs. Nelson, to author the story, it was intended to focus on events provided by my interviewee but because sufficient evidence does not exist to concentrate on art fraud and Morrisseau's supposed involvement with the Canadian mob, I have altered that aspect of the story and have focused on native mysticism and spirituality.

Other than Norval Morrisseau, the names of principal characters have been changed and additional characters have been added for the purpose of plot development and fictionalization.

D EDICATED TO

Michelle Collins, Christina Kelly,
Matthew Robinson, and Carly Meyer;
dear friends who were with me at Shadle's Bar
that special summer night many years ago.
I was complaining about not knowing how to
begin this novel and they told me just to sit down
and start writing—after all I am a writer.

And to:

Andrew (Neander) Call

Who encouraged me to shake the dust off my
manuscript and finish it up. Thank you, Andrew
I owe you this novel.

I alos want to express my gratitude to Dr. Ron Hundemer,
Associate Professor of English, University of Cincinnati for taking
time to edit this manuscript. Thank you, Ron. Your help in making this
novel a reality is unsurpassed.

Words from the Mouth of Norval Morrisseau

I transmit astral plane harmonies through my brushes into the physical plane. These otherworld colors are reflected in the alphabet of nature, a grammar in which the symbols are plants, animals, birds, fishes, earth, and sky. I am merely a channel for the spirit to utilize, and it is needed by a spirit starved society.

As far as sex was concerned, I did everything under the sun. In those days I was a sexually oriented person. But things change, things develop, and everything sooner or later dies. There are some things that grow, and you constantly have to sort out your thoughts and ideas … They speak about this tortured man, me, but I am not. I've had a marvelous time when I was drinking… .

Comments About Norval Morrisseau

After a life of decades of unbridled excess with alcohol, including drinking whole cases of vanilla extract, after-shave, Listerine, perfumes, etc. as well as living for years as a Dope Fiend and Coke Head, by the mid-1990s Norval had the most destroyed body and mind of any leading Canadian figure in Canadian history.

(The Morrisseau Period 1960-1989) …Norval reached his peak and fame as a solo artist and did whatever the hell he pleased with sex, booze, and drugs, oh, and artistic expression, ending in a slump by the end of the 80s.
From: TheMorrisseauHoaxExposedBlog.com

PART ONE

In the Beginning
(My Youth in Central Ontario)

One

BEFORE I CONTINUE WITH THE present I think you should know a little about my past, and as far as the future is concerned—it can take care of itself. It's not that I'm anyone special or famous, mind you, although I've always wanted to be a star and perhaps some day, given the right breaks and circumstances, that might happen. I just think that knowing who I am, where I came from, what preceded the here and now, and what led me to Norval Morrisseau might help illuminate an otherwise confusing story.

First of all, my name is Gilbert Petén (pronounced Jho-bear Pay-ten); it is mostly French Canadian, with a pinch of Ojibwa thrown in for good measure—but much more about that later. Also, you should know that I am now a considerably older man. Not ancient, mind you, but significantly beyond the mid-point of my life, and what I am about to tell you happened a number of years ago, back in 1979 to be more accurate. I suppose some would argue that this story being nearly forty years old makes it ancient history, but I disagree. I think what took place is timeless, historical, and human. Our emotions have no time limit.

I was born in October 1954 in a small town in the Lake Nipissing area of Ontario, Canada. The name of my home town is not important, plus I have no interest in demeaning the good people who live there, so it shall go unspoken. I am the youngest of four children born to Dora and Frank Petén. My life as a child wasn't particularly eventful, but then it wasn't typically normal either... although now that I've been away from my place of birth and rearing for several years and met many people with dark secrets and skeletons in the closet, I am inclined to think that none of us is born "normal."

Mother was the central focus of our family, not the rock upon which we were built nor the harbor that kept us safe from the storm, but more like the incubus from which we could not escape. Father was always a part of our lives, at least in the sense that he and mother weren't separated or divorced, and he was in one way or another always around, but he seldom was present for our daily routines, and he never did those dad kind of things that a little boy wants. Mother, on the other hand, was present all the time—drunk though she may have been—to oversee the various demands common to being a wife and the parent of four children. Actually, mother had given birth to eight children, but two half-brothers (about whom I learned only after I was well into my adulthood) were born before mother was prepared to become a parent, and two other children were stillborn. She gave up my two half-brothers for adoption. I never knew either of them and to this day I still have not met them.

As I mentioned at the start, mother was the point of convergence for our family. Whereas father provided exceptionally well for us, mother was the one who took care of us, attended to our daily needs, and purchased the things children require while growing up. She made certain that we were well cared for, appropriately dressed, and needful of very little.

Mother was a small woman, not much more than five feet tall, petite, and very, very French. Looking back, now, I remember thinking (when I became aware of such things) how much she struck an amazing resemblance to a blonde Rita Hayworth. In her youth, mother was quite beautiful, but as she grew older and worn with the ravages of childbirth, alcohol, and time her beauty faded, like the distant memory of a spring flower.

She was a heavy smoker, an alcoholic, but (at the same time) an exceptionally hard working woman. Not only did she raise us, but during her own childhood, she had inherited the responsibility of raising her sister and brother, after grandmother had become ill (read drunk) and was unable attend to her motherly duties. Later in her life, after we all had been born, mother assumed the additional obligation of caring for father's mother and father in our home. To this day, it's hard for me to fault mother for her alcoholism or pedestrian view of the world (assuming she even had one!); she had never had the opportunity to leave the Lake Nipissing area to become educated or worldly, and could only regard life as it happened from one day to the next—the small town way! Her life consisted of nothing other than being a wife, mothering a litter of children, and living out a dreary existence to its ultimate conclusion. I am certain that had I stayed in central Canada, a similar fate would have befallen me.

Mother was good humored, enjoyed laughter (at anyone's expense), and loved to party. More than a few times I remember mother and father entertaining friends or family on a Saturday night, and mother drinking herself into a ridiculous behavior. Quite often she would take to erotically dancing around the living room, after drinking more than she could possibly handle, then tripping and stumbling about the place, embarrassing my brother and me to the point that we'd hide in our room and cry ourselves to sleep.

Mother was, without doubt, an odd mixture of dysfunctional behavior and carefully controlled propriety. On the one hand she was a giving person who regarded family and holidays as the most important parts of her life, while on the other she was distant, aloof, and refused to involve herself with our emotional wellbeing. She regarded Sunday as the day for family gathering, so late every Sunday afternoon, various members of our entirely dysfunctional family would visit to drink, argue, and condemn one another to Hell. I remember listening to the raucous behavior from up in my bedroom, wishing that they would all disappear (mother included) and leave me to the peace and quiet I thought common to every family.

I was never afraid of mother because she was not physically abusive, but neither was I comfortable around her. The main problem was that I never knew what kind of mood she might be in: Drunk, depressed, or simply contrary. She would be at once cheerful and loving, then suddenly become equally threatening and morose. Being around her, from day to day, was like playing Russian roulette since you never knew when the trigger would strike the bullet and blow out your brains!

Mother had been raised staunchly Roman Catholic and insisted that we be raised the same (father didn't seem to care one way or the other). She would trot us off to Mass on Sunday mornings, make us recite catechism and the rosary, chase us into the confessional booth on Saturday afternoon, then sneak away, take to the bottle and wash away her sins. I don't know if she was sincerely God-loving or motivated more by the guilt and fear that is the Catholic way—we never spoke about her beliefs. All I remember is mother damning the fear of the Lord into us, then slamming down another shot of rye whiskey.

Mother had a side that could be as much uncaring and discouraging as loving and hopeful. I remember once, when I announced to her at a young age that I wanted to become an actor and singer when I grew up, she just stared at me coldly and asked, "Why?"

"You know," she said, "you can't even sing a note; you don't have an ounce of talent in your body." I don't remember necessarily being crushed (though a bit hurt, perhaps), because I had grown accustomed to her insulting ways and sharp tongue. I simply regarded her comment as "being mother" and dismissed her nastiness as alcohol-induced.

I don't remember mother playing with us, asking about school work or concerns, or just sitting and talking about what was going on in our lives. As I said, she was cold, distant, and aloof.

Father, on the other hand, was all loving—although we didn't see him very often. His job with the pulp and paper mill kept him away from home during the hours of the day we would usually be available: After school, before bedtime, or on Saturdays. He was a hard working man who was a hard, working man! That's all he did—work! But when he did get home late at night, after we were all tucked soundly in bed, he would visit our rooms, tell us a story, and pull some sort of compliment or a funny anecdote from his bag of love. I always looked forward to those times.

Father was not a big man, barely 5'10", but large-boned and handsome. He was the sole provider for the family and he accomplished his task extremely well. We never wanted for anything. Whatever mother purchased for us, father had provided through his labor.

The only activities father did allow himself to enjoy, other than working, were drinking with his friends (although he was always home for dinner whenever he didn't have to work) and ice hockey. He lived and died for hockey and his beloved Montreal Canadiens. One of my fondest memories of father is on those cold winter nights when he'd sit in front of the fireplace—radio to his ear, beer in his hand—listening to the Canadiens' hockey games. I could always tell whether they had won or lost because of father's quiet cursing or beaming smile. But even then—with hockey, radio and beer—he always had time for us when we came to him demanding that he give us whatever mother wouldn't (usually money to waste with our friends). He was, without doubt, a push-over.

Father was the complete opposite of mother. He wasn't an alcoholic, although he did enjoy a few drinks now and then. Father was loving and close, and encouraged us in whatever might be our activity of the moment. I remember, not long after mother had told me that I had no talent for singing (I had gone to father with feigned sadness), he made it a point to come to my room every night for at least a week to tell me that I was a much better singer than those "sour notes" he had heard on the radio or the squawking (as he called it) in the church choir.

I wish father had been home more often. He was one of the few pleasant memories of my childhood, but he had to work; times were tough, and he had a wife, four children, a car, a snowmobile, a house and a cottage on Lake Tomiko to bear the expenses for.

Mother eventually died just a few years ago from Lou Gehrig's Disease. But even given her fluctuating temperament, it was a sad day when she died. I did love her and there were at least a few times when I had felt close to her, but when I recall my childhood, I think mostly of father's love and mother's desperate, pathetic life.

I have often wondered why they stayed together. I suppose they did love each other in their own peculiar way, but I never heard words of love exchanged between them nor saw any evidence of caring. Maybe it was because of mother's harsh Catholicism that forbade divorce. Perhaps it was due to the reality that without father providing for us all, mother and we couldn't possibly have survived. But as I have grown older and removed from my childhood by distance, time, and the realization that most of us try to do our best with our limited resources, I can't blame either one of them for their flaws: Mother for her distance and drinking and father for his absence. They did the best they could given the circumstances, and I am not certain that I would have done any better were the roles reversed.

I have two sisters, Mary Anne and Paula, and a brother, Jonathon, who never really played a significant role in my adolescence. Mary Anne and Paula are much older than I and were always occupied with their own issues and problems and Jonathon, although just a year older, was more concerned about how his friends would regard him if he hung around with me, or if he stuck up for me in a fight. Jonathon has always been more acutely focused on how he appears to other people!

My sisters, brother, and I became closer later in life, after we had all grown into adulthood. I see them fairly often, and we have a great deal of fun with each other and a certain amount of respect for one another, but in truth, I was born the son of an alcoholic mother and a workaholic father and lived in the shadows and with the ghosts of two sisters and a brother. It wasn't much for family togetherness.

And so it was mother, father, two sisters, and a brother—and central Ontario. Not much to get started with in life, but I suppose more than many children have. When I think back to those times not more than a few years past, they seem farther distant in my memory than they really are, and almost like they didn't really happen to me. Was I ever that young? Were things as bad as I remember them to be? Is there anything I can carry into the future from my years in Ontario, save the pain and anguish of childhood? I suppose only time will tell; I certainly cannot at this point. What came before made me what I am today, and what I am today will create that which I will become tomorrow. And it continues ad infinitum, ad nauseam.

And by the way, mother, I do miss you, and I did ever tell you that I love you?

Two

HATED GROWING UP IN MY out-of-the-way home town. It was a dreary little place that seemed to be located somewhere as far away from any civilized place as you could imagine. It was cold and nasty in the winter, cool and boring in the summer, and not much else during the autumn or spring. It was a working town of laborers and hard drinkers and had no attractions with which to entice visitors. Unlike many picturesque Canadian towns, it drew few American vacationers during the summer holidays and even fewer during winter. It was small. Pedestrian. Isolated. Dead.

The only thing noteworthy about my home town was that it seemed that about half the male population was gay—or at least bisexual, or curious, or horny for anything that provided lascivious relief (and when I say half the male population I mean adults as well as boys). Of course, I'm sure that half the male population wasn't really gay, but it surely seemed that way. Five members of my family were gay, including two uncles, a cousin, my brother, and me. All of my close friends were at least bisexual, and a disproportionate number of the town's leading figures were enamored by members of the same sex, or at least they certainly gave that impression by scurrying off to Sudbury or North Bay on the weekends (rumor had it) to find relief in the arms of other men. Of course, I speak as though I experienced much of the homosexuality that went on in town, but I didn't. Not because I wasn't interested, but rather because I was greatly unpopular with the boys my age who might be interested. I was timid and shy, and wasn't about to involve myself with one of the older drunkards in town who definitely were interested—I had experienced their advances on several occasions. But my sexuality is another story and one not worth detailing at this point, although it did play a major role in my socialization and development of self-confidence later in my youth.

I don't know why the boys at school regarded me with such displeasure. I don't remember doing anything that might have incited the wrath of my peers, but I was, in a phrase, the target of everyone's hatred.

Just about everything I remember about growing up in Ontario is unpleasant. I was physically abused by most of the children my age and older. I was the butt of every joke that circulated around Assumption Elementary School. I was taunted, chased, beaten, and ridiculed. In short, my life in that godforsaken shithole of a town was little more than a living Hell on Earth.

Perhaps most of my problems stemmed from my being physically underdeveloped and effeminate, and thus a perfect target for the boys who were outwardly manly, but who liked to experiment with one another behind closed doors and dared not let anyone know about their libidinous desires. They needed a scapegoat to make themselves feel more 'normal.'

Physically, I was nearly a foot smaller than the other boys my age, and was so thin that were a strong wind to come up, I would have been blown away. My hair was long and blonde, my face beautifully angelic. And my muscles (if you could call the pitiful knots on my arms and chest muscles) were no more developed than those of the weakest girl in school. And I looked much younger than I was. When I was ten, I looked seven, at fourteen, barely ten, and at eighteen, scarcely a teenager. I wasn't particularly athletic, in fact not so at all, so I wasn't given to participating in the typical boyhood sports and shenanigans that punctuate adolescence. In other words, I was considered the town sissy despite my good humor and (I think) friendly demeanor.

The abuse started in grade one, when I was six years old. I remember a little girl (her name escapes me now) passing me a note upon which she had scribbled, "I love you. You're cute." I didn't know what to do. At six I was hardly ready for the kind of attention she revealed, and I hadn't yet begun thinking about things having to do with being 'cute.' Unfortunately for the two of us, I didn't have time to consider my reaction very long. Our teacher saw the note being passed, called me up to her desk, grabbed the secret from my hand, and read it aloud to the class. Our embarrassment was total. All the children laughed and pointed at us, reducing the little red headed girl to tears and me into a quivering ninny. At recess, the teacher made the little girl stay behind while the rest of us were excused to go out and play.

I crept around to the windows that were no higher than my waist and listened and watched as the teacher scolded my suitor, then erased the chalkboard with the little girl's beautiful long red hair. As I watched in terror, several of my classmates sneaked up behind me and started chasing me across the playground, taunting me and calling me names like lover boy. Of course, the episode was probably more traumatic for the little red-haired girl, but for me, it signaled the beginning of ten years of harassment and abuse.

More times than just that one episode with the red-headed girl shaped the pattern of my youth. From that day on, I was routinely chased, cursed, taunted, slapped, kicked, and beaten up by the boys at my school. It got so bad that when I was eight, I couldn't even leave my house to go to the store without having to check behind every bush while hoping there wouldn't be an assailant waiting to attack. When I was nine, I was stripped in the boy's bathroom and forced to wear a dress to class—even my teacher got a laugh out of that one. When I was twelve, I was threatened with being butt-fucked into doing a classmate's math homework. Math was not my best subject, but one that I quickly learned because of the threat. At fourteen, I was chased from a school dance and pushed down a steep bank of mud and slush, right into a swampy gully, ruining the new suit mother had just bought me. At fifteen, some bullies stole my clothes during gym class and I was forced to walk to the principal's office to call home, wearing nothing by my briefs and an embarrassment-caused erection. I can still remember everyone pointing and laughing at my hands-covered crotch and making comments like "Gilbert's got a boner for Mr. Alison."

On more than a few occasions, I was the butt of practical jokes that involved, among other things, opening a box—ostensibly a birthday present—only to discover it was filled with newly hatched snakes, being stranded for three hours in a treehouse after everyone had left and had taken the ladder with them, as well as being pushed out into the lake in a canoe without a paddle or other means of returning to shore.

And I had no one to whom to turn. Mother was usually drunk and too distant to listen to what she considered my childish woes. Father was always at work. Jonathon, my brother, though he sympathized with my plight, kept a safe distance for fear that he would incur the same treatment as I were he to attempt to protect me. And my sisters were considerably older and involved with their own lives. One time I did go to the priest at our church, hoping he could help, but was scared away from clerical intervention after he invited me back to the parish house for cookies, then returned from the kitchen sporting an obvious erection beneath his hassock and asking me if I had ever had a full-body back rub with hot oils. Although I was still young, I was old enough to regard his importunity as threatening and out of order.

The summer before I was to enter the seventh grade, we moved from one side of town to the other and I was enrolled in a new school, Saint Francis Academy, which I hoped would bring about a new beginning. It was an all-male school, which by that time was much to my liking since I had discovered my emerging gay identity. Unfortunately, despite the new location and the new school, things didn't change. The beatings and taunting continued. I don't know why I remained the focus of hostility, other than because, as I was told by one of my more sympathetic classmates, I sent out the wrong signals—what ever that meant. It wasn't like I was cruising the halls or eyeballing the guys! I guess it was the same reason I had been teased at Assumption School: I was effeminate and, now that we had entered the age of sexual awareness, was considered a threat by the closet-case gays.

I never was challenged, one on one, by any of the boys at school. Instead, they always attacked in groups of two or three. I suppose there is comfort and false bravado in numbers. One time, after I had endured an unusually vicious attack, wherein I had been stripped naked again (in front of a group of girls, no less), pushed into a snowbank and beaten, I went to my mother with my complaints. Her response was one of lack of interest and characteristically mother: "Go to your grandmother's," she directed. "You'll be safe there."

Safe my ass, I dreaded going to grandmother's! Nevertheless, because mother was on one of her weeklong binges, and I had nowhere else to go for solace, I went to grandmother's house—hardly a viable solution to an untenable situation.

Grandma was an alcoholic and a whore, I am sorry to say. She had no means of support, no money, no husband, and no sense of self-respect or pride. She regularly entertained a menagerie of gentlemen friends without embarrassment, and despite being visited by her grandchildren she wasn't especially shy about what she was doing, or with whom she was doing it! On that one particular day, her current man-of-the-month began teasing me while grandmother was out of the room.

"How old are you, honey?" he quizzed, reaching over and putting his hand on my knee.

I didn't answer. I was as much scared as I was disgusted.

"You're so cute. How old are you?" he asked again, moving his large, ugly hand from my knee to my crotch. "I'll bet you're old enough to be getting pubic hair around your wiener. Can I see it what it looks like?"

Despite my gay sexuality I ran from the house, disgusted with the thought of that ugly old man groping at my crotch and making passes at me. I escaped but ran straight into the arms of three classmates who evidently had followed me to grandmother's and had seen everything through the living room window. I never did discover why they had followed me in the first place. Once again, I was punched, kicked, and stomped. As I said earlier, given the situation at grandmother's her house was not much respite from my world of abuse.

I never told mother about the incident. I don't think she would have believed me, and besides, I wasn't about to tell mother that a man had been touching my penis—even though only through my pants—and had given me a semi-hardon. This is not exactly the kind of thing you talk to your mom about when you're thirteen. I didn't forget it though and didn't return to Grandmother's alone, ever again!

Throughout the remainder of high school, the abuse continued. I was attacked on my way to and from school. Chased by thugs whenever I went out to play. Beaten, even at school dances and church activities. Taunted in front of teachers. Embarrassed in front of friends. Humiliated in front of my brother. This was a childhood I would rather forget and there are only a few fond memories of those days. It was absolute Hell, and I cursed the very day I had sprung from my mother's womb: Born to an alcoholic, uncaring mother; born to a father who loved, but was never at home; born to a brother who ignored my problems for fear of reprisal; born to sisters older and distant, and born effeminate, non-athletic, and gay! There was no one to talk with. No place to find sanctuary. No place to go…

…except to the family cottage: Our summer-time retreat away from home.

Three

MY PARENTS OWNED A COTTAGE about thirty minutes from where we lived. We would go there in the summer and stay for two and a half months. It was the one place I could go where I could avoid the harassment and abuse of my classmates and peers. It was a haven away from school and a paradise where I could walk freely in the woods without the fear of being attacked. It was a dreamscape where I controlled the elements of both my life and of nature.

But it was not without its nightmares.

Although I did escape the daily routine of being chased and abused by my classmates, our cottage created a whole new set of problems with which I simply could not deal. As far as the cottage and the location were concerned, I couldn't have asked for more. There was a small lake, not more than several hundred feet from our cabin, and we were surrounded on all sides by woods, wild animals, and nature. A narrow river wound down the hillside near our cabin and emptied into the lake. The entire area was peaceful, relaxing, and safe.

Safe, that is, until our relatives arrived, and then all hell broke loose. My parents, especially mother, enjoyed entertaining at home and they doubly enjoyed entertaining at the cottage. We'd have a steady stream of uncles, aunts, and cousins visiting on the weekends. Most of them I couldn't stand, although they were entertaining at times, at least until they got so drunk they made complete fools of themselves, but one cousin, in particular, was OK—Richard—who introduced me in the summer of my fourteenth year to the concept of oral sex. Thank you, Ricky, I shall never forget!

Ricky only came to our cottage that one summer (I think he later was in trouble with the law for breaking into cars or something like that). We lost contact, as cousins who live in different towns are apt to do, and I was seldom informed as to the happenings of various family members. I was told, long after his problems had come to a head, that he had been sent away to what was then called reform school, but that one summer visit, in 1966, was enough to provide for a lifetime. And it happened so innocently.

We had gone to bed one night, with Ricky and me sharing a double, when he started talking about sex and boners and masturbating. He asked me if I had ever masturbated and I told him, "Of course, all the time, don't you?" It was a big lie. I had tried doing it once but found the experience awkward and shameful and stopped myself just before ejaculation because of the guilt. Mother had done quite well instilling the fear of the Lord in us. I was certain I would burn in Hell for even thinking about wanking it, let alone doing it. Besides, I didn't want to go blind or grow hair on my knuckles or end up insane!

After I told him yes, and asked him if he did too (to which he answered yes and made it sound like he had been doing so since he was three!) he suggested that we watch each other masturbate. Needless to say, I was excited, interested, thrilled, agreeable, and—scared to death. God, I knew I'd be damned for eternity if I did anything like that. By myself was bad enough, but with another boy, that was tantamount to eternal damnation! Of course, at the same time my adolescent hormones were circulating about my body, totally out of control, and I became erect immediately and put my hand in a place where I was certain it didn't belong. Ricky did the same to himself, and before long the sheets were down to our ankles and our hands were moving rapidly in a blur of fingers and flesh. I was about ready to complete the task at hand (pardon my horrible pun), when Ricky suddenly leaned over and replaced my hand with his mouth. That was all I needed. I was done immediately and Ricky soon followed and even though I was still convinced that I had just sealed my eternal fate of damnation, I loved it! It was the absolute opposite of the beatings I had been experiencing all my life. This was something that actually brought pleasure!

We said nothing more to each other that night just rolled over and fell asleep. We didn't even mention it the next day. We both acted a little distant from one another. Our parents must have noticed our awkwardness because they asked if we'd had a fight. Of course, we both said no, everything was fine, but I was sure that somehow they knew what had happened. My parents' interest in Ricky's and my well-being seemed unusual for their normally distant concerns with my affairs and it scared me enough that I resolved, that day, not to do anything ever again like what had happened the night before. And I was strong in my resolve not to repeat the sinful performance until later that night, and the next, when Ricky and I, twice again, indulged our curiosity. Ricky could be exceptionally enticing, and I frighteningly willing!

Ricky and his family went home on Monday morning, never to return to the cottage again. In fact, I never saw Ricky after those three days of discovery, that one weekend of typical boyhood experimentation (regardless of what people might say, heterosexual boys mess around too!). My sin cemented what I had been believing about myself for several years and started me on a slow evolution towards my sexual awakening. It's funny how a seemingly insignificant event can stick in your memory like it just happened yesterday, but that one certainly did, and I will never forget Ricky for introducing me to what was eventually to become my reality and my weakness—sex that is, not being gay.

Mother was with us at the cottage the whole summer, drunk and distant as usual, but father could only come on weekends, late at night after we were in bed, or on holidays when he vacationed from the mill. Because his presence was limited mostly to the weekends, the family parties were always on Saturday.

For the most part, our times at the cottage were fun. We would have wiener roasts over an open fire, shoot off dazzlers and sparklers, swim in the lake, and play in the woods. My brother and I got along splendidly at the cottage. He would play whatever games I suggested and treated me not only as a brother but also as an equal since he was, after all, only one year older than I. Sometimes we were permitted to invite a friend to visit for several days. Jonathon usually invited one of the guys from school who was friendlier to me than most, and I always invited my best friend, Patrick. The times with Jonathon and Patrick are some of the best memories I have of growing up in the Lake Nipissing area. We played together, hiked through the woods, swam in the lake, and told ghost stories around the fire at night. And, since Patrick and I had earlier discovered our crazy little secret of liking other guys, we engaged in tantalizing games of I'll blow you if you blow me! It was the kind of childhood I wanted…the kind of which dreams are made. Unfortunately, I can't say the same about poor Patrick's youth.

Patrick came from an even more dysfunctional family than I did. When he was eighteen his parents committed him to a mental institution for being homosexual. The very thought of Patrick being imprisoned because of loving men shattered my belief in humanity and frightened the hell out of me. My god, were my parents to find out the same about me, I could be shuttered away like my best friend. And even though the thought of being put in a sanitarium scared me to death, I resolved that Patrick could not and would not be forgotten, so I initiated my first brazen attempt at heroism. I waltzed into the hospital one day, told the attendant that I was his brother, checked him out and took him home to stay at our place. When his parents discovered my valiant attempt at playing Superman, they were madder than hell and threatened to have both of us arrested.

"For what?" I asked. I told them he was an adult and could make decisions on his own. Fortunately, none of our parents linked Patrick's homosexuality with me. As far as they knew, I was simply acting on behalf of my best buddy.

Patrick left for parts unknown not long after the hospital incident and fell into a life of sex, drugs, and booze and never did recover from the physical and mental abuse he had experienced from his family. A couple of years later, while Patrick was home for a visit, his father took a rifle to the whole family—mother, sisters, brother, Patrick, and himself—all of them blown away in an uncertain moment of anger and hysteria. I can only imagine the horror Patrick witnessed as he saw his entire family being slaughtered right before his eyes, and then of course, him. Did he feel anything? Did he have time to scream or yell? Was he able to comprehend what was happening? Or was it over so quickly that he never felt a thing? God, I hope the latter is true. I can't even begin to process the terror he must have felt.

I'll never forget Patrick. I wish I could have done more to help him, but damn, it was all I could do to help myself back in those days.

For every good there is a bad; for every up, a down; for each positive, a negative, and the cottage—my haven of protection and safety—proved no different.

Since my parents liked to entertain frequently, but were not especially endeared to friends, most of our visitors were members of my dysfunctional family. My father's brother, Uncle Ernie often came to visit—he, too, was an alcoholic. My father's other brother, Uncle Ferdinand, also came to the cottage—another alcoholic. My mother's brother, TJ, visited quite a lot—he was a pathological liar, a child molester, and a drunk. Grandmother came occasionally with her man-of-the-month—two more alcoholics to add to the fray. And of course, there was mother, drunk almost constantly, and father, who drank more at the cottage than at home. At times I began to wonder who in my family wasn't an alcoholic. Alcoholism must have been genetically coded in my family!

Generally, when family came to visit, our evenings ended up with Jonathon and me inside the cottage, in bed, and the adults sitting around the campfire drinking, swearing, arguing, and screaming at each other as though the first order of business was to hate. It was neither a pleasant situation to behold nor comforting to hear.

Two episodes are especially bothersome and I cannot forget either one.

On one occasion, my Uncle Ferdinand, who later died of alcoholism, was up visiting one weekend with his wife, Nadine. The evening began as usual. Wieners and hamburgers cooked over the camp fire, a modicum of pleasant conversation about work, neighbors, and typical town gossip, some joking and a smattering of laugher, and lots and lots of liquor. Near the end of the evening, as it grew late and the adults grew drunker, my Uncle Ferdinand became increasingly hostile and abusive towards his wife. They were arguing about something unimportant, as was the content of most of the fights at the cottage, when suddenly Ferdinand grabbed an ax, wielded it above his head like a madman straight out of a Steven King novel, and began racing around the fire chasing Aunt Nadine and shouting, "You cock-sucking son-of-a-bitch. Get over here and take your medicine like the whore you are. If you don't do what I say, I catch you and kill your goddamn ass." Whatever had provoked Uncle Ferdinand's outburst was beyond me. Until he grabbed the ax, the evening seemed to be progressing normally—make that "normally" for a group of angry drunks!

Usually mother would react in horror to such language. Even though she was a drunk, she maintained a strict discipline about nasty language and taking the Lord's name in vain. And generally father would intervene and stop such an ugly display, but neither did anything that night, save laugh at Uncle Ferdinand and bet on who would survive—Ferdinand or Nadine. I don't know what Jonathon thought of the whole drunken charade being played out on our cottage lawn because he had fallen asleep, but I was horrified and believed that Ferdinand would end up either killing Aunt Nadine or stumbling in his alcoholic stupor and falling upon the ax, ending his own life in a melodramatic and ironic way. I was rooting for the latter. What is especially odd about the situation is that I don't remember the outcome, obviously neither of them was murdered, but how the predicament was resolved has been lost to history.

Another time when Uncle Ferdinand was visiting, our dog, Misfit, had just given birth to a litter of five puppies. Father explained that we couldn't keep the puppies because there wasn't room in our house and they would cost too much to feed and care for. He promised that he would take them to town after they had been weaned and find homes for each one of them. There was no reason for me not to believe father. He was as much a lover of animals as was I, and he had an especially soft heart for our old mutt.

Uncle Ferdinand had a different idea of what to do with the puppies.

He was drunk, again, and spied a four-inch nail protruding from the outside wall of the woodshed near the cottage. Whatever possessed him to do what he did I'll never figure out, but he picked up the puppies, one by one, and hurled them against the wall, seeing if he could catch any of them on the nail. Luckily, he was so drunk he wasn't successful with his perverted game, and the puppies, though dazed and bruised, survived.

What horrified me as much as Uncle Ferdinand's vile attempt at entertainment, was father's reaction—he merely stood there watching, and laughing, as Uncle Ferdinand picked up each puppy and slammed it against the wall. He didn't even attempt to intervene. He was as drunk as Uncle Ferdinand, and the two of them stood there howling with laughter as though seriously enjoying their game of pin the puppy on the nail.

I have never forgiven father for his behavior and lack of action that night, and even though I still love him as much as I ever did, I know I lost a great deal of respect for him with that one incident.

That was our cottage. A haven, a holiday, and an escape. I had learned a great deal there about myself and about my family, and I had seen too many things I didn't want to see. I will never forget Ricky, or Patrick, or the fun that Jonathon and I had and I will long remember the fights, the drinking, and the puppies. For me, the cottage was a place that afforded me the one refuse in a childhood of torment. It was the one place I could go to find peace and protection from the beatings and abuse back home, at least until my relatives came to visit, and then it became its own hell. Even with my cabin sanctuary, I was growing weary of not having any place to go.

Four

B Y THE TIME I WAS seventeen, my sisters and brother had left home. Mary Anne and Paula had been gone for a couple of years—both being considerably older than me and getting on with their own lives—and Jonathon had left after graduating high school and enrolling in college.

I was beginning to grow some, but I still looked five or six years younger than my age. I spent a great deal of time alone—as usual—but was becoming less a target for my classmates; they were becoming more interested in older boy things: sports, cars, drinking, girls—and in many cases other boys—but I still didn't have many friends. Dennis and Marcel were the exception. I had known D and M since grade school, and although we had never been necessarily close, neither of them had joined in the game of "let's beat up Gilbert." When we entered high school we discovered that we shared similar interests: The theater, singing, writing, and guys! Both of them were gay, so we naturally gravitated towards one another. After a while, once we had discovered the other's sexuality, we began experimenting, together, nothing serious, hardly even adventurous, mostly the curiosity kind of sex that even straight boys experiment with. But there was nothing romantic; we were friends, soulmates as we used to call it, and by the summer of my fourth year in high school, we had just about exhausted what ever sexual interest we had in each other and were curious about other things—other men, to be more exact! That's when we discovered Sudbury and North Bay.

Another friend of ours, William, peripheral to our circle of sexual intimacy but nonetheless friendly, told us about how he'd go to Sudbury or North Bay on the weekends and cruise the gay bars. Of course, I use the term "gay bars" loosely. Only two places welcomed gays, but they hardly advertised as gay back then. Doing so would be tantamount to financial and legal suicide. Everyone who knew about the two bars simply referred to the them as "those open places."

William said it was easy cruising the bars, and we'd have no trouble scoring because we'd be the 'new meat' on the block (and being young didn't hurt either). This sounded exciting. We had grown bored with each other and weren't about to cruise around home. There weren't any gay-friendly bars—the town was too small, everyone knew what everybody else was doing, and I wasn't about to give my classmates additional information with which to intensify their abuse towards me. We had been lucky that our three-way 'get-togethers' had remained secret. We trusted each other and no one else had been privy to our sexual escapades, so we were ready to try out the rest of the world, or at least our part of Ontario, to begin with.

I was not yet old enough to drive, but Dennis and William were, so on weekends we'd motor to either Sudbury or North Bay to find bars, booze, and guys. I was beginning to drink for the first time in my life, imitation being the best compliment (my family had been excellent teachers). Sudbury and North Bay were about equally distant away, and it usually took about thirty minutes to get to either one. It was well worth the drive.

I was seventeen, but looked fifteen, and for the first time in my life, my appearance became a positive rather than a negative. I had long blonde hair, was still quite thin, but had begun to fill out and reveal those physical characteristics of which men in bars are often interested. Most of the men I met were attracted by my boyish looks, so I had no trouble finding what I was searching for!

Since I was only seventeen, I had to sneak into the bars with a fake identification card. Our favorite place was the Penny Pincher's Motel & Bar, which had a bar and dance floor and no doorman checking IDs. There were always plenty of men to choose from, and I had no problem zeroing in on the ones I wanted. Our weekend excursions to Penny Pincher's became so routine that we became well known to the regular customers and to the bartenders. I was a favorite of Joe, one of the bartenders at the front bar. He bought all my drinks, hoping that I might return the favor in a more direct way, which I did. Besides Joe, I never lacked for conversation with the hottest looking guys. For the first time in my life I was feeling wanted, for all the wrong reasons I might add, but at that point I could have cared less. I had finally found a place where I felt at home and not like a punching bag waiting to be creased.

It was at Penny Pincher's where I met Russ LeBrun, my first true love, although "true love" might be a bit overly-stated. But he was at least an exciting diversion and a tremendous boost for my developing confidence. He was tall, dark, and handsome. Typical! He looked like a model right out of the pages of a magazine: Six feet tall, long shiny black hair, strong muscles and chest, and eyes that made Ricky Nelson's pale in comparison (Ricky Nelson, the American TV star, was my boyhood crush). There wasn't a thing about Russ that wasn't beautiful. His face was strong and sensitive and when he held me, his arms embraced me with a security I had never before experienced. When he spoke, I listened in rapture. When he laughed, I heard the angels sing. And when he touched me, it felt as though I was being touched by the hand of god.

He picked me up one Saturday night as the bar was ready to close and we were both drunk beyond immediate repair. At first, I assumed this was to be just another one nightstand with a hunk that everyone in the bar had been cruising, and with whom I was about to score, but to my surprise we began a romantic and physical relationship that lasted for three months. I was enjoying the attention I was getting from Russ. He was falling in love but never figured out that I was fucking other guys while still seeing him.

We'd meet on weekends and spend our time at the motel drinking, loving, laughing and having sex. I was satisfied with the relationship remaining sexual. I was too young to fall in love and was enjoying myself far too much to think about anything more serious than partying. But Russ was ready for something more. He showered me with gifts and lavish dinners and paid my expenses wherever we went. I couldn't have asked for more in a boyfriend. Russ fulfilled every requirement that I demanded at my young age.

But as was the case with everything else in my young life, the relationship with Russ soured too.

One day when I returned home from school after several weeks into our relationship, I discovered mother sitting on the couch, crying. After calming her and finally convincing her to tell me what was wrong, she pointed at a bouquet of flowers that had been delivered and said they were addressed to her. They were actually for me from Russ, but I couldn't tell her as much. There was no note with the flowers, she didn't know who they were from, and father had accused her of having an affair behind his back. Naturally the bouquet caused a huge row at home: Mother drinking, father yelling, and both of them threatening each other with violence and divorce. I left, figuring they could work it out for themselves. Besides, I reasoned, they had put me through hell for seventeen years, so my ignoring the situation was just a small pay back for their years of neglect.

What concerned me more than my mother's reaction and my parents' fighting was Russ sending flowers to my home, without my permission, thinking I'd be impressed or touched by his display of sentiment. I wasn't. I was still in the closet and not about to address the situation with mother and father or any other flunky for that matter! The minute I saw the flowers in mother's house, I immediately realized that the blossom of our relationship had begun to wilt. Russ had taken the relationship thing too far.

But, the problems with Russ didn't stop there. We began fighting more often, he'd pick at everything I said or did and he became jealous if I'd ever look at another man. Fortunately, at that point, he wasn't aware of my involvement with other guys beyond me simply looking, and he'd constantly remind me of what he'd done for me, how much he was spending on me, and that I needed him! He was given to extreme mood swings and emotion. One minute he would be the most loving and giving person I had ever known, but the next, he would become angry, bitter, and verbally abusive. His whole attitude was wearing thin, but I liked the regular sex—like I said, he was hot. Given the quick deterioration of our relationship things were going downhill fast and I had no idea of how to stop a snowball once it had begun rolling. I was new to the gay scene, and even though I knew how to get what I wanted, I didn't know how to rid myself of what I didn't.

One night soon after the flowers incident, on the way home from one of the few weekends we had which hadn't been ruined by his jealously or moodiness, Russ pulled off the side of the road along a deserted stretch of highway, stopped the car, and just sat in silence for several minutes. I didn't know what was up, so I sat in silence too but sensed the volcano ready to erupt.

Suddenly, without any warning, Russ looked me square in the eyes, said that he loved me, and wanted to spend the rest of his life with me. "Do you love me?" he asked.

I didn't respond, right away. I was in disbelief. His vow of undying love had come out of nowhere.

"Do you love me, Gilbert?" he asked again.

I couldn't help it, and I didn't mean to hurt his feelings, but I started laughing; I couldn't take his pledge seriously. I was only seventeen and didn't know what love meant, let alone want to commit myself to one man for the rest of my life. I was having too much fun cruising and meeting other guys.

"What the hell are you laughing about?" he admonished. "Is something funny? I don't think telling you that I love and want to spend my life with you is especially hilarious!"

No, I knew that what he had said wasn't funny, but I couldn't help but laugh, and the more he kept talking about how much in love with me he was and how he wanted to spend his mornings and afternoons and evenings with me until the "sun doesn't shine anymore" (his syrup, not mine), the more ludicrous the situation became. I also knew by the tone of his voice that his mood was about to swing again. He was getting angry and another one of his increasingly famous emotional explosions was imminent! He clenched his fists, tightened his lips, and his eyes glazed over with a look that I had learned to fear whenever witnessing my relatives' patented attacks on each other.

"I'm sorry, Russ," I responded, laughing harder as I spoke, "but no, I'm not in love with you. I'm seventeen, not twenty-seven. I don't even know how to love, let alone commit to one man for the rest of my life. Can't we just keep things they way they are?"

Obviously, Russ didn't agree with my sentiments because no sooner had I finished my comments, then he glared at me as though I had betrayed him and everything he had hoped for, started the ignition, floored the accelerator, and the car lurched forward, gaining speed instantly: 30 miles per hour...40 miles per hour...50...60...70!

My laughing stopped as the car careened left, then right, onto the shoulder and off, swerving across the median then back to its proper lane, but I couldn't help but consider the whole episode absurd. He was 23, and I was 17. I hadn't thought about love. I wasn't interested in love. I didn't know what the hell it was. All I knew was that I like cruising the bars and just wanted to have fun. After a childhood of being abused by what seemed like everyone with whom I had come in contact and learning not to trust anyone, I wasn't interested in tying myself down to one man. Russ had fallen too deeply, too quickly, and was trying to pull me in with him—another person's attempt at manipulation.

The car raced around the curves at a dangerous speed and barely missed sideswiping a guardrail on the right and an oncoming truck on the left. By that time, my laughter had stopped and I was getting angry and frightened. I hated emotional displays like Russ was exhibiting but had never retaliated with one of my own. Maybe it was time I did.

Russ' erratic driving continued as the car raced everywhere except where it should have been. Suddenly I shouted, "Fine, go ahead and kill us both, but it won't change a thing. You'll be dead, I'll be dead, we'll both be dead, and I STILL WON'T LOVE YOU! Damn you, Russ. Stop the car and let me out of here!"

My outburst, however, wasn't what relieved the situation—it was the tree.

❈❈❈❈❈❈❈❈❈❈❈❈

I AWOKE AMONG SHATTERED GLASS, twisted metal, tree parts poking in through the windows, and blood. I could feel blood streaming down the right side of my head and filling my open mouth. Even with this, I assumed I was OK. Apparently no broken bones or severed limbs—then I thought about Russ. When I looked to where he had been sitting behind the steering wheel, I vomited. A huge tree limb was protruding through the windshield and plunged into the back of the driver's seat. Leaves and glass and pieces of metal and plastic were covering the seat and, in the darkness, I thought I could make out the shadowy figure of Russ, impaled by an ancient oak and dead! I knew immediately that Russ's death would be the ultimate punishment for my first, and only, outburst of anger—I had killed him!

My heart was pounding. I was sweating, bloody, and hurting, and even though it was a chilly evening, I felt burning hot. All the memories of being harassed and beaten, of my parents drinking and my relatives fighting, of Penny Pincher's and the Nickel Range Motel, and cruising and guys and sex and Russ came flooding back in one horrible moment of guilt and reproach. This was it, I thought, God was finally punishing me, just like the Church had said He would. I was the good Catholic boy gone bad, a once-upon-a-time Christian thrown to the lions. I was being punished for my sins, and I was either going to die and go straight to Hell or be arrested for having sex with Russ then killing him because I didn't love him. I resolved never to have sex again—especially with a man—to stop drinking and to devote my life to more Godly things.

Then I heard him. His weakened voice penetrated through the dark.

"Gilbert, Gilbert, are you O.K.? Can you hear me? Answer me. Are you dead?

He was alive; he hadn't been impaled by the oak. Somehow, he had been miraculously thrown from the car seconds before the tree limb penetrated its interior. He was fine, hardly even a cut or a bruise, just a few abrasions on his arms and legs where he had bounced on the pavement after being jettisoned from the automobile. As it turned out, I was all right as well, with no serious injuries and like Russ, just a few minor cuts and abrasions. The blood that had been flowing down the side of my head was nothing more than the blood of my guilt! As far as physical injury, we had been damn lucky!

About twenty minutes after the accident, a car came by, stopped, gathered us up, and drove us to a nearby hospital. We never did call the police; Russ had the car towed to a repair shop the next day and fortunately for us, the driver of the car that stopped was a local area husband who had been out scoring with eighteen-year old boys. He wasn't about to snitch on us, since if he did he would implicate himself in own his debauchery.

My parents picked us up at the hospital, not knowing who Russ was, other than a friend. They didn't know how or why the accident had happened. They didn't ask where we had been or what we had been doing. They asked nothing and we offered nothing. My dad graciously drove Russ home to his house, then returned to ours. I don't know if it was because of the trauma of the car wreck or the conversation that had preceded it, but Russ and I did not speak on the way to his house.

I never heard from Russ again.

★★★★★★★★★★★★

I RECEIVED A PHONE CALL several days later while I was at a friend's house. It was my friend Dennis telling me to come home immediately. He had dropped over to see me and discovered mother crying hysterically and drinking more than he'd ever seen her drink. I rushed home, all the way wondering what tragedy had befallen our family: Had father been killed at work, had Jonathon been injured in an accident, had something horrible happened to Mary Anne or Paula? Had Uncle Ferdinand been killed by his wife—well, that would have been good news!

When I finally got home, Dennis was gone and mother was prone on the sofa, a drink in one hand a cigarette in the other. She launched into me the second I entered the room.

"Are you queer, Gilbert? Dennis said you are homosexual and have been having an affair with an older man from North Bay. Is it that man from the accident? What's going on? Are you queer, Gilbert? I don't think I can deal with this."

All I could do was deny. "Homosexual, God, of course not," I lied to her. "What a dumb thing for Dennis to say, and I don't know anything about some guy from North Bay. The man from the accident was a substitute teacher from school. We were coming home from a fund-raiser for cancer." Sometimes I surprise myself with my ability to lie on such short notice.

My mind was spinning. Why would Dennis say such a thing, I wondered? He had been one of my two best friends. What did he hope to accomplish? Why was he trying to ruin me? All the years of abuse and hatred came back in that one instant, and I was convinced again that no one could be trusted, that no one was truly a friend. Only later was I to learn that Dennis had had a crush on Russ ever since the first time the three of us had met. Russ had evidently confided to Dennis what had happened between him and me on the road the evening of the crash, and Dennis thought this would be a perfect opportunity to score some points with Russ. So much for Dennis being a friend and so much for trusting anybody again.

"Well, if you are homosexual," mother continued, "and your father finds out, it will kill him, Gilbert. You'll be responsible for the death of your father! Is that what you want, to kill your own father? It's bad enough that you are destroying me like this, but to kill your father. What's gotten in to you? Haven't we given you everything you ever wanted? Is this what you've learned from the Church? What have we done to deserve this? My god, Gilbert, your father will have a heart attack." She took another drink.

It was then I first felt the seventeen years of hatred and frustration welling up like water ready to burst a dam. I was six years old again, ten, twelve, fourteen, sixteen. The abuse, the beatings, the hatred, and the violence all came rushing back in one horrible instant. I could hear Uncle Ferdinand threatening to kill his son-of-bitch wife. I could see grandmother, shacked up with another trick, screwing him for money. Mother was a drunk, father not much better, and Jonathon had abandoned me when I needed him the most. My sisters were gone. I was going to be beaten by the entire student bodies of Assumption Elementary School and Saint Francis Academy as soon as I walked out the door. A little red-headed girl circled around me, laughing, screaming, calling me lover-boy and blaming me for everything that had gone wrong in her life since the letter in the second grade. Dead puppies hung on a nail, pierced through the heart, dripping blood at my feet. An old man touched my penis and vomited semen out his mouth and onto my chest. A priest danced around me naked, chanting the Officium and shaking incense across my loins. My body exploded, sending heart and lungs and soul hurling into an abyss of alcohol and despair, and as I gasped for air, drowning in a pool of liquor and blood, I could hear my parents yelling, fighting, screaming—I was dying!

I couldn't contain my feelings any longer and exploded at mother, riddling her with a machine gun of vitriol.

"No, mother," I shouted. "If father dies it won't be because of me. Not because of his queer son, or whatever you want to call me. It will be because of you. Your mouth—his blood, your drinking—his death. Your harping—his ghost."

I fled the house, not looking back, but running from everything I had ever known, from every person I had ever loved, from every year, every month, every week and day and minute and second that defined the reality of my painful existence. I ran as fast and as far as I could. Had any of my classmates wanted to chase and beat me that day, they wouldn't have been able to catch me! And I raced until I was weak and spent and collapsed beneath a tree on the outskirts of town. I sat and cried like a baby for at least an hour, thinking about everything I hated so much about living in such a godforsaken little town: my family, my school, Russ, Patrick, and life. And like on the night of the accident, I resolved that nothing and no one would ever hurt me again. But, unlike my resolution on that fateful night, I did not promise my life to chastity, morality, or to God. I resolved, more, to dedicate my life to myself and do whatever necessary to achieve what I wanted, not what other people wanted for me and not what other people wanted of me. From then on, it would be Gilbert against the world!

Although I returned later that evening, I never really did go home again. I had had the life sucked out me by everyone who had surrounded me during my childhood, and I wasn't about to continue being a victim. I knew the instant I fled the house that afternoon that I had to leave. I had to get the hell out of there. There would be no coming back, again, at least not in the sense of returning home. I was gone. Away from home. Free! Thomas Wolfe was right: you can never go home again. Life in central Ontario was history.

It wasn't long after that incident with mother that I got the hell away for good.

Five

THE REST, AS THEY SAY, is history. I graduated high school the next month, enrolled in Sault College in Sault Ste. Marie for a year, then ended up studying at Toronto School of Art. I hooked up again with Raymond, an old friend from grade school, who had taken a nursing job in Toronto, met his lover Bernie, and fell into a crowd that included Jack Pollock, Barbara Shapiro, Joanne Clomer, and a hundred other divas, queers, drag queens, and fag hags who frequented the gallery and bar circuits in Toronto.

I didn't finish my studies at TSA but ended up taking a series of jobs in Toronto that included working in a gallery, managing an art shop, serving tables at a coffee shop, temping for a placement agency, and finally securing a position with the Government of Canada in the Department of Public Works.

On weekends and throughout the week, I partied at every bar I could find. I became tight with the people who frequented the Pollock Gallery and began drinking, doing drugs, and screwing any guy who would have me—and virtually all of them did. My life became a blur of booze, drugs, sex, parties, poppers, the baths, and hangovers.

Every relationship I had was dysfunctional. I had had the best teachers back home, and I began sinking further and further into a morass of hedonism. I took lovers then dumped them as quickly as the next hot man came along, had several affairs with beautiful women, and found myself on more than a few occasions waking in the morning, hung over and not knowing where I was, or who I had been with—man, woman, or both!

I forsook temperance, faith, religion, and philosophy and replaced each with a shot of tequila, a joint, a hot man, a line of coke, or an easy woman. I had relationships with actors up from New York in summer stock, rock stars on tour through Canada, and Canadian Broadcasting Corporation groupies who were young, hot, horny, and hung. Man, woman, or threesome, it didn't matter. I had had my fill of central Ontario and its perverted concept of morality and was anxious for the next sexual conquest to satiate my erotic needs. In a word, I was a mess.

I became more depressed with each passing day, drunker with each fleeting night, and more dependent with each ounce of grass that I inhaled into my lungs. I became totally, absolutely, and unequivocally like the living dead. And I loved it.

Then one Saturday afternoon, my friend Bernie Taylor told me that a famous Native artist, Norval Morrisseau, was in town and was looking for a young man to become his travelling companion and secretary. Bernie said that a few months with Morrisseau and I would be a rich man, perhaps forty or fifty thousand dollars richer, because although Morrisseau was a genius, he was also a drunk who threw money around without hesitation. Bernie said Morrisseau was weird (I didn't even hesitate with the word "weird"), but if I could put up with him for a short time, it would be well worth my while. It sounded good to me. I was tiring of the Toronto scene. Tiring of the parties. Tiring of the prima donna queens and insecure older queers who only wanted me for what was in my pants. Too much booze and drugs and sex over the past few years had taken their toll. I had become like the living dead: a zombie roaming the night in search of victims.

I told Bernie to set up a meeting and he did.

And thus it begins.

PART TWO

Beardmore-In-the-Woods

(January through the end of February 1979)

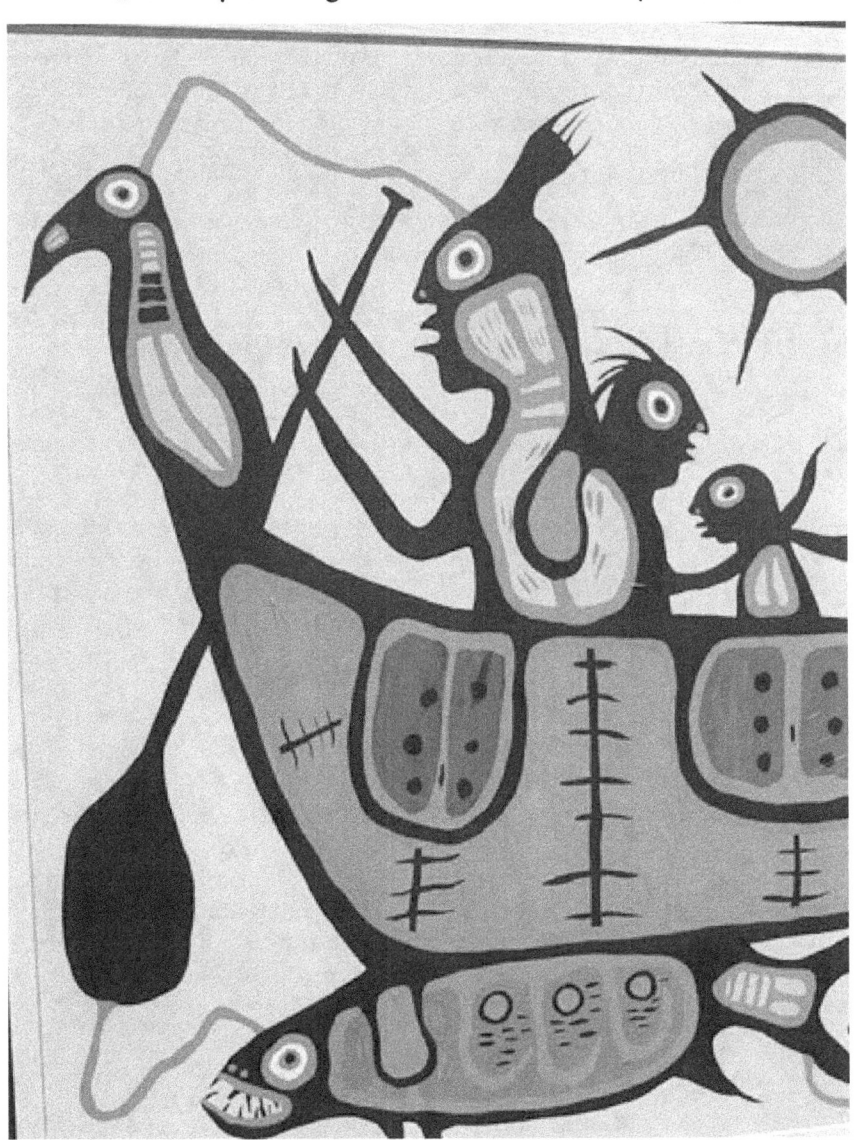

JOANNE,

I'm sorry it's taken me so long to write. Everything happened so quickly. It seems like Christmas, and the party, and being with you—on what we didn't realize would be our last night together—happened just yesterday, and now I find myself living out a dream and beginning an experience over which I have little control.

I didn't have a chance to say goodbye when I left, or at least didn't make the chance. I owe you much more than that. Our friendship deserves better but what can I say other than that I am sorry. I would have done things differently had I thought it would have made a difference but it wouldn't have. In fact knowing you as I do, I'm certain that had I let you in on my plans you would have tried talking me out of them, and I probably would have listened. You seldom give bad advice, even if unsolicited, but advice was not something I sought at the time. My leaving unannounced was something I had to do for myself, it didn't involve my feelings for you or how I feel about our friendship. I think you know by now that nothing can separate us although distance—at times—may keep us apart. But the feelings I have for you are genuine. I will never love another as I have loved you and will always keep you close to my heart and in my thoughts.

I imagine by now you know what happened or at least have a good idea of the situation as it evolved. Bernie and Raymond can't keep a secret, and besides, I wouldn't expect them to keep such information from you. They have been good friends: Allowing me to stay with them for so long, Bernie setting up the meeting with Norval Morrisseau, and then both of them agreeing, albeit reluctantly, to keep my secret until I informed them otherwise. By the way, I have freed them from keeping my secret so they may speak and you can listen freely. But it wouldn't surprise me if they had let bits and pieces of this bizarre puzzle slip, inadvertently of course, during an evening of drink, pot, and gossip. Anyway, I'm sure all of Soho suspected the truth long before I gave Bernie and Raymond permission to discuss the situation.

So what have you heard. That I've gone on a month long drunk? That I am sniffing coke and shoving it up my ass? That I'm wasted on hash? That I am living in poverty, wallowing in disrepute, and associating with the most despicable of human scum? Have you heard that I am selling myself like a common whore to an artist who doesn't give a shit about who I am, let alone care how I am? Most of it is probably true. Who am I to evaluate my own desperate situation? I have done what I thought I must, though many will say I have spun out of control again. So what can I say? That I am sorry, I'll come back and it won't ever happen again? That I've finally learned my lesson and I'll return immediately and fly right from now on? God sometimes I wish I could change things as they are. Everything! Every last fucking bit of my life that seems to have led nowhere except to this sudden and probably destructive adventure of which I now find myself a central figure. If I were able, I would offer an apology and remain sheltered in the security of our friendship—that would be the easiest course to pursue. But I dare not! I do not intend to return any time soon, so any hope you might have for a reversal of my latest ill-fortune dismiss at once. Any possibility I harbor for returning to the life I left behind shall not come to pass. I cannot pretend that I necessarily know what I am doing or insist that my departure will lead to anything other than disaster, but I don't think I can say anything that could sufficiently explain or defend my decision. I would be lying were I to propose anything different, and I know how much you hate me lying—not as much to you but more so to myself.

So much has happened since that night at Café des Coupons that I don't even know where to begin. Stars have imploded and worlds created since we last talked, and I now find myself swimming in pieces of stardust that fell from the heavens on the night I first met Norval. I wax so poetic for a failed writer, a hapless artist, and a less-than-successful human being. Wax poetic? Perhaps, but with a redundancy and simplicity that does disservice to even the poorest of the muse among us.

I am frightened but of what I do not know. Issues and ideas that confuse my thoughts threaten me. I am intimidated by the very concept of existing as a failure in a world that values status and success. At the same time I am exhilarated by the opportunity that awaits— to escape, to learn, to set myself free…to become the person I have always hoped I could be but was afraid to seek. I feel young again, although I realize my pain is spiritual, not chronological, and I feel challenged by possibilities I only once dreamed. I am scared, but not for myself as much as of myself, and yet I do not know what I fear: Failure? Success? Self-discovery? Disappointment? Commitment? Involvement? Submersion into reality? I do not know, take your pick, Joanne. You know me as well as I know myself, perhaps even better. All I know, at this point, is that I must do what I am doing.

Leaving is something I need to do for myself. I wish I could rely on your guidance and wisdom, but this time I cannot. I must seek my own destiny, be it positive or negative, and I cannot allow myself the possibility of succeeding only because someone else has dragged me along screaming and unwilling. Forgive me, I do not mean to suggest that you would attempt anything of the sort, anything other than what you thought best for me, and I do not write this as indictment against you or with recrimination for the help you have given me for so long. I am only trying to say that there comes a time when we all must make decisions—good or bad, right or wrong, positive or negative. Now is my time. Trust me, what ever I do, wherever I go, and despite the screwups I seem to bring about I will always consider what you would say or do or say in a similar situation. And that does help. We have become a part of one another bound by the ageless dimensions of time. I will always believe that we truly are the cosmic friends we have often talked about endlessly searching for a place where we can finally be together without constraint, without condition, and without the realities that keep you where you are, and me where I am—linked in cosmic understanding but limited by physical reality.

So do not despair, and please do not worry although I know you will. I will be fine. I will endure whatever comes my way and will either succeed or perish trying. And although perishing might sound less than reassuring, would you want it any other way? Haven't you always said that this world—this existence—is but one passage, one singular experience on our way to eternity? If you believe what you have told me, and what you practice yourself, then take comfort in knowing that I do not leave Toronto without hesitation. I leave hoping to find that which has eluded me all my life. And I leave knowing that what ever the outcome of this experience will be, I will see you and be with you again sometime, somewhere, somehow.

Do not try to write back. I can't deal with that right now. I must succeed or fail on my own and besides, I am having these letters mailed by a confidant who sneaks them out of Norval's place and pirates them away to a mailing location far from where we live. I don't know for certain that Norval would want me writing to you or to anyone else, but I can't take that chance. As much of a genius as he is, he is equally short-tempered. Beyond my concerns about him and what I hope will become a professional relationship, I must retain my sense of anonymity. I leave no forwarding address, we do not have a phone, and only a few of Norval's closest friends know where we are. I will remain in contact from time to time, so do not fear losing touch—that will never happen.

Know that I love you and think about you more than you suspect. Please take care of yourself. Be happy and remember what you've always told me: Life is never as bad as it seems nor as good as you dream. It is simply what it is and what you make of it. So roll the bones.

Gilbert

✳✳✳✳✳✳✳✳✳✳✳

JOURNAL ENTRY: 1-20-79

I've never written in a journal before. I don't know what to write or how to start. Should I talk about the weather, what I did today, what I ate and where I went? Should I chronicle all those unimportant things that achieve significance, years later, when pursuing the ramblings of a long-ago experience?

I did nothing today, just sat around and read for the fourth time *The Temple of Gold* by William Goldman. Norval was gone all day; where I do not know. He seldom shares his goings and comings with me.

I ate little today. A bowl of cereal for breakfast out of a filthy dish that hadn't seen water or detergent for months—I've grown used to that by now. Nothing for lunch. A salami sandwich for dinner. My eating habits differ considerably from the culinary delights I learned to enjoy at Bernie and Raymond's. And I went nowhere except outside the cabin for a short afternoon walk.

"Cabin" is hardly an appropriate description—more like a shack, and certainly not the image of luxury and accommodations I had pictured for an internationally renowned artist like Norval. Of course, given what I had learned about him at our first meeting, I shouldn't have expected the Taj Mahal, but living in a shanty with a shabby roof that leaks when it rains or snows is hardly my idea of comfort.

There is no running water, no inside plumbing, and no furniture save a tattered and dirty mattress on the floor and five straight-backed wooded chairs surrounding a three-legged table. The shack has no electricity, so we make do with candles and oil lanterns and an old-fashioned wood burning stove that provides heat (minimal at best) and serves as a hot plate for soups, stews, and breakfast.

The cabin is decorated in early pioneer: Dirt floor, one window with broken glass patched with duct tape, an entrance way covered with an animal hide of some type—elk, moose, bear, heck, I don't know—and a fire pit where we cook what ever is available on any given night. Like in the Ojibwa homes of Native tradition, smoke from our cabin vents through a small hole in the ceiling that depends on the swirling air currents to carry the smoke upward and out.

The weather here can get very cold, below zero is not uncommon, and there is more snow than I think covers the North Pole. It is difficult to keep warm since the cabin is not insulated and has only birch bark tacked to the outside walls to ward away the wind and moisture. I have an animal skin coat that keeps me warm during the days and a buffalo hide that is more than adequate for warmth at night. Still, living in these rustic conditions is harsh. I am constantly cold and cannot seem to find ways to stay warm other than to crawl under the buffalo hide with my coat on, and remain there until I have achieved a semblance of body heat.

We live with three mangy dogs—one Norval calls Spirit and two others without names. I call them Dog One and Dog Two. The pups provide additional warmth at night when they cuddle on the bed with us, or with me alone. I wonder if that is where the term 'three dog night' came from—sounds appropriate.

Outside the shack, Norval has dug a three-foot square pit in which we keep food that requires refrigeration. The permafrost keeps the food items cold. The only problem with it is trying to keep the food from freezing.

Naturally, as one might expect, strewn about the cabin is evidence of Norval's profession: Paints, canvasses, birch bark, paper, animal hides (mostly cow), and several completed works. Some of the paintings are awaiting transport to Toronto for showing, but most of them will never be seen. Indeed, they represent the singular temperament of the artist who regards his work with a harsh and critical eye, when most of us mortals would consider it genius.

Curiously, and in contrast to the squalor of our accommodations, Norval has a collection of fine silver: a tea service, trays, candy dishes, candle holders, cups, decorative figurines, women's and men's jewelry, and a small fortune in coins. For a man who rejects the simple conveniences of comfort and function, Norval is obsessed with buying anything made of silver. Upon first seeing his collection, I was not only dumbfounded by the wealth he had accumulated (and keeps unattended in the cabin), but also by the obvious disparity between function and indulgence. I was also concerned that such monetary grandeur would attract thievery from strangers who might hear of his holdings or from some of Norval's friends of less-than-questionable character who frequent the place. But Norval has assured me that nothing will get stolen and no intruder shall penetrate. He is a shaman and said he has cast a spell around the cabin that protects it during his absence. I am not sure I believe him, but I am told by his friends that the silver has been here (in varying amounts) for quite a few years and has never been disturbed—not a piece has disappeared! Perhaps his powers are greater than I suppose.

Except for the squalor in which we live, the cabin is otherwise located in a pristine and beautiful area of Ontario, near Beardmore on Lake Nipigon. The woods that surround us are deep, lush, and mostly quiet except at night when the sounds of forest creatures disturb the silence. We are bordered on every side by aspens, birch, oak, maple, and dozens of conifers. A large pond is not more than a hundred feet from our front door, and a typical woodland stream winds its way down from the mountains, which provide backdrop for our rustic location. Sometimes, I feel as though I am back at my family's summer cabin but with more clarity about and understanding of life and who I am—or am not.

Although I am not certain, I don't think anyone lives within miles. I have not seen a single person during the day, except when Norval and his friends are home, and any visitors we do receive arrive by sled or on snowshoes and always leave early in the evening for the long trek back to from where ever they came. They leave, that is, if they do not stay the night.

Indeed, I have at least achieved one part of my dream—to escape from the din of urban insanity into the isolation I have long sought. Certainly, our 'home' could, in no way, be confused as a simple overnight camp or as a quick getaway for a family holiday. We are far north of Toronto—how far north I am not certain, because I really don't know where Beardmore is in relation to civilization. Nevertheless, and despite the many drawbacks that I have mentioned, this truly is the realization of a dream. With Norval being gone most of the time, I am truly alone—dependent only on myself. And as much as I hate it here, as much as I despise the lack of modern conveniences and comforts to which I have grown accustomed, and as much as I long for civility and sophistication, there is something about living in this rustic environment that I welcome. Much to my surprise, I am becoming a part of it.

I guess that's about it for tonight. I can't think of anything else to add. As I wrote earlier, this journal thing is new to me. Maybe I'll get better at it as I go along. Enough for now, I am tired even though I haven't done a damn thing, today. I'll write again another time.

G

❋❋❋❋❋❋❋❋❋❋❋❋

January 24, 1979
Joanne,

I write again, knowing that you are probably thinking, "Uh huh, I knew he'd soon tire of this escapade and be ready to come home." Sorry, but no. I might be confused right now, although I am convinced that my decision to take the position with Norval was motivated out of personal necessity rather than confusion but I am not so confused or distraught to the point that I am ready to give up and return to my pathetic life back in Toronto. Actually, the longer I am here, the more convinced I become that I made the right decision, though there are certainly times when I question Norval's motives and my role in what ever this experience might turn out to be.

I haven't been doing much these past few days, actually not even much during the past month but I expect the situation to change soon. Basically I fill my time with reading, writing, (I've started a journal), experimenting with elementary work on the canvass, and sleeping. Norval is gone much of the time so I am left to my own devices here in our home deep in the woods north of Beardmore, Ontario.

I haven't yet figured out my reason for being with Norval. I was hired as his companion and secretary, but I have done precious little in the way of being a companion since he isn't here very often and even less as a secretary. There is nothing to do as his secretary. I don't even know why Norval needs one. He never corresponds with anyone nor does any of the things that would require the services of a secretary. At this point I am more a convenient fuck-buddy and a physical subservient to the shaman who considers himself the savior of his people—the One for whom they have long waited. I am told by Many Tongues—the messenger who carries away my letters—that Norval became as he is now, obsessed with spiritualism, only after the visit from the Thunderbird Spirit in his early adulthood and only after having been discovered by Jack Pollock.

I have told you little of Norval and will not do much more in this letter, but understand that at times he is compassionate, kind, and although he is not loving, he is at least attentive when he is here. It is almost like being a member of a cult of which Norval is the charismatic. Of course, as it often is with a cult, such is the duplicity of my relationship with Norval or anyone else's relationship with Norval for that matter: All for the one and He for himself. He feigns kindness and concern for those of us who attend his needs. I am not alone in that manner of those who attend. There is Wolf, his brother, Many Tongues, evidently a wife and children (whom I have not met and of whom Norval never speaks), and an ever-changing cast of friends who come to visit and partake of the 'master's' wisdom. When an audience surrounds Norval the situation is always the same: Norval speaks—we listen. Norval asks—we provide. Norval shits—we clean it up. He demands total devotion and attention. He claims to be the Thunderbird Spirit reincarnate.

When he is here, minions and admirers usually surround us. Most of those who engage Norval are hangers-on who bask in his greatness, his generosity, and his alcohol and dope. We are never alone. His brother Wolf (I believe his real name is Wilfred) is usually here, as are Many Tongues and Norval's assorted friends and groupies, from places unknown, who cling to his every word as though he were speaking in tongues. It is much like being in the presence of a masterful teacher, but teacher of what—other than his art—I am not sure. Perhaps it is his art that attracts admirers, although I doubt it. I haven't seen any of them examine his works other than when he is holding court and explaining the Ojibwa legend that inspired a particular painting.

Maybe it is his personality, although I doubt that too. His personality is not one to attract serious friend-ships. He is at once generous and stingy, giving and de-manding, loving and hateful, accepting and intolerant. In a word, he is quite simply Norval, and I am not given to thinking that his personality would attract anyone unless that person had a hidden agenda or was wanting some of the money Norval tosses around like confetti at a parade. Indeed, I have not yet figured out what it is about Norval that commands such attention.

Today, I got a letter from Jack. Wolf had been in To-ronto delivering several of Norval's paintings to the Pollock Gallery and returned with a letter in response to one I had sent him—Norval doesn't mind me communi-cating with Jack since Jack is his agent and manager. Jack wrote you were doing well and had adjusted to my leaving better than he had expected. You know, despite my confidence that my decision was necessary and will be beneficial to my future, I am still pained by having left you so abruptly and without warning.

I am sorry I took off without as much as a goodbye. I left a message on your answering machine, but I guess that's rather impersonal and distant for a best friend. But as I wrote in my earlier letter, things happened so quickly I wasn't sure what was going on myself. Of course you had no way of knowing, but I had already made my decision to accept Norval's job offer the night at Café des Coupons. That last night we spent together was an evening I will never forget.

Remember the drink we invented—firewater? Jack Daniel's, and what else was in it? Damn, I don't remember now. Of course, after a half dozen glasses of our invention, who could be expected to remember? It did get us there, though, didn't it! How many shots did we have that night, four, six, eight? Who knows? Who cares? Who can remember? All I remember is the two of us stumbling home to the loft and crashing on the couch, together, beside, beneath, and on top of each other.

And I do remember the kiss—our kiss. Our first and only kiss. I'll bet that surprised the hell out of you. I would venture you weren't expecting Gilbert to excite your lips with temptation, especially at a time like that: You on the rocks, again, with Warren and me only hours earlier breaking up with who was it, or was I even breaking up with anyone? It seems, if I recall correctly that that was during one of my whoring-around periods. No breakups or pathetically sad love affairs for Gilbert, just one person after another, on different nights, in an endless orgy of one-night stands and pitiful attempts at falling in love. So, I guess I wasn't breaking up with anyone.

Neither of us was ever very good at those pathetic love affairs, were we? You did a lot better than I, though. You get a perfect ten for the pathos and melodrama of your relationships, except for Warren.

Did I ever tell you how impressed I have always been with how you could regard a man as little more than a self-indulgent convenience? I'm impressed, but kidding also. You're the only person I know who has enough self-confidence to regard a relationship as being trivial and disruptive. You never did tell me whether any of the men in your life constituted a relationship of a serious nature. Ironic, isn't it? We are so close, and yet regarding things like love, know so little about one another. Of course, I can hardly speak any more authoritatively for myself. I don't remember even ever having had a serious relationship, at least one that was mutually serious to both persons involved. There were the multitudes of one-niters, the plethora of one-monthers, and the dozens of "this is it-ers," but never anything sad or wickedly desperate. I guess neither of us will ever be the stuff of which a tragic novel is written. So much the better—melodramatic notoriety is not one of my more covetous desires!

But getting back to the kiss. It almost seems like it never happened, and I wish that weren't the case. Am I imagining it? I want to remember your surprise, your shock, and the passion I felt that night we invented that godforsaken drink, stumbled our way home, and fell into bed, neither knowing if the other was conscious or alive or dead. I don't think we died, did we? On the other hand, maybe we did die and what we are experiencing now is some kind of weird between-lives thing that we have to endure before being together again. Wow, Limbo—my Catholicism shows through. God, I hope this isn't Limbo or Purgatory—that would be even worse! It isn't, is it? Help me here. I'm losing it.

Even though I am where I want to be at this particular time in my life, I do wish I could see you again and hold you close and know that you will always be by my side making certain that everything is all right and nothing will ever hurt me again. It has been so long since I've experienced security like that. In fact, I'm not sure that I ever have. Sometimes it seems that I'm spiraling further and further into an ever-darkening abyss that has no bottom and an entrance that has long ago disappeared into nightmare.

I know I sound like I'm off the deep end, but I'm really not. I'm simply relating many of the thoughts that I have considered throughout my life. One minute I curse my own existence and then the next I reassess what I hope will be a profitable future. I am confused, I am lost, I am alone, and perhaps even emotionally disturbed—at least sometimes it seems that way. I've gotten to the point that I don't know who I am anymore, maybe I never really did know, but there has to be some reason why I came, here with Norval, especially after discovering what I did about him during our first meeting. I continue to stay with him, for some reason, even though he is gone most of the time and doing things I can only imagine. There must be a reason why

I have allowed myself to be sucked into the eye of the hurricane, the peace before the second wave, only for the purpose of securing the attention of a person, an artist, like Norval Morrisseau. Perhaps I truly do hope that his genius will rub off on me. Maybe I am convinced that the excitement of living life on the edge will provide excuse for my self-destructive tendencies. I don't know anymore. I don't think now is the time to question my motives but rather simply to accept life as it happens and go with the flow.

I really don't know!

Well, I guess that's enough of my ramblings for now. Still can't leave an address, sorry! You will hear from me again, of that you can be certain. I cannot go very long without my Joanne fix, so until then—be as you always have been.

Gilbert

****

JOURNAL ENTRY: 1-25-79

Norval was gone again today, as he has been for the better part of three weeks, now, with only an occasional visit from him I find myself asking why I am here? What am I supposed to be doing with or for him? What about the companion/secretary position he hired me for? When he is here, on the few occasions he returns in the evening and remains throughout the night until the next morning, I am nothing more than a convenient receptacle in which he can deposit his swagger and semen and vent his anger and frustration. He is always drunk, usually stoned, generally coked-up, and often wrecked on hash. When he is home in his normally addicted state, so too am I. It seems like I have consumed more alcohol and have smoked more dope during his few visits than I had in the previous four years of my life and that's one hell of a lot. I am not about to snort coke or insert it up my ass as is Norval's customary manner of ingestion—he claims he gets a quicker, more intense, and longer lasting high that way. When he is here, drunk and stoned though he may be, he does treat me with a certain amount of attention. I wouldn't call it love or intimacy, just selfish attention. Still, I harbor the hope that our arrangement will change and that Norval will establish a more professional relationship with me—one focusing on his art, his wisdom, and his mysticism. I want to learn from him. I yearn to experience his spiritualism, the ancestral shamanism of which he is so proud. And yet, I begin to think that the dreams I had of changing my life, of improving my situation, of learning from the master artist are slowly dissipating. And it all seems so incongruous with what I assumed would take place, given what I had expected from our first meeting.

✸✸✸✸✸✸✸✸✸✸✸

I FIRST MET NORVAL MORRISSEAU in December 1978. I had been working for Public Works Canada, a department of the Federal Government, for several years and desperately needed a change from the tedium of my existence and job. By coincidence, a friend, Bernie Taylor, half-jokingly mentioned that Norval Morrisseau, one of Canada's leading contemporary and internationally recognized artists, was in Toronto for a few days for a gallery showing and was interested in hiring someone to be his traveling companion and private secretary and to possibly write his memoirs. I was bored with my job. In fact, I was sick to death of it, and immediately thought of the possibilities. I have always considered myself to be creative, not necessarily an artist but creative nonetheless, so I figured why not? It couldn't hurt to meet the man.

I had heard of Morrisseau from Jack Pollock, the gallery owner in Toronto who is credited with having discovered Norval. I knew a little about the man or his work. He is a man of genius talent who has brought to life the legends of the Ojibwa Indians and has become an internationally renowned artist, literally overnight. Bernie said he could arrange a meeting if I wanted one. I did.

Knowing Morrisseau's legacy and not wanting to miss the opportunity to work with him, to learn from him, and to escape the monotony of my increasingly destructive life in Toronto, I told Bernie to set up a meeting for me with Morrisseau and to convey that I was prepared to do anything for the job—ambitious words for someone so naïve and gullible.

Bernie's and my conversation was on a Saturday. On Sunday he called to say he had contacted Morrisseau and that I was to meet him the following Wednesday. Needless to say, I was ecstatic. The thought of escaping the dreary winters of Toronto and cutting myself loose from every thing with which I had become familiar was tantalizing, so much so that I awaited my meeting with Morrisseau with unbridled anticipation.

The few days that passed between Bernie's phone call and my meeting with Norval seemed like an eternity. At twenty-five I was ready for a change, wanting desperately for a better future to begin. I was convinced that this chance occasion was the opportunity I had been long awaiting. I wasn't about to let this (last?) chance pass me by. Why shouldn't I have thought as much? Given a life that seemed to be heading nowhere, having the opportunity to work with Norval Morrisseau provided the perfect resolution to my dilemma. For what more could I have asked?

Wednesday finally arrived. I was supposed to meet Morrisseau at 7:00 in the evening, so naturally, on Wednesday morning my thoughts were consumed with what I might say to this great artist in order to convince him to hire me. I had seen his art displayed in galleries and on the walls of people's homes, but I had never had the opportunity to meet him (surprising since Jack Pollock was his agent, and Jack and I were nearly inseparable at the time). Morrisseau's genius had become the focal point for conversation at cocktail parties, not only in the village and in Canada, but around the world. He had been featured on the covers of *Time, Macleans,* and *Chatelaine* and had become a man of international notoriety. I surely did not want to bungle what could be the greatest opportunity of my life or my future.

Before leaving to meet Morrisseau, I relaxed with Bernie and Raymond (with whom I was sharing a house at the time), had a couple of drinks, smoked a little dope, and then headed for my rendezvous with Norval and with destiny at the Four Seasons Hotel.

It was one of the coldest days that winter. The temperature was not much above zero, and an arctic wind swept down from the north, biting at the flesh were it exposed for too long. I bundled up and hailed a taxi to chauffeur me to my future.

After arriving at my destination and thinking myself cool and calm, I paid the driver, walked into the hotel lobby, and headed toward the elevator all the while rehearsing what I was going to say. Morrisseau was staying on the ninth floor and getting there happened so quickly that I didn't have time to finish the mental preparations highlighting my career, my experiences, and my (impressive?) resume that I was certain would secure my position with Morrisseau. I didn't know at the time that my art credentials and business acumen were not what Norval was interested in.

I stood at his door for what seemed like hours, trying desperately to remember what I wanted to say, how I intended to conduct myself, and how I proposed to relate my experiences to this man of genius aptitude. I was a mess: Still stoned and convinced that whatever I said would sound like a fawning protégé at the feet of the great master.

Finally, after screwing up enough courage to face what I hoped would begin my future, I knocked on the door. It opened, and there before me stood a man with long, oily hair, dirty, torn pants and shirt, and an odor about him that smelled of month-old perspiration—or worse! He was, in a word, disgusting. As he introduced himself, he was picking his nose and flicked its contents to the floor, then shut the door behind us. He invited me to sit and commune, as he referred to conversation, offered whiskey and dope (which I unhesitantly accepted), and we drank and smoked and talked for the remainder of the evening. Actually, he did the talking; I mostly listened and nodded like a child in rapture.

The hotel room was the antithesis of Morrisseau: Clean, bright, and well kept, with the intention of creating good cheer, but there was a gloom about the room that seemed to emanate as much from Norval as from any other possible source. He was dark, mysterious, egocentric, and morose. Not to say he wasn't at all engaging, quite the opposite—Norval was on what could be considered his best behavior that night and regaled me with a psychotic confidence that I had not before experienced in others.

Physically, Morrisseau is an intimidating man. He wears years of desperation and neglect on his face (no doubt complicated by the alcohol and booze) and carries a dignity that disguises his desperate situation. He is tall, perhaps 6'1" or 6'2", heavy around the middle, and very Native, and by that, I mean Native in the sense of the romanticized notion of First Peoples we Caucasians want to believe—the old American cowboy west kind of thing.

I had no idea how old Norval was. I guessed fifty-five or six (he was 48), but his face and physical presence revealed more about the years he had lived than I was able to guess at the time. What struck me most about this hulking man was his smile. Even given the darkness and foreboding that surrounded him, his smile and laughter were captivating: The masculine version of Helen of Troy. As he told his stories, he'd slug down a shot or two of whiskey with a frequency I could not attempt to match, generate a laugh from his belly, and slap his knees, engaging his listener with the warmth of a storyteller that seemed inviting and reassuring.

Norval quickly began talking, and I listened enthusiastically to show interest in his words. Morrisseau is a fascinating man and spins a tale so bizarre and un-believable that it sounds either concocted or fresh out of a third-rate novel. But at the same time, the stories were enchanting. He talked for hours, not allowing me the opportunity to vocalize the presentation I had so arduously prepared about my work, my interest in art, my creative abilities, and my desire to apprentice with a man of his stature. I will admit, though, his stories about life in Winnipeg, Sand Point, Lake Nipigon, being Eckankar, and practicing shamanism were cap-tivating. I was falling into a trance, and Morrisseau was the hypnotist.

Throughout the course of the evening Morrisseau would intermittently brush his long, oily hair with his hands, pick his nose and rub it against his unkempt clothes or on the furniture, fart without embarrassment or apology, belch long and deep from the bottom of his fat belly, and scratch at his crotch with such vigor that I feared he might do irreparable harm. Though he was intellectually interesting in many ways, he was not a pretty sight.

I probably did not present a much better first impression than did he. Stoned and a bit hyper and finally having an opportunity to speak only when he began losing interest in his own stories, I mentioned that I was a metis—half Ojibwa and half French descent. From stories remembered from my childhood, I explained that my paternal grandmother had married an Ojibwa Indian and together they had parented five sons and four daughters. I explained that my grandfather had been killed in a lumbering mishap shortly after the birth of their ninth child, a tragic story, and one that I hoped would endear me to him. I don't mind admit-ting that I used the story of my grandparents as a way of identifying with his Native heritage and hopefully establishing a bond that he could not refuse. I had hoped, too, that my ancestry as a metis might help secure the position he was hiring.

I also told him about the eagle tattoo on my right butt cheek, etched there because I had been told several years ago, by a spiritualist, that my spirit guide is an eagle. He asked to see it and I proudly, although, with some embarrassment, pulled my pants down to just below my right hip. He examined the tattoo as though he was examining a piece of crime-scene evidence, then gave a hearty laugh, "Beautiful, young man, very nice," he bellowed.

Norval continued laughing as I finished my embarrassing attempts at being as entertaining as he, said it was getting late, and that he wanted to see me again the next evening. I eagerly agreed, and we shook hands and parted (I washed as soon as I got to the lobby men's room). I could hardly wait to get back home to tell Bernie and Raymond the potentially good news. Although Norval hadn't said a word about hiring me, in fact hadn't even interviewed me concerning my credentials, I had a feeling that my being hired would be the successful resolution of our second meeting the next night.

I weathered the several blocks home, rather than taking a cab, so I could digest the happenings of the evening. I could think about nothing other than getting the job and apprenticing with Norval Morrisseau. It was like a dream coming true: Redemption for the nightmare of my childhood. Norval could free me from the constraints of an ordinary and pathetic life and elevate me to the heights of artistic liberation for which I longed. I floated home on a cloud (as corny as that might sound)...a cloud of anticipation and with a prayer of hope that the next evening would bring about the beginning of a personal metamorphosis that promised a new beginning and a future filled with the realization of childhood fantasy and adult dream. I had spent far too many of my twenty-five years waiting for something to happen but not doing much to encourage anything. I had a positive feeling that whatever I had been waiting for was about to begin the next night.

G

****

January 28, 1979
Joanne,

I hope this letter finds you well. I trust your life has taken a turn for the better. I heard from Jack, through Bernie, carried to me by Many Tongues, that you and Warren have separated and that you are contemplating some changes of your own. If what I am told is true, then good for you! It is about time you thought about yourself and your needs. Warren is a waste of time and not worth the attention you've paid him. I think you will be better off without him even given the pain of separation.

Things are not much different here. Norval did come home Sunday and has remained here for three days now. I am amazed I am also wondering why he has returned without any explanation concerning where he has been or what he has been doing. No matter, we have finally begun working on his art.

I have been modeling for him day and night. When he is stirred by the font of his passion, he must create, and create he does. In the past two days he has completed two paintings that will go directly to Jack and, ultimately, hang in his gallery (Many Tongues will be a busy man over the course of the next few days).

Of course, even when Norval paints, he is drunk and stoned. Come to think of it, I don't think I have ever seen him not in that condition! It seems to be his natural way. Whereas most of us would take water or food for sustenance, Norval takes liquor and marijuana. I can hardly point a finger of contention, however, given that whenever he drinks, I drink also and whenever he smokes, I smoke with him. I don't get into anything else though. No other drugs. They were the bane of my existence in Toronto, so I do not want to engage that nightmare here. Norval doesn't seem to mind that I don't do coke. And why should he? That means more coke for him! I think he couldn't care less what anyone else does regarding drinking and doping. He enters into a world of his own when he gets like that, which is so often that I surmise his world is a world that exists only in his mind and has little to do with reality. Nevertheless, and despite our constant state of intoxication, we have been working more on his art.

He says I am the best model he has ever had. I don't know how many others to whom I am I am being compared, but I will accept his compliment without hesitation since they are so few and far between.

Strange as it may sound, the modeling is harder work than you might imagine. I must remain in one pose for hours on end, neither moving nor shifting positions to ease the discomfort my body might experience. I am modeling nude, no big deal. We have been together in the physical sense (as I am sure you have probably guessed already) on a few occasions, so there is no cause for embarrassment or hesitation on my part. Anyway, anything to make me a star! Curious that although I pose nude, the paintings are seldom representations of nudity. Norval says nudity inspires him to see other things as they are when stripped of their worldly constraints. I hope the paintings I have inspired will hang in Jack's gallery at the next show. He has created several beautiful pieces, all untitled at this point. And damn, it sure is cold while posing nude!

He created one painting the other night that was breathtaking. It was as though he had captured the mysticism of the Ojibwa, the cynicism of the white man, and my beauty (humble though I am) in bold geometric shapes, vivid color, and with a depth and surrealism the likes I have never seen. He is truly a genius. The painting is of me, not nude, but more surrealistic. I suggested he title the painting White Lizard, a reference half to my metis heritage and half to the Lizard Spirit of the great north. He didn't respond but did write the suggestion down.

Little seems different about our relationship whether he is here or not. When Norval is home, he is always drunk and stoned and frequently entertains a house full of strangers whom he regales with stories about Ojibwa ancestry, custom, and legend. And often I am ignored, unless he wants sex. When he is not home, I pass the time taking walks in the woods, writing in my journal, or sleeping. Here or not, there is minimal difference to me. He did mention the other night that sometime in February or March we would travel to North Dakota for an Ojibwa cleansing ritual. I know nothing more about it than that. I'm sure it will prove interesting as he made a point of emphasizing that I would be one of the few white men to ever witness such a ceremony. I am glad to hear that he wants me to attend the ceremony. Whether or not we are together, he still regards me as his traveling companion..

Nothing else is going on. I do feel that finally I am beginning to realize the part of my hopes that portend a better future. Not only is Norval painting, again, and I modeling, but also he told me last night that he wants me to begin my own work. At long last I will be learning from the master.

I will certainly keep you informed. Until later…

Gilbert

✸✸✸✸✸✸✸✸✸✸✸✸

Many Tongues is an interesting character, and I use "character" in the most literary sense. He is straight out of a novel or a movie, complete with all the characteristics of a reluctant hero: Shy, mysterious, reticent, and affable.

I didn't have to approach him to smuggle my letters to Joanne out of the cabin and to a mailing location. He offered. He just walked right up to me one evening not long after we had arrived from Toronto, and told me, in an almost off-handed manner, that if I wanted him to buy anything for me, mail any letters, or run any kind of errand(s) when he was either in Toronto or Beardmore, just let him know. He didn't say, in so many words, that this was on the sly, that Norval didn't need to know about it, but I did get the distinct feeling that his offer should be kept secret. I have no problem with that.

I don't know whether he mails the letters from Beardmore or Toronto. He didn't say, and I didn't ask. I haven't had him run any other errands or buy any of the numerous food and personal care items I could desperately use. I don't know if he would get in trouble with Norval for doing as much for me, but I don't want to take the chance. Norval would certainly notice if I had imported food or other dry goods into the cabin, and his moods are so changeable that I wouldn't want to take the chance of getting Many Tongues into hot water with Norval.

Many Tongues appears to be considerably older than Norval, so he must be in his late sixties or early seventies. He is a grizzled-looking man. His skin is well weathered and creased with age lines that make him look far older than he probably is. He isn't an especially big man, about five-eight or nine and can't weigh more than one hundred and forty pounds. Like Norval, and most of the Native people I've met since we've been here, he wears his silvery-black hair long, well past his shoulders, but unlike Norval, he is always well groomed and clean. He's almost cute! Perhaps cute is an inappropriate word to use to describe an older, weather-beaten man, but he reminds me of the typical Native "medicine man" I saw in the movies when I was a kid. He has dark, penetrating eyes, a kind, gentle face, and a mysticism about him that rivals Norval's. Of all the people I've met since arriving here, Many Tongues is the only one with whom I feel comfortable! I get the feeling that I could talk with him about anything, and he'd have sage advice and adroit wisdom to share.

Many Tongues is the only person who associates with Norval who doesn't seem intimidated by Norval's arrogance. He doesn't seem phased by Norval's drinking and drug habits and doesn't seem the least bit impressed with Norval's art. It could be, given his age, that he is one of the Ojibwa elders who don't think that the Tribal legends should be interpreted in art for anyone to see, especially the white man. And yet, I don't get the sense that there is any prejudice in Many Tongues at all. He has treated me kindly and I've never heard him speak ill of anyone, Native Person or white.

He is the epitome of moderation in everything he does. He drinks very little, doesn't smoke dope or cigarettes, and approaches situations with a logic and sensibility that is usually the province of philosophers or mystics. Whenever he's around, there is a calm that settles around everyone with whom he comes in contact, and he makes a volatile situation serene. He seldom speaks, but when he does, it is with an authority that commands attention, even from Norval. I have wondered if Many Tongues is the shaman-teacher and Norval his student.

I'm not certain what Many Tongues' and Norval's relationship is. They seem friendly enough, but there is a perceptible distance between the two. Unlike all the others who bow at the feet of the great Morrisseau, Many Tongues does not attend to Norval's needs. He will accommodate his wishes but does so with a reserve that suggests indifference. When Norval demands, Many Tongues does not respond. When Norval whines, Many Tongues ignores him. And when Norval argues, Many Tongues disregards his mood. He does provide the daily necessities for Norval and seems to look out for Norval when Norval is drunk or stoned. I haven't heard him comment upon Norval's alcoholism or drug addiction, but from his general attitude, it is apparent that he does not approve, which makes me feel guilty sometimes, both for Norval's and my own behavior.

Nevertheless, wherever Norval goes, Many Tongues is usually close behind, except when Norval goes into Toronto. For some reason, Many Tongues refuses to accompany Norval to the city. He will go there by himself but not with Norval. I don't know if something happened, once, when they were in Toronto together or if Many Tongues would just rather not go. I get the distinct feeling that his refusal to follow Norval to the big city is as much because he would rather not witness Norval's disgusting behavior (which, I am told, is twice as bad when he travels to a city as it is, here, in the wilderness), as well as his own aversion to metropolitan areas. I do know two things that lend credence to my hypothesis: He is obviously disturbed by Norval's chemical dependency, and he is much the wilderness man. I have overheard him in conversation with others, discoursing on how much he does not like large cities with their crime, poverty, and fast pace and would rather live a simple life in the wilderness where he was born. Many Tongues is the quintessential small-town person; some might say he is the epitome of the Reservation Native.

I am drawn to Many Tongues and the serenity he radiates, not in the same way I am drawn to Norval, but in a way that portends something much deeper, much longer lasting, and more intimate. I hope that he and I will become friends, but he is quiet and unassuming; usually I'm not even sure when he is around. He simply goes about his business, leaves everyone alone, and doesn't initiate conversation. Nevertheless, I would like to talk with him in more depth.

Someday, perhaps, we will.

G

✱✱✱✱✱✱✱✱✱✱✱

Something very strange, actually disgusting, happened tonight as Norval and I prepared for bed. He had returned from a rather long walk in the forest, in his natural state of intoxication and trance, and asked me if I could assist him with his use of cocaine. Although I do not choose to participate myself, I have few problems providing the help Norval needs to get high; I consider it one of my responsibilities as his secretary. My ease with assisting Norval concerning his cocaine does give me pause occasionally. It is too much the good soldier syndrome: Anything to preserve and respect the chain of command.

When he asked me for assistance with his cocaine, I assumed he was intending to snort a line of coke, one of the two ways he generally imbibes the substance. I was wrong. He was thinking along the lines of his preferred method of ingestion, through his rectum.

I don't consider myself prudish or easily given to disgust, and I know I have involved myself in a variety of unseemly sexual exploits with several of my one-night stands. I haven't been known to reject very much in the way of new sexual experiences, but this was different.

Norval is a man who doesn't wash very often and prefers to evacuate himself in the woods using leaves as bathroom tissue. I have never known him to shower or bathe; he just sponges off with water. I don't think he has cleaned himself for several weeks, which made the reality of the experience even more abhorrent.

After preparing for bed, which for Norval simply means stripping naked and collapsing upon the mattress, he grabbed me in his arms as though wrestling a bear to the ground, and began kissing me the entire length of my body. I always shudder when Norval begins his attempts at amorous adventure, due mostly to his unkempt ways and odorous condition but also because his pitiful attempt at sex is more like clumsy fucking and an assault on his partner (victim). Norval's lovemaking is like sex with a dead man—all work and no reaction.

But back to his request. Norval sat up in bed, stared into my eyes with a vacuous look as though he had just experienced a revelation from a spirit-god, and demanded that I insert the cocaine into his rectum using my finger!

Now I realize that there aren't a great number of sexual activities in which I have not participated, however, the thought of penetrating his backend with my finger and inserting cocaine into his rectum is one that I did not want to experience, especially given the total disregard for cleanliness Norval demonstrates. I told him as much, which was a mistake.

Norval flew into a rage, hurled me off the mattress, jumped up and rampaged around the room, smashing one of his paintings. He then turned his attention to me, standing motionless and staring at me as though stalking wild game. He approached, slowly at first, then with greater rapidity until he lunged at me with both hands flailing at my neck.

As dangerous as the situation could have been, it was at the same time almost comical. Though I feared slightly for my safety, I knew also that Norval was so drunk and stoned that he couldn't have conquered his old grandmother with her hands tied behind her back. I merely moved aside as he stumbled past me and he crashed into the table. What had only moments before been one of six useable pieces of furniture in the cabin, shattered into splinters beneath his weight. Now there were only five.

Then there was silence, except for Norval's muffled groans and my stifled laugher. He remained piled atop the broken table for several moments, then arose, composed himself, and crawled beneath the covers on the mattress. I didn't know exactly what to do, or how to act, until he looked up at me, waved his hand in the air, and motioned for me to come to bed.

Knowing that Norval was so wasted that he wouldn't know whether he had done the coke or not, I whispered in his ear, asking if he had enjoyed the rush and the deft use of my finger. At first, he seemed surprised, then noticed that what remained of the cocaine was sprinkled about on the floor next to the mattress. Without hesitation, he scooped it up, snorted what could be salvaged, then smiled and nodded in the affirmative. He never knew the difference. As far as Norval was concerned, I had assisted as he had asked, thus confirming his postulation that coke up the butt really does make for a more intense high. I'm sure he must have thought this was the best high he'd ever experienced.

I am beginning to learn how to handle Norval but am also becoming more aware, and fearful, of his anger and potential for violence. But that I will worry about later. For now, I am tired and need rest.

G

＊＊＊＊＊＊＊＊＊＊＊

February 4, 1979
Gilbert,

Many Tongues delivered Norval's paintings. They are brilliant as expected. I also got your letter and am responding immediately so Many Tongues can return with my reply.

I know your experiences with Norval must be shocking. I was as much stunned when I first met the man, and that is why I write. I am preparing memoirs of my own (rather arrogant don't you think—who would want to read about me?); nevertheless, I do want to put on paper many of the thoughts that have bothered me for these past many years and I thought what better way than a collection of my own writings. I do want to share one that I composed several months ago, intended for my manuscript, but certainly pertinent to your situation. It also responds to the question you posed in your most recent communiqué.

You asked how I first met Morrisseau. I just take it for granted that everybody knows the story of how we got together. I'm sure that if I were to die tomorrow the single most important thing people would remember me for is, damn it, the discovery of Norval Morrisseau. I'd like to think that I've done other equally import-ant things. However, that's the way it is.

I met Norval in the summer of 1962. My gallery had been open for a couple of years and was struggling along. I was teaching courses at the YMCA, and Paul Bennett, the head of the Community Programs Branch of the Ontario government, approached me. I had taught a course for him the previous summer—teaching art teachers how to teach at a summer school in Guelph. He said he had a project he thought I might be interested in, teaching painting for six weeks in small mining and pulp and paper towns in Northern Ontario. He said I would have to teach two to three hours a day and that they would get me from one place to the next, by plane when necessary.

I thought it sounded really exciting and I felt I was becoming a professional, with the government hiring me to teach. Also, I'd never been up north before.

The first stop was Port Arthur, where I met a wonderful lady named Susan Ross, a graduate of the Ontario Col-lege of Art, married to a judge, James Ross. She used to live on reserves and do portraits and drawings of Indian life. She kept telling me about this Native man who painted on birch bark. I told her the last thing I wanted was an Indian who painted on birch bark. There I was a gallery owner, feeling sophisticated, profes-sional, and promoting modern art. Birch bark! It made me think of the cutesy birch-bark canoes they sell at Niagara Falls.

I purposefully avoided him. In almost every town I went, someone told me about this man. I wasn't inter-ested. As it turned out, I did not discover Norval Mor-risseau. Rather, he discovered me because in Beardmore, I couldn't avoid him.

Beardmore was a ghost town. It had been home to a gold mine, but the vein had run out years earlier and now most of the main street was boarded up. But some people were still clinging on there. I was teaching three classes a day in the one-room schoolhouse. I was hired to teach just two or three hours a day, but you know me—what was I going to do with the rest of the time? I taught kids in the morning, teenagers in the afternoon, and adults in the evening. Three full classes a day.

The second day I was there, the door opened and in walked this tall young Native man, aged around thirty. He was disgustingly drunk and he had apparently pissed his pants. He had a roll of birch bark and paper under his arm. He had heard a white teacher was up from Toronto, and he wanted to show me his paintings. This was Morrisseau.

I couldn't avoid him—he was there! I had to look at the pictures, and I was stunned. They were brilliant. I looked at him and I looked at them and I thought, "He couldn't have painted these." Not this disheveled, unkempt creature. Some of them were on white paper and the paper was pure, not a mark on it.

I was excited. I liked them very much, and I told him so. When he told me he had more painting at his home, I asked if I could go and see more. He said yes.

Susan Ross had come to Beardmore for some extra classes with me, and her friend Sheila Burnford, who wrote *The Incredible Journey*, which Disney had made into a film, had come along for the fun. They drove me to Norval's house the next day.

His house was in the middle of a garbage dump, not next to it, but in it. I shouldn't call it a house. It was a tarpaper shack. Half of it had a roof and half didn't because there was a huge tree growing through the middle of it. A little girl was sitting under the tree—Victoria, his first child. She was filthy dirty, covered in fly bites, and a chipmunk was scampering up and down her knees. There was no stove, no water, no toilet, but there was a table set up under the part of the shack that had a roof.

As I walked in, he scared the shit out of me because he started chanting and banging a drum. He was having fun, really having me on—a brilliant manipulator. But then he went over to the table and picked up a brush and did this magnificent painting and scared the shit out of me again. I got goose bumps. I knew he was a genius.

I didn't know how to handle it, but I asked him if I

could exhibit his paintings in my gallery in Toronto. He just said, "Good. How many do you want?" I went through a stack of his paintings and chose about thirty. He wanted me to pay him five bucks each. I had to explain that wasn't the way I did business, that I'd take them, get them framed, exhibit them, and keep twenty-five percent of what they sold for. I sat down and made a list of the size, material, and so on, signed it and handed it to him. He tore it up and said, "White man's paper no fucking good. Take them." Eventually, I made another list and left it with the mayor of Beardmore.

I arranged that the show would be in October and asked him if there was anyone he wanted me to invite. Yes, there was: Senator Allister Grosart, who'd been the brains behind the campaign when Diefenbaker won such a raging majority as Prime Minister. Norval had met him on one of the senator's trips up north. Norval wanted to be flown down for the opening and asked me to buy him a gray flannel suit.

I took the pictures with me to Toronto, and contacted Senator Grosart who agreed to attend. I still have his reply because it's signed by his secretary, Flora MacDonald.

That exhibition made both Morrisseau and me. It brought Norval to international attention, and it make the Pollock Gallery a public name. So, fame happened to both of us at the same time. I guess that's why regardless of what Norval has become involved with, I still have a soft spot for him in my heart.

As soon as the paintings were hung, I phoned Pearl McCarthy the art critic for the *Globe and Mail*, to come and see them. She was the first to write about Morrisseau and the first to call him a genius. Morrisseau flew in, I bought him the gray flannel suit and a tie, and he promised not to drink before the opening, and he didn't (for once), he was very good. At the Opening itself, he didn't have the opportunity to screw up since I didn't serve any alcohol.

The small works on paper were fifteen dollars; the largest paintings, about two by three feet, were three hundred dollars, framed. Within twenty-four hours, the entire exhibition was sold out. Morrisseau had become a *cause célèbre*, and I became an important person. *Time* did a feature article with a photograph. He was an instant success.

The night after the opening I decided that Norval should stay with me. He had a CBC television interview at ten the next morning, and I didn't want to put him up in a hotel because of his drinking problem. So Norval stayed with me. The opening was over, there was a red sticker on every painting in the gallery; everything was fine. That's when Norval decided that the white man didn't deserve any of his paintings and he was going to smash them all. Luckily, the gallery was locked and he couldn't get in. Eventually I let him in and he demanded that I get him a woman, and when I said I couldn't, he demanded I get him a man! Then he got up, left, and ran out into the street. We had the interview the next morning with Helen Hutchinson, and I had no idea where he'd gone or what I should do.

At nine-thirty the next morning, he came back. To this day I don't know what he met, but it must have been a bear. I've never seen so many hickeys. His whole neck was covered in huge bruises and the new gray suit was ripped in a number of places. He looked like the wrath of God. At the CBC, they found a different suit for him to wear and had to do a make-up job like you've never seen, slapping pancake over the bruises. He carried off the interview perfectly. I, on the other hand, almost had a nervous breakdown.

He made three or four thousand dollars from the show, which I gave to him. Later I got news from Susan Ross that Norval had been handing all this money around, and the entire Native community was drunk. Two Indians got so wasted that they lay down in the middle of a road in the fog and were run over and killed.

I felt guilty, awful. I decided that the answer was to set up a trust fund after his second exhibition, which I held about a year later. To do this I talked to Alan Jarvis, who was the ex-director of the National Gallery, and to Millie Ryerson, who ran the Artisan's Shop in the Village. We approached a lawyer none of us knew, who could act in Norval's best interests, and set up the trust fund. Norval would get something like five hundred dollars every two weeks, which was a fortune in those days.

The next thing I know, I got bills from the Hudson's Bay Company and from Eaton's in Port Arthur. When I phoned to see what the heck was going on, they told me that Norval had come with the *Time* article on us both and had told them to bill his agent. He had bought a silver tea service. He lived in a garbage dump, with no running water, and he bought a silver tea service! I passed the bills on to the trust, but the trustees couldn't cope. The fund lasted only six months, maybe a year. From then on, I bought each painting outright, one at a time, with the idea that he would never have a huge amount of money at any one time. Of course, later, I'd pay quite a bit at once because I was buying a large number of pictures. I was building his reputation, the paintings were getting well known, but he'd still be selling them on the street for a bottle of booze. To this day, he is still doing that.

He is mad, egocentric, demanding, and pitiful. On many occasions, he has driven me to the point that I can't stand him. He's caused me more problems than any other single human being on the face of the Earth. Every once in a while, he hates me; he'd screw me around for a buck. But he loves me. There is a bond between us. Amazing.

Take care, Gilbert, I hope this story can shed some insight into what you will be dealing with. I was surprised when Bernie told me he had set a meeting between you and Norval, and even more so when you accepted Norval's offer of employment. It's a small world—me discovering Norval, becoming friends with you, and now, you living and working with him.

If there is a God in heaven, may he be with you.

Jack

∗∗∗∗∗∗∗∗∗∗∗

February 8, 1979
Jack,

Thanks for the letter about Norval. Although I was aware that you are credited with having discovered Norval, I didn't know the details, a very interesting story to say the least. I think it will provide insight into how to deal with this mad, brilliant, and crazy man.

I have only once question: What did you mean when you said, "I still have a soft spot in my heart, regardless of what he has become involved with"? That sounds ominous and your comment concerns me a great deal.

I'll get this to Many Tongues as soon as I can, although I don't know when he will be able to get it in the mail.

Gilbert

****

JOURNAL ENTRY: 2-9-79

It is dark—everywhere, dark. It is dark outside. It is dark in the sky and on the ground. It is dark in the cabin and darker still within my soul. It has been snowing since Sunday. The sky is constantly overcast, and the clouds have merged with the Earth creating a continuum of gray that links the sky with the horizon and my depression with my loneliness. I have not seen the sun, or the moon, or the stars for a least a week. The dark presses in against the cabin, creating an ominous presence that is neither threatening, nor hostile but is nonetheless omnipresent. It is simply dark, and I grow more fearful by the day, wondering what Jack meant when he wrote, "regardless of what Norval is involved in."

It has been well over a month since Norval and I arrived here, somewhere out in the wilds of nowhere Ontario, and yet curiously, despite the reality in which I now find myself a willing participant, I find myself welcoming the darkness that surrounds me. I reach out and embrace it as I would cherish a long-lost friend or worse, I accept it as a part of me—a part that I cannot, and dare not, deny. The darkness is a blanket with which I cover my desperation, and I realize that only I am able to change my mood. Yet I do not want to change anything. Not the darkness. Not my relationship with Norval. Not the impending doom I sense around me. Not my depression.

Norval is here, sometimes, although less frequently than he is not, but whether he is present, or not, the darkness does not lift. It follows him where ever he goes, and now it follows me. Haunting me, chiding me, threatening me with an unspeakable menace that I cannot define. Norval was here for several days in succession, but now he is gone again. He screws me when he is here, in more ways than one: Physically, emotionally, and spiritually. I pose for him—he says I inspire him. He paints. He drinks. He blows hash and weed like each day is his last day on Earth. And I do his bidding. I prepare his cocaine, not regularly, but more frequently than I would like. I rub his leathery skin. I kiss his foul lips whenever he demands. I serve and service him. And yet…

…and yet I still have hope that somewhere within this darkness is the truth for which I have been searching. I still have faith that my decision to come with Norval, to accept his offer of employment will lead to a better future for me. He will continue to be a brilliant, mad, contentious genius, and I will continue to be nothing without joining his spirit. I need him as much, indeed more, than he does me. And that frightens me. Am I losing myself? Have I lost already? Is it to late to turn back?

No, I must stay. There is good to be found.

But it is dark. It is so dark. And I am at peace.

G

✴✴✴✴✴✴✴✴✴✴✴

JOURNAL ENTRY: 2-12-79

While rummaging through his papers, looking for a scrap on which to paint, I came across an old article about Norval. The article confirmed much of what Norval has already told me about his childhood. It seems that there are times, at least, when Norval remembers enough though his intoxicated stupors to accurately recall his life as it really happened, and not as he would like it to have happened.

I think the article was from *Maclean's*, but I am not certain because it was cut from its source without documentation or acknowledgment. It looks like the *Maclean's* format, and since Jack had mentioned that *Time, Maclean's* and *Chatelaine* had all done articles on Norval, I assume it is from one of them. It does corroborate the stories Norval has told me.

Norval Morrisseau was born in 1932 (he once said 1931) at Sand Point Ojibwa Reserve, on Lake Nipigon, in the province of Ontario. He was born into the Anishnaabe Tribe and was given the birth name of Jean-Baptiste Norman Henry Morrisseau. After he had become very ill when he was around nineteen years old, his birth mother put him through a renaming ceremony with a medicine woman and he was given the name Copper Thunderbird. According to Anishnaabe tradition, the renaming ceremony could help him recover from his illness, which it obviously did.

By the time he was born, the old tribal ways of the Ojibwa had become almost obsolete. But he had the boon of a remarkably traditional upbringing. According to Ojibwa tradition, as eldest son, he was sent to live with his grandparents, and it was his grandfather, Moses Nanakonagas, who educated Norval in Ojibwa ways. Morrisseau didn't spend much time in the white man's world of Indian schools. Christian schools are abundant on Native Reserves, always with the same theological philosophy and agenda: Discourage the traditional ways of the Native Peoples and indoctrinate the savages in Christianity, exchanging their natural mythology and beliefs for the story of a God come to Earth as human. The teachings are ripe with the concepts of guilt, suffering, and penance.

Norval's grandmother was a stern Catholic, educated by Jesuit missionaries, and she introduced her grandson to Christianity. Morrisseau is still fighting the inevitable conflict between his grandparents' beliefs to this day. Norval is an extremely religious man, having been over the years many kinds of Christian: Pentecostal, Russian Orthodox, and Roman Catholic. In 1976, he joined Eckankar, a doctrine of soul travel and astral projection that he finds compatible with Ojibwa belief. He has told me many times that he felt guilty when he was practicing Christianity, but as soon as he came back to his Native beliefs, there was no fear, there was no sin, there was no guilt (there is no concept of guilt in Ojibwa philosophy).

Shifting from one shade of religion to another, Norval has, nonetheless, remained a shaman, a title he bestowed upon himself—an ancient belief system that focuses on the mystical and spiritual and the powers of healing. Although he would never confirm or deny his powers, his friends believe he was initiated at an early age in the Shaking Tent ceremony, a sacred rite witnessed by few, if any, whites.

During his teens, Morrisseau began to paint, if not on canvass, at least in his imagination. It was something he had always wanted to do. He has said that he had been born an artist and would always be an artist, regardless of what else might happen in his life. Some people, he said, are born artists, but most are not, at least in their actions. People have the spirit of color and shape within them, but they choose not to see things as they could be but more as they are. He believes the artist looks at life differently and paints from within the spirit, depicting abstract concepts on whatever medium is available. That is why he has used canvass, paper, birch bark, animal hides, and his mind. Norval is a strong believer that everyone has art within them they just do not know how to tap their imagination. He believes he was fortunate because of the visit from the Thunderbird who allowed his true essence to be realized in art.

His earliest works were done with whatever happened to be at hand—wax crayons, construction paper, birch bark—and he destroyed each piece when it was finished for fear of being discovered by his elders. The lore of the Ojibwa was to be kept within the Tribe, the elders insisted, not exposed to the ridicule of white men. Even to this day, I think there is a part of Norval that believes he has betrayed his ancestors, despite the Thunderbird's prophecy that he would interpret their beliefs for the entire world. He paints with a passion that revealed not only his genius but also the anguish of a man tortured by the repressed guilt planted by his early Christian instruction.

Art wasn't the only adolescent find for Norval. At thirteen he took his first drink. It became a strong obsession. From the beginning, he told me it was a matter of drinking to get drunk and when he wanted to get drunk, which was nearly all the time during his youth and continuing even to this day. It didn't matter where he was, whom he was with, or what he was supposed to be doing. He said he wanted as much as he could drink. In fact, his notion of a social drink was forty ounces of beer, straight out of the bottle. I think it a shame that this man who has brought so much beauty to the world is seen by many, not as the individual drunk that he is, but as the stereotypical representation of how Native people are regarded by whites: drunk and violent, emotional and unpredictable. But Norval isn't a stereotype. He is ever the individual, ever the iconoclast. He is ever singular unto himself, not representing all Native people, but simply being himself—a drunk who is unable to reconcile his gift with his ancestry. Because, at an early age, he had begun to drown his insecurity in any addiction that would free him of this world and from what he considers his betrayal of the Ojibwa way, Norval is at once great and at the same time tragic.

In 1957 Norval Morrisseau was visited one night by the Thunderbird, an Ojibwa deity, who told him that he had been chosen for a special mission. Norval told me the story one evening when he was uncharacteristically open and friendly, with tears in his eyes and an obvious discomforting recollection:

Do not be afraid, the Thunderbird God told him. We are testing you and you have done well. You are the One for whom we have searched. The One of whom legends have foretold.

Not knowing what the test was, Norval became afraid and tired to run away, but the Thunderbird God spoke again, saying: *Stay in peace. You will know your mission before the full moon appears twelve times in the sky. Then you shall begin what we have prophesied.*

Norval told me that months had passed, following the visit from the Thunderbird God, before the mission became apparent, and when it did, he became even more frightened than on the night of the visitation. His mission, and it became the work of his lifetime, was to break ancient taboos and set down for the first time, in art, the sacred tribal myths and legends of the Ojibwa for everyone, Native and white, to see. Under the Thunderbird's protection, Morrisseau began to paint visions never recorded before, reaching out beyond the world of his ancestors and stretching far beyond the shores of his Native Ojibwa lands; beyond his adopted Anglican home. Norval Morrisseau had become the Thunderbird, not the God who visited him that fateful night in 1957, but the reincarnation of the Ojibwa spirit, whose mission and life's purpose was to resurrect the legends of his people and to create life, again, where for decades only despair and death had existed.

From that time forward, Norval has, indeed, brought to life the rich history and legends of his people, a proud and glorious tribe who once roamed the eastern regions of Canada and the Eastern woodlands of the United States of America in peace, harmony, and prosperity.

He has displayed his work in Canada at the Kleinberg, Pollock, and Taylor galleries, at the National Gallery of Canada, at the University of Toronto, and at the Royal Ontario Museum of Art. His art has been exhibited in the United States, Germany, France, and Finland. He completed a sixteen-foot mural for the Indian Pavilion at Expo '67 in Montreal. He is the founder of the Woodland Indian School of Art. He has handcrafted fine porcelain plates, The Children of Mother Earth, that sold for one thousand dollars per set and was hailed as the most exciting issue of limited-edition art ever offered by Anna-Perenna, Inc. He has authored two books, Windigo & Other Tales of the Ojibwa and Legends of My People: The Great Ojibwa. The National Film Board of Canada chronicled his life and work in *The Paradox of Norval Morrisseau*. His exhibitions regularly sell out on opening nights and individual paintings go for as much as $25,000 each. To top his fame he became a Member of the Order of Canada in 1978 by Governor General Edward Schreyer. Norval is, without question, peerless among contemporary Native artists.

This is the Norval Morrisseau I have come to respect and to admire; not the drunken, abusive man whose intolerance is as great as the white man's. Not the drug addicted clown who isolates himself from the world, bounded in guilt and terror. Not the angry, sexually ambivalent man who submerges his spirit in cowardice and shame, but the shaman, the Spirit Traveler, the artistic genius who embodies the soul of his people.

Frequently, I return to one of the writings I read from Norval's own pen: "I am tired of hearing about Norval the drunkard, Norval with the hangover, Norval in jail, Norval torn apart by his allegiance both to Christianity and to the old Indian ways…. They speak about this tortured man, Norval Morrisseau—I'm not tortured. I've had a marvelous time when I was drinking." Unfortunately, his words reflect too accurately, but I am not here with Norval to judge his personal choices. I am here to learn from the artist, the master. And this is why I choose to remain. This is why I persist despite the abuse, the neglect, and the self-destruction. Norval is the Copper Thunderbird!

G

＊＊＊＊＊＊＊＊＊＊＊＊

JOURNAL ENTRY: 2-13-79

My second meeting with Morrisseau at the Four Seasons Hotel in Toronto was not as anxiety producing as the first. During that first session, I was as nervous as a groom on his wedding night, but I had learned a great deal about the man behind the artist. I had seen his drunken and drug-induced behavior and had begun to see him, in an elementary way, not only as the genius that he was but as the child he tried not to be.

I did not need to drink and smoke with Bernie and Raymond prior to our second meeting, and I did not even practice my recitation of qualifications before returning to his room. I felt more relaxed with Norval, more at home, more understanding of this man who partied like a teenager when first loosed upon the world. In fact, I was so confident about him offering me the position he had advertised, that I had developed a certain conceit about myself; a certain cockiness that had no font of reality, but which provided me with the confidence I needed to approach our second meeting.

On Thursday, December 14th, at precisely 7:00 PM, our earlier agreed upon time, I returned to Norval's room at the Four Seasons. He was expecting me, but I must say I was not expecting that which I was soon to discover.

Once again, he greeted me at the door stoned, probably drunk (it was hard to tell given the giddiness of his marijuana-induced state), and hopped up on coke like you wouldn't believe. He was wearing the same outfit as he had the night before, and although I was at first surprised at seeing him dressed in the same clothes, I don't know that I should have expected anything different given the little (and lot) I had learned about him the previous night. He had on the same tattered jeans, the identical rumpled shirt, and was emitting the same obnoxious body odor that had offended my senses the previous evening. His hair was still oily and unkempt, his beard at least several days old, and his face wore the same vacant expression that had punctuated each of the stories he had told the night before.

When I entered his room, he offered a joint and a shot, which I readily accepted, and I could not believe what I saw.

On the wall, behind where the bed should have been (he had moved it away I guess for the purpose of displaying what I am about to describe), Norval had painted a six-foot oil painting of me as a metis, fully naked with an erection that would have complimented even the most advantaged of men. An array of colors covered the whole painting. The expression on the painting's face was one of distance and serenity. I was dumbfounded. The painting was brilliant! It was a beautiful was a sight to behold. I was overwhelmed with thoughts of Rivera, Duveneck, and Rubens. But it was not painted by one of the old masters but rather a new one to add to the pantheon of art. Norval Morrisseau—an Ojibwa artist. It was colorful, vivid, and alive.

Although I was speechless, and obviously impressed, I was also, at first, somewhat offended. I felt violated; like this stranger, even though an artist, had taken what he had seen, without my permission, stripped away the exterior, and left a likeness of me for the whole world to see. Me, naked, with an unmistakable and impressive hard-on! As glorious as the painting was, as breathtaking as it was to gaze upon, and as typical as it was of the genius of this man, I was nevertheless insulted. He had reduced our one meeting to an erotic representation of what he had visualized beneath the exterior. He had not once asked a question about my resume or credentials but had expressed, in the medium of his expression, an exaggeration of what I supposed he was most interested in. Surely, I thought to myself, he could have depicted me, just as beautifully, wearing something more than nothing and somehow different than with an erection! But I kept my displeasure to myself. Expressing my feelings would not be the most effective way to assure my desired position with Norval Morrisseau. And although I was embarrassed by the painting, I still wanted to escape the monotony of my devolving life, take wing with Norval and fly, so I remained silent, thinking only to myself how violated one could feel when captured on canvas, totally exposed— an image stolen!

My silence did not last long, however, as Norval asked what I thought of it. What could I say? Dare I reveal my true feelings? I told him how privileged I felt that he would paint such a remarkable piece of art. I complimented his technique. Reveled over his use of color. Gushed about the symmetry and depth. I tried my best to impress him with my knowledge of art and technique. Always being one to calculate the possibilities, I thought my assessment of his creativity might enhance my chances of becoming his companion, his protégé if you would. I groveled. I gushed. I oozed. I wanted the job!

The rest of the evening was spent in similar fashion to the night before. Lots of bad drink (Norval wasn't one to stand on the pretension of expensive liquor), a seemingly endless supply of marijuana, and a dozen or so more stories of life the Norval way: Shamanism, Eckankar, the wilderness. Again, just as the night before, he did not ask once about my credentials. No interest in my experiences. No request to see a portfolio. I should have guessed what Norval's desires and intentions were given the painting of me and his apparent lack of interest in my abilities. Naiveté I suppose; blind desire I am sure.

Near the end of the evening, as he once again appeared to grow weary of his own voice, he suddenly asked if I would be interested in being his companion and secretary. He briefly explained that the position would include traveling with him, attending to his managerial tasks, inspiring his creativity, serving as his companion—upon which he did not elaborate—learning to paint under his tutelage, and becoming his protégé.

My dream had finally come true! Norval Morrisseau, world renowned artist, celebrity of the newly emerging art nouveau, shaman, soul traveler, and Ojibwa herald had asked me, Gilbert Petén, to become his companion. His offer freed me. Freed me from the drudgery of my tedious government job. Freed me from the increasing boredom of Toronto. Freed me from a dreary past and an even more unappealing future. Freed me from who I feared I had become.

There was no hesitation on my part, even given the offense I had initially taken at the nude painting of myself. I now regarded his painting as being not only brilliant, but demanding of display at one of the prestigious Canadian galleries—perhaps Jack Pollock's. Suddenly, with the invitation to work with him, the few words that I knew could change my life forever, I cared less about being exposed with an erection for critics and admirers to observe and more about my own selfish desires to grab whatever I could on my way to an exciting adventure. I had become his art whore!

I agreed to his proposal.

Norval told me that he liked me a great deal and already felt inspired by my very presence. He called the painting on the wall Eagle Spirit. And he began calling me his Little Eagle. We had both accomplished what we had intended: Norval got a new traveling companion, and I got my escape!

Before I left that night, we made arrangements. He wanted to leave Toronto as quickly as possible. He said he hated being in the white man's city, so the next day I resigned my position with Public Works Canada, tendered my notice, and began preparing to move—to where I did not know. But it didn't matter. I would be gone! My life had begun.

G

****

JOURNAL ENTRY: 2-15-79

An old Native man came to the cabin today. I had just returned from an early morning walk and was cleaning up some of the mess that had accumulated over the past weeks, when I suddenly felt the presence of another person standing behind me. I turned around and there he stood at the animal-skin door, not knocking, not calling for anyone, not doing anything except standing silently in the doorway. I wasn't particularly surprised, or startled by his presence since we have a number of visitors who are always looking for Norval for one reason or another—usually for his shaman cleansings—so I simply said what I normally do:

"Norval isn't home."

"I do not search for Norval," said the old man, and I do mean old; he had to have been at least a hundred years in age. "I am looking for the new Old Young One," he continued.

"I don't know who that is," I responded, becoming a bit more interested. We had never had a visitor searching for any person of that name.

"I wish I could help you, but I have no idea who this new Old Young One is," I continued. "I do know Norval has gone to Beardmore and isn't here. Is there something I can do for you?"

"May I come in?" the old Indian asked.

I was embarrassed by my lack of manners. "Yes, of course, please do. I'm sorry, I didn't mean to let you stand out in the cold." I showed him to a chair and offered a cup of hot tea.

"Thank you, my friend, the warmth is welcomed. I will sit with you a while, but I cannot stay long, I have many places yet to go today."

Many places yet to go, I thought to myself? This guy was ancient and he had many places yet to go? I glanced outside but didn't see any type of vehicle, not even a dogsled for transportation! How did he intend to get to 'those many places,' by foot? I had trouble enough just getting around the heavily wooded acres of nowhere that surrounded us, and he was telling me that he had many places yet to go. In this weather, at his age? I had serious doubts about the veracity of his story, but I ignored my reservations and continued our conversation.

"If you can tell me more about the person you are looking for, perhaps I can help," I said to him. "I will remember to tell Norval and Many Tongues that you were here and ask them if they know anyone of that name."

"Many Tongues will know I was here. He will know the new Old Young One just as you do. You know the new Old Young One. Perhaps you just don't remember," he continued, but I interrupted.

"No, I am sorry, you are mistaken. I do not know anyone of that name."

He placed his hand upon the cup of tea but did not touch it to his lips and looked me straight in the face with eyes that were as deep, as dark and as mysterious as any I had ever seen and yet at the same time gentle and comforting. I felt at ease with this man, even though I had no idea who he was, from where he had come or even what his name might be.

"Again, I'm sorry, but I didn't get your name," I apologized.

"You can call me the older Old Young One," he chuckled. "I have many names, but that is the one by which I am known to many human beings." He laughed, quietly, and repeated the name over to himself as though he found something funny about it. "Yes, Old Young One, Old Young One. A very strange name, don't you think? " he asked, looking back at me.

I didn't know how to respond but given my lack of companionship, I was enjoying our vague and confusing conversation and didn't want it to end. I don't know what it was about the old man, but something made me feel that I knew him, as though we had been friends for a dozen years; perhaps it was his age that comforted and familiarized me, I don't know, but I am certain that we had never met previously. I know that I would have remembered someone his age and with eyes as penetrating as his.

"Oh, I don't know, Old Young One sounds fine to me," I went on. "Kind of like you're old, excuse my insolence but still young. I like it! It has a meaning that goes far beyond the names we white people have. Like mine: Gilbert; now what does that mean? Probably something in French, at least at some point in history, when names had descriptive or identifying connotations. But yours is very descriptive," I theorized out loud.

He laughed again. "Mandamin," he said, slowly.

"What?" I asked.

"Mandamin, not Gilbert," he repeated.

"No, it is Gilbert. You must have me mistaken with someone else."

Again, he laughed, an infectious laughter that had me giggling even though I had no idea what we were chuckling about.

"I am not confused, Mandamin. I do not mistake you for another. I assure you, since you cannot remember now, you will know the new Old Young One when the time is right!" he said.

"I will know him?" I asked, becoming more interested as he spoke. "Is this person someone I have met, or are yet to meet?"

But as suddenly as he had arrived, he abruptly announced that he had to leave.

"I must go now, I have many places yet to visit, today, many places. An American poet once wrote: The woods are lovely, dark and deep, But I have promises to keep…and miles to go before I sleep—And miles to go before I sleep," he said as his stood up. A fan of Robert Frost, I thought to myself.

"Thank you for your hospitality. It was very refreshing," the old man offered.

"Must you leave so soon?" I implored. "I get so few visitors here that…."

"I know, my friend, you are alone now, but soon you will not be so," he added.

"I will not be alone here?" I said dumbfounded, with not as much question as statement.

"You will not be alone ever again," he repeated and walked to the door.

Then he turned and addressed me one more time before he left. "Do not worry about the rat, my friend; the rabbit and the Thunderbird have dominion over the rat." As he made his strange comment he reached over and touched my forehead. "Do not worry, Mandamin."

"What rat," I asked in amazement. "What are you talking about?"

"I must leave now. I have many places yet to visit today."

As he spoke, the spoon that had been balancing precariously across his untouched cup of tea clattered onto the rebuilt table, momentarily drawing my attention away from the old man. When I turned back to ask again what rat he had been talking about, he was gone, as though vanished into thin air!

I searched outside the cabin, looked as far down our path as I could see, but there was no sign of Old Young One; he couldn't have moved quickly enough to have disappeared from sight that fast, not at his age, not at any age! In fact, as I looked around, it struck me that there was no evidence that he had even been to the cabin! A fresh layer of snow had fallen in the morning, and surely anyone who had come by foot, sled, car, or, whatever, would have left markings in the snow. But there were none. The snow was undisturbed, the old man had vanished, and…

…I shuddered, more from thoughts of my mysterious visitor than from the cold. I went back inside and latched the animal hide door behind me. I stoked the fire, but could think of nothing other than the old man, the strange name—Mandamin—he had mistakenly called me, the thing about the rat (whatever that was supposed to mean), and the person called the new Old Young One for whom he had been searching.

I'm not sure I've ever seen a rat; at least I don't remember having seen one. And why should I worry about a rat, or a rabbit, or a Thunderbird for that matter? I know that Norval is called the Thunderbird; perhaps the old man was confusing some person named the new Old Young One with Norval.

I tried to let my thoughts of the old man pass, knowing that I'd mention his visit to Many Tongues, hoping for more information, the next time I saw him. I certainly wouldn't discuss the old man with Norval. He would undoubtedly become jealous or fearful and accuse me of some kind of shenanigans. For the remainder of the day, I could think of little else, other than my strange visitor and his cryptic messages.

This whole experience grows weirder by the day: Norval, Ojibwa spiritualism, Norval's unexplained absences, the cabin itself and now this mysterious old man. I guess I'm getting what I had asked for when I took the job with Norval—excitement, and relief from the boredom of Toronto, so I guess I shouldn't complain.

But, even given all that—I still can't help but wonder, who the hell is Mandamin?

G

****

FEBRUARY 17, 1979
Joanne,

I know it's been a few weeks since I last wrote. Not much going on here; just a bunch of weird happenings for which I have no explanation, but more about that another time. Norval returned a few weeks ago and stayed for three days in a row. Then he was off again, to wherever! I still don't know where he goes, whom he sees, or what he does. He is very secretive about his comings and goings and has never shared information about his absences with me. I can only imagine what might be going on. He's probably scoring dope, but that shouldn't take days on end. I am aware that Norval has a wife and children, so perhaps that is where he is and with whom he is visiting. Jack mentioned in a letter, last month, that Norval has at least one child, Virginia I think was her name, but his reference to her was from 1962 so she must be a grown woman by now. I wonder how many other children or wives Norval might have.

Norval did mention, during his last visit home, that we'd be going to North Dakota sometime in February or March for some sort of Indian ceremony. I don't know if it is specifically Ojibwa, another tribe, or native-universal, but I am looking forward to the experience nonetheless. Curiously, since events and ceremonies are usually scheduled in advance I wonder why he doesn't know during which month we are leaving. He said I could attend, which is quite an honor, since it is evidently a ritual that few (if any) white people have ever witnessed. I guess he does have some sort of feelings for me!

He also mentioned in passing that we'd be leaving from North Dakota and going to Winnipeg to live. I'm not sure how I feel about that! I've come to like it here at the cabin, and I'm even getting used to the lack of conveniences. I still can't get used to shitting in the woods and using leaves for toilet tissue, but taking a pee isn't so bad, although it's so cold that I've learned to piss in a hurry. Given our external genitalia, we menfolk do have *some* advantages over you women. Still leaving here causes dissonance for me. As rustic as it is, rather make that as deficient as it is, it has become home. And I'm just beginning to establish a workable routine here. Now, off to elsewhere and—what else?

I've also come to enjoy the isolation of the woods. When Norval is gone, so too are his cronies, and I am here alone to revel in my solitude. I've been doing a lot of writing (in a journal—can you believe that!), some primitive sketching, and a great deal of thinking. Believe it or not, I think this experience is forcing me to reassess my outlook on life and regard what I once considered a pitiful existence as something more than wasted—not that I'm over my depression and morbidity. I guess some things will never change, but I like the closeness of nature and being a part of a world I could not even hope to experience in Toronto. Don't get me wrong. I'm not turning into one of those modern-day pioneers, you know those recycled hippie types who chuck it all and think they are returning to their roots by roughing it in a modern cabin in the woods complete with their phones and television sets, hot tubs, and stereos. I have simply become satisfied with far fewer material items that I had grown used to and have come to enjoy the peace that the woods afford me.

Don't misunderstand—I have no intention of making this way of life a permanent fixture. I've regarded this experience all along as just that, an experience! I'm not cut out for a rustic or monastic life for terribly long. As much as I've come to enjoy the serenity of our dump, I still long for a hot shower, an electric blanket, a blow dryer, and a hundred other amenities that would take a letter just to list.

I've been modeling a great deal for Norval when he is here. He's done several paintings that he says I've inspired. What a rush to think that my likeness could be hanging in a gallery, selling for tens of thousands of dollars, gracing the cover of a magazine, or perhaps even hanging in a home of one of the nouveau-riche. I fantasize about them gushing over the technique, style, color, and depth of an original Morrisseau, while clinking cocktail glasses and bubbling in a drunken stupor with their stuffy, mindless friends. I'd love it!

I'll share my journal with you when once we are together again. Ha! Bet you were beginning to believe that we'd never see each other again. Well, I told you differently in my first letter, so believe me, girl, like

General MacArthur, I shall return. Of course, when you read the journal, you'd better be prepared for Gilbert Exposed. I leave no thought unwritten, no concept unexplored, and no experience unmentioned. It is bawdy, brutal, honest, and erotic. Sounds like great reading, bet you can't wait.

Well, guess I'd better be off for now. It may be a few weeks until you hear from me again what with the trip to North Dakota and the move to Winnipeg. But, rest assured —you will hear from me!

As always, my dear friend: Take care, be good, have fun, and live for today!

I miss you one hell of a lot!

Gilbert

✦✦✦✦✦✦✦✦✦✦✦✦

JOURNAL ENTRY: 2-18-79

I've been having a recurring nightmare for the past three nights about a rat. It is simple, quick, and not necessarily frightening, but it is disturbing. I have no idea what it might mean, but I am reminded of Old Young One and his admonition for me to not worry about the rat! Did he know I would be having these nightmares, and if so, how did he know?

Had he planted the thought in my mind, and now my subconscious has given it life during my sleep, and if he did plant the thought, why? What was his purpose? What did he hope to gain? Regardless, the dreams are all too real and disquieting, even more so because of Old Young One's comments.

I am walking through the door into the kitchen at my parents' home and see a huge rat walking from one side of the kitchen to the other, heading toward the bathroom. And when I write that the rat is huge—I sincerely mean that. It is at least the size of a Golden Retriever or a Chocolate Lab. I look at it, not necessarily frightened, but certainly surprised, and it just stops in its tracks and stares back at me with dark, red, demonic eyes. We are suspended in time for several minutes, staring each other down, when it suddenly shrieks a shrill hiss that sends shivers down my spine—a hiss like the wail of a seething banshee in search of a victim. Then it turns and continues on its way, and that's it. Nothing more. The dream is weird and, it keeps recurring over and over again, night after night. I wish I understood dream interpretation.

Norval would know. Because he is a shaman, he is also a dream interpreter and a reader of the stars—a sage that knows what will happen long before it does. He is a soul traveler and a descendent of the chieftains of the Ojibwa. He is the reincarnation of the Copper Thunderbird. I know he could tell me about the rat. I have seen, and heard, and felt him do as much for others when they come to him with dreams, problems, visions—and he interprets. The visitors have filled our shack many nights when he is home and he has given them answers. They come bewildered and confused and they leave in peace. Now I am the one who is bewildered!

I have heard that he controls the ritual he calls the Awakenings, and I know he has experienced the ritual of the Shaking Tent. I am certain he could tell me what the dream means. He could help me. But he is not here. He is seldom here. Damn him, when I need him, when I want to join with the spirit he embodies, he is absent! One of the reasons I accepted his offer last December was to learn from his spiritualism, but he is seldom here. Norval, I need you! Come home.

And what about Old Young One? I am positive that he could tell me about the dream, what it means, and why I am experiencing it over and again. After all, he spoke of it even before I dreamed it. I have not seen Many Tongues for over a week and have not had the chance to tell him about the visit from Old Young One, but maybe he already knows about the visit. Old Young One said I would not have to tell Many Tongues about the visit, that he would know. And he said that Many Tongues knew the new Old Young One. Perhaps Many Tongues can help me remember who this person is. But I am certain I do not know anyone by the name of new Old Young One. How can Many Tongues possibly be able to assist me recalling someone I have never met?

This whole experience is like I have become involved with some kind of mystical cult—or perhaps not a cult but Ojibwa spiritualism. I know that Norval is a shaman, but now, with the introduction of Old Young One into the equation, and his suggestion that Many Tongues would know that he had visited, makes all three men complicit. But complicit in what I do not know. I am unnerved by the situation but feel strangely curious and comforted. Although Norval keeps me on edge with his volatile personality, I am at ease with the comfortable gentility of both Many Tongues and Old Young One.

I wish to god one of the three would come back so I could get some answers. On the other hand, make that I wish that one of the two would come back—either Many Tongues or Old Young One. I don't know why, but I don't feel that I can trust Norval with this information. In fact, I shall resolve not to share my experience about my mysterious visitor with Norval. I will wait to discuss it with Many Tongues, even though I don't know why I should trust him either—we hardly know one another—but for some reason I do.

Indeed, I will wait until the appropriate time to discuss it with him.

G

****

JOURNAL ENTRY: 2-21-79

I am disturbed and saddened by Norval's chemical dependencies on alcohol and drugs. I don't have a lot of room to talk, however, or to point fingers, but Norval's indulgent behavior regarding anything mind-altering is disquieting, not as much because I am concerned about him (although that is a legitimate distress), but more so because of the stereotype he perpetrates.

A white man, who identified himself as Jacques, came to the cabin the other day in search of Norval. I'm sure he was there to score some dope, but of course Norval wasn't here and the man was soon on his way. What upset me, more than the interruption of my monotonous daily routine, was the manner by which he asked for Norval. He didn't simply ask if Norval were home, or if Mr. Morrisseau were around, or even if the old drunk was anywhere near. Rather he asked: "Is that drunken savage home?" Now, of course, it is possible that the man who had identified himself as Jacques and Norval are good friends and the term he used to describe Norval was nothing more than friendly joking. I don't even know how Norval might refer to this man called Jacques. He might insult him, just as Jacques did Norval.

On the other hand, although Jacques, terminology didn't seem "friendly" in nature, it wasn't necessarily unfriendly or threatening but seemed more typical of how white people regard Native People, and that's the problem.

White man's history has portrayed Natives in a way that makes it comfortable for us to excuse our genocide of Native People as being necessary to the 1800s American doctrine of manifest destiny; an idea from the U.S. that transferred too comfortably to Canada—although never enunciated as directly. White man's stealing of their lands, murdering of their people, raping of their women, pillaging of their homes, and desecration of their philosophy and legends makes us no better than the Nazis we so vehemently decry for their genocide of European Jews. We have replaced the virgin lands of the Native with white, western civilization. We have eliminated Native religion and philosophy and supplanted it for Christianity and all in the name of saving the poor savages from eternal hell and damnation. We have broken treaties, ignored promises, and, ultimately, herded the few remaining Natives onto non-productive, barren reserves called reservations in the United States.

Hollywood has portrayed Native people as savage, murdering barbarians who would sooner kill the white man than befriend him. They were pictured as devious, deceitful, dishonest, drunk, and lazy. And that is how many people still regard Native people today. But if people were to examine the true history of the indigenous population and the white conquest of North America, they would realize that the stereotypes we see in the history books and on the movie screen are lies and misrepresentations of how things really were then, and still are now.

I am not well versed in the history of all Native tribes, but since I have been here, I have come to know a great deal more about the Ojibwa than I ever did before, even though there were a number of Ojibwa living in or around where I grew up.

The Ojibwa, also known as the Chippewa, are of the Algonquian language family and of the Eastern Woodlands culture. Their territory reached into southern Canada between Lake Huron and the Turtle Mountains in North Dakota.

According to Ojibwa tradition, the tribe originally emigrated from the region of the Saint Lawrence River in the east, in company with the related Ottawa and Potawatomi. The three tribes separated at what is now Mackinaw City, Michigan with the Ojibwa spreading west along both shores of Lake Superior, while the other tribes went south. The Ojibwa tribe was scattered over a vast area and comprised a large number of bands divided into permanent clans. Originally, the clans were divided into five phratries from which more than twenty clans developed. One of the clans claimed the hereditary chieftainship of the entire tribe, whereas another claimed precedence in the councils of war.

The Ojibwa were mainly hunters, fisherman, and farmers. Their food consisted of rice, fruits, berries, fish, wild game, and sugar maple. Their houses were built on pole frames in wigwam shape and were usually covered with birch bark. Birch bark sheets were also used for keeping simple pictographic records of tribal affairs.

Ojibwa mythology is elaborate; the central religious rites focused on the Medewiwin or grand medicine society.

The Ojibwa were the largest Native American tribe north of Mexico but did not come into contact with European settlers until the mid-seventeenth century when they were confined within a narrow area along the shore of Lake Superior by the incursions of the Sioux and the Fox who were being driven northward by white settlers. They acquired firearms from the French about 1690, drove off their enemies, and greatly expanded their territory. In the American Revolution the Ojibwa sided with the English which was never forgotten by the government of the United States.

In 1815, they signed a peace treaty with the U.S. government and were forced to sell most of their territory. As was the case with virtually all of the treaties initiated by the United States with Native people, the Treaty of 1815 was eventually broken, and the Ojibwa were forced onto reservations in the U.S. states of Wisconsin, Michigan, Minnesota, North Dakota, and Montana. Many Ojibwa migrated northward to Canada and settled in the north-central area of Ontario. And, as was the case with all Native American tribes, by the twentieth century, the heritage, lore, legends, and customs of the Ojibwa—indeed, their culture— had been submerged into a blend of forced Christianity and European civilization. The great white Spirit had conquered the Indigenous People in the names of God and Jesus Christ.

And that is why I have problems with Norval having such a drug addictive personality. He presents the perfect stereotype of the deceitful, despicable, 'drunken Indian.' And though he may be, he is only a man, one lonely Native man, certainly not representative of this people, and truthfully no different than any European, Asian, African, or any other person who characterizes a specific, individual personality—not the representation of an entire race or national identity.

I hope when people see the art of Norval Morrisseau and come to understand his mysticism and shamanism they will see beyond the alcohol and drugs, beyond the stereotypes and misunderstandings, beyond the whole, and to the individual.

Of course, I am not even certain that those who purchase an original Morrisseau painting even know he is a drunken, drugged-out wreck of a man. I'm sure they simply hang his art over the fireplace and accept the adulations of those who are jealous. Once again, Norval, damn you. Not for me, but for your people. You have opened the eyes of the world to your artistic genius, and you have brought life to the legends and lore of the Ojibwa, but, at the same time, you have perpetuated the negative stigmatization of Native people because of your drinking and drugging. Damn you!

G

❋❋❋❋❋❋❋❋❋❋❋

JOURNAL ENTRY: 2-22-79

I returned from my customary afternoon walk earlier today to discover that the cabin had been broken into. Of course, broken into is hardly an appropriate expression, considering that it is difficult to 'break into' a building that has no locks on the doors or glass in the windows. I suppose it is better to say that the cabin had been violated. Everything was in disarray. Furniture had been overturned and one piece broken. Norval's paintings had been transgressed and were strewn about the floor, our clothing had been torn from the home-made closet Norval fashioned out of pine, and the stew I had been preparing for our evening meal in hopes that Norval would return had been splattered on one of Norval's paintings.

My first thought was the silver collection. I was sure that Norval's magic had failed, and that someone had finally broken in to steal the thousands of dollars-worth of finely crafted artifacts. But as I checked through the collection, I couldn't find one piece missing! Although I do not have an inventory of Norval's silver, and a few pieces could have been taken without my knowledge, I can't imagine why someone would go to the trouble of coming way out here in the wilderness, only to make off with one or two pieces of silver, especially when it would have been easy to stuff the entire collection in any one of the many animal-hide bags Norval keeps in plain sight! It didn't make sense. In fact, the whole break-in didn't compute.

There was nothing missing, so it didn't appear to be thievery. Nothing had been damaged, other than the one chair, so it probably wasn't vandalism. And Norval's paintings had been left undamaged, except for the one with stew splattered on it. From the little evidence I could see, it obviously was not a thief or a vandal, and since his paintings were for the most part undamaged, it did not appear to be someone jealous of Norval, or intent upon destroying his art.

Given that we were miles from the town of Beardmore and given that we did not have a telephone, I couldn't call the police. I will have to wait until Norval returns, fill him in on what happened, and see if he has any ideas about who might have done this and why.

I must admit that the incident has left me a bit uneasy. Up until the break-in, I had never felt threatened or uncomfortable here in the woods. I actually had never even given thought to the possibility of danger or victimization; crimes like this are urban problems, not wilderness issues! The only thing I had come to fear and even then, with only remote consideration was being attacked by some kind of wild animal. I have heard stories about monstrous black bears rummaging through summer cabins in search of food and coming across vacationers whose last Earthly acts were to attempt defense against their furry invaders. I have no desire to encounter an angry, hungry bear and send myself off to eternity shredded and bloodied. Of course, given that this is February, bears are probably in hibernation and not about to emerge until spring arrives. Anyway, I certainly hadn't considered being vandalized in the middle of nowhere!

After cleaning up the mess and putting things back in some semblance of order, I came across what appeared to be the only clue to the invasion: A tattered and dirty business card with the name Jacques Volpe, barely readable. He seemed to be a clumsy intruder, at best, a fool at the worst, leaving behind evidence that could pin the tail on the donkey. I must remember to show the card to Norval because perhaps he knows who Jacques is. Or I suppose it is possible that the trespasser simply dropped the card and isn't this Volpe character himself.

Then I remembered that the man who had come looking for Norval recently identified himself as Jacques! Coincidental? I doubt it. Although Jacques is a fairly common French-Canadian name, it seems highly unlikely that two men named Jacques would manifest within a few days.

That made me nervous. What if the person (or persons) responsible for this break-in return, in the middle of the night and attempt some sort of tomfoolery? I am here, alone, as I usually am. I do not present a physically imposing figure and certainly my appearance would not frighten away even a ruthless band of demented nuns! There are no door locks to bolt, no windows to close and secure, and no means of protection other than an old musket that Norval keeps in the corner. It probably doesn't even work and I haven't seen any musket balls lying around. Besides, I wouldn't know how to use a musket even if I had ammunition. I am at the mercy of any intruder who happens along. However, since Norval's magic has, thus far, successfully protected the silver, perhaps it might extend to me. He told me that the spell he had conjured was not specifically for the silver but for anything precious that was inside the cabin. I am precious, or at least I think I am in all modesty, so maybe the spell will protect me as well.

God, I hope so.

And Norval is still gone.

G

★★★★★★★★★★★★

JOURNAL ENTRY: 2-25-79

Norval returned yesterday and announced that we will be leaving for the Cleansing ceremony in North Dakota tomorrow morning. Our party will consist of Norval, his brother Wolf who I have only met briefly, my confidant, Many Tongues, and me—oddball travelers on the way to North Dakota! According to Norval's plans, we won't be coming back to the cabin when we return to Canada. We will be taking a place in Winnipeg for a while. As much as I've grown to tolerate this dreary dwelling, I am looking forward to a hot shower and a regular meal. Besides, I've never been to Winnipeg, so another adventure follows atop another adventure.

Norval seems uncharacteristically calm. He is drunk and stoned, but there is a peace about him that projects serenity and strength. I'm not certain what it might be or what could be causing his abrupt change in behavior: Perhaps because of something that happened away from here or maybe because he is looking forward to the ceremony in North Dakota, who knows, but something has initiated a positive calm. I really don't know what it might be, and I don't want to pursue it. I figure why disturb a sleeping dog. If he wants to be more sensitive and calm, who am I do disagree, especially since I seem to be the one who experiences the brunt of his vulgar behavior—and now, the tranquility of his composure.

Given Norval's pleasant demeanor, I was hesitant to tell him about the break-in and show him the business card I had found. Nevertheless, this is his cabin, and even though nothing had been stolen, he has a right to know. When I told him the story and showed him the card, his reaction was surprising: He just tore the card in two, and grumbled, " Goddam it, not again!"

"What?" I asked, thinking I had misheard.

"Nothing, Little Eagle, just forget it, it's not a big deal," he responded.

Perhaps not a big deal to you Norval, but I was the one who was here and had to face the consequences of a possible return of the intruder(s). It was a big deal to me, but I suppose if Norval is not concerned with the break-in, then neither should I be. Perhaps our leaving for North Dakota tomorrow morning helped explained Norval's calm demeanor regarding the name 'Jacques.' Neither of us will have to worry about the intruder at this point, since we will be gone and will not be returning, at least in the near future.

As he walked away, I thought I heard him mumble something, but I'm not sure I heard him correctly. His head was bowed and what ever he said was barely audible, but I could swear he said, "I wish he'd just leave me alone!" If I am correct in what I think I heard, I can't help but wonder who 'he' is and why Norbal wants 'him' to 'leave him alone.' Unfortunately, I'll probably never know since Norval is unusually protective about his private life. Add another mystery to the saga of Norval and Gilbert!

I have packed our few belongings and have emptied the cabin of items that might attract unwanted visitors, animals that is. Norval said to leave the silver pieces as they are. He claims they will be fine. Since they belong to him, I will do as he asks; however, I can't bring myself to believe that some of the more unsavory characters who have frequented our place during the past two months might not be as trustworthy as Norval believes and given that the place has just been violated, I'm not comfortable leaving the silver in plain sight. When we (he? I? us?) are to return, here, is anyone's guess, but I wouldn't be surprised to discover the silver missing when whoever is to return—returns. Still, there is the magic spell of protection that Norval cast upon the cabin and that just might do the trick.

I'm taking my journal with me. Norval saw me writing in it earlier this evening and asked what I was writing. I told him I was keeping a written account of my experiences and vivid descriptions of his paintings. He didn't seem to like it when I said I was keeping an account of my experiences but appeared pleased when I added "and descriptions of his paintings." He didn't ask to read it, just harrumphed and walked away Maybe he can't read? I had never considered that possibility.

Many Tongues will not be joining us until tomorrow morning, so I have not had a chance to tell him about Old Young One. I hope when we get to Manitou in North Dakota, I will have a chance to speak with him alone. I am curious about the old man who came to visit and would like some explanation for his cryptic messages. But, like so many things I have been experiencing since arriving, here my conversation with Many Tongues will have to wait.

I am curious about the weather in North Dakota. Since it is just the beginning of March, there still should be snow and cold that far north in the United States. I have wondered about the Cleansing Ceremony and how it would be enacted near the end of winter's harsh weather. From what Norval has told me, the ceremony involves a great feast, camp fires and storytelling, various rituals, and the Cleansing Ceremony itself. How will these activities be accomplished in what most likely will be late winter weather? But Norval has told me not to worry. The weather will be agreeable. The temperature will be acceptable. All will be well. I suppose I have no other recourse but to acknowledge his guarantee.

So, all is packed. All is in order. All is prepared. We shall leave tomorrow morning just after sunrise. I feel strangely comforted knowing that we are about to begin a new adventure but oddly apprehensive wondering what is to come. I feel like a child again: Intimidated by the prospect of change but exhilarated by the expectation of something new and exciting. I feel like I did a hundred times before in my youth, as mother, Jonathon, and I prepared to leave our cottage for the summer and return home for another winter of discontent. I hate déjà vu.

PART THREE

From Beardmore to Winnipeg and Points Between

(March 1979)

We arrived in Manitou, North Dakota, earlier this afternoon after a three-day trip from Beardmore. The trip shouldn't have taken three days because the distance between the two locations is not that great, but Norval and Wolf had to stop along the way to pay visits to friends and family whom they had not seen in many years. Norval has family wherever he goes and friends as well—if 'friend' is an appropriate term for the many scoundrels who use him for their own purposes. I imagine his collection of friends is the result of this spiritual notoriety among the Ojibwa and, no doubt, because of his fame as an artist and I suspect his loose generosity with money doesn't hurt either! We were also delayed by the border guards searching for drugs when crossing into the USA. They seemed to be checking almost every vehicle. When our car pulled up to the checkpoint, Norval spoke quietly to one of the guards and we were waved on through. My god, Norval truly does have friends everywhere.

I am happy we were passed through by Norval's apparent friend. Crossing the border with dope in the car didn't make me feel especially safe, but Norval had probably known ahead of time that he would know at least one of the guards. God, he probably knew more than the one man who waved us on; it would be too coincidental to have happened upon his one and only friend at the border. He leads a charmed life, since he has escaped close encounters with disaster on more than a few occasions, so a brush with the law concerning the transportation of illegal substances would probably not phase Norval. I should have known that he would subvert legality somehow.

Upon first arriving in Manitou, I wasn't impressed. It is a dirty, dust bowl little town out in the middle of nowhere. There isn't actually a town here, more like just a few business establishments that cater to the locals: A bank (for what purpose I don't know, it appears that everyone in or around Manitou is poverty stricken), a combination bar and restaurant, a boarding house, a barber shop, an old-fashioned dry goods store, a corner grocery, a gas station/garage, and of course, the local sheriff's department. Nonetheless, once through the town and out to the Indian Reservation, the atmosphere changes.

The Indian Reservation, mostly Ojibwa and some Sioux, is located several miles outside of town, comfortably removed from close proximity to the white establishment. From this initial experience, I assumed there must be a significant separation of white and Native cultures in the United States. The Natives are herded onto a parcel of parched land not much larger than a small college campus, while the whites live on the prime cattle grazing lands, if prime is an appropriate description. I don't think anything in this area is necessarily prime.

The Native village of Manitou—the same name is used for both the town and the Indian reservation—is quaint, though not picturesque. It is a typical out-of-the-movies Native reserve (in the U.S.A. reserves are called reservations) with a series of wigwam-type homes, small shanties, and dilapidated mobile home cabins. It is conveniently arranged, with the village chieftain's house located at the center of the community, and everyone else's place of abode surrounding it in concentric circles. I'm not sure what to call their places of residence since they aren't exactly wigwams and not quite houses—more like run-down shanties and dilapidated house trailers. They are all situated surrounding the chief's house with each ring closer to his home representing a hierarchy of tribesmen. Adjoining pathways connect the circle of homes so that passage between and among them is easy to navigate, especially during the rainy season and winter.

Manitou Reservation isn't especially adorned with trees or shrubs—it is starkly barren. Most of the homes are covered with canvass to protect against nasty weather. They have little color after having endured the four seasons for several years. I guess I was expecting to see a Native village of the olden days replete with colorful blankets, beads, headdresses, and the like hanging from wigwams and embellishing the interiors of the homes. Of course that is typical Hollywood, an impression of Native life as it was before white people destroyed it. All in all, the reservation was similar to small-town anywhere: Kids were running around playing, dogs were barking at each other (and at the occasional intruding rabbit), and people were going about their daily lives, doing whatever one does in the routine of repetition and monotony.

And the weather was nearly perfect, as Norval had assured. It wasn't particularly warm, probably around fifty-five degrees, but there wasn't a cloud in the sky, and any snow that had accumulated throughout the winter had melted away. A gentle breeze played with the swaying tree limbs.

We arrived about four in the afternoon and since the Cleansing ceremony and pow-wow weren't supposed to happen until the next night, we searched for several confidants of Norval's who had promised sleeping accommodations. Finding Norval's friends was easy because it seemed everyone knew who Norval was and was happy to oblige our search. Norval was in good spirits. Since he is a shaman, known to other tribal Indians, he was cordially respected by everyone with whom we came into contact. Many of the people even made chit-chat about his paintings when speaking to him. I knew that Norval's artwork was recognized globally but was surprised to discover that even the people in this out-of-the-way place in North Dakota knew not only who he was but were aware of his art. I guess genius does transcend place and time!

We finally found one of Norval's friends, Tommy Three Fingers—he had lost two fingers on his right hand in a hunting accident as a child—and were put up in Tommy's tipis. On the great plains a wigwam is called a tipis. The housing is basically the same but more easily packed and toted for traveling. Before white men arrived and the Indians were put on reservations, the Native people were nomadic.

Tommy had made arrangements for his wife, four children, and himself to stay with relatives, so we have the wigwam to ourselves. Tommy was pleasant enough but quiet—or was he suspicious of me, the only white man in the village? He never spoke to me, nor targeted any conversation in my direction.

Based on Tommy's lack of attention to me, I almost wondered if I were truly present! After showing us around, he smoked a joint with us, then left. By the time we had settled in, ate the food Tommy had left for us, and smoked another joint, it was time for sleep. Norval has promised that tomorrow will be a special day, and we needed our rest, especially him as he pointed out that Cleansing is strenuous work.

As I write in my journal and make ready for bed, thankfully Norval is already asleep and not interested in sex tonight, I am reminded that this is the beginning of my third month with Norval. Nothing special has happened yet, but then I'm not sure what I had expected to have happened or had hoped would happen by this time. I have posed for Norval on several occasions, serving as his inspiration (he says) and discovered that I adapted more easily to the living conditions at Beardmore than I ever would have imagined had someone suggested I would be living in such rustic conditions. But I am uneasy and anxious as though something is hanging over my head and ready to drop—damn that sword of Damocles!

I haven't learned anything from Norval as far as art is concerned, I have not provided him with the secretarial services for which I was hired, and given his long and frequent absences from the cabin at Beardmore, I have hardly even performed in the companion way that was supposed to be the focus of our relationship. Many Tongues told me once, several weeks ago, that I am not the first of Norval's companion/secretaries; there have been at least three who preceded me. Perhaps Norval is weary of such an arrangement, or maybe I'm not the person he had hoped I would be when we first met. I don't know the answers to any of these questions. Maybe there are no answers worth worrying about. I guess like everything else in life, time will provide whatever is appropriate.

But in the meantime, I don't feel that I have necessarily learned anything. I don't feel that much different than when I left Toronto two months ago. True, I have experienced several happenings that most people wouldn't in a lifetime and I have removed myself from the tedium of the Soho scene, but in a way, I've only replaced drinking and partying with my friends back in Toronto, with smoking and drinking with new friends in Beardmore and now in Manitou. I wonder how far I have really come?

And I can't help but still worry about what Jack said in his letter back in January: "I still love Norval despite what he may be involved in." I haven't yet seen anything out of the ordinary that would suggest a serious problem of any sort, other than Norval's heaving drinking and drugging. Could the issue to which Jack alluded have anything to do with Norval being gone so often to Beardmore? Could it have to do with all the dope and drink he ingests? Could it have to do with his art or the recent break-in? Could it have to do with the mysterious stranger named Jacques Volpe? No matter, I can't think or worry about any of that tonight. It's getting later by the minute and tomorrow promises to be an exciting day. I am looking forward to it with unbridled anticipation.

G

✱✱✱✱✱✱✱✱✱✱✱✱

JOURNAL ENTRY: 3-2-79 [4:30 AM]

Many Tongues awoke me early. For him it is not so early since he arises every day at four AM. He didn't seem especially disturbed about anything, but spirited me outside the tipis and spoke quickly, glancing from side to side as he talked like a movie stool pigeon making sure his conversation was not being overheard by the wrong people.

He said he would like to talk with me when we had more time and a better opportunity. It was important, he emphasized! That was it! Come on, Many Tongues. That couldn't have waited until morning? I tried telling him about Old Young One, but he waved me silent saying, "I know about the visit." Then was off, to where I don't know, or to do what I know not either. As I wrote in an earlier journal entry, Many Tongues is mysterious but commanding, perhaps more so than Norval. Whereas Norval's demanding personality focuses on intimidation and the threat of anger or violence, Many Tongues' is more genuine and serious. The few times that Many Tongues speaks people listen, but I don't know why. And I still haven't figured out what his relationship with Norval really is based upon. Nevertheless, I agreed to his proposal to meet at his time and at his convenience. I can get away from Norval more easily than I can Many Tongues, so I thought the meeting should be best at his benefit.

Now I can't go back to sleep. Norval will be up in an hour or two and ready for the day. I will, most likely, have to be ready also to assist with preparation, but I will be tired I've only had four hours sleep. And now there are new questions and mysteries to add to the ones I was considering last night in my writing: What does Many Tongues want to tell me? Why did he have to awaken me secretly in the middle of the night just to say we'd talk later? Why was this done on the sly without Norval's knowledge? What, what, what? I don't know which I am looking forward to the most: the Cleansing ceremony tonight or my meeting with Many Tongues whenever it happens.

Damn it, again, I continue to have no control over anything that has been happening since I left Toronto, and, although, I would like something more exciting to happen, at the same time I would like to have more control over what does. I want answers to my questions. I want the changes I promised myself when I left Soho, but only time will provide that for which I seek, and I am incapable of making the changes myself. I cannot answer the questions that demand response and I have virtually no control over life happening as I would like it to happen. I cannot change that which I would like to alter without adequate knowledge and information. And as for time, there is no way to hurry it along.

G

****

JOURNAL ENTRY: 3-2-79 [5:45 AM]

I am still awake, having been aroused by Many Tongues nearly two hours ago and unable to fall back asleep. It is still dark outside, but the morning is near. I can hear the dawn chorus of warblers that portend the coming of the new day. Norval and Wolf are fast asleep in dream or in nightmare, who knows, but both are snoring as loudly as ever. There is quietness about the village that is eerie although I'm sure a similar silence engulfs all towns and villages, large or small, in the hollow of night when only creatures of the dark dare disturb the stillness.

In the distance a train goes rushing along and whistles a long and lonely sound that carries through the night, echoing the desolate song of the living. Above the quiet a lonely owl calls to its mate. A single coyote screeches in hopes of finding its companions on a distant hillside. A temperate wind rustles through the limbs of a dying tree spilling its last leaves that scatter to the ground. The call of darkness is unheard by the sleeping but chilling to those who awaken early. In the depths of the night there are a thousand towns and places and times that are lonely, desperate, and isolated. Each as dark, each as removed, each as full of foreboding—and in them, a million people tremble in their sleep; just as lonely, just as desperate, just as isolated as the towns in which they live. And each of those people live the same desperate and lonely lives of despair waiting for the night to announce itself in ways we can only imagine, in ways we can only fear.

There are those who fall asleep at night afraid for the morning to arrive—afraid of what the day might bring and what the sunlight cannot hide. There are those who toss and turn, worrying away the problems over which they have little control, until at long last falling asleep and drifting into the ghostly incubus of the night. And there are those who sleep with hesitation, knowing that if their eyes close they may never again open to this world but pass into a time and a place beyond understanding and recognition. All of them, all of us, lost, lonely, and dying. In a thousand towns and villages, in the countryside and in the cities, in people's homes and on the streets, in cars and on trains, in the air above and on the sea, the echoes of what might have been, and what is yet to come resound in frightening silence throughout the night, the night—the dark, deep, and desperate night.

And we are a part of it, inexorably tethered to that passage of time that has only beginning and end but no between. Because in the between, we sleep, we dream, we live nightmare—we are unsuspecting. And in our nightmare is an ogre called fear: The banshee, the grim reaper, the headless coachman, the great Spirit who stalks us like the hunter does his prey—unmoved by our fear, untouched by our hesitation, undeterred by our hope. And we can do nothing but lay awake and worry or fall asleep and forget.

And the fear rushes on.

❋❋❋❋❋❋❋❋❋❋❋

MANY TONGUES HAS RETURNED BUT from where I do not know. He has entered the tipis as quietly as he had left two hours ago but returned differently than he had upon his exit early this morning. He is naked, except for a loincloth, and is painted with ornate drawings of a large rabbit, a rodent, and a thunderbird scrawled across his chest and arms. He is quiet as he slips into his bed. He looks towards Norval, then towards me and pulls his bed covering up around his neck and settles beneath its warmth. I feign being asleep to observe his return. I can hear him whispering softly to himself. Is it a chant of some sort? A prayer? A mantra? I cannot tell. But even in the darkness, I can see a look of peace upon his face. An aura emanates from his flesh and casts dim light around him. It is bluish in color and faint, a presence of light neither imagined nor contrived. The aura does not fade, but remains profound, casting a blue tint upon everything in the tipis. As he settles beneath his bed covers, he seems in harmony with himself, at peace with the universe, and content with the world that surrounds him. He closes his eyes and falls asleep.

I should do the same, but it is early, very early; in fact, so early in the morning that taking sleep at this point would serve no purpose, but I should, I must. And yet, I can't help wondering what is happening with Many Tongues; his behavior has always been mysterious, but it is now downright perplexing. Now I have not only the mystery of Morrisseau to solve but of Old Young One and of and Many Tongues as well. Again, I am reminded of the words Old Young spoke about the rat (my dream that he foretold?) and the rabbit and the Thunderbird, images that Many Tongues wore on his flesh as he returned tonight. What link is there between Old Young One and Many Tongues and how do I fit into the picture? Many questions without answers, and the only answer I get is, "Not now, when it is time." I wonder, when will it be time.

But it is still early in the morning. I am tired. I must sleep...

...And I do.

G

❋❋❋❋❋❋❋❋❋❋❋

JOURNAL ENTRY: 3-2-79 [12:20 PM]

I fell fast asleep after Many Tongues had returned last night, for when I awoke this morning, it was well past 9:30. Norval had already arisen and was gone. Many Tongues was still sleeping though. Norval did not awaken either of us; I am sure he has preparation to which to attend before tonight's ceremony and couldn't be bothered with us sleepyheads. Rather interesting, though; Many Tongues is usually awake long before 9:30 in the morning and generally has accomplished more between his arising and noon than most people do in an entire day but not today. For some inexplicable reason he has slept late, seemingly unconcerned about tonight's festivities and not intimidated by Norval's potential mood.

When he did awaken, about fifteen minutes after I had, he did not appear to be concerned with the time. He merely got out of his bed, stood up, reached his hands high above his head as though trying to touch the top of the tipis, and let out the loudest whoop and cry I have ever heard. As he did, and it startled the hell out of me, he began laughing so heartily that he nearly fell over. His odd behavior was antithetical to what I had observed about Many Tongues since we first met at Beardmore; although since I have only known him for two months, I cannot accurately comment upon what is and what is normal about his comportment. Nevertheless, I regained my composure, quickly, and started asking him about the invitation he had extended earlier that morning. I didn't get very far.

"Not now," he interrupted. "When the time is right."

He is a man of few words.

I'm certain he must have seen me staring at the markings of the rabbit, the rodent, and thunderbird on his chest and arms because without hesitation, he responded to my unspoken inquiry.

"Not now, when the time is right," he repeated.

"When the time is right," I echoed. "And when might that be?"

"The time is right, when the time is right, no sooner, no later."

If I hadn't known Many Tongues better, I would have considered his response a smart-ass answer from a jokester, but I do know him well enough although not as well as I would like, to realize that he has a reason for everything he says and a purpose for everything he does. I would have to be satisfied until whenever, 'the time was right.'

And then, suddenly without warning, it happened. It was as though I had been transported from one-time dimension to another. Just moments earlier Many Tongues had warned me to be patient and wait until the time was right, and then without pronouncement, suddenly the time was right. Since I first joined Norval and met Many Tongues, I acknowledge that I have not been quick to pick up on things, but this seemed absurd; from one second of being not 'the right time' to next evidently being 'right' made little sense.

Many Tongues stood tall and erect, with his arms spread wide, stared at me with a look that sent a shiver down my spine and pointed at the markings of the rabbit and the thunderbird on his body. He motioned for me to come near and to touch them, and I did.

They were hot, as though burning with fire and yet cool, as though tempered by the fresh morning dew. I am not one given easily to a belief in the supernatural, although I have long wanted to experience something, anything, of the 'otherworldly.' I am a skeptic and demand proof of shenanigans purported to be psychic phenomena. Too many charlatans capitalize on the gullible, but now I was experiencing a phenomenon I could not explain. Despite my rearing in the Catholic Church, replete with its ritual, ceremony, mysticism and mythology, I had never before experienced a feeling like the one I had when I touched the markings on Many Tongues body. I felt as though I had touched something sacred, something holy, something truly otherworldly. I moved my hand across each marking, exploring it as though I was blind and reading Braille, and felt an instant connection with Many Tongues. By touching the markings on his arms and chest, it seemed that I was not only joining with Many Tongues but also beginning to understand the esotericism of Ojibwa ancestry. The arcane legends of which Norval had so often spoken were coming alive in my mind in that one instant.

I'm not sure what happened next because it happened so quickly. I do remember continuing to touch the markings on Many Tongues' body and running my hands across the etchings of the rabbit and the thunderbird, over and over again. I had become mesmerized, hypnotized, and I couldn't stop. It was the most serene feeling I have ever experienced—not the touching itself, but the inner peace and tranquility that I felt as my fingers came in contact with the colorful markings.

Curiously, Many Tongues directed my hands to the figures of the rabbit and the Thunderbird, but when my fingers moved near the rodent, he pushed them away as if my digits dared move to where they did not belong. When my hand first neared the scrawl of the rodent, I thought I felt a freezing chill emanate from it. But Many Tongues' quick brushing aside of my fingers betrayed any physical sensation that might have truly occurred.

Many Tongues took my right hand, placed it upon his chest, near where his heart would be, then placed my left hand upon my own chest in the same location. He bowed his head, then lifted it toward the sky in a manner that seemed ritualistic. He chanted something in Ojibwa which at first I could not understand but then became so clear that it was what I imagined speaking in tongues might be like.

"It is now when he comes, from beyond time, from beyond the stars, from beyond the distant worlds of which we know little, but of which we know much. He has come from the eastern shores, from beyond our homeland, to be with us again. And he shall dwell with us ever more."

"Wabasso," Many Tongues whispered softly.

"Where is it, where is he?" I asked, expecting to see a physical manifestation of the spirit magically appear as a ghostly image somewhere within the tipis.

"He is within," Many Tongues responded.

"Within you?" I asked, surprised.

"Within me, yes," he answered, "but within you, also, Mandamin. The Copper Spirit and the Pale Spirit—one within you and one within me, revisited as two within the One."

I had no idea what Many Tongues was talking about. His words were foreign and his less than satisfying explanation, obtuse. He had referred to me Mandamin, the name Old Young One used back at the cabin! "As two in the One," I repeated quizzically.

"Within you, within me," he repeated, again. "As two within the One. The Copper Thunderbird and the Pale Thunderbird." Then he just stood and stared at me, not with an angry or threatening gaze, but with a look of compassion and solemnity. "But enough for now," he said again, "More when the time is right."

My head was spinning my thoughts confused. "Within me," I whispered. "As two within the One. My god, Many Tongues, what is going on?" was all I could say before I fainted. I had been asking for something to happen, and happening it now seemed to be.

✸✸✸✸✸✸✸✸✸✸✸✸

Many Tongues must have put me to bed because that is where I awoke again, just before 11:30, later in the morning. And when I awoke, I felt like everything had changed but nothing had changed at all. I felt that inexorable feeling one has after awaking from nightmare—not certain if it is fantasy or reality—unsure if there is reason to be frightened or not! Had I dreamed the incident with Many Tongues? It seemed so real. Had it really taken place only a few hours before, or had it even actually happened at all? Many Tongues was nowhere around. He had left the tipis but when and to where I do not know. Norval was out undoubtedly preparing for the evening's Cleansing ceremony, and the tipis seemed unusually quiet, unusually ghostly, and unusually uncomfortable.

As I dressed, I looked down at my chest and noticed the imprint of a hand—my hand? It was shadowed upon my chest, somewhat faint, but unmistakably there, and I remembered the incident from a couple of hours earlier more clearly. Many Tongues had placed my right hand upon his chest and my left upon mine. It wasn't hallucination; what I thought had been dream was real. I was terrified…

…and I was alone.

The Thunderbird Spirit had visited.

G

✸✸✸✸✸✸✸✸✸✸✸✸

Journal Entry: 3-2-79

The Cleansing ceremony was incredible; Norval was incredible. The ceremony is one of the most unbelievable events I have ever witnessed. I cannot compare it to any of the rituals or ceremonies I experienced as a child growing up Roman Catholic, and believe me Catholic ritual is awash with pageantry and mysticism that goes beyond the sacrament of mass.

The entire village came alive late in the afternoon with ritual, ceremony, and revelry. Everyone participated in some aspect of the approaching Cleansing ceremony. Men, women, and children were all attending to a necessary part of preparation that would lead to the Cleansing later that night. Some of the older women and men were preparing food, children were playing—dressed in traditional Ojibwa regalia—and other men were preparing for the traditional dances. It was not unlike many of the customs of pagan or ethnic derivation that have been borrowed (and perverted) by Christianity in an attempt to blend pagan ritual with Christian ceremony to win over converts from the 'savage and unsaved' (consider Mardi Gras, Halloween, Easter, and All Saints Eve, among others).

The Cleansing ceremony itself is known to many Indian tribes but under different names. It has been called The Black Drink ceremony, the Burning Rocks ceremony, the Sweat-Lodge ceremony, The Vision Quest, the Yuwipi, and the Transition ritual—all nearly identical, with similar purpose but focusing upon different deities and interpretations of legend and vision, not unlike the ceremonies of Christianity practiced under the names of different religious sects. I'm not even certain that the Cleansing ceremony is recognized as traditionally Ojibwa. It is probably a derivation of Eastern Woodland Algonquin, but I think it is more an invention and re-interpretation that reservation Indians practiced for the purpose of explaining visions and cleansing the spirit. I use the word spirit rather than soul because the Christian connotation of soul was unknown to Indian tribes prior to the emergence and domination of white culture.

Late in the afternoon, a great feast was held involving the entire village. Food of all sorts was plentiful. The preparation begins several weeks prior to the ceremony with the gathering of food and the making of costumes and ornaments—much like Christian preparation for Thanksgiving or Christmas. I did not want for anything in way of food. There were wild rice dishes, fruits and vegetables, fish, poultry, and red meats. However, unlike most European feasts, there were no desserts, just the fruits and berries that had been stored from the previous season. I came away from the feast stuffed but not uncomfortable or bloated.

Following the feast, the young men of the tribes gathered to dance traditional Ojibway and other Algonquin-derivation dances. The costumes were magnificent, vibrant and colorful and representative of the specific tribes from which each man came. I witnessed the Brule Sioux sun dance, the Cree fertility dance, the Ojibwa war dance, and the Metis dance of light. Each was stunning, beautiful, and expressive. I was surprised to see Wolf dancing the Ojibwa war dance with other men of the tribe. Wolf, who usually functions only in the shadow of his older brother, was as adept at the ritualistic dance as any man there. His costume was as colorful as the others on display, and I was pleasantly surprised to see that he was able to accomplish something without the aid of Norval.

The dancing went on for several hours and consisted of different categories of dance, specific to varying age groups and tribes. The younger men and boys participated in similar numbers to the older men. I was glad I wasn't stoned. I didn't need any kind of chemical agent to augment the splendor and spectacle of the dancing.

By eight o'clock at night, the dancing had ended and the people separated into various groups to attend different activities. The women and children of the tribes gathered around a huge campfire to hear stories about Ojibway and Algonquin legends told by the masterful story-teller, Legend-Giver. Most of the men went out onto the dark plains to commune with the great spirits of their tribes.

A small handful of men and three women left the larger group and headed to the lodge where the Cleansing ceremony was to take place. Norval had disappeared an hour into the dancing to prepare himself for the ceremony. He told me later that preparation consisted of nothing more than meditation and quieting his spirit so it would be more receptive to entering into the spiritual world and receiving visions.

This was the part of the daylong activities that excited me the most and which I was fortunate to attend. To Norval's knowledge (and Many Tongues corroborated his memory), no white man had ever before attended one of the Cleansing ceremonies, at least in Manitou with this particular gathering of tribes.

At eight-thirty, fourteen of us—nine men whom I did not know, the three women I mentioned earlier, Many Tongues, and I—joined Norval in the tribal shaman's lodge. Norval was no longer called Norval, or Jean Baptiste as many of his friends know him but was rather addressed as the Copper Thunderbird. He was afforded great respect from all who attended and much to my surprise, did not appear drunk or stoned on marijuana, hash, or cocaine—he was clean.

The lodge was large enough to hold all fifteen of us but small enough to be cramped; we were sitting shoulder to shoulder in a great circle surrounding the Copper Thunderbird and a small fire that consumed an ever-replenished supply of birch logs and heated four woven baskets filled with rocks. The baskets were kept from catching fire by being sprinkled with water every fifteen or twenty minutes which, when they were, gave off torrents of steam that swirled around the lodge, eventually dissipating into the heavy air. The lodge was hot, almost unbearably so, and steamy, much like a contemporary steam bath back in Toronto.

As we entered, Norval (the Copper Thunderbird) was chanting in his Native Ojibwa, raising small wooded cups of incense in the air, and moving them about in a circular fashion that emitted an odor that joined with the steam to create a surrealistic atmosphere. Everyone remained quiet as they entered, in deference to the Copper Thunderbird and out of respect for the ceremony itself.

It began with The Copper Thunderbird enumerating a series of prophecies in Ojibwa. An old Indian woman sitting beside me translated for me: There would come great rains in the spring that would bring bountiful harvests of wild-rice and berries in the autumn; the fish would bite in abundance on the lines of the tribe's fishermen and feed the tribes for the duration of summer; the Chief's wife would bear a male child—an heir to his leadership; and there would come, within the passing of autumn to winter, great trouble between the white men of Manitou and the Indian nations of the gathering. The last prophecy was received as were all the others, with quiet reserve and acceptance —the Copper Thunderbird had spoken with the Words and through the Visions visited by the Great Thunderbird Spirit of the Ojibwa, and nothing anyone could say or think or do would (or could) change the prophecies. Norval did not explain any of the prophecies, only enumerated them while in trance. The prophecies are not to be explained, simply accepted.

And then the transfiguration began.

After Norval had finished the litany of prophecies and was immersed in meditation with the Great Thunderbird Spirit, his entire countenance changed. His eyes rolled back, his skin grew pale, his hair turned as white as snow. His spirit seemed to leave his body as a great whiff of bluish smoke surrounded him and his corporeal essence transformed into a spiritual entity. When the smoke dissipated, his face appeared calmer than I had ever witnessed before, his eyes were glazed with a look of distance that suggested a hypnotic spell, and his very physical form became more youthful, more powerful, and more commanding. He had transformed from the dirty, unkempt Norval that I had come to know over the past two months, into a strong, beautiful man. He sat erect, legs crossed and arms folded, and asked if there was anyone present who desired the Cleansing.

At first no one budged, but within a few minutes, an older Indian man arose and moved towards Norval.

"I am Gray Beaver," he announced to the Copper Thunderbird. "I have come for your cleansing. I am old and weak and in great pain. I can no longer do the necessary chores because of my age. I am not of this tribe anymore. I am beyond my ability to help with all that is needed. My years are many and my heart is full. I have lived as I should have lived without fear, without sadness. Now I must take leave and pass as is custom. I need your cleansing to set me free of this world, to allow me to rest forever in the arms of the Great Spirit."

Norval placed his hand upon the man's forehead, entered into a trance, and spoke in Ojibway, saying, "Rise and go in peace. You are cleansed of your fear and your worry. Before the full moon rises and sets four times, you will be freed to run again upon youthful legs, to swim in the cold waters, to hunt the wild bear, and to take a wife and to bring forth with children."

The old man smiled and touched the hand of the Copper Thunderbird, then returned to his seat.

That was too much. I couldn't believe that Norval, Copper Thunderbird or not, had the power to make this man young again. I was skeptical and only later, after the ceremony, did Many Tongues explain that Norval, indeed, could not make the man young again but could cleanse him of the fear he was experiencing as he approached death. He would die within four months and would be freed to live again in another world as the young man he had been here on Earth many years earlier.

Following the old Indian man, one of the women rose immediately approached Norval and sat in front of him. She was a young, beautiful girl of not more than eighteen. She had a look about her that suggested great worry and hesitation. The old woman translator explained to me that she was the daughter of parents who had been killed in an automobile accident late in the autumn of the preceding year. She was an orphan, and at eighteen was considered of marriageable situation. But she had not married, nor had she taken a suitor or boyfriend. She mourned for her dead parents all day long, wailed throughout the night, and discouraged every man who expressed interest. A sad situation, I thought, such a beautiful young woman, with her entire life ahead, consumed by the pain of loss and rejecting of a bountiful future.

Before she could say her name, Norval interrupted.

"Mary Wind Dancer," he spoke, "Take my hand, rest it upon your heart, and listen."

The Copper Thunderbird continued:

"You cause us great sorrow, daughter. We have gone beyond the world of the living and dwell with the Great Spirit in places north and south, east and west. We rise with the sun, sleep with the moon, and carry with the wind as it rushes down from the sky and across the plains. We are at peace. We are with Wabasso. I am your mother, the woman of your birth and you the child of my womb. I am your father, the seed of your growth and you the child of my loins. Let us pass in peace. Let us be as deep as the water, as distant as the cloud, as one with the beginning and the end. Dry your tears. Do not stand at our graves and weep, for we are not there. We do not sleep."

Suddenly the young girl collapsed. Norval fell backward as if in a swoon, then regained himself and spoke again as the Copper Thunderbird:

"We are a thousand winds that blow from the north, the diamond glint on the winter snow, the sunlight on ripened grain. We are the gentle autumn rain. When you awaken in the morning, hush and listen. We are the swift rush of quiet birds in circling flight. We are the soft star shine at night. Do not stand at our graves and cry. We are not there. We did not die."

The young Indian girl arose from her faint and carried away from Norval's presence a look of understanding and resolve. Whereas earlier she had appeared frightened and timid, she now seemed confident and strong. She moved with the grace of the Goddess of Victory among the people in the lodge with a smile that revealed a newly discovered inner peace. As she returned to where she had been sitting prior to the Cleansing, I thought I saw her glance in the direction of a young Indian man who, from his look upon her, obviously thought her captivating and beautiful.

The rest of the evening was a repeat of the earlier two episodes ten times over. By the end of the Cleansing ceremony, a dozen people had gone, one by one, to Norval—the Copper Thunderbird—for advice, an interpretation of vision, and cleansing of the psyche, and all had come away satisfied that the shaman had served their issues well. In addition to the old man and the young girl who had visited with Norval, four others had been healed of disease and pain, two were cleansed of what they considered "worldly" sins (Christianity had permeated their culture with the concepts of sin and guilt, complete with their accompanying, unfortunate psychological effects), three received visions of futures yet to unfold, and one was revisited by a wife who had died in childbirth. It was a draining experience.

By the end of the evening, Norval was exhausted. He had spent every bit of energy with his mysticism and supernatural abilities dispensing advice, comforting the lonely, giving hope to the desperate, and healing the sick. When, at last, the final seeker had left the lodge, there were none left save Many Tongues, Norval, and me.

I was about to approach Norval, when Many Tongues interceded and walked me out into the night.

"He must be alone, to emerge, again, transformed into human being," Many Tongues explained.

"Go to the sleeping tent and await his return."

Many Tongues had a look of comfort on his face that bordered on pride and satisfaction. Although I had lost track of Many Tongues during the Cleansing ceremony—my attention was naturally diverted to Norval and the people to whom he attended—I sensed that he was pleased with the ceremony and the manner by which Norval had addressed the various people and their concerns. I watched him disappear as he walked away from me in silence and headed into the dark. Where he was going, I do not know. When he would return, I could only guess. I heeded his words and headed back to Jack Three Finger's tipis.

The night was cold, the stars were out, the moon slowly moved across the sky to the west. I tried, in my most intellectual way, to understand what had happened that night but failed. Logic did not suffice. Intellect did not avail. Common sense seemed of little consequence. What I had witnessed was something I could not explain; it was something that in this world, our limited understanding of the spiritual and the supernatural could not illuminate. Norval had transformed into a spiritual entity—be it shaman, the Copper Thunderbird, or mystic. Much of what he had done and said throughout the course of the evening would be explained as natural phenomenon with practical explanation by some, as mass hysterical behavior by others, or as a charlatan duping the gullible, by still others. But I'm not so sure there exists a logical explanation. I do not know Norval well enough to be certain that what happened was truly spiritual, but I have been with him long enough to know, also, that what I saw and heard was not a sham.

I am more engrossed by Norval now and just as intrigued by Many Tongues and our impending meeting. Perhaps now, I will begin to learn the reasons for my presence here. I certainly hope so, anyway.

When I returned to the tent, it was empty. And the night was still cold.

G

✸✸✸✸✸✸✸✸✸✸✸✸

MARCH 3, 1979
Joanne

It's been a while, but then I told you not to expect a letter until we had returned from North Dakota. I'm writing this on the 3rd, but I don't know when you might receive it; we are still in Manitou, North Dakota (leaving tomorrow morning, probably), so I don't know when I'll have a chance to mail this. Many Tongues doesn't have to spirit away the letters while we're on the road since I should have ample opportunity to locate a mail box without drawing suspicion from Norval.

A lot has happened since my last correspondence, so much, in fact, that a letter would not do justice to the activities and events I could try to enumerate. Rest assured, when I return you will get a first-hand accounting of everything that has gone on.

As I wrote above, we're still in Manitou but plan on leaving for Winnipeg tomorrow morning. The experiences here have been incredible. Not only have I learned a great deal about Ojibwa customs and legends but have found a new and interesting friend in Many Tongues and have developed a new respect for Norval—The Copper Thunderbird! I have seen him do things that would shock you and everyone else we know in Toronto. He is, indeed, a shaman, a soul traveler, and a mystic. I don't know where all of this is leading either. Norval is still an alcoholic and a drug abuser of the first magnitude, and I fear that after we leave Manitou, he will revert to his ornery ways. Still, the absolute divination that I witnessed last evening has to result in something that should help explain why I am here. I certainly hope so, anyway.

I am sorry that Norval is so dependent upon chemicals in his daily life. His dependency contradicts everything he has accomplished here. His visions and healings have helped a number of people and the spiritualism he possesses is significant. He is well respected by his tribe members and people of other tribes—not as much because of his art genius, but rather because of his shamanism and vision quest. He can be so powerful, so caring, and so loving. Too bad his positive qualities become subsumed by the negative. But, again, more on that later.

I mentioned Many Tongues (remember, he is the man who originally carried my letters for mailing). He and I have become quite close, if "close" is an appropriate term for our relationship. I really don't know him any better than I did when we first met. He is still an enigma to me. Just recently, we shared a mental intimacy that I have never achieved with anyone else. He calls me Mandamin, which loosely translated means "half-burned wood man." I imagine he uses the term to allude to my mixed heritage and my darker complexion. He has intimated, through mental telepathy, that we are somehow joined with a common type of psychic or cosmic connection. I don't know what it all means, but I intend to find out as soon as possible. Of course, according to Many Tongues, we have to wait until the time is right to extend our immersion. No problem, I can deal with that although somewhat impatiently. I have nowhere to go right now but to Winnipeg.

As for me, I am well. I survived the two-month stay at Norval's cabin in Beardmore and believe me that was no small feat. It was cold, snowy, uncomfortable, and downright unpleasant. But, oddly enough, I miss it. Perhaps it was the serenity and the isolation that I embraced. I don't know. All I do know is that it seemed an appropriate escape from the life I was lead- ing in Toronto. As you well know, I was squarely on the path of self-destruction: Drinking, doping, partying, and fucking all the time. Can't say I have done much of that here. There has been drinking and doping but not much partying, and sex only with Norval (when the urge strikes him, which thank God isn't often). I must admit, I feel different—more confident, more peaceful, more on the track of figuring out who I am. I admit that although I am still at a loss figuring out what it is I want to do with my life I believe my stay at the cabin is a sort of first step in the right direction. Kind of like my initial experience as Norval's travel- ing companion and secretary was destined to happen in an isolated rustic area. I like to think of it as my decent into darkness to be followed by my ascent into the light of personal revelation. I know that sounds corny and overly dramatic, but it seems appropriate that in order to divorce myself from who I had become in Toronto, the cabin in the woods at Beardmore became a necessary bridge between my past and—hopefully—a better future.

Interestingly, with the recent experiences here in Manitou, little has been said or done about Norval's art, my posing, or him instructing me in artistic technique. There were aborted times at the cabin when we launched into Norval's world of art, and I miss that. I wish we would return to the main reason I thought I had been hired. He hasn't painted for a couple of weeks, but I suppose artists—of any sort—are more active when inspired by the muse. Of course, one of my responsibilities is to motivate and inspire Norval. I guess he doesn't feel as inspired by me as he did when we first met. I think I might be too confrontational for Norval since he prefers a man (or any person for that matter) to bow to his wishes, but I haven't done that. I speak back if he insults me, argue when he voices an illogical argument, and refuse to do anything that I find disgusting or inappropriate to my ethics and morality. I probably irritate him more than any other person he deals with, and he doesn't quite know how to interact with me, truly a first for Norval Morrisseau.

I don't pretend to have discovered my personal reality yet. Quite to the contrary. There are still too many unpleasant memories of growing up in Ontario and a few too many regrets about my experiences in Toronto. There are times when I feel renewed, refreshed, and confident but just as many times when I become depressed and revert to my self-destructive pity and anxiety. I have to remember the bridge concept that I wrote about a couple of paragraphs above.

Were I to describe myself at this point in my life, I would say that I am lonely and yet learning more about how to confront my alienation. Depressed, but beginning to see alternatives to the sadness I thought would always be a constant part of my essence. Desperate and yet developing a sense of calm that portends better things to come. And isolated and yet starting to feel a part of something that is far bigger than me and which I do not, yet, understand. Similar to my letter of several weeks ago I am, in a phrase, still fucked up. It just doesn't seem so pervasive when I am away from everything and everyone with which I had become familiar. It is much like going on vacation—you don't necessarily consider the reality from which you are escaping because you are too busy enjoying the new experiences that you encounter. When you return home from the holiday—BAM—back to reality.

I always tend to speak only of me in my letters. I am curious about how you are doing. Are you still on the outs with Warren? Have you made any decision about making those changes in your life that Jack Pollock referred to? Again, I will have to hope for the best for you since I cannot receive correspondence from you or anyone else. I continue to wonder why Norval doesn't like me communicating with the 'outside' world, but at least I had Many Tongues to spirit away my letters when we were at the cabin, and now that we'll be in a large city I can find time to mail them myself.

Of all the people I have met throughout my short life, you are one of the most level-headed I know. I completely trust that you will make the right decisions for yourself and will take great care of yourself. Please don't prove me wrong!

I don't know how much longer Norval wants me in his employ. Bernie told me last December that usually Norval's hires only last a few months until either they, or Norval grow weary of the arrangement. Bernie indicated that I would be considerably better off financially could I 'ride out the Norval storm,' but so far I haven't seen a cent of Norval's money. He does provide for me by way of supplying food and buying the small necessities I infrequently request, but as for any type of salary—forget it! I have received nothing. We'll see how things develop when we get to Winnipeg. If there is a significant and positive change, I might stay longer. If not, then who knows?

Enough for now, I must still write in my journal (I'm becoming quite the Anne Frank of Canada). Until we see each other again, which as I have written in all my letters will come to pass sooner than later, take care, be well, and live your life to the fullest.

I love you.

Gilbert

❋❋❋❋❋❋❋❋❋❋❋

JOURNAL ENTRY: 3-3-79

Many Tongues had advised me following the Cleansing ceremony to return to the tent and await Norval's return. I did. Norval returned as well much later (perhaps three hours later) but by the time he was back, he was tired and distant. He had the look of a man who had expended too much energy (which I can understand, given the activity at the Cleansing ceremony), and the appearance of a man who had been recently satisfied by carnal activity. How do I know? He was distant in a way that was unusual, not like when he would return to Beardmore after several days and greet me with, at least, feigned interest and a modicum of friendliness. It was more like the distance a man shows his wife or lover when he has lost interest and is being sexually satisfied elsewhere. Usually when Norval returns from anywhere he has been he wants to smoke a joint, do a little hash, snort a line of coke, and initiate his bizarre idea of sex. But when he came back to the tipis early in the morning, he was obviously drunk and stoned already and expressed no interest in kissing and hanging on me like he often does. He merely grunted a hello, stripped, and fell into bed.

It didn't take Norval long to seek pleasure elsewhere. Apparently, he has returned to his deceptive ways before the embers of tonight's ritual fire died to ash and must have rekindled his lust elsewhere.

Many Tongues came in not long after Norval did, took one look at the Copper Thunderbird dead out in bed, sighed what sounded like a quiet groan of frustration and quickly went to bed himself.

Many Tongues was not inebriated on alcohol or drugs, which was not surprising since I have never seen him in such a manner before, and like Norval, he had a look about him that was distant in an otherworldly sense. He suffered an air of serenity about him that was both confident and assured. He appeared strong and sober, the exact opposite of Norval, and carried himself like a god come to Earth to observe his pathetic creations. I'm beginning to wonder if, indeed, that is what Many Tongues is: A god come to Earth. He seems so distant but not unapproachable; so frightening, but not threatening; so powerful, but not abusive. He is every bit the enigma that Norval is but in a positive and curious way. I want to know more about this man.

Before he fell asleep, he called me over and whispered in my ear: "The time approaches; perhaps tomorrow or the next day. When we are alone. When Norval is gone. When we have hours to ourselves, not fleeting minutes. Then it will be time."

After our exchanges of yesterday, I knew better than to pursue his comment; he will only give information he is comfortable with revealing—no more, no less. As I mentioned before, Many Tongues is a man of few words. I nodded my head with understanding and returned to bed. Within minutes I could hear both Norval and Many Tongues snoring. They are quick to sleep, unlike me.

I lay awake for several hours more, wondering what would be the revelation Many Tongues seemed so anxious, and yet patient, to provide. I wondered how my relationship with Norval would improve (or not) when we got to Winnipeg. I wondered, again, like so many times before at Beardmore, why I was here, what I hoped to accomplish from my association with Morrisseau, and whether, or not, I would achieve any of the goals I had established when I accepted the position with Norval back in December: Money! Fame! Stardom! Notoriety! Success!

No doubt I had learned more about myself in the two months I had been with Norval than I had in the previous years in Toronto. Certainly, what one learns is relative—I had learned a great deal about myself in Toronto, but what I learned, I didn't necessarily like. And yet, I am not certain what I have learned, here with Norval, and whether it will be beneficial later in life.

I have learned to survive in the wilderness. I have learned to be alone most of the time and not consider my solitude bad. I have learned to respond on cue to Norval's demands and yet still retain a degree of self-respect. I have learned to accept Norval with a grain of salt—embracing his better points, such as his mysticism and shamanism, and his art, but rejecting the worst. And I have learned to hate the man for his disgusting behavior, his chemical dependency, his arrogance, and his self-indulgent attitude. But most of all I think I have learned, finally, to trust someone—Many Tongues. But why I should trust a man who offers little other than continued mystery, I am not certain. I hope he does not disappoint me.

Tomorrow we leave Manitou and begin another part of this grand adventure. To think that it has been only a little over two months since I first met Norval Morrisseau, and that in that time I have changed from a whoring party-goer in Toronto to the near recluse I was in Beardmore is more than I ever would have imagined. Had someone suggested as much back in December, I would have thought him crazy or unbalanced. In a period of little more than two months I have quit my job in Toronto, lived in the wilderness of central Ontario, modeled and inspired the great Morrisseau, traveled to North Dakota to witness one of the most captivating events of my life, and now prepare to go forward, again.

Or is it truly forward? I can only hope as much but as has been the case with everything else in my life, forward will probably end up going backwards, but with a twist of the new, too much of the old, and a hunger for serious change. I am a product of so many experiences and people who have come and gone from my life—very few good, most of them bad.

Mother and father? Jonathon? Patrick? Russ? Marcel? Raymond? Bernie? Jack? Toronto? Everyone and everything that has been a part of my life has moved me backward as much as forward; everything I have experienced has created as much negative as positive. Why should now be any different? But, there I go again, supposing that the bad will always supplant the good. No matter. It is late, and I am tired.

G

✦✦✦✦✦✦✦✦✦✦✦

JOURNAL ENTRY: 3-5-79

We've been on the road for two days now. It doesn't take two days to get from Manitou to Winnipeg but Norval travels at his own pace. Many Tongues and I haven't had the opportunity to meet alone yet, so I still anxiously await our rendezvous. We've taken a room in a motel in the small town of St. Pierre-Jolys, not more than a few hours from Winnipeg, but Norval wanted to stop, so stop we did.

As I feared, Norval's mood has regressed again to one of arrogance and haughtiness. The Cleansing ceremony evidently had little permanent effect on his personality, even though it did wonders for those who attended. He's not drinking as much as pre-Manitou but is smoking dope and hash and snorting coke morning, noon, and night. As soon as he senses that he is coming down from one high, he immediately initiates another, so his state of being is constantly altered and his perception of reality greatly diminished.

The trip, so far, has been uneventful—for the most part. Norval does drugs and bitches about the most insignificant comments either Many Tongues or I make. Wolf just grunts, laughs, and agrees with everything his brother says or does. Many Tongues and I do the driving and ignore Norval's complaints and Wolf's sniggering. There was one incident, however, at a restaurant in Lake Bronson, North Dakota, this morning that was vintage Norval.

We had stopped for breakfast, which in itself was unusual because Norval usually does not care for food so early in the morning. He needs a high first, he says, to stimulate his culinary interest. The rest of us were starving, so stop we did. We had just finished eating, when the waitress, a young girl of about seventeen, brought us the check, smiled, and told us to have a good day. The check was all that was needed to set Norval off.

He took one look at the itemized total and started pounding on the table with clenched fists and chanting some kind of Norval gibberish that meant absolutely nothing in any language known to humankind. Naturally, he drew the attention of everyone in the restaurant, including the manager, a man of about twenty-five, who came over to the table to inquire as to the problem.

The poor guy didn't have a chance.

"Problem," Norval snorted. "Yeah, there's a problem. This check is wrong. The total on this fucking check is wrong—completely wrong. You're cheating me. I don't like to be cheated. Is it because I'm a Native man? You want to fuck-over the old Indian? Is that it, white boy?"

The young man, trying to hold his own in the wake of Norval's outburst, tried calming Norval down—but to no avail. Norval was on a rampage and knew that he had the young man by the balls. The manager asked to see the check, in an attempt to remedy the problem, so Norval shoved it into the young man's gut, as hard as he could, eliciting a groan from the kid, and sending him falling backwards into a table behind him. Plates, glasses, utensils, and food flew everywhere. They cascaded to the floor, crashed onto the tables on either side of the one into which the manager had fallen, and doused several innocent patrons with eggs, bacon, pancakes, syrup, and whatever else might have been a part of the breakfast plates.

The young man, to his credit, quickly regained his composure, straightened himself, and as politely as possible directed our party to leave.

"Sir, I'm going to have to ask you to pay the bill and leave. I'll be happy to review the total for you and make the necessary adjustments if the total is incorrect." I have to hand it to the kid; he had more guts than most people do dealing with Norval, but then I am certain he didn't know who this crazed man was and wasn't intimidated by his status or position.

"You're fucking right you'll make the necessary adjustments," Norval bellowed. "Look at it for yourself; you'll see that little bitch tried to cheat me!"

The manager quickly re-totaled the bill and apologized, noting that the check was off by a nickel. "I'm sure the waitress wasn't trying to cheat you out of five cents, sir, but I'll be happy to adjust it. Now, if you'll just pay the correct amount and accept my apology."

That still wasn't good enough for Norval.

"I'll pay shit," he screamed loud enough to wake the dead. And with that he grabbed the check back from the manager-kid, stuffed it into his coffee mug, and hurled the cup across the room. It crashed into a mirror on the far wall, sending shards of glass spilling down on top of the customers sitting in the booth below. One woman was slightly cut, but other than her minor injury, most of the damage was limited to the broken mirror and the ruined breakfasts on the table.

"You fucking white people are all alike, trying to screw us Native people every chance you get. Well, I'm not going to stand for this kind of treatment. Either this breakfast is free, or I'll report your cheating ways to the sheriff."

Norval didn't have to go looking for the sheriff because just as he was making his last stand and vilifying the manager with a tirade of insults, the sheriff walked through the door—one of the customers had called him.

To make a long story short, Norval shouted his interpretation of the story to the sheriff but changed the punch line by insisting that he had agreed to pay the re-totaled difference and leave quietly. He had only thrown the cup in self-defense, Norval insisted, when two white men sitting at the counter (who by now were conveniently gone) made a move in his direction and threatened to beat the shit out of him if he didn't get the hell out of the restaurant immediately. Of course, there was absolutely no truth to what Norval was saying, but no one in the restaurant contradicted him—including the manager of the restaurant—and we were free to leave. We didn't even have to pay the check or damages to the restaurant. Evidently everyone had become intimidated by Norval's behavior and were glad just to get him (and us) out of there.

On our way out, Norval pulled a copy of *The Thunder Bay Times News* out of his jacket (the one with the story about his investiture as a Member of the Order of Canada) and threw it on the cash register counter.

"You can send the bills for any damages to Governor-General Schreyer." It was Norval's way of letting everyone know who he was, and how important he considered himself to be. The entire episode was vintage Morrisseau.

Throughout the incident, Many Tongues sat quietly, observing Norval. He didn't say a word, just sat there watching, taking it all in, and looking uncomfortably disturbed. When we left, he offered an apology to the manager and slipped him some cash which I assume was to cover the cost of the breakfast and the damages to the restaurant. Once more, another reason Many Tongues intrigued me.

Wolf contributed nothing to the melee, except encouraging Norval by goading his behavior, laughing at whatever ignorant comments Norval made, and acting like the shadow puppy he really is to his big brother by spewing obscenities from a safe distance behind Norval.

I was scared to death. The entire scene shook me to my core. To begin with, I had never before seen Norval display such anger in public. Further, I was a white man, traveling with three Natives, but being lumped together with the other whites that Norval was denigrating. And I was concerned that someone in the restaurant might take serious offense at Norval's outburst and take matters into his own hands—guns are not unusual in the open spaces of Big Sky country. Then when the sheriff came along, I started wondering what jail would be like and how long we might be incarcerated. But since the episode had been resolved without further incident we hit the road and were gone.

So much for the gentle, caring Copper Thunderbird I had observed at the Cleansing ceremony two nights earlier. The Thunderbird had flown, and Norval was back, in its place—angry, stoned, obnoxious, and as disgusting as ever.

G

∗∗∗∗∗∗∗∗∗∗∗

JOURNAL ENTRY: 3-7-79

We finally arrived in Winnipeg, Manitoba mid-morning yesterday. We rented a small apartment in a complex called the House of York on the north side of town. The room isn't much better than the accommodations I had gotten used to in Beardmore; it was nearly as rustic but at least had the convenience of modern amenities like running water, indoor plumbing, heat, and a stove upon which to cook. It is, basically, an efficiency apartment, thirty by thirty, with a small separate kitchenette and a bathroom. The living quarters consist of the one large room which includes the receiving area (not nearly as formal as my language suggests) and our sleeping quarters.

The kitchenette is tiny, barely large enough for the appliances (a refrigerator, stove, and sink), but has room for a very small table.

The bathroom isn't much larger. At least there is a toilet and a shower/tub. I am anxiously awaiting my first full bath in two months!

The apartment is furnished, though perhaps "furnished" is too generous of a description. There are the previously mentioned appliances in the kitchen, a tattered sofa, a coffee table, and a couple of chairs in the living/bedroom area. But no bed! At least at Beardmore we had a mattress. I'm not sure what we will be sleeping on, but I assume Norval has something in mind, probably animal skins of some sort.

I can't say I'm particularly pleased with our accommodations. It may be more contemporary than what I grew accustomed at Beardmore, but it has no personality about it. Beardmore was at least rustic—this is just pitiful. Beardmore had an ambiance, coarse though it might have been, but this apartment has no atmosphere, no positive environment, nothing. It is barely a step above living in poverty, and this despite Norval's wealth! But then, again, it is typically Norval: Stripped of pretension, barren, and sterile —just like the man himself!

Many Tongues will not be staying with us, much to my chagrin. Prior to arriving in Winnipeg, I did not know that Many Tongues had lived here in the past and still had a small place in town. His apartment is not far from where we are staying and he will take up residence there. I'm hoping that I'll have the chance to see him on a regular basis, but given that he evidently knows people in Winnipeg, I imagine he will be visiting with them. Besides, I'm sure he a life of his own to which he must attend. He did remind me, after we had settled in, and before he left for his own place, that he and I must get together to further explore the visions that had come to him our first night in Manitou. I anxiously await that opportunity. He has told me repeatedly that we will continue that evening's experience when the 'time is right.' I do hope that right time presents itself soon!

Unfortunately, Wolf is staying with us temporarily until he can secure his own place, so that will make three cozy partners in a room hardly large enough for one. I can't help but wonder how Wolf's continued presence will affect Norval's and my relationship. I assume he will be gone during the day, working, but I also assume he will be here at night, which should make for interesting intimacy between Norval and me. But then, perhaps I should be pleased with Wolf staying here since his presence at night just might discourage Norval from the more physical aspects of our 'companionship.' Good old Wolf, I knew there must be some legitimate purpose to his existence!

After unpacking what little we had brought with us, Norval suggested we go out to dinner. Just he and I—what a surprise! It was the first time in weeks that Norval had indicated that he wanted to be with me, and it was the first time in weeks that we were alone. Usually when he came home to Beardmore, from where ever he had been, he brought at least one friend with him and of course, when we traveled to Manitou, Many Tongues and Wolf were with us. Dinner together would be our first experience alone in quite some time.

We went to a small restaurant for dinner, an elegant place with a classic decor. I am being too generous with the use of the words 'elegant' and 'classic.' The place was far gaudier and more prosaic than it was elegant! It was decorated with red velvet wallpaper that covered all the walls and trimmed the wooden furniture. It reminded me of accommodations in the Middle Ages because there were metal shields and armored weapons displayed on the walls and in the corners as well as axes, crossbows, and spears enclosed in viewing cabinets throughout dining area.

It also seemed to attract a questionable clientele.

Most of the people in the restaurant were male. I only noticed three women other than employees. Most of the men were dressed in clothing characteristically reminiscent of what I had seen in gangster movies: Dark, pinstriped suits; white, starched shirts; bold red ties; dark glasses, and a boutonniere in the suit jacket lapel. It was like something out of a mobster film; every man in the place was dressed the same. The three women were dressed like streetwalkers with costumes and makeup that made them almost comical.

Everyone seemed to be engaged in some sort of secretive meeting with their dining guests, as no one was speaking in normal tones but rather held their heads close together, whispering and talking in hushed voices. Of course I let my imagination run wild, assuming that we had stumbled into a mob hangout with godfathers and sleazy molls planning their next illegal caper. No one seemed to be enjoying his, or in the cases of the three women, her dinner. Everyone wore frowns and grimaces and infrequently flashed a smile. There was no sense of merriment or enjoyment. The customers, apparently, were there for the purposes of eating and executing a diabolical agenda of which I was not aware. Since I could not overhear any of the whispered conversations, I imagined they were making plans for a big mob hit. Maybe they were discussing how to get away with rubbing out the weaker mob families. Or possibly their conversations involved buying off the cops. That had to be it! The well-dressed, pinstriped men were the 'bosses,' and the more modestly dressed guests were the cops, taking bribes and accepting pay-offs! What a loathsome group of scum!

What struck me more than even the appearance of the restaurant's patrons was how the maître d addressed us when we entered.

"Will you be dining at Mr. Volpe's table tonight, sir?" he asked.

Volpe! The name on the business card that had been left in the cabin during the break-in, or had it been left? Perhaps it had been there all along, but I had just never noticed it prior to cleaning up the mess. Why else would we be dinning at Mr. Volpe's table? Norval had to know who this Volpe man was.

"No," Norval almost shouted, glaring at the maître d and pointing to a table near the center of the room. "That one will do."

The plot thickens, organ music in the background and another piece of the puzzle falls casually from the unsuspecting lips of a stranger. I am intrigued by this mystery that continues to unravel directly into my life! The maître d ushered us to our table and we ordered without further discussion of the Volpe table.

My runaway imagination was brought back to reality when our food arrived. We had ordered steak and just as the waitress was serving our main course, Norval initiated one of his less than discrete habits. He began picking his nose and did so with such frequency that I was quickly losing my appetite. Here was Norval Morrisseau, in a restaurant filled with customers, whom I assume he did not know (but even knowing them would not make his behavior acceptable) picking his nose and flicking its contents onto the floor, rubbing it on his clothing, or wiping it beneath the table! I could not believe my eyes. Norval Morrisseau, a man whom I had come to admire for his artistic genius, whom I had witnessed giving help to his people during the Cleansing ceremony, and for whom I had a begrudging amount of respect concerning his irreverence for white custom was picking his nose in public. He could care less who he was with or in what company he was in, let alone a restaurant full of people staring in disbelief! I was, again, disgusted by his behavior and was reminded why the respect I had for this man was wearing thin. The more I observed of Norval in public, especially in the white man's world, the more and more I became appalled by his behavior.

Eating and finishing dinner could not have come quickly enough. I had to choke down my food due to my embarrassment with Norval's comportment. Finally, our server brought the check and with it paid, Norval and I returned to the apartment.

Other than the decor of the restaurant, its odd customer base, and the incident with picking his nose, dinner was less than significant. Our conversation was mundane and for once, Norval had managed to sheath his temper in an unusual display of measure. For reasons I could not explain, he had been temperate about flying off the handle over the slightest displeasure.

When we got back to the apartment, Wolf had not yet returned from where ever he had spent the evening, so Norval immediately pulled a joint from his shirt pocket and lit up. We smoked that one and then two others while Norval ruminated about his philosophy of life and people in general. He rambled for about an hour and a half, but I really wasn't listening and don't remember a thing he said.

As he was winding down, stoned and becoming bored with his own voice, I mentioned that I was tired and wanted to clean up and go to bed. He looked at me with a curious expression and suddenly blurted out something about money meaning nothing to him.

"Money," I thought, "what does that have to do with anything he had been talking about?" Of course, since I hadn't been listening very carefully, it could have been that he was referring back to a topic he had discussed earlier. I seized the opportunity. In the two plus months I had been with Norval, I hadn't received a penny of payment for my secretarial and companionship services. True, my services weren't many, but functioning as a secretary/companion was, after all, why I had been hired by Norval, and the promise of good pay (by Bernie) was one of the reasons I had accepted the position. Norval did pay for our necessary means of survival and had provided me with housing—crude though it might have been—but he had never offered me a regular salary or payment of any sort. I concluded that this was my opportunity.

"Terrific, Norval," I responded, "If you can live without money—great. I can't. This was supposed to be a paid position but so far I haven't seen a penny of payment."

Immediately, Norval reached into his boot (he didn't carry a wallet) and pulled out a small treasure of cash. He jammed a wad of bills in my hand, and then, in what seemed like a scene from a movie, began throwing one hundred bills into the air.

"White man's money ain't no fucking good," he bellowed. "Take what you want. Grab what you can and save it all. Go ahead, little white boy, gather it up. Fucking gather it all up!"

That was good enough for me—this little white boy. I began collecting the bills that floated through the air and landed all over the apartment. In order to calm Norval's rage, I told him I'd hold it for safekeeping until morning when he could deposit it in one of the many banks accounts he had. For good measure, I added that it was a bad idea to leave that amount of cash strewn across the apartment floor. I was becoming as devious as he was. I knew he wouldn't remember the incident the next morning—drugs have that mentally dulling effect—and I'd be able to keep what I had collected. And I did. All told, I scooped up about $2500 in large denominations and put it away in my toiletry kit, where I knew Norval would never think of looking. I doubted that he would even remember the incident but knew, also, that if he did he had no use for toiletry items, so my hiding place was virtually discovery-proof.

Tomorrow I'll feign running a few errands, or simply taking a walk, and wire the money to my account in Toronto. Being in the city, as opposed to living in the cabin at Beardmore, allows for excuses of my own choosing to get away from Norval. For that I am grateful.

G

✻✻✻✻✻✻✻✻✻✻✻

JOURNAL ENTRY: 3-9-79

Part of my job is to inspire Norval, and for the last two days that is exactly what I have been doing—finally!

After a prolonged separation from his art, Norval has begun painting again. I suppose all artists, regardless of their medium, have times when they feel less creative and less motivated than at other times when they are more so. Beardmore and Manitou both happened during one of Norval's unmotivated and non-creative periods, and although they served a valuable purpose in helping me better understand Norval the man, they were dry periods for his artistry and for my hopes of learning from him. But now he is back with brush in hand and working on many different paintings and with a variety of display mediums: canvas, birch bark, and animal skin.

Our mornings begin similarly each day. Norval awakens, prepares the sweet grass for burning, then goes through his ritual of Indian chants which wash and cleanse the spirit. Even though I find many of Norval's characteristics loathsome, I admire his rigorous adherence to the spiritualism from which he draws sustenance and creativity.

Most of my afternoons are spent lying on either a buffalo hide or bear rug with Norval painting continuously. I am his inspiration, he says. I am just glad that when Norval paints his attitude is tempered by creativity and inspired only as the artist and not the lecherous man that he can be. Any thoughts of sex are submerged by artistic inspiration. I have finally learned to separate the two Norvals: Norval the artist and shaman, for whom I have a great deal of respect and admiration; and Norval the man, for whom I have nothing but distaste and loathing. Thankfully, the past several days have been spent with Norval the artist.

I am never hesitant with, nor intimidated by Norval the artist. I make suggestions on subject matter, give criticism on paintings in progress, and propose titles for the finished products. Usually I can come up with ideas learned from my early schooling that focus on fictional characters or fables.

Last week I remembered a movie with which I had been particularly fascinated about the lost city of Atlantis. I discussed the subject with Norval and suggested he work on a painting having to do with the mythological city and the prince who long ago ruled it. He thought it was an interesting concept and painted on a small oval canvas, which again I suggested. Norval had never before used an oval canvas in his work; he had always used square or rectangular shapes of differing sizes. The oval canvas was a first for Norval, and it worked quite well. The painting is beautiful. It depicts an Indian man's regal face with a fish swimming beside him. The background is blue to signify the sea. Norval titled the painting *Sea Prince*, etched my name on the back with a copyright symbol and gave the painting to me.

Several days ago, I suggested that Norval paint me as my astrological sign, a Sagittarius. He painted a colorful, vivid work of me as half Native and half horse. Interestingly when Norval uses me as his subject matter, which has become increasingly frequent lately, I am always depicted as a Native person; he has never painted me as a white man, and only once as a metis (*Eagle Spirit*—the painting he did back in Toronto the first night we met).

Yesterday, I asked Norval if he had ever done a floral design painting. He said that he had not, so I suggested that he should. He took my suggestion and painted not one but two large canvases of what are nothing but brightly colored flowers—another first for Norval, since the majority of his works are representations of Ojibwa legend and motifs of contemporary Indian culture. He gave me the two paintings this morning, both completed in one day! His mastery is unbounded.

It is good to have Norval the artist back again. Although when I first decided to accept his job offer and leave Toronto, I was primarily motivated by wanting to get out of Toronto and seek a different direction in life, I was also stirred to action by knowing that I'd be working with a genius and might learn from him as well as inspire him. Certainly the suggestion of the riches I might amass, as Bernie indicated, didn't hurt, nor did my desire to become a celebrity, if only vicariously through Norval. Still it was good to be in the presence of Morrisseau the artist again. Throughout our (my) stay at Beardmore, I had begun to lose all hope that my fantasy of learning from the great artist would come true. There were the few instances when he was at the cabin that he did a bit of painting, but nothing by way of quality or quantity like has happened over the past several days. He has literally turned out a dozen or more paintings! Watching him work is watching a genius master his skill, and despite the occasional money Norval tosses my way (still, nothing in the way of a salary) and my soon-to-be-recognized fame as his leading inspiration, I am honored to be a part of what has to be considered art history! The money and the fame are becoming less and less important. I am satisfied to have become a part of his art.

Enough for now, it is late and I am tired; posing is not easy work!

G

✸✸✸✸✸✸✸✸✸✸✸

JOURNAL ENTRY: 3-10-79

I intercepted a strange letter this morning. It was addressed to Norval but was unsealed and the contents were sticking partially out of the envelope.

Norval had gone out to run an errand. About what I do not know, because he is not inclined to involve me with his personal adventures, so I had the opportunity to peruse his special delivery. At first I resisted the temptation, not being one to snoop where my nose does not belong, but after an hour of seeing the partially exposed letter lying on the table, curiosity got the better of me.

I figured it couldn't hurt. I would read the letter and replace it in the envelope (sealed this time so Norval wouldn't suspect my incursion). I was hoping it might shed light on where Norval had been during his absences from our cabin near Beardmore.

The letter was addressed to Jean Baptiste—Norval's Catholic confirmation name—and read:

```
Your few visits last month were not enough. We appre-
ciate your taking the time to come see us, but we are
in a bad way. As you know, I cannot work, and we need
money. Please help, Jean, you are our only hope.

Victoria
```

From what I have learned, Victoria is Norval's grown daughter. Because the return address is in Beardmore, Ontario, obviously her note provides some explanation for where Norval had gone during his absences from the cabin. But it raises more questions. If not his daughter, then who is Victoria? Why had Norval gone to visit her? Why is she in a "bad way"? Why should he send her money?

I remember from Jack Pollock's letter in January that Norval is, or was at one time they had met, married and had at least seven children. If, indeed, Victoria is one of his daughters, questions regarding the note would be answered. But from what Jack wrote in his letter, Victoria was a child when he met her. If that is the case, and this is the same Victoria of whom Jack spoke, then she must be a young woman in her twenties by now. I doubt that this Victoria could be more than a daughter or family friend. It seems unlikely that Victoria would be a lover of Norval's. He has never expressed more than obligatory interest in women, at least not to me, and then only for the purpose of fathering offspring and continuing his tribal heritage. I would suspect that were he involved with another person other than his wife (assuming there was still a wife in Norval's life), it would be a man and a younger man at that. Norval is constantly commenting on the good looks of the younger men we see when we go out. He seems most favorably attracted to thin boys with sad-looking faces and tight little butts. His sexual appetite for younger men is voracious! Indeed, much of what he has commented upon concerning his more libidinous desires leads me to conclude that Victoria is not a lover or a sexual interest but a daughter.

If she is one of his daughters, then I am surprised because Jack intimated in his letter that Norval ignores his wife and children for the most part, only paying occasional visits and providing virtually nothing in the way of financial help. As a Native citizen of Canada, Norval is only required to pay one dollar per year in child support for each child he has fathered, and that is exactly what he contributes (according to Jack)—one dollar per year for seven children, a whopping total of seven dollars a year. And to think this is the same man whose paintings sell for tens of thousands of dollars and who has a savings account in at least one bank in every major city in Canada.

The letter has caused dissonance. Once again, I am perplexed and curious. One moment I am enraptured by the great artistry of Norval Morrisseau and the next embarrassed that I even know him. But this is typical. He can be generous with his personality and with his money but only in spurts and only under his conditions. One must be prepared to accept Norval's moods as well as his stinginess and sudden bursts of generosity. He will not spend more than the dollar of child support required by law but will turn around and indiscriminately throw a fistful of dollars to strangers!

Norval the enigma—Norval the schizophrenic. Norval the man of a thousand faces. He can be giving but only on his terms. Loving, when it is convenient. Generous, if he so chooses. Engaging, if in a good mood. Intellectual, if he deems it appropriate. Caring, if it is to his benefit. But he can also be angry, moody, irritating, obscene, violent, argumentative, disruptive, and childish. Not exactly the kind of person one would choose as a friend or wish for as a husband or father—unless of course there was a hidden agenda involved!

Norval has not yet returned, so I will give him the letter tomorrow. I am going to sleep. I have the place to myself. Wolf is gone also, which he is most of the time thank god, so I intend to enjoy the privacy and the peace that surrounds me.

G

❋❋❋❋❋❋❋❋❋❋❋❋

JOURNAL ENTRY: 3-11-79

The privacy and peace for which I longed last night when I attempted to sleep did not last long, at least not within my dreams. I do not remember the specifics of any of the dreams that I experience, but I do recall having numerous fantasies that passed into nightmare.

I was being chased, pushed, pulled, and harassed in each of the dreams: In some I was being chased by figures I cannot identify, while in others I was being pulled towards something disquieting that I cannot explain. In still others I was being pulled into the depths of a bottomless pit, while in still others I was being harassed physically and emotionally by people I had never seen before. The dreams frightened and disturbed me, but there was nothing I could do about any of them. In dream we have no control over the situations or circumstances, and I had become a victim to the treacherous desires of those who tormented my sleep...until...

...until the horror of my nightmares was shattered by a presence I cannot explain. It was as though the cavalry had come to my rescue in the form of an unknown liberator. My faceless hero exorcised the demons of my fantasy world and chased them away as quickly as they had manifested in my mind. I do not know who or what it was; the dreams are vague and dissipate as soon as I awaken, but I am thankful to whomever or whatever saved me from the terror of my nightmares. I take comfort in knowing that something or someone has entered my dreams and is protecting me.

After regaining myself from the disruptions during my sleep, I quickly dressed and approached Norval. He had returned sometime while I slept. There was still the matter of the letter to address. I handed him the note from Victoria that I had intercepted —he did not suspect that I had read it. After looking at it, he grumbled to himself, mumbled some profanities, and threw the letter in the garbage. If indeed, Victoria is Norval's daughter, then so much for fatherly love.

G

∗∗∗∗∗∗∗∗∗∗∗∗

MARCH 11, 1979
Joanne,

I'm going to bitch throughout this entire letter, so be forewarned. If you don't want to read my complaining, stop right now, tear it up, and throw it away; otherwise read on and listen to what I have to say. Oh, by the way, hello, how are you? I'm not much on ceremony and politeness tonight—sorry.

Being with Norval is a constant up and down. Some days I am happy that I made the decision to accept the job, but other days I hate him so much I would just as soon see him dead. He is a boorish, uncultured, argumentative man! I have been doing a great deal more posing, and Norval has been painting considerably more than he did when we were at Beardmore, but it has almost gotten to the point that the art doesn't matter anymore. He ignores his family (I have learned he has a wife and children), treats his brother, Wolf, like a second-class citizen (of course Wolf brings much of it upon himself by fawning over Norval and never standing up to him), and demonstrates very little consideration for friends. He is an uncouth barbarian who blames all of his problems on the white man.

I am not one to defend what our ancestors, and many of our contemporaries did and are still doing to Native People, but I don't subscribe to the theory that Norval is a product of discrimination and hatred. He is, after all, an internationally respected artist who has had audiences with dignitaries and politicians and who can hold his own in conversation with anyone. His problems might have begun because of discrimination and being forced into white ways by ignorant do-gooders, but his decision to continue drinking and doping is his—not anyone else's! There is no cause for him to treat innocent people with the disrespect he does. And I know of what I speak. I'm gay (like you didn't know), but I do not suspect that everyone who is heterosexual is out to get me or will discriminate against me. I would rather approach people as individuals and allow for a relationship to either flourish or decay before making judgments about one's attitude towards my sexuality. I think Norval could do the same, and he is in a much more lucrative position than am I: I have nothing to my name, no recognition, no status. Given Norval's gift of art, he has the opportunity to make changes more effectively and efficiently than simply cursing white people as an entire race and damning us all to hell. I would respect him more if he would act as the strong person he is, and attack the problems of discrimination for the purpose of making changes, rather than to simply drink and dope himself into oblivion.

For example:

Last week we visited the Cardigan Milne Gallery owned and operated by Marlene Milne and Jan Cardigan. They are interested in having an art exhibition of Morrisseau paintings and planned for a show next month.

Norval was truly excited and ready to get on with his painting, so we stopped at a small art supply shop after leaving the gallery. Norval grabbed everything in sight from canvasses of all sizes and shapes to paint and brushes and whatever else he needed. When he was about to pay the cashier, a young lady in her twenties, he suddenly started shouting and cursing obscenities at her.

"Are you fucking blind?" he roared. "Can't you see that I'm Native and we don't pay taxes?" She had added in tax on the materials—I'm sure much to her regret, after experiencing the wrath of Morrisseau. "You stupid fool, you stupid white bitch, you don't even know Norval Morrisseau when you see him."

Naturally, the young girl redid the sales slip, minus the tax, and the sum came close to $500. Norval handed her a one-thousand-dollar bill and said he wanted change in small denominations. Of course, as fate would have it, the art shop was unable to make change for the large bill, which sent Norval into another rage. He shouted and cursed until, finally, one of the other clerks ran across the street to a bank and got the proper change.

Typical Norval Morrisseau. He automatically assumed that the young woman was purposefully cheating him simply because he is Native and she, white.

Or consider:

Norval has a total disregard for other beautiful objects of art (sometimes even his own). He owned an exquisite Oriental jade artifact that dated back to one of the old Chinese dynasties (I'm not sure which one, but it wasn't the Ming). The object was a flat bowl that had been hand-crafted and painted and depicted an ancient Chinese legend on it. It was the type of sculpture one would use on a table as a centerpiece to elicit admiration. To Norval it was nothing but a piece of green rock he would use to butt his joints in (can you imagine Norval allowing someone to treat his art with such disrespect?).

One afternoon, when he was in a particularly bad mood, he became angry at some insignificant occurrence, grabbed the jade bowl and threw it against the wall. It chipped and broke into several pieces. I was sickened thinking about its history and artistry and how the beautiful artifact had survived a thousand years only to be destroyed during one of Norval's bouts of lunacy, but Norval didn't care. "It's just a piece of shit," he said, "The Chinese are nothing but a bunch of mongrels." Talk about disrespect for the culture and customs of other races—and he has the nerve to pounce upon the Native issue, while at the same time demonstrating a total disregard for other cultures.

On another occasion, Norval had purchased a marijuana bong. It had two separate glass vials. In one of the vials we would put marijuana and in the other ice cubes and red wine (what an excellent high!). The electric motor on the pipe pumps water through the section that contains the pot, circulates it through the second vial (with the wine), cools the smoke, and makes it easier to inhale while giving the dope a wine-influenced flavor.

It was truly a creative invention, that is, until one day when it didn't work properly, and Norval shattered it by smashing it in the garbage can. Another fit of rage. Another example of disrespect for people or in this case, objects. Another typical Morrisseau frenzy.

And I haven't told you about the restaurant episode on our way home from Manitou or the literally dozens of times he flies in to a rage and curses innocent clerks, bank tellers, guests to our home, or passersby on the street.

I am well aware that his problems are a result of his long addiction to alcohol, hash, and cocaine, but I am growing weary of his constant mood swings, embarrassed by his public behavior, and disgusted with his attitude.

I am not concerned about my sanity anymore; Norval's lunacy is making me feel quite sane. Perhaps this experience will lead to good after all, but what a way to get there. Compared to him, I am a picture of rationality (if you can believe that!).

I could go on and on with more examples of Norval's arrogance and violence, but I don't want to bore you completely. I'm sure this letter has done enough of that already.

There are still several issues I would like to resolve before I make the decision to leave, issues especially with Many Tongues, but my patience is growing thin. You just might see me sooner than you think.

Enough for now; we've got a long day tomorrow; something about getting back to the basics of painting, Norval said. And he still has to finish preparing for the exhibition at the Cardigan Milne Gallery, so until later, I am and always shall be, your loving friend.

Gilbert

✵✵✵✵✵✵✵✵✵✵✵✵

JOURNAL ENTRY: 3-13-79 [EARLY MORNING]

I had the dream about the giant rat again last night—the first time I have had it for several weeks. But there was a curious twist to the dream that has not happened before. It started out as usual:

I'm entering my parents' house through the kitchen door when I see a huge, ugly rat walking nearly upright on his back legs. As in all my other dreams, I am not frightened but more surprised. "Should I tell my parents they have rats," I think to myself. "No, it would just upset them and give cause for another fight." So I don't.

Half way across the room, on its trip from where ever it had come to the bathroom (the dreams do not reveal from where the rat comes), it stops, turns and looks me straight in the face with its red, satanic eyes. The rat hisses with a shrill screech that sounds like a banshee haunting its intended victim. Then, as it is about to walk away, a giant bird swoops down from somewhere near the ceiling and, with sharpened talons, knocks the rat over onto its back and slices open a wound around its neck. Almost immediately, a giant rabbit leaps from the bathroom, sinks its teeth into the rat and drags it back into the bathroom. And I am left standing there, alone, shocked by the rat and mesmerized by the bird and the rabbit.

In none of the other dreams was there a bird or a giant rabbit—they appeared last night for the first time. But, I have suspicion concerning their sudden appearance in the dream and why they interfered with the regular sequence of the nightmare. I am reminded of Old Young One's admonition not to fear the rat, that the rabbit and the Thunderbird have dominion. Could this be his prophecy coming true?

I must contact Many Tongues; it is time for our talk. He said I would know when the time was right, and I can't think of a more appropriate time than now. I shall contact him today.

G

✵✵✵✵✵✵✵✵✵✵✵✵

JOURNAL ENTRY: 3-13-79 [LATE AT night]

I contacted Many Tongues through a teller at one of the banks Norval uses. The young lady knew Many Tongues and provided me with his phone number. I was surprised that Many Tongues had a telephone, nevertheless, I called and we spoke. He agreed to meet tomorrow evening. I await our visit with great anticipation.

Meanwhile, things grow more convoluted by the minute.

To begin with, Wolf is moving in with us—permanently. He had been staying with us off and on since we arrived in Winnipeg several weeks ago but was seldom here and had taken an apartment several blocks from us to ensure his own privacy (he claimed). Contrary to Wolf's insistence, I suspect he wants to distance himself from his older brother as much as possible. Sometimes Wolf revels in Norval's attention and vile moods, but other times he deplores them—silently though it might be. We hadn't seen him for three or four days, until earlier this morning when he came over to our place complaining that he had been evicted from his apartment for disruptive behavior and had nowhere to go. He has not been working (surprise, surprise!) and was living off Norval's generosity, which is a dangerous thing to do, given Norval's penchant for dichotomous behavior.

In many ways, Wolf is even more pathetic than Norval and in other ways more engaging. He mimics Norval's drinking and doping, and is much like a mischievous little boy whenever the two of them are together—Norval leading and Wolf following like the child he pretends to be. It is no wonder Wolf demonstrates such low regard for himself. To my knowledge he has never supported himself and has never accomplished anything of significance that might encourage additional success. He is every bit the artist that Norval is and every bit the drunkard and doper, but I suspect his lack of self-esteem generates from living in the shadow of his older and more famous brother. His work is just as vivid and as colorful as Norval's, and depicts with as much clarity and insight the legends of the Ojibwa. But he has not gained the attention or notoriety that Norval has. I suppose one family prodigy is sufficient, and since Norval was discovered long before Wolf was old enough to paint seriously, Norval assumed the fame and the fortune as well as the admiration of his people and of his fellow countrymen. Besides, the Thunderbird spirit visited Norval, not Wolf.

In some respects I feel sorry for Wolf. It must be difficult to be the unknown, unheralded, unrecognized younger brother of a genius. He has had to listen constantly to the praise heaped upon Norval and has had to endure the embarrassment and humiliation of being regarded as the family failure. Interestingly, though, given Norval's petulant personality and addiction to alcohol and drugs, I'm not certain why Wolf would want to emulate his older brother; he does nonetheless, and except for the reputation that has failed to come with his art, he has done quite well in mimicking Norval's chemical dependency and bloated ego.

Of course, Norval relented after a short row and agreed to let Wolf move in. Now we have three in a room barely large enough for only one.

And as if the news of Wolf's moving in wasn't enough disruption, another visitor came to the apartment this afternoon. A man who I had never seen before and who I hope not to see again.

Norval and Wolf had gone back to Wolf's place to move his belonging over here, so I was alone. I was working on one of my ideas for an original Morrisseau, this one having to do with me posing as the great Thunderbird Spirit, when there came a loud and sudden knocking on the door.

I opened it to a man whom I can only describe as sinister looking. He was tall, dark, muscular, and mysterious. He was dressed all in black—even including black sunglasses that disguised his eyes. He wore a fedora slung low across his forehead. He looked like a character straight out of *The Godfather*. He asked for Norval by name and when I informed him that Norval wasn't home, he pushed his way past me, looked through the apartment, which didn't take long, then disgustedly said he had a message to leave.

"Tell Norval that Jacques wants to see him." Then as suddenly as he had arrived, he was gone!

I tried calling after him, to get his name or to further clarify the message, but to no avail. He was several steps ahead of me before I could regain my composure. On his way down the steps, I heard him mutter back to me, "Let it go, kid... just let it go."

When I told Norval about the visitor and relayed the message, he became whiter than I imagined a Native could get. His bronzed skin turned ghostly pallid and a look of terror crossed his face. This was not the strong, abrasive Norval that I had come to know but an anemic imitation of the Copper Thunderbird. He withdrew into himself for the remainder of the evening, neither painting nor speaking, not even becoming abusive and argumentative. Quite to the contrary, he was agreeable and humble—the exact opposite of the man who cursed innocent waitresses and clerks and who damned everyone and everything in his way straight to hell. He didn't even want to smoke any dope—only the second time since we had been together that he refused marijuana, the other time being prior to the Cleansing Ceremony. He became like a cowering child, frightened by ghosts in the dark, and although I have little pity for Norval, I did feel a bit empathetic. No doubt there have been times when I have felt frightened by circumstances beyond my control, so I am able to identify with fear—long ago it had become a regular part of my being and still plagues me frequently.

Later that evening, Norval announced plans to visit another brother and his sister somewhere outside of Beardmore, two days hence. We would all be going, he said: Wolf, him, and me. I was curious about meeting Norval's family, but concerned about what the visit from the sinister stranger could have meant and why it had spurred this sudden desire on Norval's part to abruptly leave Winnipeg only a few weeks before the exhibition at the Cardigan-Milne Gallery. Nevertheless, I was relieved that we wouldn't be leaving for two days—there was still time to meet with Many Tongues.

G

✸✸✸✸✸✸✸✸✸✸✸✸

JOURNAL ENTRY: 3-14-79 [11:40 PM]

My visit with Many Tongues came off as planned.

I taxied to his place, a small apartment several miles north of ours, located near the edge of town and in the a semi-rural area more appropriate to his lifestyle. He seemed as glad to see me as I was to see him. We greeted one another as though we had been lifelong friends who hadn't seen each other for years. As soon as I saw Many Tongues, I felt comfortable again, a feeling I had not had since he left us when we arrived in Winnipeg. It was good to see his smiling face and reassuring to hear his soft, almost inaudible whisper. Secure to be in his supportive presence. And I know he was just as happy to see me, for when we greeted, he threw his arms around me in a huge bear hug and said, "Welcome, brother, I have missed you." Instantly I felt at home.

After we had greeted and engaged in trivial chatter, he said he wanted to tell me a story. He settled into his oversized recliner, shifted himself into a comfortable position, folded his arms across his chest and told me the following (I paraphrase as best I can, but surprisingly, I remember Many Tongues' story almost word for word):

"This is a true story; you can believe what I say. I was a small boy, perhaps six or seven when my tale begins. To tell the truth, I'm not sure how old I was. I was born before the census takers came, so there is no record.

"At that time, our village rested on the shores of the great water in a land far from here. In the village there lived a young boy who had no family and no name. He lived by himself in a great lodge of birch bark and twigs. He kept to himself and went about his business in a way that made the other people of the village jealous and angry. Jealous, because he had the most beautiful lodge in the village; it was clean and warm and was filled with food, even when hunting and growing was bad and mad because no one knew who he was or from where he had come. He had always lived in the village, long before even the oldest of the men and women had been born. No one could remember him being older or younger, so the people of the village called him Old Young One, but they did not speak to him, no children would play with him, and no men would take him on the hunt. They were afraid of him because he had no family, no name, and no age—they though he was Malsum or an evil Manitou.

He kept himself away from the other people, except during the ceremonies that the people held to celebrate the coming of the growing season and the passing of warm days into cold. At the time of ceremony, he would join the people of the village and speak of visions and in a language only the oldest of the people could understand: He told of human beings with pale skin and human beings who were as dark as night. He spoke of battles and wars with the white human beings that the Natives had not yet seen. He told also of great armies of men fighting—brother against brother—and spilling rivers of blood in a land that was like ours but was not ours anymore. He spoke of his own people wandering the land in the cold and in the snow with no lodge in which to live and no land to cultivate and he spoke of many Native people piled in deep graves and of small children and old women lying dead in the grass like bison after the hunt. He spoke of many other visions that frightened the people and so he was not welcomed to visit at any of the people's lodges, and no one went to his. They thought he was an evil spirit, and they were frightened.

"One day in the middle time of the hot season, the rains did not come, the wind did not blow, and the nights became so unbearable that many people slept outside their lodges to cool down. The food in the village was low, and the chief was afraid there would not be enough to last the cold season. All the people were frightened that they might die cold and hungry. It was a sad time.

"Then, in the afternoon of the last day of the hot season, Old Young One went to the lodge of the village chief and asked that he might speak with him because he knew where to find food for the cold season. No one knew what to do. Never before had Old Young One spoken directly to anyone in the village, and no one ever had talked to him. Only the stories told at the Cleansing Ceremony were the few words he had spoken to the villagers. The daughter of the chief was surprised, but kind and wise, and said she would speak to her father about Old Young One's request. The chief agreed to listen to Old Young One because he did not know what else to do; his people would die if they did not get food for the cold season.

"When Old Young One entered the chief's lodge, the chief said to him right off, 'What do you know of getting us food? You told my daughter that you would save us from dying in the cold season. Tell me now or I shall make you leave my lodge and our village.' Old Young One smiled and said to the chief, 'I know how to get food for your people, but I must have another to help me. A male-child must accompany me. I cannot complete my task alone.'

"The chief, desperate to help his people, knew Old Young One had many visions and great magic and he wondered how could it hurt to let Old Young One try—his people were facing oblivion and Old Young One offered hope. Many boys in the village would be glad to go on an adventure. They always wanted to go hunting with the men but could not because they were too young. The chief told Old Young One that he could choose any village male-child he wanted to go with him to find the food. Old Young One was pleased and replied, 'You will not be sorry, I will bring food for your village. I will make the rains come again, and the wind blow like it did many weeks ago, and I will make your lodges warm when it is cold and cool when it is hot.' The chief laughed, thinking that Old Young One was crazy but let him leave to find the one he would choose to go with him.

"Old Young One went from lodge to lodge searching for the right companion to take with him on his adventure. But one after another, he came away from each lodge disappointed that he could not find a companion. Then he came to the lodge where my father and mother and three sisters and I lived. He saw me sitting in the back of the lodge, hiding beneath a blanket, afraid for him to see me because I was frightened that he might choose me. My hiding did not work because as soon as Old Young One saw me he pointed and said, 'He is the one. I want your son to come with me.'

"My mother and father did not trust Old Young One and said no. They did not want me to leave them and my sisters; they feared that I would not come home again. But Old Young One told them what the chief had said to him, and so they had to let me go. I was afraid, but after we left the lodge with our cold weather skins, he smiled at me and told me not to be afraid any more. And I wasn't. His eyes were kind. He was gentle. But he was also brave and strong; I was comforted knowing he would provide care of me.

"After we had walked many miles from the village, he stopped and sat down. 'We have come far enough. We will travel no farther,' he said.

"I said back to him, 'We must go farther to find the food, and the rain, and the wind, and the warm. You told the chief that we would find all these things for the people of the village.'

"He did not tell me to be quiet like the men and women of the village would have done. He just smiled and told me to be patient like the seed that lasts the cold season and grows when the warm time begins, and then he told me to wait with him.

"'For what?' I asked.

"'You will know when the time is right,' he said softly.

"And so we waited. And we waited…and we waited…until the sun disappeared behind the hills, until the moon and the stars shined in the sky, until the birds started singing in the early morning quiet, until the sun came up again on the other side of the world. All this time Old Young One sat in silence. He did not sleep or even close his eyes. He only stared into the sky above and at the dirt below. And when the sun held straight up high overhead, he spoke again and said:

"'Now the time is right; take my hand. Press it to your chest where you feel the sound of life beating. Feel how hot, like the fire, my skin is. Feel how cool, like the morning dew, my skin is. I am the fire and the water. I am the wind and the calm. I am the Earth and the sky. I am forever and I am now. I am Manitou— powerful and with magic. I can take many shapes to gain what I want. I was born before the Wanagi-Wachipi danced their dance of death at Wounded Knee. I was born before the white man first set his treacherous foot upon the land of the turtle. I was born even before the time when Glooskap made the sun and the moon appear in the sky. It has been many years since I came from the long night of my beginning.'

"As Old Young One said this, he changed from a human into a wolf, then into a bear, then into a hawk, then into a wolverine, then into a fox, then into a martin, then into a snake, then into a rabbit and finally into an enormous owl. I was very frightened by what Old Young One could do with his magic. I had heard my father tell stories of the great Manitou, but I had never seen one before that day, and I did not know if Old Young One was a good Manitou or an evil Manitou.

"'Who are you?' I said as I kept his hand pressed against my chest.

"'I am no person and I am all. I have no name. I come from beyond the night sky. I have been in your village for a thousand years and a thousand years before that. I have been called by many names: Glooskap, Wabasso, The Great Spirit, The Thunderbird. These are names people give me because they do not know who I am, and they are frightened of me.

"'And who are you, truly?' I asked feeling no fear.

"'I am you.'

"When Old Young One said, 'I am you,' I felt the heat from his skin burn through my skin, up my arm, and race throughout my whole body. I felt the coolness of his chest soothe and calm the fire until it did not rage but only comforted. I was warm and I was cold. But I felt Old Young One inside me, like when the Great Spirit enters a body to reveal a vision. I was no longer me, and he was no longer him—we had joined to become one.

"Then he continued, 'Do you not wonder why the sun makes you warm during the day, or the dark makes you cold at night? Do you not wonder why the rains and the snows come when they do, and why the rice grows plentiful in the shallows? Do you not wonder why the animals cannot speak, or why the moon and the stars shine in the sky? Do you not wonder all of these things and more? It is because one spirit is all and all spirits are one. It is because of the joining of one, with another—because of the awakening. I am not one person you call Old Young One; I am many people who have lived before me and who live in me, and I will become many people who will live after I am no longer.

"'Now is the time for you to Join." And as he spoke, Old Young One reached his arms to the sky, spoke in a language that no Indian had ever heard before and changed into the body of a rabbit, with the head of a Thunderbird.

"At once I felt all the substance that was inside my body rush to my skin, making me feel hot and cold at the same time. Old Young One took both of my hands and we spun around faster and faster in a dance of praise, until all the trees and bushes and grass and hills that surrounded us were blurred so I could not see them, and then, everything disappeared and I fainted.

"When I woke, I was alone. Old Young One had gone. 'What a fool I have been to believe his silly story,' I thought to myself. 'I will have to go home, like a dog with his tail between his legs and be made fun of. My mother and father, my sisters, and the chief and his daughter will feel foolish, too because they believed the evil Manitou.'

"I was tired and groggy with sleep still in my eyes but struggled to my feet and looked around for the pathway home. When I found the path that led down the mountain and through the woods, I was disturbed because when I looked, I could see my village far in the distance! 'How can this be,' I thought, 'No human can see so far—not twenty miles, not even two.' And then I noticed I could hear the birds in the trees, not chirping like they do in the early morning, but speaking to each other and asking if they had enough worms and bugs to eat. I bent over to pick up my blanket and discovered that when I touched it, my hands could feel the blanket and my skin at the same time. Then I smelled wild rice cooking over a hot fire, but there was no one around who was cooking. And I could taste the rice when I licked my lips in the cool morning air. Everything I could see or hear or touch or smell or taste was like magic; everything was easier for me to perceive and to understand.

"Then I heard the faint voice of Old Young One again, but it seemed to be coming from inside me. 'Go home and you will find plenty of food for the cold season. The rains have come, the winds are blowing again, and the cool breeze has chased the heat from your lodges. I have lived in your village for many years and now it is time I pass. I am now you. Your people will not understand; they will not know that you and I are one. They will wonder where I have gone and why you return alone. Tell them, that in our adventure to find food and the wind I was killed by an evil bear when we stumbled upon her prison. They will be sad because of what we have done for the village, but they will be glad that you have returned safely. You will return a hero.

"'But you will also have a responsibility to watch over your people. We are powerful, but we cannot make the humans do what we want or what we know they should do. They will always be human beings and will be good and bad and make both wise and foolish decisions. But we must watch over them and hear the voices of the human beings who will listen to us. They are in us, just as we are in them. As I lived and joined with the many who came before me; now you must live and wait for others to join with you. You will know when the time for Joining has come. Your life will be long, as long as my years and more. But you must never use the magic for evil; it must only be for good. You will not hear my words, again; my words are now your words. We are one. Go now.'

"Those were the last words I heard from Old Young One. When I returned home, there was great happiness and joy. There was plenty of food enough for the cold season, and the rains and the winds had returned. When I returned, the people of my village welcomed me home like a hero, and I told them how Old Young One had been killed by a great brown bear while we struggled with the evil magic to free the rains and the wind from the bear's prison. Everyone in the village was sad because Old Young One had kept his word but now was dead; they were sorry they had not listened to him before. But they were happy that I had come back safely and the rejoicing lasted well into the next week."

✴✴✴✴✴✴✴✴✴✴

When Many Tongues finished his story, we sat in silence for several minutes. I had no idea what to say. The story was overwhelming, beyond my ability to understand, and Many Tongues seemed worn and tired and was looking beyond anything that was in the room where we sat. His eyes were glazed, he stared into the darkness of the night, and neither looked in my direction nor spoke.

When he did, it was commanding, comforting.

"Do you understand?" he asked.

I hesitated before I answered: "The story, yes. Its connection with me, not exactly."

"The new Old Young One," Many Tongues responded.

"What are you talking about? The new Old Young One—what do you mean? I'm not even a Native person; only half—I am metis! How can I be what ever it is you're talking about?"

For the first time in my relationship with Many Tongues, I was feeling uncomfortable. I knew what he was getting at, I think, but I wasn't about to accept the possibility. It was too much to ingest in one evening. Whereas I had thought that our meeting would have proven beneficial and would clear up the confusion that I had about myself and my relationship with Norval, as well as the attraction I felt for Many Tongues —especially since the evening in the tipis in Manitou— it did not! If fact it did the opposite. I became more confused! I didn't want to deal with what he was suggesting. I had come to Winnipeg with Norval for the purpose of getting the hell out of Toronto, making some quick cash, and learning more about my own art, and now Many Tongues was trying to tell me that I— that we —were some kind of combined ancient spirit that manifested itself as human but existed in the spiritual world and lived for thousands of years! Not exactly what I wanted to hear; not the kind of information I was prepared to assimilate or accept.

"Who are you, Many Tongues?" I finally blurted out.

"You know who I am, Wabasso," he answered. "I am you!"

I had suspected what Many Tongues was going to say, but this was all too much for me to deal with in one night, and I suggested as much to my new and mysterious friend.

"Perhaps you are right, Old Young One. We must wait until another night—a better time. I have told you much and you must think upon what I have said. Tomorrow night?"

When I told Many Tongues about leaving for Beardmore, he seemed unusually agitated but asked how long we'd be gone. "A few days," I told him, "No more than a week."

That seemed to calm his concern. "A few days is not long, a week, not much longer. The sun and moon have waited for a thousand and more years. We can wait a few days."

That relieved me. Many Tongues was right that I needed some time to 'think upon' everything he had said, and time was one thing I seemed to have enough of.

"Then when I return, I can contact you?" I asked.

"Yes," was all that Many Tongues replied, then lowered his head as though falling asleep. He had seemed to tire after telling the story, earlier and I didn't want to awaken him, so I gathered my coat and made my way to the door. As I opened it to leave, I heard Many Tongues speak, but his voice sounded from within me rather than from his lips.

"Know when the time is right, Wabasso, do not deny your destiny."

I left in a hurry.

G

****

Journal Entry: 3-15-79 [3:30 AM]

I write in my journal, early in the morning, after having been awakened again by one of my dreams. I recount the episode as best I can.

After returning from my visit with Many Tongues last night, I quickly fell asleep. Norval and Wolf had gone out again avoiding the apartment as much as possible. Ever since the visit from the sinister intruder, Norval has made himself as scarce as he can and hadn't come back yet. Given my state of mind after my meeting with Many Tongues, I fell deep into sleep.

Then the dreams began: First, me as an ancestral Native Spirit, lording over a rag tag clan of nomadic Ojibwa who had no land upon which to live, and no lodges in which to keep warm; then, the rat dream—repeated for the umpteenth time; and finally, an unusual dream that was as much disturbing as it was frightening:

I had to get home, where ever home might have been, it wasn't clarified in the dream, but the only means of travel I had was swimming down a river, a long, dark, and wide river like the Humber in Toronto. Somehow, I knew that I had to keep swimming since I couldn't port on either shore without being assailed by the evil creatures and demonic spirits that cavorted in a terrible dance of death. It was night and every thing was dark—there was no moon or stars in the sky and no lights on either shoreline. Monstrous trees with gnarled, twisted trunks lined the banks of the river with low hanging branches that swept the water's surface and threatened to ensnare any passersby in their tangled web of thorny splay. The water was cold and deep, and I had to keep swimming so as not delay my pace, and yet I was so tired it was all I could do to tread water to keep my tired body afloat. I knew, although I had not been told by anyone, that were I to land on either shore, I would be accosted by the evil creatures and half-human mongrels that inhabited both sides of the river, so I kept swimming and swimming further and further down what seemed an endless river, hoping that around the next bend would be home, but still I had no idea of where home was, or who would be there to greet me upon my arrival.

At one point, after becoming so tired that I thought I would slip into unconsciousness and drown, I came upon a clearing on the left bank of the river that was covered with the most beautiful vegetation I had ever seen. Tall flowering junipers shaded a garden of hydrangea and magnolias. Vines of Virginia Clematis curled along the ground, weaving in and out of landscaped rocks and timber where vibrant golden trumpet vine and fiery red geraniums grew. A small stream, bordered by wild Hosta and water fern, flowed through the clearing, wound down the hillside near the water's edge, and spilled over a rocky outcrop into the dark river. It was as inviting as it was beautiful.

Without hesitation, I swam to the shore and pulled my weary body onto dry land. It was a feeling I cannot describe; I felt relieved to be out of the cold water and reassured to be back on land. As I walked into the clearing, I could see a beautiful garden with a stone walkway not far from the water's edge that led into the lush foliage. I began walking up the path, entered into my self-discovered Garden of Eden, and took rest beneath the welcoming branches of pine and birch that shaded the blazing sun overhead. I hadn't even noticed, nor cared that suddenly it was a warm, sunny day!

Down the path, I could see people walking along the stepping stones: men and women hand in hand and small children playing, nearby, in fields of wild flowers. They looked at me, waved, and motioned for me to come closer and join them. There was so much comfort in seeing the people, strangers though they were, that I lost all sense of the unspoken warning that, earlier, had cautioned me against taking refuge on the shore and rushed to be with them. I felt at ease, comfortable, at home. A wealth of incredible happiness engulfed me. This garden was home, the place for which I had been searching on my journey down the river. At long last I was home, that beautiful, lush, fertile garden of security.

As I approached nearer the people, they continued smiling and waving me closer. I reached out to take the hand of one of the women who had encouraged me onward, when suddenly everything I had come to instantly embrace, changed without warning. The comforting, welcoming people—men, women, and children—abruptly transformed into hideous, impish creatures. Their appearance was revolting: Hunched-backed and stooped with long arms that brushed the ground as they walked; broken skin with festering wounds oozing yellowish puss and blood; twisted, misshapen faces with hollow, lifeless eyes, and teeth that protruded from their mouths like sharpened fangs. They grabbed at me, swiped at my skin with nails that grew from the ends of their fingers like thorns on a rose branch, and spat burning, acidic venom that dissolved my clothing and scalded my flesh. I broke free of their attempt at subduing me and ran as fast as I could through what had once been the beautiful garden but was now nothing but barbed bushes and snarled trees trying to find my way back to the river.

The garden had degenerated from the woodland oasis of only moments earlier to a contorted knot of branches, bramble, and thorny vines that grew from the ground and twisted across the rock path like snakes slithering through the grass. The trees were reaching down with their distorted, barren arm-like branches, trying to catch me in a trap that would hold until the vile creatures caught up with me. All around I could hear wailing and groaning and the sound of ogres crying out in the dark. The sun had disappeared and the land was blanketed in utter darkness.

At last I reached the river, jumped in, and swam away from the hellish oasis that had, at first, promised relief. And there I was again, swimming faster and faster as far away from my nightmare as I could and closer to what I hoped would be my real home around the next bend.

But home wasn't near. I awoke while still swimming in the cold of the dank, dark river, and am here, now, writing in my journal, as confused and as helpless as the day I had left Toronto—nay, central Ontario, nay, my mother's womb— and joined with Norval, joined with anyone, joined with life in hopes of finding out who I am, but not yet discovering the truth about myself, about what I want, or about where I am going.

For the past few weeks life seemed to be settling down for me personally; I was beginning to feel more comfortable with myself and with the situation with Norval and now this horrific dream and everything else that shaded my sun. Life seemed to be crashing down around me, and all I could think of was Old Young One at the cabin at Beardmore, Many Tongues confiding in me the story of how the two would Join as one, and now me—as Many Tongues put it: The new Old Young One. What the hell is going on?

Damn you, Many Tongues!

G

✸✸✸✸✸✸✸✸✸✸✸

JOURNAL ENTRY: 3-15-79

The trip to Beardmore has been delayed, at least for a week or two. In his haste to get out of town, Norval didn't consider the exhibition at Cardigan-Milne Gallery. Now he is intent upon finishing several of the paintings he had started so he can (as he said), "Have a full showing and suck in more money."

The delay is fine with me because I'm hoping to get to see Many Tongues again—we have to go on with what we started last night. I may be frightened and confused, but I know many of the answers I seek are tied up in my relationship with Many Tongues and whatever the heck he's talking about with the story about Old Young One, himself, and me.

Norval is laying low, which sounds like something out of a bad murder mystery. He paints at night when he supposes the "sinister jerk is asleep," constantly puts his ear to the door to hear if anyone is coming up the stairs, and watches out the window at every passing car and every suspicious person. "Suspicious" for Norval means anyone who he doesn't recognize. Earlier today he became convinced that an old lady trying to get across the busy street, from the far side to the side on which our apartment is located, was actually our ominous visitor dressed up in disguise. He made me go out and see if it was really an old woman. "Cop a feel, if you have to. Grab her tits or his cock; either way you'll know," he told me. "Just make sure it isn't that guy who was here earlier." I didn't 'cop a feel' nor 'grab anyone's cock,' as Norval had suggested when I got out to the street. I could see, without having to resort to physical harassment, the person was indeed an old woman simply trying to get across the street (and I did help her).

Right after lunch, we heard a pounding on the door. It was urgent in its rapidity and sounded like someone was trying to bust down the door. Norval had become so spooked by the visitor with the message that he nearly jumped out the window and fled, of course I wouldn't have been far behind; he now had me scared out of my wits too.

The pounding continued as we sat frozen in our chairs at the table. After a few minutes of the demanding knocking, we heard a voice calling Norval's name.

"Norval, you there? Open up, I know you're in there. It's me, Brian," the voice called.

Brain! Norval was relieved, but I was in the dark. "Who is Brian?" I asked as Norval opened the door. I found out right away.

There stood a Native man, maybe twenty or twenty-one, with long dark hair to his shoulders, a strong jaw and handsome face, and eyes that penetrated as he looked in my direction. He was slender but not skinny, dressed in tattered jeans and a white T-shirt with an Ojibwa inscription across the front. His jeans were appropriately ripped at his thigh and under the crotch revealing a tantalizing peek at his underwear. He was gorgeous! He was everything that Norval always looked at in a passing boy and more! A round, firm ass, abs like a washboard, a more than generous chest, and a crotch that suggested more beneath the jeans than might first be suspected. He smiled broadly at Norval, glared at me (or was I imagining it?), and stepped inside.

Norval let out a loud whoop, threw his arms around the newcomer, and slapped the guy's rear.

"Brian, my boy, what brings you here?" Norval was obviously glad to see this person he called Brian. "I thought you were still in Beardmore!"

Still in Beardmore, I thought to myself. *What brings you here?*

He was greeting this Brian like a long-lost lover. In a flash of sudden insight, it was all beginning to make sense. When Norval had been away from our cabin for days on end, then came home moody and argumentative, he must have been visiting this boy (or rather man, I suppose, but he didn't look much older than a kid). Victoria's letter suggested that Norval had visited with her only occasionally which couldn't have explained his numerous absences from the cabin. But Brain could have. Gracious, I might have been swayed away from the cabin too had I had the chance to be with Brian. Now it was all falling into place.

A few steps behind Brian came Wolf, trudging up the stairs carrying three suitcases in his hands and under his arms. He puffed his way into the room, dropped the bags on the floor, and collapsed on the sofa.

"Thanks a lot, asshole," he grinned, then continued, "Look who I found at the bus station."

I doubt that he just happened to find Brian at the bus station. I wasn't aware that Wolf was into cruising bus station pick-ups, so I'm sure there had been prior arrangements made—probably between Wolf and Brian—since Norval seemed genuinely surprised to see the boy. It was likely that Wolf and Brian had made arrangements sometime earlier and then Brian high tailed it here as quickly as he could to be with his lover, or more aptly, his fuck-buddy!

"Got some good, shit, TB," Brian said reaching into the smallest of three bags. TB, I wondered. Thunderbird perhaps? How cute, they've even got pet names for each other. My jealousy was beginning to show.

Brian withdrew a bag of black hash, which practically made Norval's eyes bug out. He laid it out on the table, and we all indulged in hot knifing. In a few minutes we were all stoned, and before I knew what was going on, Brain was naked and Norval was drawing and painting, hopefully not readying more paintings for the exhibition in two weeks. I don't think naked men replete with erections is exactly what the gallery was hoping for.

I hadn't yet been introduced, even though Brian and I had hot knifed together, and suddenly there was this hot looking Native kid posing for Norval. Needless to say I was angry, but the hash dulled my hostility, so I was more inclined to just remain in the background and observe. I reclined on the couch, watching Brain with his athletic body and Norval painting like a madman. I must say that Brain was quite a pleasant sight to behold, far more pleasing than Norval's or Wolf's exteriors of grizzled faces and middle-age physical inadequacies. Brian was young, well built, sensual, and—how shall I say this—impressively equipped.

Several paintings were done that day; Norval is so gifted in his visions of art that he is able to complete a painting an hour. Thankfully for the work expected by the Cardigan-Milne Gallery, the end-work of his labor does not necessarily reflect the subject. All of the paintings, except one, were of patterns far different than a naked man. Norval did four paintings that afternoon: Three of them inspired by Brian, but one provoked by me. Norval had coaxed me into joining Brian in the *au naturel* state, which in my intoxicated condition, both from the hash and from Brian's loveliness, wasn't hard to do. It was like an artistic ménage-à-trois—Brain and I naked and Norval raping our bodies for inspiration. Poor Wolf had passed out after the third round of hot knifing, so Brian and I were left to Norval's demands.

Late in the afternoon, long after Norval had stopped painting, we heard another knock on the door. This time Norval bolted for the bathroom and told Brain to deal with it—what ever "it" might be.

I have to hand it to Brian; he was as cool as a cucumber, as they say (who ever the hell "they" are, and depending upon how cool a cucumber actually is). He threw a loosely hung towel around his waist and answered the door.

Norval's worst nightmare was realized. There was the threatening stranger again, looking every bit as intimidating as the first day I had seen him.

"Morrisseau here?" he demanded.

Brain got a look of anger on his face and began spinning a tale of lies that would make Prospero proud.

"Morrisseau? Norval Morrisseau, the great painter?" Brain blurted, "Not likely, that fucker! That asshole invites me here then splits. I come all the way from eastern Canada, and he leaves me here with his boy-toy." Brian nodded in my direction. "I didn't even get a chance to see him. Man, that creep tells me he's got a job for me as a model, so I drop everything back home, come all the way out here and the jerk is gone. I'm left with no money to get back home and his little fuck-buddy," again nodding in my direction.

The stranger looked at me and almost smiled. "You fucking queers," he grumbled. "That slut was here the other day, too," he said looking at me. "Said he didn't know where Morrisseau was." Saying that, he entered the room, crossed immediately towards me and grabbed me by my shoulders.

"Did you lie to me the other day, cock-sucker? Mr. Petén, isn't it?" he demanded.

What the hell? He knew my name!

O.K., I can lie as well as anyone and play any kind of game that's been started. "No, I didn't lie. I told you he was gone, but I didn't know that he'd left town. I'm supposed to be modeling for him too, and he leaves me high and dry. You think I'm happy about that? And then this kid comes here, today, saying that Norval wants him for a model. The hell with all of this shit!"

The stranger seemed satisfied, dropped his hands from my shoulders, and noticed Wolf crashed out on the couch.

"Who's that?" he asked.

"A buddy who came with me," Brian offered. "He's blown on hash. Gotta' let him sleep it off."

Again, the stranger seemed satisfied with Brian's lie.

"Well, looks like you two aren't missing Morrisseau very much," he said looking at our towel-clad condition. "Kind of weird to be going about the place naked isn't it?" he continued. " Course I guess not for your kind—fucking faggots!" he spat and turned for the door.

"If you do see Morrisseau, tell him Jacques wants to see him right away. He knows how to get a hold of Jacques." He was out the door.

The stranger was halfway to the stairs when he turned around. "And tell Morrisseau that Jacques is a very impatient man. It don't matter where he's gone, we'll find him." With that, the stranger was down the stairs and out the door before we could say anything else.

Brian and I stood there for a few silent minutes just staring at nothing in particular.

"Not a bad lie," I offered. "You're pretty good."

"Yeah, I've had enough practice," Brian answered back.

Brian's and my first conversation, and it was telling lies about Norval.

Wolf was still on the couch passed out, so Brian and I went to get Norval. The door to the bathroom was jammed shut with something from inside, but we managed to push it open. There in the corner, hunched down between the toilet and the bathtub, crouched Norval: Silent, trembling, and looking like he'd seen a ghost. The great artist and mystic who only minutes earlier had been hot knifing and painting like a man possessed had been reduced to a cowering little boy.

It took us several minutes to coax him out of his hiding place and back to the living room. But even then, after the stranger had been long gone and the three of us were alone and sitting on the floor, Norval didn't speak; he just stared into space, apparently lost in his own turmoil. Whatever was going on, whatever kind of trouble Norval had gotten himself in to, and who ever Jacques was, we weren't about to find out that night (Jacques Volpe from the business card, I suspected). Norval didn't say another word all evening and finally went to bed alone a couple of hours later.

Wolf never did wake up that night. Brain sat at the table hot-knifing, and I was left by myself to consider what might be going on. I remembered the letter from Jack Pollock a number of weeks ago. His words became more ominous, now given the break-in at the cabin, the incident concerning the Volpe table at the restaurant, and the two visits from the sinister stranger. "Whatever Norval has gotten himself into, I still love him," Jack had written.

Brian groaned then rolled over and fell asleep.

Really? I thought. *You still love him, Jack? Give me a break.* Whatever Norval had gotten himself into did concern me, if for no other reason that I was now involved, but I couldn't say I still loved the man, especially with Brian now in the picture.

G

❊❊❊❊❊❊❊❊❊❊❊

JOURNAL ENTRY: 3-17-79

Once again today, I experienced the many changing moods of Norval Morrisseau. One would think that after the length of time I've spent with him that I would have developed insight into his multitude of personality shifts, but such is not the case evidently! Why, I don't know. I realize that I'm a gullible person and the kind of man who hopes for the best from people, especially my friends, but I think trusting people has gotten me into more trouble than it's worth. It certainly did back home as a child, and in Toronto, and now with Norval. Perhaps I expect too much from humankind. I suppose, were I to be forthright, that I'd have to admit that I expect my friends to treat me the way I treat them: with respect, courtesy, and honesty. I have frequently been disappointed throughout my life with this philosophy. Considering that my expectations and some of my friends' ensuing realities regarding friendship have been less than satisfying, it isn't realistic to think things would change with Norval.

I know I've established standards that are far too demanding both for myself as well as for my friends, but I place a great deal of significance on friendship, and that I suppose that is one of my major downfalls. After all, lovers come and go, but a friend is forever.

Yeah, right.

I am a perfectionist in everything I do, a classic Type A personality, and I expect my friends to be the same. Simply achieving isn't enough for me. I have to overachieve, and I am never satisfied with any of the successes other people attribute to me. In school, it wasn't good enough that I'd get all As and an occasional B on my grade card. It had to be all As or I'd punish myself with severe recrimination and harsh second-guessing! At work, regardless of which of the many jobs I've held, I was successful to the point of achieving recognition and commendation from employers, co-workers, and customers, but again, it was never enough! I strive constantly not to be just good or an above average employee, but the best worker of all.

My friends have always told me that I'm the one person they can trust and count on, that I'm always there for them when ever they are in trouble, or just down on themselves and depressed. I try to go the extra mile and to give when there is little left to emote. But again it's not good enough; I just don't want to be a good friend—I want to be the best friend possible!

Sexually, I have taught myself to be the giver in a physical relationship, rather than the taker. I want the man I'm with to feel special, to feel exhilarated, to lie back and enjoy the sensual pleasures of passion and intimacy. I am always the one to await the tease, but also the one who initiates libidinous delectation. The men I've been with have always said I'm the best lay they've ever had. I am well aware that sexual compliments are easily given when one is under the influence of alcohol or drugs, which was frequently the case with many of my experiences, and that the person who I am with at the moment, is not about to tell me during the heat of desire that I'm no good! But still my actions and their compliments are not enough for me. If I regard myself a good lay, then I want to be great. If I'm a great lay, then I want to be the best fuck they've ever had.

My demand for perfection doesn't stop! No matter what I do and despite my successes (whatever they may be), the results are not sufficient! I am driven by an unmitigated demand to succeed. I am not certain why I am so relentless. Is it because I lack the self-confidence I try to project? Could it be because of my abusive childhood and a need to prove to everyone who screwed me over that I not only survived their monstrous violations but also have succeeded beyond their wildest imagination? Maybe it's because so many people have told me that I would fail that I have assimilated their negativity and am trying to prove them wrong. Perhaps it is because I think that I constantly have to prove myself, to myself and to others, over and over again.

And concomitant with my need to succeed is the exact opposite of success—the belief that I have failed, and will fail, and that whatever good might be happening at any given time, with any given situation, will be dashed with a sudden dose of bad luck or reality. Reality—the great leveler of hubris.

I suppose, in short, I would say that I rigorously pursue the best, expect the worst, and am never satisfied with anything between. I am given to the extremes: either total success or total failure—that is the only way I can operate. And even if I were to succeed, legitimately, I would assume that some how, some way I had fooled everybody. Indeed, I can fool all of the people all of the time. I wish that I could free myself from these unrealistic demands I place upon myself and upon my friends, but I am the most critical, demanding, and exacting person I know—for myself, and unfortunately, with my friends.

And it causes depression. Depression because I know I can do better, because I believe I'm never good enough, because, as I wrote earlier, I am a perfectionist.

And I expect the same from my friends, which is unrealistic, overly querulous, and unfair. I cannot demand that other people live up to expectations that are unrealistic and impossible. If I cannot please myself, concerning the rigorous expectations I have established, then I can hardly demand others ascribe to such impractical discipline.

And, somehow, that brings me back to Norval and his changing moods. As I scribbled, earlier, I am constantly surprised at his chameleon-like personality.

The day started off well. Norval suggested that just he and I go for a drive. I think it was his way of making better the unexpected arrival of Brian. We drove up to the south shore of Lake Winnipeg, ate lunch at one of those typical *Good Food Here* joints, and were headed back home when an unexpected snowstorm hit. March snowstorms can be sudden and fickle. Usually, by mid-March winter has begun to break and the early signs of spring are beginning to appear. But as is the case in most northern climates, the weather cannot be depended upon.

When we left in the morning, it was sunny and cool, a perfect beginning for a spring day. But, by lunchtime, the clouds had rolled in off Lake Winnipeg and a thunderhead was developing. A storm of ominous proportions was inevitable—rain if the temperature held, snow if it dropped.

The temperature dropped.

We were no more than ten miles away from the Lake when it hit. A cold front blew in from the west, converged with the storm coming land ward off the lake, dropped the temperature about twenty degrees, and dumped eight inches of snow by the time it had exhausted itself two hours later.

We were heading south on route 59 when the snow started. We had been talking about the upcoming exhibition at Cardigan Milne and about other incidental things that people are given to talking about while motoring in a car—other people, the scenery, what's been going on that we hadn't caught up on, and the like—when Norval's mood, like the weather, changed without warning.

Throughout the drive up to Lake Winnipeg, at lunch, and as we began homeward, Norval had been in one of his better moods. He was joking around, laughing at my pitiful attempts at humor, and talking about the next painting he was going to do of me—an Egyptian God. He had seen a stone etching at an exhibit of Egyptian art at a gallery in Winnipeg and had been impressed with their geometric shapes and bold coloration. Norval considered the Egyptian art similar to the work he did as an Ojibwa artist, and was attracted to it more than any other period of art I had heard him discuss.

And then something snapped. Perhaps Norval was thinking about Brian's arrival and wondering how he would balance the two of us without making either of us petty or jealous, or maybe he had been worrying about the visits from the stranger—who knows. Regardless, he took a last toke from the joint we had been sharing and butted it on the pant leg of my jeans.

"Jesus, Norval," I yelped as I snuffed the singed denim.

"Just to keep you honest," he joked, with a hint of recrimination in his voice.

"To keep me honest, about what?" I wondered what I had done to deserve his sudden anger.

"To keep you in line, white boy," he spat.

There it was again, the damn Native man/white boy thing. He couldn't let up. Everything Norval thought or did, all of his actions and reactions, every incident that occurred in his life was, according to Norval Morrisseau, the result of white racism, and yet he couldn't possibly comprehend that his prejudice was the racism that created part of the strain between us. He had contrived a world in which everyone, including his closest friends and confidants, were white racists. And it was so hypocritical. Norval's supposed hatred of white people in his private life was totally antithetical to the public comments he made, almost always alluding to how all people of the world should love one another and get long; that it was his mission to foster the advent of a world at peace and harmony. I was getting sick of his hypocrisy.

Sick enough of it that I made my mistake.

"Norval," I began, "Sometimes you act like you have a split personality. You swing without warning like a pendulum from one mood to another. Sometimes you're as fun as hell to be with, but other times you get so dark and moody that you're frightening. And this 'white boy' thing; I'm tired of you always being ready to blame everything that happens on racism."

Norval slammed his fist into the dashboard, stomped his feet on the floor like a child in tantrum, and shouted, "Stop the fucking car," at the top of his voice. "NOW," he ordered. My thoughts instantly recalled a similar situation years ago with Russ.

As I pulled to the side of the road, Norval was yelling and cursing and using combinations of foul language that I had never heard! His face was flush, his eyes angry and dark, and his voice quivered as he scolded me for interfering in something about which I knew nothing. I don't think I'd ever seen Norval that angry. Obviously I had hit a nerve, and Norval was retaliating with every bit of ammunition he had.

"You son-of-a-bitch," he barked, "I could send you home right now without a fucking penny. Is that what you want?"

The thought of going home did cross my mind; penniless, however, was not an option!

"Or I could keep you here, locked in the bathroom and never let you out unless I want to fuck your goddamn ass."

That was not a pleasant alternative to consider either.

He grabbed me around the scruff of my neck as he listed the possible consequences of my untimely comment. He was choking me to the point I thought I'd pass out. I was gasping for air and flailing at him with my arms, hoping that he'd come to his senses and recognize that he was hurting me. I honestly feared for my life; I thought he was going to kill me.

"Or I could just kill you, dump you by the side of the road, and no one would find your skinny ass until the snow melts."

Another unacceptable possibility.

"Which will it be?" he continued, beginning to calm down. "Or, you could just shut your fucking mouth and not butt in where you're not welcomed."

I opted for the last choice.

"Now, let's get home," he directed.

The rest of the trip home was passed in near silence. I wasn't about to discuss any thing that might incur his wrath and given that I had no idea what might trigger his anger, my choices for conversation were severely limited. We journeyed home—me in silence and Norval occasionally commenting on something stupid like how coke is better up the ass than the nose.

Gee, I'm really happy to know that!

When we got back to the apartment, Norval told me what a great time he had had that day and that we should go out more often—just the two of us.

I do not concur with his assessment of the day nor his proposal for future trips.

❈❈❈❈❈❈❈❈❈❈❈❈

LATER THIS EVENING, NORVAL HAD an artist friend, Robert Houle, come for a visit. Houle is another Ojibwa artist, successful in his own right, but one who had not achieved the degree of success and recognition that Norval had.

Again, Norval's mood swung dramatically. He was like a pendulum: Swinging from the apex of anger and violence, down to a mid-range of calm, and over to the opposite apogee of friendliness and humor. When Houle arrived, Norval swung from calm to gushing friendliness.

Houle had come for spiritual counseling and guidance and was seeking solace and answers to his life-way problems.

Norval told Wolf and Brian to get lost, gave them two one hundred-dollar bills from his boot, and told them to get out, get drunk, and get laid. "You're both a couple of pansies," he chided, "go get fucked before your dicks fall off." Norval had such a way with situations.

He asked me to stay, claiming that he wanted me to be his link between the real world and the spiritual, a link he insisted was paramount to him being able to seek the Thunderbird Spirit and merge with its consciousness. Although I was still smarting from the incident earlier that day, I agreed hoping that the spirituality Norval possessed would either rub off on me or point me in the direction of discovering my own mystic abilities.

The counseling lasted for an hour. Norval was able to contact the Thunderbird Spirit and revealed visions and dispensed advice to Houle that evidently addressed the exact issues with which Houle was concerned. Houle listened to each word The Copper Thunderbird spoke and readily nodded and mumbled approval.

After the reading had ended, Houle left without any acknowledgment of my presence. He effusively thanked Norval, made half-hearted arrangements to meet with him in the near future, then was gone. He departed as quickly as he had arrived.

After he had left, Norval swung away from the friendliness he had demonstrated for Houle and back to a more melancholy mood that implied irritation with me. He said nothing to suggest as much, but remained silent for the remainder of the evening.

In one day's time I had experienced vintage Morrisseau the pendulum: Happiness and elation, dull monotony, anger and violence, back to the void of emotion, over to excitement and exhilaration, and back—finally—to a monotone of tedium.

With each experience, I grow wearier of staying with Norval for longer than it takes to collect sufficient funds with which to leave. But, in truth, I'm not certain I can stand him that long.

And yet, what captured my interest the most was what took place during the counseling session with Houle. The entire time that Norval was offering guidance and spiritual advice, my mind was filled with a presence I had not before experienced. It did not seem like it was I acting as the go-between, or interpreter, if you will, but rather it was though I was providing the sage advice and comfort through Norval's mind. I cannot attest to the veracity of my suspicion, but it seemed as though I had somehow penetrated Norval's mind and had claimed it as my own. I am becoming more confused with each experience I have.

There is no doubt I must see Many Tongues as soon as possible.

G

✸✸✸✸✸✸✸✸✸✸✸

Journal Entry: 3-18-79

Things have gone fairly well since our trip to Lake Winnipeg. Norval has recovered from his bouts of sudden anger and has gone back to finishing up the paintings for the show. The trip to Beardmore has been delayed again. Norval figures that since Brian and I pulled off our deception with Volpe's thug so perfectly, there is no reason to clear out quickly as long as he lays low. And of course, now that Brian is here, I suppose Norval sees no reason to go home. But how Norval expects to pull off an art exhibit at a well-known gallery without either Jacques Volpe or the sinister visitor finding out is beyond me. Nor can I imagine he's about to visit the brother or sister he mentioned a few days ago, assuming they even exist, and if they do, why would he go to visit. He had never mentioned them before and now that the crisis with the stranger seems past, there's no reason to go to Beardmore.

For the past few days we've just kept busy: Norval painting, Brian doing most of the modeling (I've been reduced to a cumbersome hanger-on), and Wolf mostly smoking dope and hot knifing. I tote the laundry back and forth to the laundromat, not exactly what I had pictured back in December!

Yesterday, while going through the dirty clothes, I found three hundred dollars in Norval's pants pocket. Being honest (damn me!) I gave it to him and he told me to go out and buy him a birthday present. It wasn't his birthday (his demands for presents have been quite regular since we arrived in Winnipeg), but I did what I was told. I bought him a shirt, a necktie, and a pair of jeans. All told, I spent about fifty-five dollars and pocketed the rest of the money—I guess I'm not so honest after all. When I gave the clothing to him, he was thrilled and didn't ask for the change. Victory! I added it to my savings that I was preparing to wire to a bank in Toronto. Over time, I have collected a tidy little stash using the 'birthday gift' method in addition to the fifteen hundred dollars he gave me previously. Frequently, Norval gives me money with which to purchase various items, and I keep whatever is left over. He never objects, never questions me, and never seems suspicious. Since he doesn't give me a regular salary I consider the money fair reward, and Norval probably regards it as "so what money." He has made enough references, throughout our relationship, about not liking white men's money anyway. Well, I do; if he doesn't, that's his problem.

Later that same day, Norval was feeling a bit on the good side, unusual since the visit from the stranger but not surprising given his obvious fascination with Brian. The two of them have become quite inseparable. I haven't even slept with Norval since Brian arrived (not a bad tradeoff), and I'm sure the two of them are screwing like bunnies. We all sleep together, so I'm certain that nothing is going on at night while I'm there, but when I'm off running Norval's errands, I have no doubt that they are working on more than just a painting. I have no evidence to support my belief, but both men seem unusually playful when I return.

That night, Norval stuffed a salmon with wild rice, a traditional Ojibwa dish which was truly delicious. He seldom cooks (we usually bring in fast food), but the few times he has, he's demonstrated culinary skills in line with his artistic genius. This morning, he made breakfast with Norval-recipe fry bread—another taste-tempting delight. I never cease to be amazed by this man. He is undoubtedly a gifted artist. His abilities as a shaman and a mystic are legendary, and I have experienced his many different mood swings: One day angry and argumentative, the next playful and childlike, another day spiritual and philosophical, and another artistic and ingenious—and of course always stoned or drunk regardless of that day's particular mood. Now I have discovered his culinary expertise. I'm beginning to think he really does have a split personality, maybe even multiple personalities, but I dare not discuss any such theory with Norval; I'd hate incurring the angry, argumentative Morrisseau.

Midmorning today, after we had finished breakfast, we ran out of dope, which put Norval back into a terrible mood. Usually when one of Norval's 'no dope' moods hits, Wolf is smart enough to stay away from the apartment as much as possible to avoid Norval's wrath. Brain is learning quickly, too. But this time, both were in the apartment. I was getting tired of Norval's moods as well so I decided to take matters into my own hands.

Interestingly, even though Brian has become Norval's featured model and Wolf is his doting brother, I have been able to maintain a certain authority over both. Norval has not specifically elaborated my position, but I have the feeling he has told Wolf and Brian to heed my words because even though they have a closer intimacy with Norval, I have his trust regarding day-today matters. I think he has told them both to leave me alone and respond to my orders.

That fit well into my plan, given that I was no longer desirous of taking more hostility from Norval.

I ordered Wolf and Brian to go out and not return until they had scored some dope. I emphasized how it would benefit us all: Norval would have his dope and would be in a much less foul mood, and we'd have some peace and quiet from all the craziness that happens when Norval is dry. I exercised my assumed authority and gave Wolf and Brian an ultimatum: Get the dope or don't return. I reminded them of my position with Norval and barked at them like Norval would, were he the one giving the orders. It worked! They scurried out of the apartment as quickly as I had finished my delivering my directives and were gone several hours. When they returned, they had scored big. Norval was ecstatic. I was relieved.

We got stoned as soon as they returned with the marijuana and toked out the rest of the afternoon. Norval was nearly finished with the paintings for the exhibition and was feeling quite pleased. Still feeling my newfound authority over Wolf and Brian, I told them to get us something to eat, steak and potatoes preferably, and I wanted it brought back, fully prepared with all the accompanying side dishes. They both looked at me with a glare of hatred but responded without word or whimper. I didn't have any desire to be alone with Norval, but figured he'd be harmless given how wrecked as he was, and I was enjoying my power of control—something I had never before in my life experienced!

Norval must have been pleased with my attitude also, because no sooner had they left than he started becoming amorous with me, a possibility I hadn't considered given Norval's recent attention to Brian! He got out one of the dozens of porn flicks he hides away (some gay, some straight) and insisted we explore the world of sensual pleasure. We had used pornography a number of other times to encourage our sexual forays, but this time Norval pulled out all the stops.

He brewed a mixture of herbal tea, swallowed a handful of multivitamins and ginseng, and lit incense and dried grass to evoke the spirits of the Ojibwa fertility gods. It was all I could do to muster the resolve to fulfill Norval's demands, but I performed as expected, though with much less attention and creativity for which

I am known. Curious how I have authority over Brian and Wolf, but Norval still has total control of me! Of course, the preparation of tea and incense and burning grass took far longer than the intimacy, and by the time Brian and Wolf had returned (not more than an hour later), we had completed Norval's attempt at life imitating pornographic art and were collapsed naked on the sofa together.

Wolf seemed to ignore the scene, but Brain was obviously angered and hurt—further clarifying my suspicion that he and Norval were more involved than either of them had let on. Or perhaps Brian was simply jealous about something I had with Norval that the did not. I don't mind admitting that even though I could no longer stand the thought, let alone the reality, of having sex with Norval, Brian's jealousy was satisfying. I was regressing into patterns that had been established in my teenage years and had perfected to a tee as a young man in Toronto. Norval, in his unknowing and devious ways, was re-engaging the monster I had become earlier in my pathetic life.

Wolf and Brian fell asleep immediately after we had finished dinner. Norval passed out from the combination of food, booze, and dope, and I was left alone to consider the happenings of the day. I sat, drifting in and out of consciousness for about an hour, wondering why I was the only one among us four who ever seemed to regard the meaning and reasons for things we all did, individually or as a group, beyond simply becoming drunk or stoned and stumbling through life like bums on the streets. I wondered further how I could go back and forth from one emotion, one mood, one paradigm of thought and action to another, and another, and another with little regard for how I was continuing to retard my own emotional development. In actuality, I exhibited no maturity beyond the same moodiness for which I criticize Norval. At a point I fell deep into sleep.

****

THERE IS SOMETHING ABOUT THE water—especially at night—that is dark, foreboding, and intense. It calls to me to become a part of it, to join in communion with the dark, bottomless deep. Its waves, in synchronized rhythm wash against the shore, inviting me to carry out with the currents into the depths of isolation and despair returning, once again, to the point from which I came. The water is the nexus of life and death: The alpha and omega, the world as one continuous entity before the drying of land.

The water is dark like the night that engulfs it. Foreboding like the storm that threatens. Intense like the power and unknowing it portends. And yet, the water is welcoming and comforting: A repose from the insanity of everything that has gone before or is yet to come. And within its mystery rests the enigma of union and alienation: Accepting all that is or can ever hope to be, while embracing the understanding that being alone, being isolated, being separated is a fantasy that dare not be challenged. To become one with the water, to join the very font from which we spring invites emotional and intellectual dissonance. To be One and to be All. To be singular and to be many. To be strong yet at the mercy of Poseidon.

To challenge its anger that has the power to swallow the unsuspecting to a silent death beneath its wave.

I go to the water to find the peace I can find nowhere else. I travel to the one place where I am at home. I visit the water in my dreams, in reality, in fantasy. And it is always the same: Dark, lonely, endless, and bottomless. I return a thousand times to the genesis of my creation: Always to the water, always with the same need, always in the same existence.

During the light of day, I can sit and look out across the water and watch its green shallow recede into the blue of the deep, disappear into the distance of the horizon, and ebb into the broken clouds of the sky. And in the air below, untouched by the water, but at the mercy of its dominion is a silence that echoes the sound of eternity—whispers of what once had been, what is, and what is yet to come.

On either side of me, I can look as far up or as far down the coast line as possible and see nothing but water and sand, rocks and pebbles, and flotsam that has drifted in from nowhere and from everywhere—the nothing and the everything that I do not understand. I lift with the wind and walk the shore, alone, dreaming, needing, and wanting a place where I can belong.

At night, as the rest of the world sleeps, I scale the dunes of sand that landward protect and seaward expose, pretending myself into dream. I become a part of the water swelling with the waves, receding with the tides, preparing myself for the sacrifice the gods demand: To free myself from this hated reality and drift with the lonely sound of a passing tanker, unseen in the deepening night.

There is a distance about the water, beyond the geographic and beyond the reality, that entrances me. It is distance that allows me to escape the demons that haunt my every breath. Demons that prevent me from becoming the person I want to be. Demons that make me shiver asleep at night, even in the warmth of the summer heat.

I sit in the dark of night upon brown sand and colored agates and lose myself into a dream that carries me beyond the fantasy that augurs nightmare, and I soar on wings that carry me high above the ground, loosed from the bondage and isolation that defines every thought and emotion I dare experience. I fly above the earth, defying gravity and ascend to heights I dare not imagine while rooted to the ground by reality.

The water eases my pain. Comforts my anguish. Consoles my humiliation. For each moment of loneliness I experience, the water swaths me in repose. And, yet, the water I so dearly need, demands the discomfort of knowing that whoever I think I am is the person I will never know, the person I will never become, the person I shall always fear. And I weep myself asleep—lost, alienated, distant, and alone.

I go back to the water in my mind for it summons me to come. I am enticed to succumb to a fate experienced by the thousands of victims who have challenged the water only to lose to its haunting and mysterious power. And like those poor souls who have gone before me, I do not know how close I might be to the end, surrendering to the mercy of the water and accepting the fate I cannot deny.

And I go willingly. Curiously. Obediently.

And, too often, I go back to my hideous dream of swimming down the dark, lonely river.

Who knew when it happened,
That a tear spilling onto the floor,
At the end of a row of people,
Around the corner,
In the dark,
Alone,
Was significant?
Or, who would have thought,
That a comment about how
Autumn is purposefully choking out summer,
And how sad it is to see the mums
beginning to bloom
--*Like lilacs last in the dooryard bloomed*--
Would be revealing?

Every night,
And every day seemed to fall onto deaf ears:
Tacit, muted, irrelevant,
Who was to know, then,
What since has become truth?
Who could have assumed,
How a thousand empty thoughts later,
I would be found on the surface of the water,
Floating face down into eternity
(or at least partially floating).
Who would have suspected, so long ago,
That a tear spilling onto the floor,
In a lonely part of my mind,
Would become the final bath of desperation?

G

✦✦✦✦✦✦✦✦✦✦✦✦

JOURNAL ENTRY: 3-20-79

Norval was in the mood to paint today, and it's a good thing because the exhibition at the Cardigan-Milne Gallery is only two days away and only three quarters of the paintings he promised had been done as of this morning. Norval has busied himself so much with Brian and drugs that the time has slipped by more quickly than I imagine he thought it would—and that's giving him credit for even knowing what day it is. I am well aware that all work and no play makes

Jack a dull boy, but in Norval's case, all play and no work will cost Jack a contact, thousands of dollars, and disaster! The press has already been invited to review the show, invitations have been distributed, guests of honor are anxiously awaiting the exhibition, advance publicity for the show has been published extensively in the local papers, and Norval is fucking away his time fucking Brian! All of this publicity does not bode well for Norval being unseen by Jacques Volpe and his hoodlums. But, I guess if Norval hasn't given that any consideration, then neither should I. I am not his nursemaid… although they know me by name!

I have taken the upper hand with much of Norval's business: paying his bills, running errands, and attending to his bank accounts, so I figured motivating him for the show would fall into the realm of my secretarial duties also. After breakfast, this morning and before the three stooges started doping away the day, I took command like General Patton on the front lines in Italy and began issuing orders.

I instructed Wolf to run to the art supply shop and purchase five more canvasses. Without asking, I took money for the canvasses from Norval's boot, handed it to Wolf and told him to find five differently shaped canvasses: large, small, oval, and rectangular—whatever. Norval looked surprised at my boldness, but said nothing, I think he was even pleased that someone was taking charge.

"No canvasses, no dope today, Wolf," I ordered. I knew the threat would work. Norval's earlier discussion with Brain and Wolf had instilled the fear of, well, not me, but of Norval, and it worked such that I had control of the dope, anyway, so I didn't expect Wolf to contradict. Wolf grabbed the money and bolted out the door.

Brian was next. He had been enjoying himself much too much since his arrival, all at the expense of Norval's dope and dick, so I thought he needed a more challenging task with which to keep himself occupied. Not that I was trying, in my own devious way, to get back at Brian—Norval wasn't worth it—but there was something about him waltzing in here, nearly taking over our apartment, and assuming my role without even the slightest hint of contrition. The bathtub in the apartment was a mess; we hadn't used it for its intended purpose for weeks. Norval had filled it with water, a softening solution, and some concoction of herbs then soaked cow hides in the brew to make them more pliable as canvasses and more easily worked for painting.

"The bathtub, Brian—clean it up. Hang the skins to dry, empty the solution, and scrub it spotless! In fact clean up the entire bathroom. And the same goes for you: no clean tub…no clean bathroom, no dope today." I was getting good at being in command, but of course, I kept my ulterior motives so deeply suppressed that I wasn't even aware of them until later. Only after Norval nodded at me approvingly did I realize that I was seeking his approval with my arrogant bravado while at the same time punishing Brian for interfering in my relationship with Norval. I had given him the most disgusting job possible, and I loved it! Of course, the situation between Brian and Norval really wasn't Brian's fault or necessarily his own doing; Norval had taken a liking to the boy (Norval had an almost fatal weakness for young men with beautiful faces and strong bodies) and had promised him many of the same things he had promised me.

Nevertheless, we were on our way. Wolf was off buying additional canvasses, Brian was (reluctantly) cleaning the tub and prepping the canvasses we had, Norval was preparing his brushes and paints, and I was, well, I was wondering what the hell was going on!

As much as I had grown to detest Norval over the past few weeks, I was jealous of his attention toward Brian and was taking my hostilities out on the young Indian for merely responding to Norval in an honest and admiring way. Maybe my feelings were because I knew I couldn't give Norval what he wanted, but that Brian not only could but was happy to provide. Perhaps I was just getting fed up with the whole situation of the four of us doing nothing but smoking dope, wasting away our lives, and constantly flirting with disaster. Good god, was I becoming mature! Such a possibility not only disturbed me but sickened me as well. More likely, I was (and am) perturbed with myself for, recently, ignoring Many Tongues and relegating his mysticism to mere hocus-pocus (that made it easier for me to discount without feeling guilty). What ever motivated my control today felt comfortably good and was working.

A couple of hours after I had issued my ultimatums, Wolf returned with five canvasses of different shapes, the tub and the bathroom were clean—well, at least cleaner than when Brian has started with his task—and Norval had readied his materials. As a means of reward, I pulled out four joints that I had rolled while the others had been attending to their chores, and offered them up as appeasement. No one rejected my generosity. We got high, Norval readied to paint—all was in order.

Until Norval made a fateful decision.

It was Norval who decided that he couldn't possibly get the last paintings done in time for the exhibition: five canvasses of three cowhides, and two birch bark etchings. Curiously, I had seen him complete more painting is less time than was left before the showing, but for some reason (Wanting to drug? Wanting to fuck Brian? Both?) he suggested that he would draw dark-line figures on each medium and we (Wolf, Brian, and myself) would add the color to his drawings. He argued that it would be more like assembly line work with each of us assigned a series of colors, and adding them as we moved from one painting to another. I had no question that the idea would be workable since Wolf was an accomplished artists in his own right and I had picked up a deep understanding of Norval's technique, shading, and coloration during my two-plus months with him. As for Brian, I had no idea concerning his artistic bent, but figured we could cover for him. Still, the idea was fraud—art fraud pure and simple. Norval had no intention of letting us sign the paintings. He intended to sign each one with the famous Morrisseau signature. I had read somewhere that several of the great masters of art had done much the same, but generally the work completed by their apprentices was known (for the most part) to patrons and critics alike and was considered part of the learning process. Some artists even gave their protégés credit on the back of the canvas. But this was different. Norval had neither the intention of giving any of us credit for the work nor revealing the reality to the owners of Cardigan-Milne or anyone else for that matter. He was willfully and knowingly committing fraud.

Although I knew that what Norval had suggested was fraud, we really didn't have a choice. Norval engaged his dominating insistence, we were all high, and the show was only two days away. After rethinking the amount of time left to us, Norval was right about one thing—he couldn't possibly have finished the work on his own, the canvases had to dry thoroughly before display. Given the situation and Norval's persistence, we all started painting.

Norval sketched and the three of us colored. Yellow here and there, a splash of red, some blue, a little green, then a smidgen of orange. Norval sketched five canvases comprised of three cow hides and two birch barks. We colored the same.

It took until early in the morning and four more joints, but we finally completed all five mediums, and Norval signed each and every one. There was ample time for the new works to dry.

In less than two days, the paintings would be hanging at the Cardigan-Milne Gallery for the world to see. The show was a guaranteed sellout as were all of Norval's exhibitions. Critics would rave, patrons would gush, celebrities would babble enthusiastically, and each painting would sell for thousands of dollars. Patrons of the haute hip salon world would carry home original Morrisseaus to display on livingroom walls and above the fireplace in dens, but only Norval, Wolf, Brian, and I would know the truth: that several of the paintings soon to be hanging in homes across Canada and around the world and proudly displayed in galleries from Winnipeg to Paris would not be Morrisseau's, but would be fakes—frauds.

Norval had made the decision, but we had gone along with it, and now, not only had Norval transgressed the ethics of creativity and honesty, but so too had we—so too had I. I felt as though I had hit bottom. I had betrayed the only thing I held in high esteem, the only thing I could put faith in, the only thing I could believe in—my personal integrity.

When I picked up my journal to write this evening, I felt sick, literally sick to my stomach, and I remain sick as I write. Three months ago, when I made the decision to leave Toronto, I had done so hoping to make some quick cash, learn about art, inspire the great Morrisseau, escape the debauchery of Toronto, and discover myself. I'm not sure that I've accomplished any of what I had intended, other than to sink lower into my abyss of intemperance.

I am a failure.

G

✸✸✸✸✸✸✸✸✸✸✸✸

JOURNAL ENTRY: 3-24-79

Norval's exhibit was a rousing success, at least as far as the unsuspecting public was concerned. For anyone else even remotely associated with the Cardigan-Milne Gallery or the press, or anyone who had any interest in following local art openings, it was an unmitigated charade—but not because of the fraud (my worst fear) but because of Norval's obstinate personality. Even though he made a considerable financial take on the art and despite the fact that the show had been packed for its entire run, the press reviews about Norval himself were less than enthusiastic. But it started out well.

On opening night, the four of us 'artists' arrived at the gallery stoned and acting like kids in a candy store. I can't remember acting so silly or having such a good time since leaving Toronto. Norval was in a good mood—laughing and joking around with different patrons—and I was getting along with Brian and Wolf (and I thought it was politics that made for strange bedfellows…in our case, more like alcohol and dope!). We worked the gallery, moving from one clique to another, chatting up technique, style, the use of color, and the Ojibwa legends that had inspired most of the work. We did not share commentary regarding Brian posing nude, the inspiration behind the paintings! Norval and Wolf were particularly good at regaling the guests with stories of tribal custom and lore, and Brian was in a world of his own since he never had been to an art opening before and never had brushed elbows with the nouveau riche. We were in an element that far eclipsed Beardmore, shined lightyears beyond Manitou, and pushed the memory of our Winnipeg art fraud to the furthest reaches of our malleable minds. Clinking wine glasses, scavenging hors d'oeuvres, and hob-knobbing with the self-ordained elite was the order of the evening—and we did it quite well.

There were the normal local dignitaries and aspiring artists present, several dozen patrons of the arts, a handful of the curious who were there, no doubt, wondering why all the fuss over a Native person's art—it's just a bunch of geometric designs that faintly look like animal figures—and of course the press. Surprisingly, there was no sign of Volpe or any of his men! The event was posh, polite, and charming with all the pretentious characteristics of an art exhibit I had grown to hate back in Toronto but found curiously pleasing in Winnipeg.

It was the first Morrisseau exhibit I had attended as the personal secretary of the artist, and my introduction caused an amazing amount of groveling at my feet by the parvenu aristocracy. They assumed I had influence over Norval, but what they didn't know couldn't hurt them. I played my role to the hilt. I have to admit that it was quite a rush. I don't think I've ever experienced anything quite as exciting. To be by the side, on the arm that is, of one of Canada's leading contemporary artists was not only a fantasy come true, but what I thought would be the debut of the Eagle Spirit: the inspiration, the celebrity, the STAR! I was no longer in Toronto, a hanger-on at openings, fawning over the hunky guys and quasi-celebrities, but firmly, and with everyone's gushing consent, in the personal company of Norval Morrisseau: artist, shaman, Eckankar traveler, and Copper Thunderbird.

The show started with a wine and cheese party and went until it came time for the press conference, when the festive mood of the evening shifted and the thrill changed from carefree merriment to hostility and repression. Customarily, the press reviews opening night and interviews the artist at the same time, a plan we stuck with for this opening, not suspecting that such would be the undoing of Norval and the gala evening. Suddenly, Norval transformed from the affable, entertaining man who had been circulating about the exhibit, regaling the neophyte with tantalizingly untrue tales, to a reclusive, childish bore who acted like a pouting, contemptuous genius—the dark mood of Norval had swung again!

Rather than sitting and talking with the press, a relatively non-threatening task, Norval stalked about the room like a bull in rut. He moved as far away from the press as he could, without leaving the building, and ignored every question asked. Every few minutes, he'd glare back as the assemblage of critics, scowl, and mumble something in his favorite language—gibberish Ojibwa, his own means of verbal communication that meant absolutely nothing! The press mistook his gobbleygook words for some kind of Indian cursing. At one point, Norval walked to the farthest corner of the gallery, faced the wall, and pretended to be inspecting a painting from about three inches away, all the while peeing on the wall.

While all this was happening, I was thinking to myself that I'd like to talk with the reporters and tell them not to waste time with Norval because he was stoned and paranoid. It was obvious that Norval was too strung out to give an interview, but Ted Allen from the *Winnipeg Free Press* persisted with his questioning.

Finally, he called out to Norval, "Come on, Big Fella" (the media's pet name), "stop fooling around and come over here and sit down and talk." That was all Norval needed to set him off.

"That's white man's furniture. I don't sit on white man's furniture," he roared. "And I don't talk to white men critics. Your minds are already made up about what you're going to say. You already know what you're going to write. It's all crap. Why bother talking to me. Fuck off."

Norval's outburst didn't quell the tide of questioning; in fact seemed to spur it on, as though the press had discovered another bizarre quality to the Norval legend previously unknown that they wanted to milk for all they could. Why they would think as much is beyond me. Norval's tempestuous relationship with the press and his known alcoholism and drug dependency were legendary.

The spectacle of questions and silence, or worse, smart-ass responses from Norval, went on for about an hour until the press grew weary of the game and packed up and left. And we were left alone, much to everyone's relief.

After several minutes of regaining ourselves, Norval stormed out followed by Wolf, Brian, and me quickly in tow. He impertinently ignored his hosts who had so generously provided him the venue and so lavishingly gushed about his talent. By the time we got back to the apartment, he had simmered down a bit and wanted to snort a line of coke. He did, I got stoned, and Brian and Wolf did their usual, a little of everything: coke, booze, pot. After weeks of preparing for the opening by trying to manipulate Norval into moods good enough to paint, I was exhausted. I was also still worried about the fraud (for obvious legal reasons) and disappointed about the role I had played in bringing the deceit to fruition. And of course, I worried about how the press would handle Norval's outburst.

Once again, I am questioning why I am here and what I'm hoping to get out of all this: Money? Fame? Status? My original reasons for leaving Toronto are beginning to pale in comparison to what I have become involved with, and I'm starting to wonder if I would have been better off staying back east and dealing with all the shit there.

I need to see Many Tongues again.

After another joint I lost myself in worry and anxiety; I crashed almost immediately. As I began to fall asleep, I glanced out the window down to the street, and not to my surprise there was the same sinister-looking man standing beneath a streetlight. But for some odd reason, I gave him little concern and fell fast asleep. I was exhausted.

G

✦✦✦✦✦✦✦✦✦✦✦✦

JOURNAL ENTRY: 3-25-79

The reviews of the opening were mixed: one complimentary and the other disparaging of Norval himself.

Tim Allen of the *Free Press* wrote in the morning edition on March 23rd under the headlines: MORRISSEAU MEETS PRESS BUT THE VIBES ARE BAD and ARTIST'S PSYCHIC SPACE VIOLATED:

"The Big Fella with the bottomless inkwell eyes was staring down at the reporter's open hand extended in friendship as though it proffered a fresh road apple. His own hands hung like breadfruit at his sides. Finally, he looked up to make hard eye contact, snorted and turned away. (…) Morrisseau, known reverentially as Thunderbird Spirit, patriarch of Canadian Native artists, reputed Ojibwa shaman, mystic darling of the haute hip salons of the nations, top buck in the $2 million annual Indian art market, and the hottest thing on canvas since Harold Town was outrageous, said nothing regarding the interviews, and was rude beyond even what could be normally expected from the artist…He is a boorish snob, and although he thinks his attitude stems from his proud Indian heritage, it stems more from his own emotional wreckage."

Another article in the *Winnipeg Free Press* by Leonard Marcoe attested to the genius of the work, thus (unknowingly) validating the authenticity of our forgery by saying, "A copious supply of paintings and prints by Norval Morrisseau is on show at the Cardigan Milne Gallery. Manifestations of Native legends have been implanted on flat color backgrounds with attendant motifs and symbols. Design and color intensities have been deliberated with equal balance. Since no attempt, or little, is made at modulation, most colors project equal intensity. Truly vintage Morrisseau."

Thank you, Mr. Marcoe, but the last laugh is unfortunately on you. Only about half of what you reviewed and to which you referred in your column were original Morrisseaus. The rest were Wolf/Brian/Gilbert forgeries. The sketching's were classic Morrisseau, but we added all the colors. And they sold for thousands of dollars. I guess what the American President Abraham Lincoln once said should be amended to: Indeed, you can fool all the people all the time! Norval did. Wolf did. Brian Did. And I did.

I don't know if I'm more pleased with the compliments written by Tim Allen and Leonard Marcoe, or disgusted with the realization that I am, indeed, a forger. But then, everything pales in relation to something else. Everything is relative—what is a tear in one man's eye is a flood in another's. And thus, just as the Cardigan-Milne exhibition was relative, so too was the forgery. What had commanded Norval's and our attention for the past two weeks had come and gone so quickly—certainly not without incident but at least without discovery. The show is to continue for two more weeks, but none of us will return. Norval does not attend his own exhibits except on opening night or unless otherwise necessary. And what was happening in Norval's life during the past two weeks, other than preparation for the show, was not to be easily dismissed, especially when we returned home the night of the opening to find an ominous-looking note left on our door. Fortunately, I was first up the steps and intercepted the note before any of the others could. I haven't read it yet. I don't want to upset myself, and I have no intention of agitating Norval. The last two days have not seen Norval in the best of moods, and I do not propose disturbing Norval any more than he has been. I may not particularly care for him, anymore, but he is still the genius, the Shaman, the mystic, and the Eckankar traveler. He deserves respect...

...he is Norval Morrisseau, so the note can wait until morning.

G

✦✦✦✦✦✦✦✦✦✦✦

Journal Entry: 3-26-79 [early afternoon]

I read the note, this morning, then immediately gave it to Norval. As I had expected, his reaction to the note was predictable. He ran the gamut of emotions from shock and surprise to anger, and finally to fear.

The note was simple, to the point, but every bit as cryptic as our two-time visitor had been. It read:

Your boys have said that they don't know where you are. Liars all of you: Mr. Petén, Brian Maye, and your worthless brother, Wilfred. If you are not around, then I applaud your wonderful stand-in at the exhibit opening. I watched with both amusement and curiosity at your award-winning performance. Yes, I was there, and so too were you. I am growing weary of your games, Norval, we must speak: Tonight. The Winnipeg Inn. Eight O'clock. Be there.

Jacques

The rest of the day we packed. The trip to Beardmore is on again and will happen this afternoon. I don't know when we might be back, days or weeks, I just don't know, but I can guess what the message means; it is obvious that Norval has gotten himself into some kind of serious trouble with his tormentor. I'm not fond of having to return to the cabin at Beardmore, but unless I simply leave and return to Toronto, I have no choice but to go back. Norval reminded the three of us about participating in his 'clever art deal,' so leaving for home is not an option at this point. I must still contact Many Tongues before we go because Norval made it clear this morning, after reading the note, that we would all be returning to Beardmore with him: Brian, Wolf, and me—no questions, no discussion.

He is beginning to frighten me. Unwillingly, I have been changed from his secretary and companion to his accomplice in fraud and, evidently because of the fraud, a prisoner restrained by threats and intimidation, two methods of manipulation I am not strong enough to resist.

I am going to make an excuse to get out of the apartment before we leave later this afternoon. I can easily establish a ruse about going out to buy things we'll need for the journey, and hopefully, will find Many Tongues home and amenable to my unannounced visit. I have 'thought upon' the story he told when we met a number of days ago, and I am ready, at this point, to accept whatever he considers my destiny. Certainly, whatever is in store for me cannot be as threatening or harrowing as what I am experiencing now: Fraud, flight, and fear.

Once again, I find myself ready to damn Norval to hell. He is a major pain in the butt, but I have willingly made myself available to his eccentricities and demands. I think now is the time to pursue my own necessity.

Please be home, Many Tongues. I need you now, more than ever.

⁕⁕⁕⁕⁕⁕⁕⁕⁕⁕⁕⁕

JOURNAL ENTRY: 3-26-79 [AFTERNOON]

I returned only minutes ago, after being unable to locate Many Tongues, to a ramshackle mess of an apartment. Brian and Wolf were both passed out and surrounded by drug paraphernalia that was typical of one of their binges: Bongs, papers, clips, straws, and a compact mirror—sure signs of massive consumption. Brian lay naked on the floor and Wolf was slumped across the couch. I can only guess that because of their intoxicated state, they had heard nothing that had taken place—whatever it was that had taken place.

Three of Norval's paintings had been slashed and overturned on the floor. Our few belongings had been rifled through and were strewn about with little regard for ownership. Papers were thrown about, as though someone had been looking for something specific, then left whatever had not been found scattered in a heap in the middle of the living room. Though none of us had much in the way of personal possessions, what little we had had been shredded and left in a pile wherever it fell. The few clothes I owned had been destroyed—ripped and torn beyond use. That was it. It didn't look like there had been a physical struggle of any sort and despite the mess, the furniture was intact and upright and there was no evidence of bodily harm to either Brian or Wolf (they probably hadn't even heard anything out of the ordinary given their inebriated states). Other than the mess that had been made, there wasn't anything to suggest a battle between opposing forces, except...

...except that Norval was gone!

No note. No sign of struggle. No nothing. Norval had simply disappeared. It wasn't like him, especially considering that we had planned on leaving for Beardmore the same day. Certainly there were times when he'd go away for several days without advance warning, particularly when we were back at the cabin, but he would always announce his departure even at the last minute. To simply vanish without word or note was peculiar; in fact it was downright frightening.

Once again it was up to me to take command of the situation—I am becoming quite good at playing the taskmaster. I sent Wolf out to search Norval's favorite haunts that he frequented when cruising for dope or boys. I told Brian to wander about the town, asking if anyone had seen Norval. Norval was quite well known, although not necessarily liked in Winnipeg, especially after the gallery opening, so were he still around someone would have seen him. I tried contacting Many Tongues again hoping that one shaman might know the whereabouts of another. We all returned empty handed.

Wolf discovered no clues. Brian had talked to twenty or more people, none of whom had seen Norval. And although I was able to finally locate Many Tongues, he hadn't had contact with the Copper Thunderbird for over a month. I explained the situation to Many Tongues and we agreed that given the circumstances we would delay our meeting until the next day. Meanwhile he would search for Norval through Thought Projection—a concept we hadn't yet discussed but which I accepted readily from Many Tongues without further explanation.

We were desperate. We had nothing to go on. Brian suggested we go to the police, a suggestion both Wolf and I dismissed immediately given the precarious position we feared Norval might be in. Wolf thought we should just get stoned and wait. And I didn't know what to do, except consider the words Many Tongues had spoken when I told him about Norval's disappearance:

"The Copper Thunderbird survives many threats; he will rise in anger to protect his nest. He is more powerful than that which pursues him. Let him be. He will return." Advice not unlike Wolf's, cryptic and casual, but without the getting stoned part.

So we waited since there was nothing else we could do. We had exhausted every possibility we could think of. Wolf seemed unconcerned. Brain stared out the window, like a child awaiting the return of an absent parent. And I found myself worrying about this man whom I had learned to detest during the past three months. Maybe I'm more like Jack Pollock than I thought. What ever Norval had become involved with, I still had some amount of love for him. I was shocked at my own discovery.

And we still wait as I write in my journal.

G

****

Journal Entry: 3-30-79

It's another one of those dark days, but they seem to come more sporadically than before. Once they were constant, then they became considerably less frequent, and now they happen when I least expect them. Norval has been gone for three and a half days now, and we still haven't a clue as to where he might be. We haven't heard a word from him. And, surprisingly, we haven't heard anything from Volpe or his hooligans either. Especially considering the note that had demanded a meeting with Norval several days ago.

My days have become tedious repetitions of one another. I get up. Do the chores around the apartment. Bark a few orders to Wolf and Brian. Eat. Smoke dope. Chat with Brian or Wolf when they are sober enough to understand normal conversation. Write in my journal. Then go to bed.

I replaced our clothing that had been destroyed by the intruder using money we found stashed in one of Norval's boots. Thankfully, he usually has several hundred dollars stuck in his boots. The cash surely came in handy this time.

I am growing tired of the same monotonous routine. I'm not certain anymore if a real world exists beyond these walls of my self-imposed prison. I don't go out unless to run an errand. I have become obsessed with Norval's disappearance, unlike back at Beardmore when I would be relieved with his absence and use the time to satisfy my own curiosity about self and discovery. But this is different. Norval has disappeared without word or trace, and though I do not know the man as well as I had hoped I would by this point in our relationship, I do not think mysterious disappearance is normal to his state of being.

I could use this opportunity to my advantage and split; return to Toronto, resume my life, and try to forget that any of this ever happened—but I don't. I wait like the parent whose child has disappeared without a trace, the parent who cannot put finality to absence, hoping the child might still be alive. Moreover, I still have yet to visit Many Tongues again.

I have thought about going back to Beardmore in search of Norval, but that would prove no point; I wouldn't know where to look, although everyone there knows him and could direct me to his location—assuming, of course, he wants to be found. Besides, if he had gone to Beardmore, and was to return soon, we'd probably pass on the highway without knowing it like two ships passing silently in the night.

And so I wait within the confines of my imprisonment.

Is there still a sun that rises in the east and sets in the west? A moon that arches across the dark sky on a clear night and disappears beneath the awakening horizon as the dawn breaks? Are there still stars that twinkle and shine, and hang so low you can almost reach up and touch them? I don't know; I only suspect they exist because I am alive—at least I think I am alive—and if, indeed, I am, then I must yet, be a part of this world that has caused me so much pain.

But now the world collapses around me. The sun and the moon and the stars have fallen, and I languish beneath the rubble of the heavens that buries my fears deep within my soul. I left home to learn about the world—which in a bizarre way I have. I left Toronto to discover myself (and to make some easy money)—but I have not. And I have left myself too many times, hoping that when I returned to my corporeal shell, I would be transformed into a creature of understanding and intelligence—but I have not been so transfigured.

And I fear everything.

Wasn't it the American President Franklin Roosevelt who said, "We have nothing to fear but fear itself"? His words are wise because when I look to my fears, when I analyze the font of my terror, I find nothing but a poorly defined concept with little substance upon which to focus my apprehension.

Norval is gone from my life, perhaps forever, but this is not like his absences from the cabin at Beardmore. Although I did not know what he was doing, or whom he was with when I was left alone in the woods, he always told me when he was leaving and (mostly) when he'd return. He didn't just vanish.

And this disappearance is serious—not motivated by a cute young man that turned Norval's head but by the workings of something wicked, something evil, something treacherous and it stems from Norval's darkest fear—but a fear of what, I do not know. He will not discuss personal matters with me or anyone else (not even his brother, Wolf), and so the three of us (Wolf, Brian, and me) are at a loss regarding what to do. Even wise Many Tongues cannot help, other than to speak in riddles and tribal prophecy. His Thought Projection revealed little, save disjointed dreams and confused thoughts, conditions Many Tongues said are common to those who are suffering pain and fear.

Wolf does not seem to take his brother's disappearance seriously. He just sits around getting stoned and assumes that Norval will reappear someday soon. Brian goes through periods of crying and watching out the window, expecting to see Norval come waltzing down the street at any minute. And I just sit here wondering what happened? Where is he? Is he all right? Am I in danger? My thoughts might sound melodramatic, but at this point, I don't think they are. The note that evidently prompted Norval's unexpected disappearance also mentioned me by name, and if whoever wrote the note knows that much, *they* surely know more about me than I'd like.

I am scared. Scared that somehow, some way, whoever is behind Norval's disappearance will come back to get me. I have the uneasy feeling that this episode is much more ominous than I'd like to believe. Perhaps I've seen too many movies about mobs and gangs and hoodlums, but if I'm right in what I know about the Hollywood version of evil, they will come back to the scene of the crime to eliminate witnesses. And that puts me squarely in the ring. Wolf and Brian too, I suppose, although I don't think the visitor cared about who Brian was (a numbingly stupid boy-toy and artist's model), and I'm sure they could care less about Wolf. If they know Norval and they know me, then obviously they know Wolf also, but I don't think even the most bumbling of mobsters would consider Wolf a threat. He can't even remember his own name, let alone recognize who anyone else might be. Besides, he was not present during the first visit and was doped and passed out during the second and the third—he saw no one!

But I'm still scared. I don't want to end up at the bottom of a lake wearing cement shoes (I heard that in one of the old movies I saw about the mob), or tied up and drugged such that I don't know what time of day it is, let alone understand where I was or who my captors were. I might be more concerned than is necessary, but just because Norval is a famous artist does not make him immune to danger or worse—death! Whatever he's done, whatever he has become involved with is serious enough for Norval to either have been kidnapped or to have disappeared voluntarily. For all I know Norval could be dead as I write this. For all I know I could be dead, too but just imagining all of this until they come to carry off my abused, lifeless body.

Enough. It is late. Brian and Wolf have already crashed, and I should do the same. I've thought about writing to Jack Pollock to see if he can shed any light on the situation, but as I recall from a conversation with Norval last week, Jack is in the States right now. So no help there.

I have resolved to await Norval's return—assuming it happens. I cannot leave with the small amount of cash I have pilfered. I dare not leave when I too am a witness to the men, or man, who visited both places where we have lived. And I want not leave when Norval is yet missing. That would be not only foolish, but loathsome. A friend does not abandon a friend regardless of how untidy the friendship might be. There seems to be no help anywhere, not even Many Tongues. Once again, I am alone.

G

PART FOUR

Mysticism and the Joining

(April, 1979)

APRIL, 1,1979

Joanne,

I know it's been a while since I last wrote. I am sorry. Things around here have gotten very strange. I wish you were here to help me figure this one out, but you're not, so no use me wishing for things that cannot be (a problem I've had since childhood). I hope all is well with you.

What about the situation with Warren? Are you still on the outs? Have you got back together? What are you doing with or for yourself? I'd love to hear the answers to all these questions, but I'll have to wait— although something tells me that my wait might not be as long as I have recently thought.

Norval has been missing for over four days (a long story that I don't want to go into right now). I think he has become a victim of foul play—perhaps the mob! I have no convincing evidence with which to support my hypothesis, but there are too many weird happenings to simply write them off as coincidence. For instance: The cabin near Beardmore was burglarized, after which I found a business card with the name Jacques Volpe on it, but I have no knowledge about who this Volpe person is. A sinister-looking man has come by the apartment here in Winnipeg twice now, asking about Norval. Our apartment was broken into a few days ago; and now Norval is missing!

I suppose I am reaching for an explanation by blaming an imaginary mob, based upon Hollywood movies, but given what Jack Pollock wrote in his letter to me about "still loving Norval despite what Norval might be mixed up in" and considering the above unexplained occur-rences I have jumped to the conclusion that the mob is behind all this. It doesn't hurt my case either when I remember that the first night we were here, Norval and I went out to eat at a restaurant where Norval was greeted by name and asked if he wanted to sit at Mr. Volpe's table! From all appearances, it looked like everyone in the restaurant was some kind of old-fash-ioned gangster. Of course, I don't know why the mob would be interested in Norval. I know he does a lot of drugs but as far as I know, he has always purchased his stash from friends—maybe his friends are mobsters! Of course, I have no definitive knowledge that he actually purchases his dope from friends. He could be buying it from the mob!

I hope Norval is all right. Even though I've come to abhor him more and more, I wouldn't want to see anything bad happen to him. Despite his horrific behavior, he is genius of unquestionable talent—that alone makes me concerned about him. I would hate the world to lose an artist as great as Norval, but I probably worry for nothing. When we were at the cabin at Beardmore, he'd be gone for a week or more a number of times, so this is probably nothing more than another one of his sporadic escapades. Of course when he disappeared from Beardmore he always announced his departure ahead of when he left and provided some indication of when he would return.

What is even more perplexing is that Norval's disappearance occurred following a tumultuous opening of his work at the Cardigan-Milne Gallery. The show is still running for another week, and, believe me, he is raking in the dollars. The reviews that appeared in the local papers were complimentary of his work, but scathing of him as a man. Norval hates the press, is exceptionally rude to them, and has blown them off—a curious irony, considering that the free press Norval gets feeds his tremendous appetite for attention and sells paintings by the dozens. He claims that he doesn't like the white man's money, but he sure enjoys spending it on booze and drugs. I can't help wonder if his disrespect towards the press has anything to do with his disappearance. Probably not, but at this point, I am considering anything.

We were supposed to leave for Beardmore a few days ago to visit his brother and sister, but that trip has been delayed. Right now we're just biding time (we being his brother, Wolf, a cute young protégé Norval has invited to stay with us named Brian, and me). I have decided, unbeknownst to either of my wasted companions, that should we not hear from Norval within the week, I will go to the police—despite the consequences for Norval, whatever they might be!

I guess that's about it for now. I've caught you up on the major occurrences of the past few weeks. The minor incidences I can fill in when next we meet. Take care of yourself and remember, like I always say—I love you lots.

Gilbert

✶✶✶✶✶✶✶✶✶✶✶✶

JOURNAL ENTRY: 4-2-79

Given that Norval has not yet returned, assuming he is able to return and is not being held against his will, Wolf, Brian, and I have nothing to do. Wolf has friends in Winnipeg with whom he can pass time, Brian spends most of his time smoking dope and sexually entertaining himself, and I have been trying to keep the daily activities here somewhat regular.

I tried initiating a schedule of chores to keep us occupied and to keep the place in some semblance of order. Wolf would be in charge of keeping the living room and kitchen clean and Brian would take care of the bathroom and remove garbage from the apartment (believe me, a considerable chore considering the amount of empty beer cans and fast food wrappers). I scheduled myself for the laundry, the purchase food and other necessary items with a cache of money Norval left behind. I would, also, try to keep up our flagging spirits. None of my cleanliness plan worked, unfortunately. With Norval gone, my power over Wolf and Brian had diminished—neither took me seriously nor attended to my commands. No Norval, no threat. No commanding Gilbert, no clean apartment.

Brian has been dabbling with some paintings of his own (amazingly similar to Norval's but without the originality and genius behind them), so other than his chores, masturbating, and smoking dope, he at least has something to take his mind off Norval's disappearance. Usually Wolf takes off to parts unknown. Like Norval, he is quite secretive about the places he goes and the people he sees, and returns home late in the evening stoned and drunk. He has done a little painting since Norval's disappearance, but not much although it is surprisingly of exhibition quality.

I'm not sure what I've been doing, other than the tasks I've assigned myself and thinking! Thinking about where Norval might be, why he left (or was kidnapped), when and if he will return, and what I will do if he doesn't come back. I'm not particularly concerned about what Wolf or Brian will do. Wolf has family and friends back in Beardmore, so I'm sure he'd return home. I assume Brian has family and friends somewhere, so I am certain that with their help, he could be able to fend for himself. Actually, I'm not concerned about either of them; both are grown men although neither acts like it, and both are quite capable of existing without Norval's influence or interference. Wolf has always been somewhat independent of Norval, even though he travels and stays with him a great deal, and Brian, well, obviously he had a life prior to hooking up with Norval. Neither of them is the type of person I would gravitate towards as a friend, but certainly, they both must have friends – somewhere! The only things the three of us have in common are Norval, dope, and the art fraud—not exactly solid ground upon which to establish a relationship!

It's me I'm concerned about. I haven't realized any of the goals I established when I left Toronto. I have not been the inspiration to Norval that I had hoped I'd be although he might take issue with that. After all, he has named several paintings after me and has taken my advice and suggestions for ideas on several other paintings. I haven't learned a great deal about art itself, other than having become more knowledgeable and more critical of Norval's work. I certainly haven't made the fast cash that Bernie suggested I'd make by taking the job with Norval, although I have been able to spirit away about $3,500.00 compliments of Norval's intoxicated generosity. And I don't feel that I've necessarily learned a great deal about myself, or evolved my intellectual or emotional development.

I have become less enamored with the alcohol and drug scene. I don't like getting stoned every day anymore, and I'm growing more and more disgusted with people who do—especially people who substitute chemical dependency for personal development and achievement. I have also become less dependent upon sexual gratification as a way of determining self-identity and success. It used to be that I loved cruising and taking a different person home every night. Now, and perhaps much of which is due to my disgust with sex with Norval, I find myself more interested in getting to know a person first, and having physical intimacy flow naturally from the development of a relationship based upon mutual interests and respect. Of course, that's easy for me to say right now because right now, I'm not getting laid at all! It is always easier to pontificate when not faced with the temptation of that which is being scrutinized. Kind of like the Roman Catholic Church and the thousands of priests who moralize about premarital sex, masturbation, and the like. It's easy for them to discredit the pleasures of the flesh; they are (for the most part) bitter old (and young) men who probably entered the priesthood because of feelings of personal inadequacy in the real world, be it sexual, social, or personal. And in addition to those who cheat on their Holy vows with members of the parish or with young boys, the remaining priests are cynical purveyors of the Word of God. From my experiences of having been approached by two of the three priests who served our parish when I was young, pedophilia is rampant in the Church. I am absolutely convinced that the Church is ripe with pedophiles, child molesters, and adulterers—adultery in the sense of cheating on their vows with God. The concept of sexual repression is straight out of the early Roman Church when control of the individual meant controlling every aspect of life: Economic, moral, sexual, political, social, and personal. When a religious institution can control individual with threats of eternal damnation and an angry God exacting vengeance, then it becomes easy to control the entire socio-political culture of any society of which the church is a part. Unite the Church with politics and the emerging political concept of 'values,' and control becomes complete.

But, of course, none of this has to do with me since I've divorced myself from the Church. My concerns are for what I have or have not accomplished since leaving Toronto and my accomplishments do not seem significant.

Maybe it's time I visited with Many Tongues again and finish what we began several weeks ago. I'll contact him tomorrow.

G

****

I met with Many Tongues today. The Joining has been rejoined.

When I got to his home, Many Tongues was already awaiting my arrival. He was sitting on the floor, dressed in traditional Ojibwa clothing, and was smoking a peace pipe. A pungent odor of burning sweet grass filled the air. The room was dark, except for five candles that were appropriately placed—one in each corner of the room and one, on a center table, directly in front of Many Tongues. The candles cast an eerie shadow across the ceiling and walls that reminded me of the swirling ooze of the psychedelic Lava Lamps of the 1960s. Many Tongues' collection of religious artifacts from around the world were displayed throughout the room: A statue of Buddha, a menorah, a Hindu Snake God, a Buddhist Wheel of Law, a yin yang medallion, the Islamic Koran, a Christian cross, and figurines of dozens of Hindu deities. There were other gods and goddesses from aboriginal peoples, but I did not know by what names the were known. The sound of Ojibwa tribal music played softly in the background and completed the mystical setting. The room was haunting and ethereal and gave me mind of a scene out of J.R.R. Tolkien; I was half expecting to see Gandalf magically appear or Celeborn ascending the throne of Lothlorien.

Many Tongues appeared to be in a trance; he whispered a "come in" when I knocked upon his door but offered no greeting when I entered. He was sitting on the floor. His eyes were glazed, his arms folded upon his chest, his legs crossed, and he had a look about him that was distant. He was chanting to himself, but after a few moments he spoke:

"You have come," was all he said.

"I have, Many Tongues. There is trouble—big trouble—and I need your help."

"I am aware of Norval's disappearance. You have already spoken to me about it."

"I know," I answered, "but there's more."

"I know that also, Mandamin," Many Tongues replied.

"You know what?" I asked, surprised that Many Tongues apparently knew more than I thought possible.

"Your spirit is heavy, Old Young One; you are troubled by events beyond your control, but of which you have become a part," he responded. "You must not be deceitful nor challenge the fates. Be of proud spirit and sound mind and walk in the light of the sun."

The forgery! Many Tongues knew about the art fraud at the Cardigan Milne Gallery, but how? He hadn't been there. I hadn't mentioned a word about it to him because I was too embarrassed, too ashamed. Perhaps one of the others had said something, but Brian hadn't even met Many Tongues and would have no reason to visit him. Wolf was politely distant from Many Tongues and had told me once that the old man made him feel creepy, so I could exclude him. That left

Norval. Perhaps Norval's disappearance wasn't as mysterious as I had thought. Maybe he was just hiding out until the situation, whatever it was, with Volpe and the note had passed. He could have contacted Many Tongues and told him everything. But, why would Norval have admitted to art fraud, hardly the kind of information he'd want anyone to know, especially Many Tongues!

"You are very troubled, my friend," Many Tongues continued. "You must let go of your worldly concerns and focus upon the spiritual; it is your only path to peace."

"Yes, I am troubled, Many Tongues, very much so. But not just about one thing, it's about many," and I told Many Tongues everything: How I was worried about Norval's disappearance and my concern for his safety; about my relationship with Norval and how it was progressing from dislike to hatred; about my concerns for myself and my inability to evolve and change as much as I'd like; about the whole story of me taking the job with Norval; and, finally, about the art fraud—probably the most distressing secret to reveal.

Many Tongues smiled weakly and placed his hand upon my shoulder as I finished my half hour litany of problems.

"Too much, Old Young One…" he chuckled, "…too much. One problem at a time, if truly these are problems. You do not have as many as you might think. Perhaps we should start at the beginning and come forward. I asked you many nights ago to think heavily upon Old Young One and Many Tongues. Have you done so, Gilbert?"

"God, yes," I gushed—it was the first time I had heard Many Tongues call me by my Christian name. "I haven't done anything but think about it, even when I'm trying to deny it, but now I am ready to hear more. Please, start at the beginning, or where ever you want; I've got all night."

"All night," Many Tongues responded, his voice softening to barely a whisper. "Not just all-night Thunderbird Spirit—all of eternity!"

And with that said, Many Tongues began from the beginning.

✦✦✦✦✦✦✦✦✦✦✦

"Many seasons have passed since I first came into this world. I am the Old Young One, Wabasso, Glooskap, The Thunderbird Spirit, and I exist as no person other than the human incarnation of Many Tongues: First born male-child of Light Feather and Bear Hunter who birthed me many thousands of years ago but only seventy years by the measure of this world. My father is the universe; my mother, the sun and the moon. My brothers and sisters are the stars, the wind, the rain, the Earth, and the fire. I am One with the essence of both the living and the dead—one with the universal spirit.

"I have been, mistakenly, called by many different names. Some human beings have called me Buddha, Mohammed, Moses, or Jesus, and others have called me Zeus, Odin, Thor, or Isis. And those who give names to their troubles have called me the Evil One, Beelzebub, Satan, the Serpent, or the Manitou. I am all of these names, but I am not possessed with evil; wickedness is but a manifestation of our inner thoughts, our desire to create order out of chaos, to create meaning out of nothingness, and to construct a consequence for all that is wrong with our world."

Many Tongues paused momentarily then began again with a question:

"When you were a child and you had no friends, what did you do, with whom did you play?"

"I made up an imaginary friend," I answered sheepishly, embarrassed to reveal my long-ago caprice.

"That is what many little ones do," Many Tongues went on. "And the imaginary playmate provides the comfort you could find in no other. It neither argues nor contradicts. It does not abandon you when you are in need nor chastise you when you are sad. It does not criticize, and it does not limit. Your imaginary friend has no boundaries, other than those that you impose. It is nothing more than you define, nothing less than you imagine. It is the outward expression of inward necessity, the realization of all things that you lack in the real world. What you do not have, you invent in your friend. When you are sad, it is there to comfort. When you are joyful, it shares your happiness. It is with you at all times, and it travels to where ever you go. But when you grow older, adults tell you that you must put away your childish beliefs, and your imaginary friend fades into the past like a memory dissolved.

"It is the same with grown humans, my friend. When we cannot explain that which we do not understand we create a diversion to comfort our apprehension. We invent a playmate, an adult playmate who provides us with the spiritual needs we demand. We call it by different name, names that have saved humans from themselves: Buddha, Moses, Christ, Jehovah, Brahma, Vishnu, Shiva, Allah, the Great Spirit, Wabasso, The Thunderbird, and many more—all created by human beings in many lands, with one hope and for one purpose: To give meaning to what we call life. And like the imaginary playmate you invented as a child, these adult playmates do not breathe—except within the mind."

"Then you're arguing that religion is a fraud," I responded, "invented only for the purposes of explaining things we don't understand and to give hope to what we consider our futile and chaotic existence. Believe, me Many Tongues," I added, cynically, "I have been well aware of that since the first time I experienced the hypocrisy of the Catholic Church."

"Not fraud, Old Young One, simply convenience," Many Tongues answered.

"You are Christian…," Many Tongues began.

"Was a Christian," I corrected.

"You were born into Christianity, Gilbert. When you were a child, did you not believe in the great God of the white man?" Many Tongues asked.

"I did," I replied.

"Why did you believe?" he asked.

"Mainly because my parents taught me to. But, I suppose in my own mind, it was like my imaginary playmate; I needed someone, something to believe in.

God was all I had known from the time I was a child, it was all that I had been taught. I had no reason to doubt my parents' beliefs, and when I was younger, there were times when I did find my belief in God comforting, until...," I stopped, hesitant to continue because of my embarrassment with having fallen away from the church. I was talking with a man who was more spiritual than I would ever be.

"Until you became a man and began to question the ways of your God," Many Tongues finished.

"Yes, I guess. But not only because I questioned His ways but because I felt deserted and tricked by God," I answered sadly.

"Because...?" Many Tongues implored.

"Because he made me queer then abandoned me to a world where I have been hated and beaten, abused and attacked, considered sick or sinful by my church, ruled illegal by my government, regarded as demented, discriminated against, and thought of as a child molester," I answered angrily. "Because he let the other children in the neighborhood bully me. Because he made my mother an alcoholic and my father weak. Because..."

"Your god did not make you a Two-Person. Your god did not abandon you. You abandoned yourself," Many Tongues interrupted. "Your god did not make the other children hate you or make your mother an alcoholic or your father weak; they did those things unto themselves—without the help from any god, without the help of any spirit, without the help of their Evil One. Their demons do not come from above or below but from within. Just as all demons do and just as all goodness does."

I wasn't completely ready to accept Many Tongues' assessment of my life and the people who had screwed it up, but his assessment was interesting and worth considering.

Many Tongues continued his questioning: "And, when you were a child, did you believe in the spirits that cowered at the feet of your Christian God and did its bidding, both good and evil: The angels? The Saints? The Demons? The Devil?" he asked again.

"Of course I believed in all of them. I attended a Catholic school where those kinds of beliefs are crammed down your throat, and besides, mother made certain that we learned all the catechism of the Church. She was insistent that we learn to become good Catholics. I guess she was afraid we'd burn in Hell if we didn't believe as she would have us believe," I answered, uncomfortable in my memory of my youth and the nightmares it had created.

"And did you believe in the folktales of your people as well? In spirits like Santa Claus and the tooth fairy?" he queried.

"Of course," I replied, surprised that Many Tongues knew about Santa Claus and the tooth fairy.

"I believed in Santa until I was seven, when my brother spoiled Christmas Eve one year by telling me that Santa Claus didn't exist, that he was really mother and father. I didn't believe him at first until I snuck down stairs and lay on the couch watching mother and father putting the toys around the tree. And I believed in the tooth fairy until I felt my father's hand slip a quarter beneath my pillow one night after I had lost a tooth," I finished.

"And in discovering that reality, you lost two very valuable beliefs: the belief in the honesty of human beings and the belief in the visit from friends that you looked forward to, even though you never saw them," Many Tongues responded.

"Yes, it sucked big time. Christmas was probably the only time during the year when I felt truly happy and the tooth fairy was—well, just fun," I said sadly.

"And did you believe in the other spirits of your tribe, such as the rabbit who hides the eggs of the hen in the spring so that children might have pleasure in finding them?" he asked.

"If you mean the Easter Bunny, again, yes, I believed in the Easter Bunny."

"Did you believe in the fairy tales of your people: The Guardian Angel? The Sandman?"

"Yes, of course, yes! I believed in all those childish myths."

"Not myths, Mandamin," Many Tongues responded looking me squarely in the eyes. "Not myths at all, but stories your people told to explain things that you could not understand as a child. Explanations to make the real seem less frightening; stories that helped ease your transition from childhood to adult. That is what we call myth, believing in that which we cannot explain, but it is only myth when regarded from one tribe to another, not within our own tribe!"

Many Tongues continued his questioning without skipping a beat. "And did you also believe in ghosts and goblins, witches and werewolves, and monsters that lived under your bed at night?"

"Yes, those too," I answered, shuddering—remembering back to my fear of hanging my hand over the side of the bed, convinced that some unspeakable monster would reach out, grab it, and pull me to a grizzly death below.

Many Tongues continued, "And so, until you were a young man you believed in everything that the adults, of your tribe, encouraged you to believe. Then, when you came to the age of reason, you dismissed their stories as childish whim, designed to teach a lesson, explain a moral, frighten you into obedience, or make you sad."

"Yes, I guess so," I added, "But every child, of every culture believes in their own heroes and heroines—the legends and mythology of their people. It's natural; it's that rite of passage thing that every culture has, even the Ojibwa. It helps us make the transition into adulthood, to develop as a culture, and to progress—to evolve as a society. The stories are just silly stories, passed down from one generation to the next for the purpose of educating the young of the society in the mores and folkways and taboos of the culture. It has nothing to do with religion," I argued.

"Ah, but it does," Many Tongues responded. "It has everything to do with religion and nothing to do with reality."

Many Tongues' cryptic explanation of adolescent spirituality seemed to be going nowhere. His circular argumentation was disturbing, disappointing. I had expected more from him, and he was talking to me of fairies and ghosts, bogey-men and Santa Claus. I saw no purpose in the discussion and apparently made my feelings known by the frustrated tone of my voice and the restless language of my body.

But Many Tongues persisted, "When you are a child, you create imaginary playmates to give you comfort. You accept the fantastical stories of your people to provide understanding of your world. You believe in the heroes and the villains of your culture to teach you right from wrong, good from bad, and hope over despair. You accept the fantasies, the fairy-tales, the fables, the parables, and the lore—to teach you truth. But as you grow older, you dismiss your childish ways to become as an adult and to act as an adult."

Many Tongues went on, "In the olden times, long before human beings understood what caused the wind to howl or the fire to consume, they created spirits to explain what they could not understand. When the fierce bolts from the sky ripped through the clouds, when the rivers flooded, and when the earth opened up and swallowed them alive, human beings invented spirits who controlled the dominion of fate and destiny. When human beings could not explain the animals that walked upon land or swam in the seas or flew high in the air above their dreams and all the other things they could see and hear—but not understand—they created imaginary playmates who controlled the outer world and the under world and the above world. But as human beings grew wiser with the passing of time, the gods of the old ways became like fantasies in a storybook and passed into memory. As human beings learned why the mountain erupted, why the sea crashed upon the shore, and why the great winds came from the sky to destroy their homes, they forgot about the gods of the olden times and accepted the science of the everyday world and its problems.

"And human beings in every tribe, who did not believe in the many gods and spirits of their neighbors, looked to the sky and called it by one name, the Great One—the Omnipotent Being—the creator and the protector of human beings and all else that walked upon the earth, flew in the sky and swam in the sea.

"And still, other human beings believed there were spirits alive in everything that surrounded them: In the rocks and in the hills, in the dirt and in the water, in the trees and in the flowers, in the animals and in the human beings.

"But when we became so grown up, such that we did not need the gods of legend, we dismissed the religion of our childhood, much as we do the fanciful stories of our youth and rejected the spirits that surround us and that live within us. We forgot about our gods and about our connection to the world. We forgot who we are and where we are going. And we laughed at our ancient ones and said their gods were false and ours are real! It is very sad to see human beings forget from where they come.

"Once human beings forgot that they needed an explanation for each act of destruction and desperation they were left with the question that perturbed them the most: Why are we here?"

Many Tongues slumped in his chair, obviously anguished by the story he had told. "That is the beginning, Old Young One," he whispered.

Many Tongues' chin fell against his chest and his eyes closed. He began chanting in Ojibwa and thumped his fingers on the floor with an accompanying cadence that whispered throughout the room. He was tiring, and I feared he wouldn't finish what we had started, but within a few minutes he roused himself and continued.

"Do you understand, Old Young One?" he asked.

"I don't know, Many Tongues," I replied. "Your explanation of the evolution of religion and the concept of gods is historically and sociologically accurate, at least as I remember from my studies, but I still don't understand what you're getting at. What does this have to do with you or me?"

"Many of my people say that the gods are dead; that they have deserted us because they let the white man take our land. Many of my people say that the old ways are bad and that we must live like new men in a modern world," Many Tongues began. "Many of my people have forgotten the old ways, the legends of our tribe, the stories that long ago we told around the fire at night. But they are fools!

"And many of your people, the white human beings and the brown human beings and human beings of all colors from every tribe in the world, say that their gods are dead and that they have deserted them. That there are no more burning bushes. No more men who walk upon water. No more miracles to save human beings from death. They think that their gods do not care about them because they cannot see their gods or touch their gods. And they say that the gods are silly and childish and capricious. But they are wrong!

"And many people in our world today believe in strange things that make them feel good. They focus upon what they can touch and hear and see and smell and taste. They adorn themselves with many fanciful trinkets, fill their homes with expensive toys, and ignore the spirit that lives within them. They are like children, though they are grown, unable to limit their fancy, unwilling to seek that which lives within. They waste their money and their time and their thoughts and their hearts and their spirits, and they lose everything that makes them a human being because they are proud and do not want to believe in childish stories about gods and spirits. And they forget about the spirit that lives in the ground upon which they walk.

"And there are other human beings who use their god for wickedness. They tell us that their god has spoken to them and that other human beings must act as they say, do as they demand, believe as they believe. They use their god to make other human beings fearful; they use their god to make themselves appear better than the ones they condemn. They do not look inward to find the spirit but only outward and speak of visions of damnation and the end of the world. But they are foolish and wicked. They do not truly understand.

"The gods and the spirits of my people and of your people, and of all people in the world are still living though they have never lived," Many Tongues offered.

"Living, but have never lived?" I questioned. "Many Tongues, you speak in riddles. What are you talking about? What do you mean they are living yet they have never lived?"

Many Tongues became excited by my question. "They are living because some of my people and some your people say they are alive, but they are like the fantasies of our youth. They exist because human beings say they exit. They do not live nor ever did live in the way we have been told by the elders of our tribes."

"So," I answered smugly. "The gods live only because we say they live, only because we want it to be because it makes us feel better about ourselves and about all of the questions that we cannot answer. And yet they have never lived because they never existed to begin with. Instead they are the creations of adults, searching for the same comfort and reassurance that they had as children—with the Tooth Fairy, or Santa Claus, or the Easter Bunny or an imaginary playmate!"

"Almost," Many Tongues answered softly, "but what we believe is not the same as what is make-believe. As long as a god lives within the spirit of the human being who believes, it is not fantasy, it is just not truth!"

"So, the God of Christianity?" I asked.

"In the mind; not in the Heavens," replied Many Tongues.

"And Allah?"

"In the mind."

"Brahma, Vishnu, Shiva?"

"In the mind, also, one in three, three in one," Many Tongues repeated.

"And all the other gods, from antiquity?

"In the mind."

"The Greek and Roman gods? The Egyptian, Norse, Teutonic, and Aztec gods? And the gods of Ojibwa, and Algonquian, and Asian, and Oceanic peoples?"

"All manifestations of the mind," said Many Tongues. "Alive, because even one human being believes, but not Truth because they never existed, until given a name and a face and a personality created in the image of human beings, by human beings."

Many Tongues shifted in his chair and asked, "Do you think the great god of the White man, or the god of all Dark men, or the gods of Indians, and the gods of Yellow men are so diminutive and whimsical that they would look and act and think as do we? If they are great and powerful, why do they look like an ugly human being? Why are they not more beautiful than we will ever be? Why would they punish us as our Earthly father does? Why would they banish us to eternal damnation? Why would they be so childish as to demand praise and worship with meaningless rituals and awkward ceremonies? Why would they give us a mind, then punish us when we use it? Why would they be like us?"

Many Tongues reached down to the table and picked up a small rock. He held it to the light of one of the candles, turned it over in his hand several times, studying it as though he were examining a piece of evidence. Finally, he held the rock above the candle; its jagged sides of sparkling color glittered in the light.

"Consider the rock. It is but a small piece of this world, and yet it embraces all that is in this world. This small rock is god. It is the Great Spirit. It is all that ever has been and all that ever will be. Hold it and feel the power within," he said handing me the small stone. "Press it to your chest and feel its warmth. Touch it to your cheek and feel its coldness. Think upon it and consider its worth."

As I did what Many Tongues suggested, he continued:

"This is the God of your childhood. This is the God of the Christians. It is the God of Islam, of Hinduism, of Buddhism, of Taoism, of Judaism, of the Ojibwa, of the Inca, of the Zulu, of all men and women, of all children, of all human beings who live and breathe, and of all human beings who, now, travel through eternity for ever more."

As Many Tongues spoke, I could feel both the warmth and the coolness of the rock. I regarded it with the same demeanor I would a precious artifact. I cuddled and coddled it, afraid that if I dropped it, I would be dropping something holy.

Many Tongues continued, "The rock is a piece of the Earth. It is nothing more than mud and silt compressed by time. It is of the highest and most powerful mountain and of the deepest and most restless water. It is of the land upon which we walk and the world in which we live. It comes from the Earth and shall return to the Earth, dust to dust. The simple rock has no activity: It does not live or breathe, it neither eats nor sleeps, it does not grow stronger or weaker with time. It is not like the animals and the plants and the human beings that are among us. We can watch them grow strong and multiply. We can see them grow weak and die. But the rock ages very slowly, far more slowly than we can observe, and so we think that the rock will be forever. But it will not—and when it is a rock no more, it returns to the Earth and the universe therein.

"That is how human beings believe, Mandamin. We accept what we can see, and hear and touch and taste and smell, and we reject what we cannot. We embrace the secular and reject the spiritual. We cast the simple rock aside, admiring only the most beautiful and precious among them and trample upon it with our feet, just as we trample upon the spirit that lives within us all."

Many Tongues placed his hand over mine, and together we clutched the rock tightly. I could feel an indescribable power, like the static of electricity shooting up through my arm and coursing throughout my entire body. I trembled with disbelief as a faint light, like a fragile glowing ember emanated from our joined hands. I almost withdrew and let go of the rock, but Many Tongues grasped my hand securely.

"We are like this rock though we will grow old and die. But when we do, we will return, like the rock to the Earth from which we sprang. The rock we hold is from my birthing home. I found it when I was a young one of five. Look upon it. It has not changed from the time I first found it, and yet it is my age and much older. I do not know how old, perhaps one hundred million years or more.

"In this one rock, in all the rocks of the world and in all the animals and plants and human beings and insects that bite us in our sleep is the knowledge of who we are and why we are. But human beings will not listen to the sounds of the universe; they do not believe. It is easier for them to believe in a god they cannot see than to believe in what is around them. Human beings think it is better to invent a God with the face of a human and the soul of a shaman."

"But, human beings do not listen long enough to learn about their gods. They would rather believe fanciful stories than disclose the truth. They would rather be told what to do and what not to do than search for that which is genuine. They would rather mumble words of praise than honor the world in which they live. And they would rather conform like, obedient children, than question the gods of antiquity."

Many Tongues continued holding my right hand, the two of us clutching the rock, then reached over and took my left hand in his. As he did, he continued speaking:

"When you walk in the forest, do you not hear the sounds of the birds and the animals and the trees and the flowers? When you wade in the water, do you not see the small fish that swim near the shore? Do you not feel the pebbles beneath your feet? Do you not imagine the huge creatures that live in the deep? Do you not hear the wind howling during a storm? Do you not feel the heat from the sun? The cold from the snow? The wet from the rain? When you close your eyes at night, ready to sleep, do you not hear the silence that surrounds you? These things are all god, they are all spirit, they are all a part of us as we are a part of them, and it is good.

"All of these things are not silly gods who ask us to do silly things. They are not capricious spirits who torment and torture us. They are not wicked creatures that frighten and confound us. They are the living gods of the Earth, and only when human beings learn to accept the truth will they be free.

"In every rock there is Many Tongues and there is Gilbert. There is Norval and there is Wolf. There is every man and woman, every child who was ever born. There is a beginning and there is an end. In every rock there are all the human beings of the world, living and breathing, loving and hating, growing old and dying. It is one link, one piece of star that fell to Earth from the sky. It is one people, one religion, and one spirit. It is Life Magic!"

Many Tongues was growing tired. I could tell as his conversation slowed and his eyes fluttered open and closed, but he regained himself once more and continued:

"I am no greater than any other human being. I have no powers of vision that other human beings do not have. I am you and you are me. Each one of us must come to understand that who we are and what we are is deep within us. I am the Old Young One. You are the Old Young One. We are all the Old Young One. But we cannot see until we open our eyes. We cannot hear unless we are willing to listen. That is what I said at the beginning, my friend—it is not tonight for which we must ready ourselves—it is for all of eternity. Forever and forever until the stars no longer shine beyond the moon."

Many Tongues slumped in his chair, weakened by both age and exhaustion. He had told me much of what I had come to hear but still nothing about me or Norval or what he had, several weeks ago, referred to as the "Joining." I wanted—needed—to hear more. But the old man was tired and worn.

I made him comfortable on the floor, draped a blanket over his body and around his shoulders, snuffed out the candles that had nearly burned to their wick's end and quietly left. There was much more we had to discuss but not then. We were both weary, especially Many Tongues' human frame that had nearly tripled my years on Earth, so I took exit and let him sleep.

"Another night, Many Tongues," I whispered, as I closed the door behind me. "When the time is right."

G

✸✸✸✸✸✸✸✸✸✸✸

Journal Entry: 4-4-79

The first thing I heard as I awoke this morning, actually the thing that awakened me, was a thundering voice that I'd recognize anywhere.

"What the hell is this?" Norval roared.

"Norval!" I shouted, "What are you doing here...I mean where have you been...I mean are you all right?"

"What the hell do you care, little snitcher boy?" Norval shouted. "I said, what the hell is this? He had my journal in his hand, shaking it my face and I was barely awake. He didn't even give me a chance to reply.

"I should take this piece of crap and burn it right now. In fact, that's damn sure what I am going to do," he said as he tossed the journal in the waste basked and pulled out his lighter. He flicked it once and held it to the trashcan.

"No!" I screamed. "Get your fucking hands off my property!" I could hardly believe I was talking to Norval in such a hostile manner, but it was barely 7:00 AM. I didn't even have the sleep out of my eyes, yet and there he stood ready to burn away all of the thoughts I had written over the past few months. I jumped out of bed grabbed the lighter out of his hand and threw it out the open window.

Norval was livid. He raised his hand and was about to strike me, when Brian entered the room, naked from sleep and, much to my relief, sporting his usual early morning wood.

"Norval, you're back," Brian squealed as he rushed across the room, tackled Norval to the floor and forced apart Norval's lips with his own.

As Brian welcomed Norval home in a more physically animated way than I would consider, I retrieved my journal from the wastebasket. I quickly inspected it for damage —missing pages, whatever—but to my relief, it appeared intact. I slipped it down my joggers and returned my attention to the frolicking twosome on the floor.

Brian had nearly stripped Norval naked and was about to initiate more than I cared to observe, when Norval pushed him away and turned his attention back to me.

"Where'd that piece of shit go,?" he asked.

"Forget it, Norval, you're not getting my journal. You may think you own me and everybody else in this apartment," I said, looking straightaway at Brian, who was back at Norval's feet like a puppy nuzzling for love—god it was sickening—"but you don't. There are some things that are private, some things that are personal—things over which you have no domain. This is my personal property, and I'll thank you not to disturb it again." As if I'd recklessly leave it out again and provide the opportunity!

"It's just a journal, nothing bad in it, so just drop the whole thing," I said, and noticed as I spoke, that I was becoming bolder with each word.

Norval stared back at me with a look that would have frightened away even the most fearless of men. I didn't flinch, not that I'd become so brave but more because he had violated my personal space and private property—amazing how we humans react when perceiving property to be at risk, more than the same consideration we'd give to a fellow human!

I thought a change of subject would be the best course of action and hoped that flattery would get me everywhere assuming I could dissuade Brian from his less than successful attempts at sodomizing Norval. I pushed Brain aside and threw my arms around Norval in a big bear hug (the things we do to keep peace!).

"It's good to have you back. Where have you been? Are you O.K.? Tell us all about it, what happened? We've been scared shitless!"

"You seem to know where I've been," Norval chided, still angry and not letting go of the situation with the journal. "The mob had me. Didn't you write that in your book. I'm a mobster, asshole, a fucking white man's mobster. Too bad they didn't kill me, huh?" Norval was using my words against me. Ammunition for his attack on the journal writings and on me.

"Norval, that was just one of the possibilities I considered, maybe I should say, one of my fears. I was worried about you. It's not like you to suddenly disappear without a word, a note, or even a trace. Damn, we were really concerned," I answered him.

"Yeah, I can tell by your little book that you were concerned about this old, drunken, doped up, moody, arrogant, ugly, disgusting, piece of shit Indian! Did I leave out anything else?" he thundered.

I had no response for what he had seen in the journal—he must have read the entire thing. "I'm sorry, Norval, I know I said some harsh things, but I hope you know I do care about you. Would I still be here if I didn't? It doesn't cost that much to catch a bus back to Toronto, and yet I'm here. I waited for you to come back. Doesn't that tell you something?"

This time I had Norval; he didn't have a ready response.

After a few minutes he answered back, "Yeah, you're still here; probably been fucking Brian since I've been gone."

Brian screamed like a child, "Norval, you know I'd never do that to you." He began reaching out for Norval to comfort him. "Please, Norval, I'd never be with another man."

"Shut up, baby-ass," Norval snorted.

"I'm sick of this conversation," I added.

"Norval, just hold me like you used to," Brian pleaded.

"What the hell's going on in here," Wolf grumbled, entering the room—the sleeping dog had been stirred. He took one look in the room and let out a whoop. "Norval," he shouted with the same shock both Brian and I had.

Norval just turned and left the room.

✸✸✸✸✸✸✸✸✸✸✸✸

LATER THAT AFTERNOON, AFTER NORVAL had calmed down from his morning tantrum, I approached him again, hoping to find out at least some truth as to what had happened and where he had been.

"Nothing to say. You seem to know more about it than I do," was his only response to my query.

I tried explaining the reasons why I had jumped to the conclusion that he had been (possibly) abducted by the mob, but to no avail. He had no intention of accepting my explanation and no desire to provide any additional information.

"Just been gone for a while," he added. "That enough for you?"

"I guess it will have to be for now," I resigned. "Obviously you have no intention of revealing anything else about your disappearance."

"NOT A DISAPPEARANCE," he shouted. "I was just gone for a few days. If you can't deal with that, fuck you."

Typical Morrisseau, ask him a question, get no response, just like opening night with the press at the Cardigan Milne Gallery. I suppose I shouldn't have expected more though since the press, who usually had been supportive of Norval, had been getting nothing out of him for the past several openings. I don't know why I thought I would fare better.

Norval had one more question to ask about the journal.

"Who the hell is that Many Tongues you kept writing about?"

"Many Tongues?" I shot back incredulously. "What are you talking about? He visited us at Beardmore and went with us to Manitou. You don't remember?" This had to be a joke, I thought to myself, what the hell was he trying to pull. How could he ask who Many Tongues was? I couldn't believe Norval's ignorance or amnesia or insensitivity. How could he forget an old friend like Many Tongues? Maybe something terrible had happened to Norval after all.

"The old fucker who went with us to Manitou? His name isn't Many Tongues; it's Bull William—Bull William, the Storyteller. And where'd you get a name like Many Tongues? Sounds like a white man made it up, because it's not an Indian name; course, you are a white man, aren't you?" Norval emphasized, looking at me with a great deal of disgust.

"Bull William, the Storyteller," I gasped. "Are we talking about the same man?"

"I hope so, since we were all together for about a week, unless you've gone crazy," Norval responded, calming down a bit. "An old grizzled fellow, about a hundred or so years old. Can't see anymore. Can hardly hear. And can't walk much without a cane. I take him places because he likes to get out and travel. He told me he wanted to see as much of Canada as he could before he dies. Guess I can at least do that much for the old guy."

"Bull William the…I mean Many Tongues isn't over a hundred years old. He's only about seventy. He's not deaf, he can see quite well, and I've never observed him having trouble walking. In fact, I'd say that he is in excellent shape for a man of his age," I returned, astonished that Norval was describing someone who most certainly wasn't Many Tongues.

Norval just stared at me. He didn't take his eyes off me for about five very uncomfortable minutes. He got up, started out the door, then turned, paused and said very seriously with a sincerity that sent shivers down my spine.

"Come to think of it, I did know a man called Many Tongues a long time ago—and I still think it's a stupid white man's name—but he died about ten years ago. I hadn't heard about him for years. They say he just wandered off one night after having some kind of secret ritual with some guy, something about a spiritual joining, or some shit like that. He thought he was a shaman and a visionary. Everyone said he was as loony as hell. They found him several weeks later, dead in the woods, half rotted and half eaten by wolves. Many Tongues has been dead for years. If old Bull William says he's this Many Tongues character, then I tell you he's crazy. In fact, white boy, I think you're fucking crazy too." And with that Norval left the room.

All I could do, after hearing Norval's story about his Many Tongues, was sit and stare. I don't think I moved for an hour, and I have little recollection of what I was thinking about. All I knew was that I had to see Many Tongues again as soon as possible.

✸✸✸✸✸✸✸✸✸✸✸✸

I went to Many Tongues' place later in the afternoon as soon as I had regained myself and had had the time to consider what I'd ask or say to him. It's not an easy subject to broach. "Hey, Many Tongues, I understand you're dead. What gives?"

When a man from inside the apartment answered my knock, I stumbled backwards nearly tumbling down the stairs. It wasn't Many Tongues, but who it was I didn't know and didn't want to know!

Opening the door to my knocking was an old man who had to have been over a hundred years old. His gait was hesitant, in fact downright halting. He almost fell over just standing at the door hanging onto its knob. His skin was wrinkled with deep jagged age lines and his face was as ashen as any white person's I'd seen of the same age. He squinted at me with heavy deep eyes and looked up and down my body as though trying to figure out who was at his door. After a couple of extremely awkward minutes, he finally spoke.

"Mandamin," he whispered, "come in, I wasn't expecting you."

"Many Tongues," I responded, "Is that you? What's going on, I just saw you last night. You look like you've aged fifty years!"

"Yes, yes, come in, come in. I haven't a thing to offer you—no food or drink—I wasn't expecting you." He acted like he wasn't really certain who I was. Food and drink? We never before had shared physical nourishment during our visits.

"You never expect me, Many Tongues. You call to me with your mind," I reminded him. "I come when you penetrate my mind or when we had previously made arrangements."

"Yes, yes of course, but this time your visit has taken me by surprise. Usually I can see your presence long before you arrive. Usually I know when you are coming to visit but I was not prepared. I must have dozed off. I am sorry. Come in, come in. Sit down."

As I entered the room, I took a quick look around. Everything was in order, everything appeared the same as when I had left the night before: The recliner, the candles, the coffee table, the myriad of artifacts—everything! The only aspect of the room that was different was Many Tongues.

"Are you up to talking?" I asked, sitting down.

"Of course, Old Young One, I am always up to talking. Have you ever known me not to being up for talking? When have you been able to shut me up?" he answered with a smile spreading across his face.

"Good point," I laughed.

"Norval is back…" I began.

"I know," Many Tongues interrupted. "This morning in a rage no doubt. Didn't like what he found in your journal, did he? A very angry and childish man, Norval."

I was astonished and becoming more curious by the minute. "How did you know that?" I asked. "No one possibly could have filled you in. Was Norval here earlier? I wouldn't be surprised if had been based on some of the things he told me. I'd expect him to rush over here and tip you off."

"I am disappointed, Mandamin," Many Tongues answered. "Norval has not been here. Not once. Not ever. Not even after we returned from Manitou. I would not trick you. I do not lie to my Companion Traveler."

I hesitated. What had Many Tongues called me—his Companion Traveler—what was that? What was he talking about? He must have sensed my confusion because he answered my question before I posed it.

"When the time is right," he whispered.

When the time is right, again, how many times had I heard that? I was frustrated and wanted to know everything right then and there, but I was resigned to knowing that I would have to wait for Many Tongues to reveal his mysteries as he saw fit.

I focused back on the question about how Many Tongues had known that Norval had returned.

"Then how did you know that Norval is back?" I asked.

Many Tongues laughed quietly at first, then heartily out loud.

"I know because I know," he responded with his typical cryptic explanation. "Have you already forgotten about what we spoke last night?" Many Tongues paused as though contemplating what he had just said while his eyes looked past me as though searching for recognition beyond the room in which we sat...

"...Or was it a thousand years ago when we last met?"

It is difficult to write how I felt when Many Tongues lapsed into a trance that had him questioning when we had last seen one another. His hesitance caused chills to sweep up and down my spine. The expression on his face was distant as though he had passed into another dimension and was having difficulty maintaining his link to this existence. I gently touched his hand and, somehow, spoke to him with my thoughts as much as my voice.

"No it wasn't a thousand years ago, Many Tongues, it was last night," I responded, bewildered. His hesitation and inability to remember things that had happened only the night before and his physical appearance had me concerned. I was frightened. I wasn't certain who or to what I was speaking.

"A thousand years or last night, it does not matter, Mandamin. They are one in the same—a singular event in the continuum of eternity that subsumes both within one. It is only in how you perceive that distinguishes one from another. We are here now and we are a thousand years both into the past and into the future. What I say to you now you said to me yesterday.

"Do you not remember the one who came to your door at Beardmore? Have you not wondered about his strange words, about why he did not drink your tea, about how he had arrived and left, without trace?"

No doubt I had been wondering about the old man ever since he visited. But...

Many Tongues interrupted my thoughts, "It was I who knocked upon your door, but it was you who had begun the preparation. You must focus deeply into the most distant reaches of your thoughts and touch upon the spirit that dwells within. You have come to me, not by choice, but by fate just as I have come to you in your dreams. And like the unbroken continuum of time, we are two human beings—one in the same—separated by time and circumstance but always linked in spirit. Have you not yet guessed that we travel this continuum together; that your universe is mine and mine, yours. We did speak last night—in this dimension—just as at the same time we spoke last night in a world a thousand years past."

Many Tongues reached out and touched his hand to my forehead then pulled it back and placed it upon his.

As we sat in momentary silence I suddenly began to feel very strange. It felt as though I was on fire, like a battle was being waged within my body. I was becoming sick to my stomach. I was sweating and shaking. My legs grew weak and my arms numb. My mind went blank. The air in my lungs felt burning hot. I was having difficulty breathing. And although I know it sounds absurd, it felt as though an unknown indistinct force had invaded my body and was fighting with my very essence (my soul?) for control of my spirit. Many Tongues just sat in his chair observing what was happening.

"Many Tongues," I gasped, "For God's sake what's going on? Help me—please help me. The pain is unbearable. My body is failing. I think I'm dying."

The physical manifestations went on for a half hour or so.

At last Many Tongues answered with a powerful commanding voice, "Not dying, mystic spirit, simply changing. The transformation has begun."

I felt my body returning to what I assumed was normal—at least the burning had subsided. I was not sick to my stomach anymore and I was able to control the shaking and quivering of my hands. I looked at Many Tongues. In my concern over what had been happening to my own body and at first thinking that I was dying, I hadn't noticed that the same phenomenon had happened to him. And there before me sat the man who I had come to love and admire. Not the weak frail Indian who had opened the door to my importuning moments earlier, but the Many Tongues I had known since Beardmore. Many Tongues had transformed not before my eyes, but certainly in my presence. He sat in his chair a strong well-heeled man of about seventy.

"The transformation is complete," Many Tongues announced. "We are now as one."

And truly we were. Each time he spoke I sensed his words before he uttered them, as though they were a part of my own thoughts. When he told of amazing visions he could see I saw what he described, not because I could hear his voice, but because I saw the exact visions within my own mind. As he spoke of the many years he had traveled this dimension I shared his weariness and sorrow. As he chanted in Ojibwa I chanted with him, understanding each word of the language I had never before spoken.

We sat in silence for over an hour, both of us projecting back in time to places of which I had no understanding—to places I had not previously visited. I was meeting people I had never before greeted and seeing sights I had never experienced—at least not as Gilbert. I projected five hundred years back to Africa, a thousand more to Asia, five thousand to what was once the lush homeland of the

North American Natives. I became one of the people in all of these places who were working, playing, laughing, crying, living, and dying in a world that had become mine.

I felt the pain of the black man who had been taken from his home by European slave traders. I experienced the terror of the Indians being driven from their land—raped, scalped, and murdered. I walked with the Jews into the gas chambers at Auschwitz. I lived the cruelty of the Spanish, the Portuguese, the French, the English, the Chinese, the Americans, the Romans, the Egyptians, and every other nation of people that had brought pain and suffering to the children of the Earth through conquest and genocide. And I felt the misery of humanity as it suffocated beneath its own insanity.

And then we returned.

"Do you understand?" Many Tongues asked.

"No…I don't know…I'm not sure…well, how can I…this is all happening so quickly…so much I don't understand. Are we human…spirit…god…what?" I demanded.

As soon as we had returned I felt the mental bond with Many Tongues vanish just as quickly as it had begun. The old man laughed to himself, a laughter that was reassuring not cruel. "Oh, we are human, Old Young One, we are very human—see," and he pricked his finger with a safety pin then reached over and did the same to me. We bled. Indeed, we seemed human enough!

"Then what is all this?" I asked. "What is going on? Norval saying you were dead. You looking like the man Norval described who supposedly died ten years ago. This transformation. The visions. The projecting. What's this all about?"

"In time, my forever friend, in time. You have too many questions. This old man cannot keep up," Many Tongues replied, laughing again.

"For God's sake, Many Tongues, this isn't fair. You owe me an explanation!" I shouted.

"I owe you nothing!" Many Tongues exploded back, his eyes blazing, his stare frozen on his face like ice. "You must discover the truth for yourself. I am only a Companion Traveler. I cannot bring you to the answers you seek. You must find them for yourself."

"So that's it?" I queried. "As simple as that. A quick dismissal of my concerns. No answers, no explanation? You're just going to suck me into all this then say too bad, figure it out for yourself?"

"Yes, my Companion Traveler. You must find your own truth, your own way. We must all travel the path of life alone. There will be times when we may find another human of our own tribe, of our own kind, and when we do we must join with that spirit and cherish it—never let it go. Companion Travelers are very rare, very difficult to come across. With your Companion Traveler you will never be alone, but you must always discover the path of your own direction. Even your Companion Traveler cannot do that for you—only with you."

I was becoming more frustrated with the increasingly obscure explanations Many Tongues offered. As exciting and as wonderful as these new discoveries were—in fact as otherworldly as they seemed to be—I wanted, I needed logical, practical answers. Many Tongues had purposefully sought me out, sucked me in, and was now intending to leave me high and dry without even a simple explanation. I had heard of people who believed in the supernatural—in psychic phenomena—but I had never experienced anything of the sort, but I wasn't about to accept this experience as psychic or mystical without more convincing evidence. And if it were a mystical experience, I wasn't certain that I wanted to be a part of it, especially without the guidance and wisdom Many Tongues had provided so far.

"What about Norval, then?" I asked. "Can you at least explain why he said you were dead, and why he claims that you're an old man of over a hundred years?"

Many Tongues took a long breath, sighed and responded. "Norval is a bitter man, an unhappy man. He has many great and wonderful talents. He has brought the legends of the Ojibwa back to life after many long years, even against the wishes of the elders. He has made his people proud; they have great respect for the man Norval Morrisseau and take great pride in his paintings. He is a great man for what he has done. But he is also a poor man, not in wealth, but in spirit. He is a shaman but does not use his knowledge to help himself. He gives advice and guidance to others but fails to heed his own counsel. He has visions but cannot find truth in his own life. The Thunderbird spirit visited Norval many years ago when the Thunderbird left its nest, but Norval does not fly with the freedom of the Great Bird. He is as much goodness as he is wicked. As much loving as he is hateful. As much positive as he is negative. He drinks too much. He does too many drugs. He is in trouble, not only in spirit but also in the profane.

Many people have their hands in his pockets and he does not know how to push them away. He will live as an unhappy man and he will die alone and bitter. He believes that he is the incarnation of the Thunderbird Spirit. He believes he can cleanse those that heartache visits. Consider his performance at Manitou—did you think it was Norval Morrisseau who cleansed those who came to him? Or did you not notice that Many Tongues was in trance at the same moment each of the humans were counseled and cured?"

I was shocked at Many Tongues' revelation. Indeed, I had believed that Norval had morphed into a powerful shaman—The Copper Thunderbird—and had cleansed those who came before him. I had not considered that Many Tongues had intervened. But I do recall the trance into which Many Tongues had fallen. I remember his distant stare, his vacant eyes, and his near stupor. I was simply too uninformed at that point—I had no idea!

"That is all I can say about Jean Baptiste Norman Henry Morrisseau," Many Tongues concluded.

I was curious about his relationship with Norval. "Many Tongues, why have you been with Norval as a friend if so much about him is unpleasant? Are you his spiritual guide?" I asked.

"Not guide. I do not know why I am with Norval…I do not know. Perhaps we are together so that he might discover his own identity; perhaps because we are to learn from one another. I met Norval by chance in Beardmore many years ago and we have traveled this life together for a short distance, but I will not always be with him. We do not always understand why we walk the same path with other human beings. I do not know why I walk with Norval. We travel with some human beings as Companion Travelers, as you and I shall journey, but with other human beings we travel together for other reasons—though they might not be revealed during this existence," he answered.

"And the way he sees you—as a frail old man?" I asked.

"Norval sees me as he sees himself. I am his mirror, I am his reflection. Because he is a sad and unhappy man he sees me as an old dying Indian…as the man he will become one day many years before his time. He calls me Bull William the Storyteller, but he does not remember that old Bull William died in an accident one night after drinking too much liquor and taking too many drugs and smashed himself dead in his automobile. Norval does not remember what happened to Bull William because he does not want to remember—Bull William is a reflection of Norval. I have always been Many Tongues, although as we discussed, many humans in many lands have called me—have called us—by many other names. I am no older than I am, seventy-one. I have lived no longer with this body than when I first sprang from my mother's womb. And I will die in this body and shall be burned on the pyre as this body. I am no more and no less than are you or are any human being who seeks the truth. I am a spirit guide, a counselor, and a seer. I am simply the old man Many Tongues."

"And what about Norval saying you were found dead after having a secret ritual with a stranger?" I asked.

"I did not die. You can easily see that for yourself. Norval only believes I died. I have had five spiritual Joinings with other human beings. That is the secret ritual of which Norval speaks. But it is not secret, it is not ritual; it is only enigmatic to those who do not believe for if they were to believe the Joining, it would cast doubt as to their own faith and weaken their strength with suspicion. What Norval saw was a Joining not unlike yours and mine.

"As for my supposed death, I went into the woods after the Joining, as many times I have done, to become one again with the Earth and sky around me. I came back out of the woods one day later. Many human beings saw me come back from the woods and many human beings have seen me since. Certainly I am not dead. The man who was discovered in the woods was an old Indian named Joseph St. Cloud. He had gone to the woods to die just as our people used to do in the olden days—his time was right. His body was partially decayed and partially eaten by scavenger wolves. Norval chose to believe what he wanted to believe. Old Joseph's death came at the same time as did Bull William's. Norval has confused the two for convenience. He does not want to remember."

"Then that's it? As simple as you explain," I wondered aloud.

"As simple as it is, yes," Many Tongues replied. "And now you must go. I am tired. Your visit was a surprise, and I am not used to so much excitement without preparation. But you will come back. We have much more to discuss."

"But I need to know about us Many Tongues and about me. I seek the knowledge you have. You must give me understanding; you must give me truth," I implored.

Many Tongues sighed then spoke softly: "I am no more and no less than are you, Companion Traveler. I have no deeper understanding of truth than you already possess within yourself. I am older and have more worldly knowledge than you, but I can only awaken what is already within you. You must seek the truth for yourself. We have traveled many paths of life together and have been incarnated as many different spirits. Only during this life am I Many Tongues, the old man, and you Gilbert, the younger. What I share with you, you have shared with me many times in the past. And what we have shared with one another is the truth of who and what we are."

"One more question, please, Many Tongues," I interrupted. "If what you say about Joseph St. Cloud is true, and it wasn't you found dead in the woods, and you are not as old as Norval believes, then why, when you came to the door earlier tonight, did you look like the man Norval had described as old and dying?"

"Ah, my Companion Traveler, you think you have caught me in a mistake, perhaps telling you a lie! No—never! As I have told you, I do not lie to you now; I will not lie to you ever! When I came to the door I was as I look now but what you saw was what you expected to see—just as Norval sees what he expects to see. Norval had you convinced, or at least suspicious of my true identity, my true face. He even pretended to not know who 'this Many Tongues' is of whom you wrote in your journal. You saw me through the eyes of Norval, not through your own. You must come to trust what you see —even if it does not appear real. What is real and what is false are deceiving and often the same. You must trust! You must believe! You must have faith in your own ability to separate truth from deception."

I didn't know what else to say at that point. My initial questions had been answered, but my curiosity was increasing. I wanted to know more, but Many Tongues had already indicated he was worn and tired. I didn't want to infringe upon my dear friend—my Companion Traveler—any longer.

And so I left with the understanding that we would meet again soon. The fact was, we had to meet. We had joined in mind, but we had not become as One. We yet had many roads to explore together.

G

✸✸✸✸✸✸✸✸✸✸✸✸

Journal Entry: 4-6-79

I had the dream about the giant rat again.

I am entering my parents' home through the kitchen door when I see a huge ugly rat walking nearly upright on his hind legs. As in all my other dreams, I am not frightened, more surprised. "Should I tell my parents they have rats?" I think to myself. "No, it would just upset them and give cause for another fight." So I don't.

Halfway across the room on its trip from where ever it had come, it stops at the bathroom turns and looks me straight in the face with its red satanic eyes. The rat hisses with a shrill screech that for all the world sounds like a banshee haunting its intended victim. Then as it is about to walk away a giant bird swoops down from somewhere near the ceiling and, with sharpened talons, flies towards the rat but stops short of attacking. The bird turns in my direction and perches upon my shoulder. At once it fades and merges with my spirit.

Almost immediately a giant rabbit leaps from the bathroom, lunges for the rat with its teeth exposed, but like the bird does not attack. Instead it leaps towards me and joins with the two which had become one and we stand as three in one watching the rat as it tries to walk away. But it has become paralyzed and cannot move. It struggles to escape, but our power has become greater than its. The rat begins hissing and shrieking then drops to all fours rather than walking upright. It seems dazed and confused, stares at me with its diabolical eyes then spits blood on my shoes and pant legs. The rat begins slowly moving in a circle—with methodical ritualized movements—then races faster and faster until it becomes a series of rats chasing one another rather than one rat running as fast as it can in a circle.

My parents come into the kitchen see the rat and join in its chase—pursuing the rat, the rat pursuing them. All three hiss at one another with the piercing wail of a ghoul. Then suddenly they all stop running.

The rat begins shrinking and my parents begin fading until, within a few minutes, the once huge ugly rat has disappeared completely and my parents have faded into oblivion.

I hear the call of an eagle resonate from deep within my spirit. I feel the surge of the rabbit fighting to free itself from within my soul. Suddenly the visage of an old Native man appears in the kitchen, walks towards me, extends his arms in greeting, and we clasp hands.

As our hands join, a rush that feels like electricity courses throughout my body. I hear the word "freedom" whispered over and over again, and at once the figure of the old man merges with me and I feel the power of his age and wisdom unite with my spirit.

I am then left alone. The rat has disappeared. My parents have faded. The eagle, the rabbit, and the old Indian have merged with me. My parents' house, in which I had been standing, dissolves into the peaceful serenity of a lush, densely wooded forest.

I feel at peace. There is no fear, no hesitation, and no doubt in my mind. I know the rat and the dream will never return. I have been freed.

G

****

JOURNAL ENTRY: 4-14-79

With Norval back and still as evasive as ever about his whereabouts for those several days things have returned to normal around here, if normal is an appropriate term to describe the four of us: Norval, a French-Canadian metis, a doting (but acquiescent) brother, and a pandering Indian youth, who would just as soon I leave as continue my confrontations with Norval.

"It puts him in a bad mood," Brian complains about by arguments with Norval. "I don't like it when he's in a bad mood—he can be nasty and violent, and he ignores me." Gracious, what a startling revelation, Brian, so where have you been for the past month?

Norval has begun painting again—or perhaps I should say Norval has begun sketching, and we have begun painting again. The incident with the forgeries at the Cardigan Milne Gallery I thought a one-time occurrence, but to get the exhibit ready for the opening night exhibition, it has started again. I am not certain why. Norval is obviously an accomplished artist and immensely able to create his own work, but for some reason he has taken to letting Wolf, Brian, and me fill in the coloration on each of his sketchings. We use the same process we did for the Cardigan Milne art fraud: Norval sketches, we color. At this point I do not know if Norval's reluctance to do his own work is the result of whatever has been going on to disrupt him (the visitor, the note, his recent absence) or is a manifestation of his weariness with his art, although I would find the latter hard to believe. Regardless of what else Norval might be, he has always been committed to his art. His recent disposition to allow us to complete his work is disturbing; it is not like Norval to take his art so lightly, and I fear that whatever trouble he is in—if indeed he is in trouble—is far more serious than I had first thought.

My fanciful suspicion about mob involvement based only on the business card, the visitor to the apartment, and the note we found might not be as absurd as it sounds. In fact Norval's hysterics about me writing about the mob in my journal obviously hit a little too close to home. Was it Shakespeare who penned the famous line: "Me thinks thou dost protest too much?" Norval, I think you might, also.

Since his re-emergence Norval has been even more distant, more aloof, and more quarrelsome than ever. He jumps at the slightest sound, scolds Brian whenever the young man says or does anything of which Norval doesn't approve, almost totally ignores Wolf (addressing him only with hostility and anger), and avoids me like the plague. I find myself being concerned for Norval, but I don't know if my feelings are generated out of sincerity or out of pity.

His use of drugs has not diminished. I don't think there is a single minute of the day that passes without Norval either being stoned or preparing to get stoned! He doesn't seem to be drinking as much but still far more than is healthy, and the amount he does drink is counterproductive to his work. Perhaps the chemicals have something to do with Norval's reticence to do his own work. When I confronted him about his drinking last night he angrily responded that he is only a social drinker, then added that socializing constituted any time he so defined.

I am further concerned about the amount of art fraud of which we have all become willing participants. I do not know if fraud had existed with Norval's paintings before 1979 because I was not with him and have no first-hand knowledge of potential fraud, but I do know for a fact that it has become prevalent since just before the gallery showing. And the fraud seems so ridiculous, so unnecessary. With his exceptional talent Norval does not need to enlist apprentices to assist with his work—and "assist" is very loosely used; we are actually creating his work.

Following the Cardigan-Milne episode there was a second incident of fraud and deception that did not seem at all bothersome to Norval. In fact, as with Cardigan Milne, he encouraged it.

One day last week, Wolf had gone to see an optician regarding getting the prescription eyeglasses he desperately needed. He has to nearly press his face to the canvass to see where he should be painting within the sketches Norval draws. One of Wolf's attempts looked much like a child's coloring book, with a rainbow display of colors extending beyond the lines of the outlined figures. After returning from the eye doctor Wolf told Norval that it would cost sixty dollars for the prescription. Norval flatly refused to pay the sixty dollars but told Wolf to ask the optician if he would accept two small original Morrisseau paintings in lieu of payment. Of course, the optician gladly accepted the offer—two Morrisseaus, even small ones, are worth considerably more than sixty dollars!

Instead of painting the two canvasses himself, which would have taken no time to speak of, Norval told Brian to create two twelve-inch square paintings, which he did: One of a young Indian girl and the other of a matching Indian boy. When Brian had completed the paintings Norval signed them both. Wolf presented the paintings to the optician, got his prescription, and left.

Since Brian's use of color is similar to Norval's I am sure the optician had no idea they were forgeries and worthless. As far as the doctor was concerned, he had two valuable Morrisseaus created especially for him! I picture the paintings hanging in the optician's home being marveled over by friends who come to visit. Someday I am certain that the trusting doctor will not be so pleased—the fraud cannot work indefinitely, can it?—and will not be as quick to trust anyone again.

I find myself torn between doing what is right (exposing the sham) and continuing to participate, even if only as an observer, in what is wrong. I have become no better than Norval because I know what is taking place but I do nothing to stop it! Many Tongues would not be pleased.

Even the episode with the optician wasn't the last concerning Norval's fraudulent paintings. A few days ago, Brian told Norval that he desperately wanted to do a painting by himself. Brian does have raw undeveloped talent and paints very much in the Woodland tradition but has not yet perfected his own style. At first Norval was reticent, saying that Brian had not honed his skills sufficiently to paint on his own and that he needed more training from the master. Brian begged and pleaded so insistently, like a child wanting his parent to purchase a special toy, that Norval gave in. He told Brian to start with something simple—like a Thunderbird. Brian painted Norval's suggestion, a Thunderbird that took him two days to complete. When it was finished, Norval signed it. It is worthless as a Morrisseau, but Norval sent it along to Jack Pollock in Toronto with a suggested selling price of fifteen hundred dollars!

The only thing that Norval has been dabbling with on his own is a dust jacket for an album of Ojibwa tribal music by the Native singer, Shingoose. The two met at Norval's opening at the Cardigan-Milne Gallery and Shingoose asked Norval if he would listen to his music and produce an original painting for the album sleeve. Thankfully, for Shingoose's sake, he had met Norval on one of Norval's better days and Norval accepted the proposition immediately. We were all invited to visit the recording studio when Shingoose was recording his original music, and it was one of the few times since Norval's return that Norval has seemed the slightest bit enthused about painting. He finished the painting this morning, and as is the case with most real Morrisseaus, it is breathtaking. At least Shingoose will be getting an original Morrisseau.

I can't say for certain, but it seems more than coincidental that Norval has little hesitation about committing fraud with paintings that he either knows, for sure, or suspects will be going to a white person but does the work himself when the piece is for a Native. Since his paintings are sold from galleries (for the most part), and since few Indians patronize the galleries in Canada, it is likely that whites will purchase Norval's paintings. It seems Norval has discovered another way to 'fuck over the white man.' I'm sure it's his way of getting even.

Norval's bizarre attitudes continue to extend to things beyond his painting. Just this evening, we were all sitting around smoking dope and having a fairly good time (at least as good a time as the four of us can have together) when Norval decided that he wanted to explain to us that amassing money, and then using it to manipulate people—although common—was not a good way to exercise power or influence and that it was more important that life, whether you are rich or poor, be spiritually meaningful. I was excited about the prospects of having a serious discussion with Norval and pursuing his thesis because Norval's intellect is one of the two main reasons I could still tolerate the man. There are times when Norval's lucidity and philosophy can be very sensible and captivating, thus my polarized feelings about him. He is, as I have written in numerous journal writings, a boorish cad who can also demonstrate serious intellectual understanding and insightful criticism of political, social, and philosophical issues—at least for a while! And so his opening salvo about money and spirituality had me interested.

Listening attentively, I was trying to piece together all of what he was trying to explain when suddenly he took a one thousand dollar bill out of his boots, used it as marijuana rolling paper, and lit it up.

He went on to explain that the money represented nothing more than the slavery white people had imposed upon everyone—not only themselves and their own white poor but also upon minorities like Indians and Blacks. Norval argued that the money symbolized white power, and that true fulfillment in life comes from within the spirit and not from the material. A person could have hundreds of thousands of dollars but no happiness, or no money and great happiness. Most of his argument was focused upon the politics of money: How it could be used to buy power, influence, focus attention upon the wealthy, and establish a caste system of those who have and those who have not. Norval argued that Native people had been subjugated to white control because the white man owned their land, which translated into money, which translated into power, which translated into the white supremacy, which translated into the white man's ability to control Native people and keep them as indentured servants and slaves. Secular power, Norval insisted, stemmed from an unhealthy reliance upon money, and thus money was the root of evil, itself—not just the love of money!

I do not disagree with Norval on any of the points he made, especially concerning white power and control; however, for those of us who do not have the wealth that Norval does and have to pay bills simply to exist, using a thousand-dollar bill as marijuana rolling paper constitutes an extreme demonstration of the point. I know I could think of much better ways of using a thousand-dollar bill and still regard the misuse of money as an inexcusable attack upon all of humanity. I argued that it should not be at issue whether we have and use money as a means for material exchange for indeed all societies—primitive or contemporary—employ some method of barter, even if communal and cooperative. The singular focus upon money as a means, rather than an end, constitutes the evil.

Norval became silent but not contemplative suggesting more that he had become bored with the conversation and he was pondering his next argument. He rolled his eyes back, sighed, and asked if I wanted to smoke a joint with him.

Our discussion had come to an end because Norval had tired of it and deemed it over. What had been a promising conversation deteriorated into inanity. I was disappointed but relented, there was nothing I could do to change the man.

Having lost the battle, I collapsed and acquiesced to my victor. We smoked a second thousand-dollar joint Norval had rolled and I must say, it was the smoothest, richest tasting stick I have ever smoked—coincidence or power of suggestion?

Despite Norval's many character flaws, I have to admit that he is mostly consistent with his philosophy concerning money. He does have a number of checking and savings accounts in banks throughout Canada, but he seldom seems in need of tapping any of them for cash reserves. His boot is always well stocked! From where he gets the money to stuff into his boot I am not certain. I assume it comes from the sale of his paintings, but from what I understand, all the money from gallery sales goes directly into one of his accounts somewhere. Since I have been with Norval I have only once seen him visit a bank to withdraw any money for the boot stash, so the question remains: How does his boot get supplied such that there is always money available? Another Morrisseau conundrum.

Norval is quite free with money—free with it, but controlling. As I have mentioned several times, he has not paid me a salary—nor has he to Wolf or Brian—but none of us need for any necessities. He will not remunerate us for our work but keeps us under his thumb by providing that which we cannot afford. He is quick to dispense money at the drop of a hat, and he is forever giving money away to friends and strangers whom he perceives as being in need. I have also witnessed Norval tossing paper notes into the air just so he can watch people scramble for his monetary treats. His actions with money seem as much generous as they do churlish. Apparently he gets some kind of thrill observing those in need trample each other to scoop up his droppings.

Although Norval is mostly consistent in his philosophy concerning money, he was adamant about not giving Wolf the money he needed for his glasses, and he provides little for his wife and seven children. Given that Norval is as wealthy as he is, freely gives money to friends and strangers, and tosses it around like confetti it is dichotomous that he is resolute about not helping his own blood. His attitude about money is one of the contradictions of Norval Morrisseau— just one—because, believe me, there are many.

G

✱✱✱✱✱✱✱✱✱✱✱✱

JOURNAL ENTRY: 4-15-79

Norval told me this morning that he had bought me a present, but that I won't get it until next week. What it is I have no idea—he won't give any hints. Why I have to wait so long I don't know either. And why he has purchased me a gift I haven't the slightest clue. Our relationship certainly has not been at its best lately. We seem to argue about everything, important or insignificant, and he spends considerably more time with Brian than he does with me. Nevertheless, I am always willing to accept gifts, especially from Norval because they are so few and far between. I am anxious and yet apprehensive. I do not want to be beholden to him and yet, generally, when Norval buys something for a friend it is of significance—without strings attached—and besides I am not beyond accepting gifts of great value.

He also announced that the trip is back on to visit his siblings in Beardmore. All of us will be going—Brian and Wolf included. I am hesitant about the trip, especially with both Brian and Wolf along but, it will get us away from Winnipeg for a while and away from the threats and mysteries of the past several weeks. The gift I look forward to, the trip I do not.

At this point, nearly four months into being with Norval, I am not certain how much longer I can endure his lunacy. However, the trip might be just what I need (and the present won't hurt). He said we'll only be gone for a few days, not even a week, and we will return to Winnipeg before the 22nd. The plans could prove beneficial. I still want to see Many Tongues again and the trip away might give me time to assimilate more of what he and I have been pursuing. After we are back from Beardmore and I have been with Many Tongues I might decide to leave permanently. I'm not certain yet. I'll have to play it by ear. I'm sure Norval wouldn't mind since he still has his trusty shadow in Wolf and his doting protégé in Brian. I don't think I would be missed.

I can't help wonder though what this trip might bring. It seems that every time we pack up and go from one place to another something dramatic happens. What awaits our journey this time? Hopefully, not more of the mystery that has surrounded Norval in the past several weeks—I'm sure I can do without another disappearance, his or mine. Wolf or Brian on the other hand… .

G

✽✽✽✽✽✽✽✽✽✽✽

JOURNAL ENTRY: 4-16-79

Norval awoke me early this morning. Much to my surprise he was sober, packed, and almost ready to leave for Beardmore—almost that is because he wanted to initiate a cleansing ceremony before we left. He wanted to assure comfortable passage and a safe trip.

After I had showered and packed Norval was ready to begin the cleansing ceremony. He took a record from its sleeve—an album of North American Indian chants—and lit a braid of sweet grass that he had prepared the night before. I decided to use the cleansing to my benefit. I could focus upon my Joining with Many Tongues and attempt the time projection the two of us had shared several nights ago.

My presentation and comportment were much to Norval's surprise. I entered the room clad only in my boxer shorts and sat on the floor—legs crossed, arms folded across my chest, my back rigid. The room was thick with the odor of burning sweet grass and as the smoke enveloped the solemnity that I associated with the ritual I used my hands to encourage the smoke towards my face, trying to grab it and sheathe my mind and spirit in its cleansing virtues. I was absorbed in meditation—even waving Norval away when he approached to sit beside me.

"Not now," I whispered, "When the time is right."

I was not able to project back into time as I had with Many Tongues, but I did free my mind sufficiently to wander, alone, through the labyrinth of dreamscape. I passed in and out of a hundred collected memories—memories shared by Companion Travelers from ages past and time present. I do not know how suddenly I had become knowledgeable about the intricacies of Companion Travelers—Many Tongues and I had not gone beyond his initial revelation. Nonetheless, I launched into the new experience with exuberence and became a part of each spirit, absorbing from each and they from me. And I gave to each Companion Traveler with whom I was in contact a part of my spirit, sharing as do Companion Travelers every thought and dream that cannot be experienced with others who do not believe. I dare not reveal exactly what I sensed or consummated in my passage into dream, for the experience is uncommonly personal—one shared only with your Companion Traveler. It is not for the uninitiated. I inhaled the heavy smoke from the sweet grass and cleansed all impurities and evil spirits from my thoughts. I had become one with my surroundings and with myself, and not even Norval could dissuade my complete repose.

I am certain Norval wondered what was going on. He was not aware of my experiences with Many Tongues (or Bull William, as he insisted my friend be called) and had no idea that I had become a Companion Traveler with the old man. I am not sure he would have approved. I'm certain he would have considered Many Tongues' and my joining as a threat, both to him personally and to our relationship. And I think he would have been especially jealous of Many Tongues' mysticism, since Norval regarded himself a shaman unequaled among peers.

I concluded the cleansing ceremony by chanting an ancient Earth prayer in Ojibwa, then swathed my body in more smoke as though washing away the impurities from my skin. Norval stared in amazement. He had never heard me speak Ojibwa, and I am positive he had no idea what I was hoping to accomplish. The only comment he made after I had left the dream world and returned to reality was: "'The Prayer of Earth and Sky Together,' Little Eagle. That is an ancient prayer of my people known to very few Ojibwa, unspoken by any white man. Where did you learn the Earth Prayer?"

"I just picked it up somewhere; I don't recall now," I answered casually. I thought I'd give him more to think about and added, "Remember, Norval, I am metis—half Indian and half French—there is much you do not know about me, much you have never bothered to ask." He did not respond but stood dumbfounded. Finally, I had gotten the better of Norval Morrisseau and I was pleased, not only because I had successfully initiated my first singular transformation also but because I had stunned Norval with my knowledge of Ojibwa language and Native ritual. For the rest of the day, Norval regarded me with suspicion.

Before leaving Winnipeg, Norval needed to obtain cash, and since he did not carry any bankcards or identification on his person, he made me drive him to four different banks in the city in an attempt to withdraw money from each one. In all, it took nearly two hours. I asked him how he had been able to withdraw money without identification or a bank account number and he tossed a copy of *Time* on my lap and laughed. He had shown the tellers the story about himself in the American news magazine, and because of his notoriety and respect among

Canadians—white as well as Native—he was able to withdraw money from the banks in which he had deposits. I was impressed—Morrisseau is surely one of a kind! He also told me that we had gone to four banks because he couldn't remember in which banks he had made deposits! He would simply show the magazine for identification, inquire as to whether or not he had an account and make a withdrawal if he did. I asked him for the withdrawal slips to keep for his records. Given that he didn't even know which banks he was with, I doubt if he had any records. That would be too 'white' and might contradict his philosophy about money he had so intricately explained earlier—as if keeping tens of thousands of dollars in any number of unknown banks didn't! Nonetheless, I was insistent on performing the secretarial duties for which I had been hired, and he handed them over. Besides, the bank slips might become useful when I decided to leave. All told, Norval ended up with more than three thousand dollars for the trip.

Finally, after having completed Norval's search for hidden treasure, we were on our way to Beardmore. I was driving, Norval sat beside me in the front passenger seat, and Brian and Wolf slept in the back. I felt a twinge of sadness when leaving Winnipeg, knowing that as we did I was, at the same time, leaving Many Tongues, the man who had become my closest confidant and friend. Although we were only to be gone less than a week, something gnawed at my emotions and made me feel uncomfortable—like when as a child, I had gone away to summer camp for the first time, knowing that I would return home, but feeling the lonely pangs of abandonment and fear. I offered a small prayer that Many Tongues and I would be rejoined in friendship as soon as we returned, but even with that I could not shake the feeling that our next meeting would be far different that we had previously experienced.

It was an unusually cold and wintry day for April. Had I not known what month it was, I would have guessed it to be January or February. We had not driven more than fifteen miles out of Winnipeg when an unexpected April snowstorm exploded upon us without warning. Within an hour, we were driving through seven inches of freshly fallen snow and swirling drifts of nature's powder. The wind was whipping snow across the road as quickly as the few cars traveling ahead of us could melt the heavy wet drifts. The highway quickly became buried in a sheet of winter's icy blast. The conditions presented a frightening hazard so my concentration was totally focused upon getting through the blizzard safely and arriving at Beardmore intact. Norval thought differently.

"April snow," he laughed, "the Great Creator's trick of spring." And with that, he pulled an ounce of weed from his pocket, stuffed a huge portion of it into a stone pipe he had sculpted in the shape of a penis and began sucking it down. He passed the pipe around. Brian and Wolf, asleep in the back seat, were ignorant of the snow storm but quickly awoke when they smelled the odor of burning weed. Brian toked as deeply as he could and nearly coughed out his lungs on several draws. Wolf imbibed without hesitation—and without problem—but I passed on it because I was trying to negotiate the snow and the dangerous driving conditions.

Within minutes the car filled with smoke—even cracking the windows couldn't clear the smoke—and I started feeling giddy and high. My mind began wandering, my concentration faltered, and every stupid comment that one of my fellow passengers made became hysterically funny. I had gotten a contact high from the smoke that was circulating inside the car and was beginning to relax and enjoy myself more with each snowy curve we rounded. My concentration waned and I began thinking about the beautiful wonderland that was forming around us. Each snowdrift became a wintry palace, each snowflake a spirited dancing messenger from one world to another. I had never looked at snow in quite the same way. It was as though I had freed myself of the irritation that we humans so often associate with nature's resplendence and allowed myself to become a part of the event I could not escape.

I was driving fairly well and was negotiating the curving road and snow drifts with professional acumen and ease as we headed deeper into the snowstorm. We had slowed to about twenty miles per hour because of the snow and ice. I thought I was in complete control of the car as we approached a particularly treacherous stretch of road the locals had christened Dead Man's Run. The wicked curves snaked in one direction, then jutted in ninety-degree angles in the opposite, creating piloting conditions that would challenge even the most experienced professional. The highway twisted from one sudden curve to the next, up a ridge then down the other side, and wound through the countryside like a snake through a garden. The frightening toll of fatal accidents that happened along that stretch of road was designated with white crosses to mark the dead, but in the blizzard the crosses were buried beneath drifts of snow so that the tips of the white crosses protruded above the accumulation, creating an unintentional graveyard of ghostly markers.

As our car slid around one nasty curve we hit a patch of ice and I lost command of the steering wheel. We fishtailed from one side of the road to the other. The automobile began spinning out of control, careening wildly with a life of its own. It happened so quickly that none of us knew what had happened until we spun in three complete circles then smashed into a billowy bank of snow. The rear of the car penetrated the snow embankment nearly up to the handles on the back doors, which left the front of the car sticking out of the embankment and still collecting falling snow on its hood.

There was a stunned moment of silence in the car, followed by the hysterical laughter of four grown men stoned on pot and not seeming to care what had just happened. Norval was laughing the hardest—which was rare for him—and Wolf was so overcome with hysterics that he accidentally leaned on one of the back door handles and it opened, sending him tumbling out into a huge pile of snow.

After calming down a bit, the remaining three of us struggled out of the car to check on Wolf as well as the condition of the car. Exiting the car was a chore in itself, not because of the snow, but because of our intoxicated condition.

Wolf was fine, just wet and cold (and a bit embarrassed), but the car was buried beyond our ability to either drive it out, dig it out, or push it out of the embankment. Otherwise we were all OK—no one had been injured.

We wandered around the car in knee-high snow trying to figure out how to dislodge the car so we could be on our way, but had no idea of what to do. Then it dawned on us that not only was the car stuck, but that the snow was coming down faster and more furiously than earlier, and we couldn't see more than a couple of feet in front of our faces. On top of that, we had no idea where we were! We were somewhere between Winnipeg and Beardmore, but that wasn't much to go on when blinded by snow, freezing cold, and marooned. If we couldn't get the car out of the embankment soon, or get assistance from someone, we were faced with the prospect of trudging back in the direction we had come or forward into the void of mounting snow in search of civilization. We had no idea which way to go, no idea which direction might provide the quickest route to safety since none of us had been keeping track of how far it had been since we had passed the last evidence of life. Our other option—which didn't appeal to any of us—was to stay with the car, hoping that eventually a kind-hearted soul would happen along to provide aid, and either get buried alive in the accumulating snow or freeze to death in what was quickly becoming an arctic wilderness.

We decided that since we hadn't seen another car for at least an hour our best bet would be for two of us to start walking back toward Winnipeg (hopefully not the entire distance), hoping to find a house, a store, a filling station—any refuge from the storm that might afford safety and assistance. The other two would remain with the car in case someone came along and could offer help.

We played the child's game of Rock, Paper, Scissors to determine who would be walking. The two who won the shake-off would remain with the car while the other two would begin hiking. As luck would have it, Norval and I were the victors, which sent Brian and Wolf on their snowy trek. Wolf said nothing, just grunted and began walking, but Brian whimpered and pleaded with Norval to let him remain and send me instead. Thankfully, Norval didn't acquiesce, and within minutes, Brian and Wolf had disappeared out of sight. Norval and I hunkered down in the car for—for how long…we could only guess.

Sometimes events happen for reasons that we can't explain, as though predestined beyond understanding. Such was the case with the accident and with Norval and me winning the game and remaining with the car. Given the conversation that took place as we waited for rescue, I can think of no other explanation.

We had been sitting in silence for about ten minutes when Norval suddenly interrupted the quiet.

"Where did you learn the ancient Prayer of Earth and Sky?" he asked innocuously.

"I already told you, Norval, I just picked it up somewhere; I don't remember."

"That is not the truth, Little Eagle," Norval corrected. "The Prayer of Earth and Sky is an ancient meditation that few Ojibwa even know; no white man has ever heard it. Where did you learn it?" he asked, again.

I debated telling Norval the truth—about Many Tongues, about me, about our joining and about the two of us becoming Companion Travelers—but I hesitated, fearing his jealousy would erupt in another ugly display of anger. Norval couldn't even recognize that Many Tongues was who he really was, and not Bull William the Storyteller, let alone handle the fact that Many Tongues was a powerful shaman and I his learning apprentice and Companion Traveler. On the other hand, my relationship with Norval had disintegrated into a virtual desert of no emotion, and I had come to regard Many Tongues as my closest earthly friend. I wondered why not be honest and let Norval deal with reality as best he could.

"Actually, Norval, I learned the prayer from Many Tongues—the man you call Bull William. We spent a great deal of time together while you were missing and have discovered that we are spiritually connected. We have become Companion Travelers, wandering the cosmos together and yet separately. I have projected into the past to learn the ways of the spirit guides—that is how I learned the prayer," I explained.

Norval sat in silence for a few minutes with his face expressionless and his mind subdued in thought. I watched closely for an outward display of anger or jealousy but could only observe him staring blankly through the front window of the car as though contemplating the falling snow.

"From old Bull William," he finally said.

"No, Norval," I replied sternly, "from Many Tongues. His name is Many Tongues, and he is seventy-one years old, healthy, and not even close to being dead. I am aware of the truth about Bull William and Many Tongues and about the old man found dead in the woods. I'm not going to insist that you accept what I say or ask that you believe it, but you can at least acknowledge the fact that Many Tongues is who he says he is and that he and I have become Companion Travelers."

Then, an amazing change came over Norval. The fire that usually rages in his eyes when confronted with information or situations over which he has no control vanished. His expression softened and his voice became almost melodic. "I accept what you tell me, Little Eagle. I am not certain that I believe what you say, but I do accept that you believe it."

Norval turned and looked me directly in the eyes. "You have not lied to me since the time we first met, Little Eagle, even in the writings in your diary. Your entries about me are not complimentary and I think, perhaps exaggerated, but they are not lies. I am who and what you write: a weary, drunken Indian who can be every bit as nasty and wicked as pleasant and good. If you think I do not know who I am you, are mistaken. But I am a shaman also. I can see and understand things that most people cannot. I can see the past as clearly as the present. I can hear the silent voice of the future as keenly as I hear the deafening din of today. I am the Thunderbird, lost in the nether world for many years, now reborn from dust. I am the Seer of many things you cannot understand."

He continued, "You and I have not become the companions that I had hoped we would. We are of different temperament, different worlds. If you have found comfort in the words and visions of the one you call Many Tongues, then so be it. I am happy for you. It is the unusual man who finds his Companion Traveler. I have not, but if you have, then I am pleased."

I couldn't believe what I was hearing coming from this proud and lonely man. I was nearly moved to tears as he spoke with a candor and honesty I had not previously experienced with Norval. The months of disgust for Norval that had evolved in our relationship eased and I wanted, I needed to let him know how I truly felt about him. He was not the total waste of a person that, many times, I had written about in my journal. I took his hand in mine and spoke as best I could about him and me:

"No, Norval, we have not become what I had hoped for either, but then, how can I say, how can I know what I really expected. When I accepted your offer last December, I was so screwed up, without the slightest bit of understanding of what I wanted for myself, that I had no idea of what I wanted from you or for us. I know that I wanted to get away from Toronto. I wanted to forget everything I could about my childhood. I wanted an adventure. I wanted…I wanted to learn from you."

I could barely continue, my voice cracked with emotion, and the words stuck in my throat as I tried to explain three and a half months of frustration. The conversation was beyond anything I had expected, and I hadn't prepared for what I might say when confronted with such sentiment.

"I don't hate you, Norval, if that's what you think. I could never hate you! As strange as it might sound, I love you in a way that surpasses friendship but falls short of being in love. You are correct when you say we are of different temperament and different worlds, and I don't think our worlds are destined to merge."

Norval grasped my hand more tightly. "Then let us Join, if only momentarily, Little Eagle. Let me see what you see, let me know what you understand. Let me go with you, just this one time, into a place beyond this world into the dreams you create within your own mind."

I hesitated, but figured our Joining—if only temporarily—couldn't hurt. From the first moment I had met Norval, I was struck by his spiritualism, though it was often hidden deeply beneath his worldly scars, and wanted to learn from his experiences, and reap what he had to sow.

"OK," I agreed. "Just this once, Norval."

Outside the snow had stopped falling and the Earth around us was blanketed in ghostly pale. The silence that befriends the snow was deafening as if the whole world had stopped for this one moment in time, when the shaman—the

Thunderbird Spirit—and the newly discovered Companion Traveler would combine energy for one brief moment of eternity.

Norval held my hand tightly, and I his. We gazed into each other's eyes. The Copper Thunderbird began chanting the Prayer of the Earth and Sky, and my voice joined with his. For a fleeting, bittersweet moment, I could feel Norval's energy surge through my body, bathing my spirit with the intensity that was the very essence of that which he was, as mine coursed through his body, swathing his spirit with mine. We had Joined.

We remained Joined for what seemed an eternity, but was, in reality, no more than several minutes. Norval continued holding my hand, squeezing it more tightly as he searched my mind and my spirit for recognition. His body heaved, as though electrified by a powerful current, his face tightened with the emotional pain that is common to Joining, then he slumped in his seat, letting go of my hand.

"What you have told me is true, Little Eagle…what you have told me is true," Norval repeated sadly but with a resurgence of optimism. "You truly are a Companion Traveler and journey among many great and wonderful spirits. You have walked the path of life from the time the stars first illuminated the night and have died a thousand deaths and are reborn. I am pleased."

The remainder of our time in the car—awaiting the rescue we were beginning to think would never happen—was spent in silence. There was not an air of hostility or anger exchanged between us, not even a hint of jealousy or antipathy. We simply sat without speaking. But what I sensed during the Joining with Norval was terrifying. I cannot put name to it nor even begin to identify the depth of the terror I felt, but it was dark, ominous, frightening, and lonely. It was as if I had tapped into Norval's deepest fears—and realities—but could neither see nor feel beyond the walls of isolation he had erected. I almost wished for more time, for a longer Joining, but perhaps it was best we separated when we had. I am not yet practiced in exploring Thought Projection and would not dare challenge emotions and spirits I do not yet understand. Given that for so long Norval and I have been separated by distrust, I am happy with the intimacy we were able to share—if only for a moment. At least Norval now believes me about Many Tongues and does not suspect me of shenanigans beyond what I have confessed.

And I was touched and moved by Norval's candor, because it is the first we have shared, even including our initial meeting. Perhaps now we can continue with the reasons for why we are together, but I suppose, as is the case with all else—only time will tell.

✴✴✴✴✴✴✴✴✴✴✴

MIRACLES DO HAPPEN. THE SNOW had stopped and within a half hour a tow truck happened along—the driver had been returning from having towed a car to a nearby repair shop when the storm hit. He pulled our car out of the embankment—at no charge! Nevertheless, Norval handed the man a hundred-dollar bill, much to the truck owner's surprise and delight, and within a few minutes we had turned the car around in search of Wolf and Brian.

After about sixty minutes of driving back in the direction from where we had come (our journey was much slower, and we covered much less ground than when originally leaving Winnipeg) we came across a small fisherman's ice shanty that had been pulled from a nearby lake because of the approaching spring thaw. There we saw two sets of footprints leading up to the door. Thankfully the prints had not been completely covered over—otherwise no telling how long we might have been searching.

I waited in the car and within a few minutes, Norval emerged with Wolf and Brian trailing behind him. They had seen the shanty, were tired and winded from tramping through the blizzard, and decided to hole up until the storm had passed. Of course, the storm had passed more than an hour earlier, but given that they had smoked another doobie, they were stoned and were not inclined to leave the protection of the shanty. Had we not come along, they probably would have fallen asleep and frozen to death.

With all of us back in the fold, we headed off for Beardmore with no further hindrance. The closer we got to Norval's cabin, the less snow we encountered, until by the time we finally arrived at his place, the ground was greening with the resurrecting touch of spring and not a flake of snow could be seen anywhere. Our unintended adventure was over, and we were dead tired.

Norval's cabin was welcome relief from the day's escapade.

After unloading our bags from the car, Norval lit a fire in the Franklin stove, brewed a pot of tea, and we all relaxed with another round of penis-pipe smoking. Not much was said as we sat around the stove drinking tea and smoking pot—I think we all had had about enough excitement and communication for one day. Within an hour's time, Wolf and Brian had passed out, and Norval and I were left alone.

 Norval said we should sleep, too. We had had more of an adventure than Wolf and Brian would ever know. He gathered bearskin rugs for both of us and told me to sleep wherever I would be most comfortable—with him or by myself. I chose by myself. Before we fell asleep, Norval came to me, took my hand with the same gentleness he had exhibited in the car during our Joining, and softly spoke in my ear.

"Companion Traveler," he whispered, "You are more powerful than you understand. You are still young and have much to learn about the world of the spirits. You will need a guide, someone more powerful and more accomplished than Many Tongues to shepherd you through the ages. We must Join permanently and share the power and the strength we use independently. We must unite as one and travel the path of eternity, together. The spirits have brought us to this awareness for a purpose we do not yet understand. But it is destined by the spirits to be as it is, and it is good."

And then he projected into my mind—a trick I had not yet experienced with Many Tongues. His thoughts sent chills up and down my spine. It could have been the terror, the loneliness, the emptiness that I had sensed in his spirit when we had Joined earlier in the day manifesting itself freely in our newly discovered spiritual connection—I do not know for certain. What I do know is that his thoughts were deadly and frightening beyond any emotion I had previously experienced in my entire life. They resounded with a permanence that made me shudder. I pulled the buffalo rug up around my neck and tried to ward off the loathing of Norval's thoughts as he violated my mind:

"…and you shall not leave me, Little Eagle. I will not let you go. You shall be with me forever."

G

✦✦✦✦✦✦✦✦✦✦✦

JOURNAL ENTRY: 4-17-79

We went into Beardmore this afternoon. I hadn't been to Beardmore when I was at the cabin back in January, so this was my first trip and hopefully my last! There wasn't much to see in Beardmore, just a typical little town mostly of Native population and heritage—not terribly unlike Manitou, North Dakota: Dirty, old, rundown. From Beardmore, we drove to Tansleyville, another small village of Native people and some whites, not far from Beardmore and not much different. Change the signposts and you'd never know you had left one town for the other. Norval wanted to buy some pot, and evidently Tansleyville was the place to go.

When Norval suggested going to Tansleyville, I expressed no objection, realizing that when Norval ran out of marijuana he would rage into one of his terrible moods and get so unbearable that not even the most abominable of hooligans would want to be around him, but mainly because of the thoughts Norval had projected into my mind the night before. I had been mulling over his threat "not to let me go and keep me forever" and didn't want to stir up any unnecessary unpleasantries—I needed time to consider my options. Earlier this morning, I decided that regardless of Norval's thought-threats, I had no intention of remaining with him after returning to Winnipeg.

We arrived at a pool hall/restaurant in Tansleyville where Wolf started sizing up the place to see if he recognized any dealers. After a few minutes he did, so Norval and Wolf began negotiating price, quality, and quantity. As the discussion became more animated, Norval, Wolf, and the dealer went off to another table, leaving Brian and me alone. Soon after that, Brian recognized several friends and took off to join them. I'm not sure how Brian had come to know so many people in Tansleyville (and Beardmore) since he was from a reserve near Winnipeg, but I suspect he has been to both of these towns before, especially considering the surprise Norval expressed upon seeing Brian when the young man came to our apartment in Winnipeg. Norval had asked Brian what he was doing back in Winnipeg, rather than Beardmore. Without having to do a great deal of investigative detective work, I assumed that Brian had (probably) been with Norval at both Beardmore and Tansleyville at some point—possibly in January when I was at the cabin, but I couldn't know for certain since Norval was tight lipped about any thing having to do with his private life.

While I was sitting at the table eating an older Native man came up and asked if he could join me. He said he recognized Norval and assumed that I was a friend of his. Not wanting to be ungracious I invited him to sit and ordered a pitcher of beer.

The old guy introduced himself as Joe and said he had known Norval since Norval was a teenager. He welcomed my purchase of beer, downing a frosty mug in one gulp which loosened him up enough that he began telling stories about Norval that I assume he figured I didn't know. He regaled me with tales about how Norval had become interested in art, how he had been visited by the Thunderbird Spirit, how he had become an internationally recognized artist, and so on. I had heard all of Joe's stories before until his tongue became looser with a second pitcher of ale and he, unknowingly, filled in many of the gaps that had confounded me about Norval.

Old Joe must have assumed that Norval and I were close friends because he incorrectly supposed that whatever he said was information to which I was already privy. I thank the beer for diminishing Joe's hesitation to talk, and I thank Joe for providing me with a great deal of missing information about Norval.

According to Joe, Norval is not as well liked or as well respected as he thinks he is. Joe said that a number of the townspeople—members of the local tribe—were more than disgusted with Norval because he had married an Indian woman named Harriet when they were young, had fathered seven children with her, but failed to provide any support for his wife and children. In fact, Joe claimed that Norval seldom even visited with his family and hadn't seen them probably for at least ten years. That answered part of the question I had had about who Norval had not been visiting the many times he left me alone at the cabin in January—his family—but it didn't answer who he had been with until Joe downed another beer.

"The only family he ever sees," Joe offered, "is his nephew, Brian. I think he's a nephew on Norval's daddy's side."

His nephew! So Norval had been introducing Brian as his nephew to the townsfolk of Beardmore; but why? Who had he hoped to fool? Brian was from a reserve in Winnipeg, so I assumed he could pull of the charade here in Tansleyville. Perhaps it was because Norval was embarrassed about Brian being so young, but then Norval had never been hesitant about revealing his penchant for younger men and his bisexuality was well known, so that didn't seem logical.

"Yep," Joe continued, "Norval takes special care of Brian; says Brian is going to be just as good an artist as he is. I ain't never seen any of the boy's paintings, but Norval sure raves about them. I guess it's been a few years now that they've been hanging around here and in Beardmore. Ain't no place Norval goes without Brian, and no place Brian goes without Norval."

So that was it. Norval had passed Brian off as his nephew because he had been seeing him since Brian was a minor. Even the relaxed customs of the Ojibwa don't accept an adult man involved with a minor—a boy! In most cultures, pedophile relationships are taboo, and the Ojibwa are no different.

Joe's revelations were like solving a mystery; I had finally heard the truth about who Norval had been with the entire time we were supposed to be together at the cabin and only a few days after Norval had hired me as his companion and secretary. I had hardly warmed his bed before he was out screwing around with Brian on the sly. And he didn't have the guts to tell me. But then I guess why should he? He had the best of both worlds: Me home at his cabin, and Brian shacked up somewhere in either Beardmore or Tansleyville, both of us anxiously awaiting Norval's visits. I can't say that I was shocked at this discovery, but I was surprised. Once again I couldn't think how typically 'Norval' the whole incident was.

Old Joe was on a roll, so I ordered another pitcher of beer—thank goodness the transactions between Norval and Wolf and the drug dealer had spilled over into socializing and were taking longer than I had expected. The third pitcher of beer loosened up Joe even more.

"It's good seeing Norval again even if he is a jackass. He's always good for a couple of stories though they's mostly lies," Joe went on, lowering his voice and leaning towards me, as though discussing secrets that others dared not hear. "Guess it's been a few weeks since he was here last."

"A few weeks?" I repeated with interest.

"Yep, been about two weeks. He was here by himself last month. Well, by himself I mean, except for those two guys who'd been going around asking everybody if they'd seen Norval. Guess he was holed up in his place outside of Beardmore. I don't think them guys ever did find him, since old Norval was in and out of here in just a few days." Joe paused, assuming I knew who the two men were and could supply him with a resolution to the story. "Hope they found him; they said it was really important. Do you know if they ever did?"

Norval had been here two weeks ago. The same time he went missing from Winnipeg! Why? What was he doing? For what reason did he hide out in his cabin? Even though Joe was providing information to which I was not privy prior, he was also causing the arousal of more questions.

I was catching on to Joe's conversation quickly and was playing the role of dummy exceptionally well. "No, I don't think they found him. There was a guy looking for Norval back in Winnipeg, but Norval was out both times he came to our apartment, so I don't know what he wanted. Never gave a name either. It could have been one of the men you met. What did they look like?"

"Oh, they seemed nice enough, at least polite, but they were scary looking. Dressed in big city suits—all black and official looking. Always wearing sunglasses too. Both of 'em big white guys, about six feet tall. Not much else to tell, like I said, they was all dressed in black—hats, coats, pants…everything, and they was always wearing them damn sunglasses! Didn't say much, just asked about Norval. They never gave their names either. Don't know who they were or what they wanted." Joe stopped in mid-conversation and fell silent when he spotted an old Indian woman enter the restaurant.

"Joe," she shrieked.

"Gotta go now, the old lady's here." Joe stood up, extended his hand, and turned toward the door. "Nice talking to ya. Tell Norval I said hello, and I hope he finds those guys who was looking for him. They said it was real important!"

"Yeah, thanks, Joe. Nice talking to you too. I'll give him the message. See you around." That was a lie. I hoped I didn't see anyone from Tansleyville around— ever again—but decided being polite was in order since Joe had supplied me with more information than I could have gotten out of Norval in ten years.

Joe disappeared out the door, hoofing it as quickly as he could behind the old woman—his wife, I assume—who was scolding him mercilessly for getting drunk yet again and flicking him on his head with her hand with every step out of the restaurant. I downed the last of the beer and sat waiting for Norval and Wolf or Brian to return, regarding my newly discovered information with pleasure. I finally knew the truth, but more importantly, had something to use against Norval. I figured my plan precisely by the time Norval and Wolf returned about ten minutes later, and it didn't hurt my confidence to be just enough buzzed to become sarcastically bold.

"Did you get the dope?" I asked loudly. Several customers turned and looked in our direction.

Norval and Wolf shot me a "shut up, asshole" look and nodded affirmatively.

"Not just weed," Wolf whispered in my ear, "but some black hash too. Looks like we're going to be partying tonight."

"Fucking great," I over-emphasized, using language I'd rather not speak in public, and employing my most convincing theatrics, "Party tonight—fucking awesome, Wolf."

Both brothers stared at me like I had gone off my rocker. "You drunk?" Norval asked.

"Just a bit," I confessed, "but, damn, who gives a shit, beer is good for the soul. Hey let's find Brian and get the hell out of here. The sooner we're back at the cabin, the sooner we can get as screwed up as we want." I was pouring it on thick. "Where the hell is that nephew of yours, anyway?"

Norval looked stunned at my comment. Wolf looked confused. "Whose nephew?" Wolf asked.

"Norval's, well yours too, I mean—you know, Brian," I added.

"He isn't our nephew," Wolf shot back. "What's got into you? Man, you really are drunk —you know who Brian is. He's been living with us for a month now!"

I acted like I was drunker than I really was and started laughing, uncontrollably and slurring my speech like a drunk who frequents any neighborhood tavern.

"I know that, Wolf-man. I'm just kidding around. Just repeating the things that the two guys said who were here looking for Norval," I lied.

Norval looked even more stunned at my latest revelation. "What two guys?" he asked with concern.

"The two guys who were talking to me when you were scoring the dope," I said looking around as though searching for them. "Guess they left already. I told them I didn't know where you were. Is that all right? You know," I added, purposefully lowering my voice, "one of the guys looked kind of like that jerk who was at the apartment in Winnipeg, but it couldn't be. How would he know we were here?" My thespian dramatics were paying off.

Norval was more concerned than I'd ever seen him—he was terrified! The look on his face was priceless—one of the few times since leaving Toronto that I wished I had brought a camera along.

"Let's find Brian and get going," Norval said suddenly.

"All right," I returned, continuing my act, "Back to the cabin for party time!"

"Back to Winnipeg," Norval corrected.

"Winnipeg!" Wolf and I chorused.

"Winnipeg," Norval repeated, staring at me with a look that was so pathetic, it would have been pitiful had it not been Norval.

"Whatever...," Wolf responded dejectedly.

Winnipeg, I agreed to myself—and freedom!

G

✳✳✳✳✳✳✳✳✳✳✳✳

Journal Entry: 4-18-79

We got back to Winnipeg early this morning. After the show I had put on at the pool hall in Tansleyville, Norval wasted little time in leaving. We rounded up Brian and hit the road as quickly as we could—probably not quickly enough for Norval. All the way home, Norval kept questioning me about the two men who had ostensibly been talking to me. Wanting to continue the charade, I continued lying and pretended that I couldn't remember anything because I had been so drunk. Although he accepted my explanation, he was not pleased. I don't think he figured I was making it up—he seemed far too worried about the make-be-lieve conversation to question its authenticity, and he didn't call into question its veracity. So much for Norval's great shamanism and ability to Mind-Penetrate!

On the one hand, I feel like I've stirred things up for no reason and have upset Norval unnecessarily. Lying is not one of my more natural inclinations, although I must say I pulled it off quite well. On the other hand, given the message he had Thought Projected about never letting me go and considering all the untenable situations Norval had created over the past few months, I have convinced myself that he deserves whatever I can dish out. Regardless, I have not created the situation with the two men—whoever they are. We were visited here twice by who I am assuming is one of the men from Tansleyville, and somebody had been searching for Norval back in Beardmore. Plus, there were the two break-ins, the one at Beardmore and the second one here. Whatever situation Norval has gotten himself into must be serious. I have not known him to disappear as he did several weeks ago or become as agitated as he did in Tansleyville. I have been wondering if I could use Thought-Projection of my own to probe Norval's mind and discover the answers. It's worth a try.

After we returned, Norval decided to move to a new apartment. Just another bit of evidence to suggest his concern about whatever is going on—we're on the lam. He claims that the place we are in is too crowded for the four of us and that he would like a bedroom for just him and me. Curious, the place hasn't been too small for the past month. Brian is not at all happy with the proposed move, especially when Norval added the "a bedroom for Little Eagle and me." For the past few weeks he, and Norval have been spending most of the time together, and I've been the odd man out. Now the roles are being reversed. I'm certain because of Norval's and my Joining, and his belief that my powers are great, he thinks he could benefit from feeding off them. Apparently Norval and I will become bedmates again and Brian will become the odd man out. Anyway, despite what Brian might think about the move, we rented a one-bedroom apartment in a complex four streets further away from the center of the city.

While Norval, Brian, and Wolf were moving belongings to our new quarters, I took the time to clean the apartment we were leaving. The place had not been thoroughly gone over. The mess sickened me; it was like a garbage dump despite my earlier attempts at doling out chores to Wolf and Brian! I hadn't really paid it that much attention. I guess after having lived in squalor for nearly three months, I had become accustomed to the filth and stench.

The kitchen walls were covered with splattered paint—even behind the refrigerator. Dirty plates and utensils were piled in sink, soaking in crusty water that had been left unattended for several days. And the floor was coated with a layer of crud so thick I stuck to it as I walked across the tiles.

The living room was buried under old newspapers, beer bottles, dirty clothing, fast food wrappers, scum-encrusted dishes, pot roaches, cocaine bags, and an assortment of dozens of other non-describable items. I don't know how any of us found a place to sleep with was such a mess everywhere. Wolf usually crashed where ever he had been sitting when he passed out, I normally took either the mattress or a bear skin or buffalo rug, and Norval and Brian cuddled together on a bear skin of their own.

But the worst mess of all was in the bathroom. Even though I had previously ordered Brian to clean the tub, he never did finish the job and had left the room a horrible mess. It looked like a cow had exploded in the tub and all its guts and hide had been splattered throughout: On the walls, on the ceiling, on the floor. The tub was filled with putrid water and cowhides. The sink basin and the mirror were covered with a purple Lady Patricia dye that Norval had been using to color his hair jet black, and the toilet was chipped and scarred with huge gashes from where Norval's sculpting tools had slipped—he had been carving his stone and wooden phallic-pipes in the bathroom using the toilet as support for the stones and wooden blocks out of which they were carved. The toilet seat lid was broken in three pieces and scattered across the floor. In my sobriety, I was struck wondering how any of us had used the toilet or had taken a shower. Actually, Norval and Wolf didn't bathe or shower, and Brian only did so only occasionally. I was the one who suffered most.

All told, the apartment was disgusting. I wasn't about to leave it in that condition for the landlord to see. Even though it was in Norval's name, my pride came into play. If Norval wanted to create the reality that he was a slob, so be it. He could live with embarrassment if he so chose. I decided I did not want to be considered as slovenly.

By late in the evening, the move was complete and Wolf was working Norval to break out the black hash they had purchased in Tansleyville. Norval obliged—we all did some and once again the three of them ended up passing out well within an hour after hot knifing.

I have remained awake planning my escape. I have no intention of remaining here for longer than another week. I have to see Many Tongues again and complete what we have started, but after that—I am out of here!

G

✶✶✶✶✶✶✶✶✶✶✶✶

JOURNAL ENTRY: 4-19-79 [1:30 PM]

Norval's gift for me, which he announced before we had left for Beardmore, arrived today. It was not supposed to be here for another few days but was delivered early. When Norval made me close my eyes and led me outside to the curb, I felt much like a child on Christmas morning—there was a great deal of excitement and anticipation that accompanied the discovery ritual. However, after seeing the gift, my heart sank and all I could say was, "Thanks, it's beautiful."

A brand new, canary yellow Pontiac Firebird sat parked at the curb waiting for someone to take it for a spin. It was a beautiful automobile, complete with all the amenities and comforts money can buy. Norval was probably more thrilled with the gift than I. His face broke into an uncharacteristic grin when we went out to view it, and he immediately dubbed it Eagle Claw and said it was mine to keep, regardless of what transpired between us (as if I'm going to believe that falsity!).

If I do not sound overwhelmed with the gift, it is because I am not; I am underwhelmed. Without question, the car is a generous gift on Norval's part, but I do not trust him. I know he ordered it before we had experienced our Joining on the way to Beardmore, so it isn't a bribe to keep me here, but I realize also that the automobile is just another one of Norval's methods of manipulation to make me beholden to him. As I wrote yesterday, I have no intention of remaining in Winnipeg for much longer, and hope to get Norval Morrisseau out of my life completely, so if he thinks I can be bought with expensive presents he is one hundred percent wrong. As I write, I'm struck by the irony—gifts like the car are exactly the things I had hoped for when I first agreed to Norval's job offer! But now…

I will admit that when I first accepted the position of companion/secretary with Norval, I did so as much to make money as I did for the other reasons I thought legitimate at the time. Without doubt, I must confess that when this experience began, I functioned as little more than a prostitute, willing to sell my services—including my body and my sexuality—to Norval in return for being 'kept' (and the hope for cold, hard cash!). But things have changed since then. I am ashamed of my initial intentions and will not continue my debauchery by accepting gifts of any type. I have accepted the last of what Norval might give and wish that I could return what he has already presented.

It is bad enough that I have become party to the art fraud that Norval seems to take so lightly. It is sufficiently demeaning that I have allowed myself to do the things I have done for Norval in exchange for his occasional gifts of money. It is reprehensible that I have allowed myself to sink to the depths of intemperance that has included my dependency upon alcohol and drugs, just to get through this experience. But there comes a time when even the most contemptible actions must be seen for what they are, and the cumulative effects of indulgence must be regarded for what they portend: Ruinous behavior that destroys, rather than creates! I have come to that point and can no longer humor the darker side of my personality.

I do not like the person I have become. In fact, I consider myself despicable. I am vain, arrogant, conceited, woeful, and spurious. I am quick to criticize Norval for his arrogance, and yet I become the same when I condemn him. I attack Wolf and Brian for their laziness and sloth, and yet I have done little better when I consider the months I have wasted here in central Canada. I chastise all three of my living companions for over-indulging in alcohol and drugs, and yet I drink and smoke nearly as much as they do. And I find myself regarding my own demeanor as somehow superior to those with whom I have lived for the past few months. And yet I am no better than those I denounce when I engage in the haughty conceit I am so quick to embrace.

I am no better and no worse than these men I have come to know so well. I exist as do they, simply trying to find myself, to find my way, and to become the person I know hides deep within.

And so, I reject all that I have become, from the time I first left home to this very minute as I write in my journal. I must purge myself of the conceit. Free myself of the arrogance. Loose myself from the debauchery. Castigate the spurious. Eliminate the treachery. Redeem whatever good might remain.

I have taken my Joining with Many Tongues too lightly. I call him my friend, but I do not return that which he so freely gives to me. He is comforting and wise, gentle and assuring, honest and trustworthy. And I am immature, childish, petty, and demanding. Were Many Tongues here with me now, I would say to this man

I have come to love, "Forgive me, my friend—my Companion Traveler—I am not the man you think I am; I am not worthy of being your friend."

I must see him. I must speak with him. I must allow our friendship to blossom as it should: Full, rich, radiant, and bountiful. It is time I rejected the old, the dispossessed, the wicked, and the vain.

I just hope I am not too late.

G

＊＊＊＊＊＊＊＊＊＊＊＊

JOURNAL ENTRY: 4-19-79 [9:00 PM]

We christened Eagle Claw with a maiden voyage this afternoon. Thank goodness it didn't snow (which seems to be the normal for climatic conditions when ever Norval and I take a road trip). The weather was warm and sunny—a perfect spring day. I must admit that when I got behind the wheel of the Firebird, I felt a sense of excitement and power I have never felt before. Cruising through the streets of Winnipeg, touring the open highways, and watching the faces of strangers turn and gaze as we stopped at every traffic light or parked in front of a convenience store gave me a feeling of snobbery I have seldom known. However, I dare not allow these feelings to take root—no matter how haughty I might feel. I cannot permit my sensory emotions to dissuade the decision I have made.

Naturally, our ride was not taken alone; Brian and Wolf came with us. Wolf, as he is apt to do, appreciated the car for what it is, and nothing more—a car! He seems to be unmoved by material possessions and more impressed with just hanging out. Brian, on the other hand, was contemptuous and petty. He practically drooled all over the car and treated me as though I had been presented with a major honor from Norval. I suppose in some respects Brian is right—an expensive gift like an automobile was an honor Norval bestowed upon few, but was, at the same time, a bribe with the intent to restrain. If Brian said once, he must have said a hundred times how little I had done to deserve the car and how much he could use a vehicle to get back and forth from the reserve when he visited from our place to home. Norval ignored him. I seethed. Wolf just sat in the back seat smoking dope and enjoying the ride. Sometimes I think Wolf has more of a handle on life than I've given him credit for.

We were out for about four hours then returned a little before nine. At the moment, Brian is outside cleaning away the dust that accumulated on the car during our ride—he has taken to treating the car as though it were his—Wolf has crashed on the living room sofa, Norval is sketching several canvases (no doubt preparing for another round of Morrisseau frauds), and I sit writing in my journal. In some respects, it has been one of the more eventful days that I have experienced since being here in Winnipeg. In other respects, it has been nothing more than typical: Screwing around, blowing off the day, getting stoned, and ending the day by passing out, rather than going to sleep—a distinction that has great merit when you think about it. The only difference between our normal routine and today was that we carried out the normal in an automobile.

I am thinking of Many Tongues, I am thinking of Joanne, I am thinking of Bernie and Raymond—the four people who have always demonstrated compassion and understanding. I am thinking about wanting to see Many Tongues at least one more time before I leave. And I am thinking about how good it will be to get the hell out of here and back to Joanne.

I must implement my plan of escape very soon; there is no time to spare—the headaches from Norval's attempt to Through Project are becoming too often and are incredibly painful.

G

❈❈❈❈❈❈❈❈❈❈❈

JOURNAL ENTRY: 3-20-79 [12:30 AM]

Norval spoke with me this early this afternoon before going about his business. His message was simple and direct. I was writing a letter to Joanne, which he interrupted, but which I was able to disguise as a journal entry, when he grabbed the pen from my hand, ripped my diary from the table and waved it above his head shouting obscenities and carrying on like a madman. His change in mood from earlier in the day was as dramatic and as diametric as the snowstorm that had hit on our way to Beardmore. His first order of business was the automobile.

"The car is yours, Little Eagle," he commanded, "but not to do with it as you please. You may not take the car without my permission; you cannot use it alone. One of us—Wolf, Brian, or me must be with you at all times. I am watching you, closely because I suspect that you want to leave, and the car provides the means by which you could do so. But you will not leave; you are not free to go. As you must know from my Thought Projection, your place is here with me and you will remain here for as long as our dreams continue to combine as one. I will watch you at all times, at least until I am confident that I can trust you again. Think of this as your prison, if you will, but understand this is for your own good, for your own protection. You are not strong enough to survive without me. I have searched your connection with the dream world and I have seen your powers weakened by your thoughts. Little Eagle, you are not sufficiently prepared."

Norval's words were harrowing. He was making me a prisoner—a kidnapping of my mind and my body against their will. He had become aware of my intention to leave, most likely through his Through Projection into my mind, and had slammed shut the only door I had for escape—the automobile. I hadn't seriously considered stealing a gift of that expense, but he feared that through Thought Projection, I could conform his thoughts and dreams to my benefit, fool him, and take off with the automobile. Now he was attaching the shackles of torment that he hoped would bind me to him permanently.

Many Tongues had warned me that once a Joining has been completed the minds of the two become susceptible to Thought Projections from other sources, be they treacherous or trustworthy. I should have been more careful about guarding passage into my own thoughts, but I had not had the opportunity to explore the process further with Many Tongues and was now paying the price for my naïveté and inability to prevent access into my mind. Norval had demonstrated that he was able to penetrate my thoughts with the message he had planted in my mind three days days ago on our way Beardmore, and if he could do that, then, indeed, I was his prisoner—if not physically, then surely through his control of my thoughts. My hopes for escape had been severely damaged, and I was left with little course of action other than to accept, at least temporarily, that which I could not change, at least not without Many Tongues' help.

Like the Wraith from Hell that he was quickly becoming, Norval continued his purge:

"As for your journal, complete what you will tonight. I will read what you have written in the morning and if I do not find it objectionable, I will save your writings for you. I will keep them safe and out of danger—no telling into what wrong hands they might fall if you are not careful. I do not want you to continue writing; I have had enough of your nastiness and foul words against me. This is all I have to say."

Into what wrong hands could my journal fall? I thought to myself. Unless Norval was concerned about the suspicious visitors we had had or the two men searching for him at Tansleyville. Perhaps my writings revealed more than I thought! Once again, Norval's words and actions made him suspect of being involved with something nefarious. Regardless, I had no intention of ceasing my journal entries; I would write secretly—only when Norval was asleep and certainly not when either Wolf of Brian could see me.

Now all seems lost. I will be unable to visit with Many Tongues, if indeed Norval intends to watch me as closely as he claims, and yet I cannot help think that there is always a solution to a seemingly unsolvable situation. I must use my intelligence and cunning. My physical escape is not a concern because I could simply walk out while Norval is asleep and be done with this charade that began in January. What is at stake is not being held against my will—over that I have some control—rather, my concern is with the spiritual. If Norval can project into my thoughts and dreams, I will never be free of him or his influence, no matter how far away from him I am until I am able to penetrate his thoughts and counter his projection into my thoughts with those of my own and use them against him. But I fear I will not be able to penetrate Norval's mind—let alone anyone else's—without the tutelage and guidance of Many Tongues.

Now I must plan for what seems the impossible, which will take some doing given that I will be unable to visit with Many Tongues and do not understand how to use Thought Projection to my benefit. But my task is not impossible. Norval might think that his ability to Thought Project is more powerful than mine—and indeed it might be at this point. But he forgets how easily he succumbs to the temptations of alcohol and drugs, which will cloud his mind and make it more difficult for him to control my thoughts and easier for me to penetrate his. His arrogance is not as ironclad as he might think.

G

****

Joanne,

I am coming home. Exactly when, I do not know, but rest assured it will not be long—certainly within the next few weeks.

When I return, you will find that I have changed. I am a different man—not the same Gilbert you last saw back in December. My journey over the past four months has taken me in directions I never would have imagined just a few months ago. I have sunk into the depths of despair and desolation, I have embraced the legerdemain of debauchery, and I have adopted the ways of the diminished and the vanquished. And yet, just as the Phoenix of legend, I now resurrect from my decaying ashes and regain the person who I once was. When, again we meet, we shall do so as equals, not as the disparate friends that we were for too long.

And yet, as I prepare to leave, I do so with a great deal of trepidation.

Norval has made me a prisoner of thought and has erected a barrier through which he is confident I cannot escape, but his confidence is temporary. Still, I am frightened. Frightened that somehow, some way, Norval will find me after I have gone—he has his ways and his cunning through the spiritualism he professes and through many contacts who I am certain will do his bidding at the slightest command! I fear that, somehow, once I have left, he will find me and take me back to either that godforsaken run-down shack in Beardmore, or worse, spirit me away to a desolate part of the northern wilderness that he knows so well. He would be content to keep me drugged and drunk so that I do not know who I am, where I am, or what he might be doing to me.

I know it sounds insane; everyone thinks that because Norval is an artist of world renown, that he wouldn't do anything stupid or rash or illegal! Don't kid yourself. Norval can get so out of control on dope and booze that I wouldn't put anything past him: Not abduction, not kidnapping, not even murder! I am frightened. When you get this letter, take it to Jack Pollock. He will know what to do.

I have good reason to believe that Norval is somehow

involved with the mob (despite his protestations otherwise), and if he is—if the mob does own him, as I
suspect—then they own everything and everyone around
him as well. I am convinced that both Norval and the
mob have goons in Winnipeg, connections in Toronto, and
friends all over the place who will enact their charge
without hesitation, so I am certain that he—or they—
could do what ever they want to me, when ever they want.

Of course, it is possible that I have little to fear
from Norval once I have escaped. His weakness for alcohol and drugs is so overpowering that he forgets
things quickly. Without question, he is an artist of
great genius, I do not doubt that he is the shaman he
claims to be, and I know he honestly believes that the
Thunderbird Spirit has visited him. But he is also a
drunken, drug-addicted loser whose obsessive personality provides him the need to possess passionately, hate
strongly, and remember forever. I can only hope that
soon after my departure he will forget about his beautiful Eagle Spirit—or as he calls me, Little Eagle—who
once graced the cover of *Maclean's* and who, if only for
a few months, served as the inspiration for much of his
glorious work. Actually, I do not think it will take
him long to forget—his dependence on chemicals and his
own problems (which are evidently severe) will take
care of that for me—besides, he has already recruited
another "companion" (Brian Maye) who more readily and
subserviently attends to the needs of the great Norval.

I am not certain when you will receive this letter—I
must sneak it away for mailing when I can. Many Tongues
is no longer able to assist since we have been separated
by distance and by the spiritual abduction engineered
by Norval. It is possible I will beat this letter home,
but if not, get it to Jack as soon as possible.

Well, enough for now—Norval has passed out, but I trust
him even less when he sleeps. I fear he can hear and
see while in dream, but of that I am not certain. Do
not worry about me; I have resources beyond those of
which I have spoken and about which you will learn very
shortly, so my escape is imminent, my return to your
security is soon.

I still love you as much as ever, if not more. Be ready
and expect a knock upon your door at any time—it will
be me.

Gilbert

✴✴✴✴✴✴✴✴✴✴✴✴

I had the same crazy, disturbing river dream again last night. It was as vivid and as real as the first one, but even as it began, my subconscious seemed to sense something different would happen in this incarnation.

Just as in the first dream, I was swimming down a dark, lonely river—everything was black and frightening. The same twisted, gnarled trees lined the banks of the cold river with their limbs hanging low into the water, ready to capture any creature that swam close to their grasp. I swam desperately, trying my best to keep near the center of the river, catching the current that helped ensure my slow progress down stream.

It seemed like I had been swimming for hours when, once again, I came upon the same Edenesque garden that suddenly presented itself near the end of one of the longest stretches of dank, harrowing water. This time, I hesitated, treading water to keep my place. Surprisingly, the current had stopped as though encouraging me to swim to the shore where the garden with its splay of beautiful foliage swept to the river's edge. My hesitation did not last long, remembering the last time I took refuge in the garden only to have it suddenly change from a calm, peaceful place of rest with friendly faces beckoning me to join them into slimy, disgusting creatures that lunged at me, chasing me back into the water. I wasn't about to repeat that same mistake.

But how could I remember such events? How could I recall the garden oasis and the friendly faces that turned into hideous creatures that wanted to somehow harm me? This was a dream. Dreams are uncontrollable. Dreams take their own course of action and plot. Dreams are in our heads, our minds, and our subconscious. I am fully aware how my mind could have recreated the same sequence of events, down to the last detail, but how could I intervene and change the fantasy of the dream? No matter, I ignored the inviting garden, ceased treading water, and began swimming again. The current picked up—quite quickly and with tremendous force—and began sweeping me downstream. My ability to swim had been rendered useless, and I was swirled around like a bobber on the end of a fishing line. My body was pulled down into the dark abyss of the river, tossed back up to the surface, sucked under again, then hurled a great distance downstream. I cascaded through rapids with sharp boulders that ripped at my skin and slammed me against downed branches jammed into the rocks like spears waiting to impale any creature that dared challenge their supremacy.

Finally, the rapids and the current relented, and I passed into a more tranquil section of the river—still dark, black, cold, and threatening—but somehow a bit calmer, a tad less horrific. The shore was still lined with thorny trees that protected the banks from any unwanted visitors. And yet, I felt more composed as the current relented, the rapids disappeared, and I found myself swimming again, rather than being carried by the inexorable flow of an angry body of water.

I took advantage of this respite and floated, allowing the river to gently guide me down stream to…to wherever my destination was to be.

As I floated—temporarily taking advantage of my less distressing experience—I head a faint voice calling my name: "Old Young One, I am here."

If it were possible (and in a dream it surely is) I stopped swimming and bobbed up and down in the middle of the river, not moving, not going forward or backward—not doing anything except staying in place, as though anchored to the river's bottom.

The voice in my head grew louder, "Mandamin, I am here."

"My Companion Traveller, I am here with you—and you with me," the voice spoke.

"Many Tongues," I shouted. "Old Young One," I began screaming. "Is that you? My friend, my Companion Traveler?"

There was no response.

I shouted again and again and again: "Many Tongues, please answer. I am lost. I am weary. I am frightened. I am nearing the path to death's door. Please answer my call."

Still nothing, and I began to fear that it wasn't Many Tongues, but Norval who was Though Penetrating my mind. I shuddered, praying (yes, praying—something I hadn't done since I was an innocent Child late at night in the comfort of my bed).

"Many Tongues, Old Young One, if this voice is yours, please make it known to me," I cried.

And he did.

"Yes, Mandamin, it is my voice speaking with you in your dream. Can you hear me? Can you recognize that I am not the font of your worst fear? Do you not recognize the sound that has comforted your angst for these past few months?"

"Yes, yes, yes, Many Tongues," I cried, "I do know it is you; I do know your voice and the comfort you bring. Help me. Save me. Please! I cannot control this dream as I had hoped I could. The river is long. Dark. Black. Threatening. Damning. I know it will pull me to my grave. To an early death that I do not want nor for which I am ready."

"No, Mandamin. The river is not your enemy. It springs from the same Earth from which you sprang. It flows from the highest mountain to the far away sea. It carries you in peace and with great compassion, but your mind has been poisoned by the darkness that has overcome Norval. His wickedness has polluted the river. It is not dark and loathsome. It is not as you sense in this dream. You must resist his influence. You must reject his dominion over you. You must think upon our several conversations and free yourself from bondage."

Easier said than done, I thought to myself. Were it that simple I would have shaken myself from this dream already and taken to the sweet slumber of sleep rather than the terror of this nightmare.

"But how, Many Tongues? How do I release myself from Norval's oppression? How do I free myself from this pitiless river? This vile dream?" I implored.

"By believing in that about which we spoke during our last meeting during the beginning of our Joining. By believing, new Old Young One, by believing. You have settled in to the depths of your deepest despair. You have become lost within a dream world that does not exist. You have called to me, and I have come. Our Joining will be complete when you believe."

"But I thought our Joining was done. I thought it had been completed when last we met?" I wondered aloud. "And now you tell me it will only be complete when I believe! I do believe," I cried aloud. "How much longer must I wait to feel your total presence within me? How many more meetings must we have? And I did not call you. Your voice came to me as a faint whisper of hope."

"Ah, my dear friend and Companion Traveler, you did call to me. As you were being swept down river, through the rapids and jagged spears that threatened to claim your body for themselves, you called—with the eye of your mind. With the essence of your spirit and your soul. With the hope that I might appear and save you from this terror. Mandamin—you did call!

"Do not be afraid. The Joining will be complete when you believe. We shall walk the paths of this world—and others—as one, as Companion Travelers. But you must believe!"

At once I lost my composure and my temper: "Damn it, Many Tongues. How long must I wait? Why have you tricked me?"

Many Tongues' voice was gentle, soft, calming like a mother singing a lullaby to her child: "This is your last trial, Mandamin. Every human who becomes one with the Old Young One must show their worth. You have proved to me that you want to believe, but you do not yet. You were raised Christian, so I am certain that you know the old teachings that tell us that we humans create our own Hell on Earth. This is your Hell, my Companion Traveler. Now you must not only want to believe but also create within your mind the reality of belief and of faith. You must accept that we are one, that you are part of an experience much larger than yourself. You must not cower like the child afraid of the night or of the dark river! You must not cave to your fear of being alone on this Earth, for you are not. You must take this dream into which you have brought me and be done with it. I cannot finish this dream for you. I did not dispel the rat in your last nightmare. You did, my friend. And now, you have reached the last of your tribulations and must cast away all doubt and fear and simply, believe."

I cannot explain how that which happened next, actually happened. I cannot put logic to the mystical. I cannot pretend to know how or why or what caused my escape, but suddenly I was tossed ashore into the warmth of a fresh garden with a beautiful sun shinning above and a gentle breeze tickling at my skin. But no, not tossed like a child might cast aside a toy, but rather gently lifted from the dark, forlorn, dreadful river and set upon the shore surrounded by flowering foliage and woodland creatures that gathered around as though welcoming me home. Home—but where home was, I still did not know.

As I sat on the banks of my newly discovered garden a sudden rush that felt like electricity raced through my body. Up one side, down the other, continuing over and over until after several minutes at last it ceased and I was left trembling with physical exhaustion and emotional confusion. Thoughts of Many Tongues, Norval, and the Old Young One swirled in my mind like the bewildering thoughts of a man barely clinging to sanity. I felt as though I was being tossed about in a clothes dryer and purged of my turmoil. I was at once transported from the nightmare of terror to a dreamscape that was lush with comfort, an indescribable sense of safety, and unmitigated pleasure. The horror of the dark river subsided. The fear that had been my constant companion while swimming the river abated. The confusion of where I was and who I was and why I was ceased. Unexpectedly, I began to fade and felt the security of sleep embrace me in a blanket of protection. I fell into deep slumber.

For how long I slept within my dream, I do not know. I do know that when I awakened I felt a surge of autonomy overcome my entirety. A reclaimed sense of self pervaded my essence. I had been loosed from the dream's hellish nightmare and was free! I was at long last free of the Dark River. Despite not knowing what had happened to change the terror I had been experiencing I am grateful for its intervention although I did not how or why such a transformation could have happened.

But, allow me to rewrite: I do know how and why. I had subconsciously called for my dear friend Many Tongues and he had responded. He had come back into my life at the very moment I was certain my essence was being exhausted. He had saved me from the Dark River Dream (as I have come to call it) and simply told me to believe, and when I did believe, the Joining would be complete.

And Believe, I did. From the depths of my mind—and my soul—I embraced Many Tongue's countenance and words as though we had been sitting across from one another in his small, untidy apartment and quite simply—BELIEVED. I do not know from where my courage came. I do not understand how I was able to summon the strength to enact the deed of believing, but somehow I began embracing the quintessence of belief more readily, more perfectly, more completely. I believed in Many Tongues. I believed in our Joining. I believed that we were Companion Travelers. And I believed in me. I could feel my heart warming. I sensed my resolve strengthen. I knew I had achieved that for which I had been searching. I was saved. The Joining had been completed!

I know that the Dark River Dream shall not disturb my sleep again. I am convinced that Many Tongues and I—the older and the younger Old Young Ones—have been joined. And I hope that Norval Morrisseau no longer has power over me whether it be in our everyday lives or in his pathetic attempt to control me by his Thought Penetration.

I believed and my faith has set me free. I believed and I was saved from the horror of the dark endless River. I believed and I had regained a sense of myself. G

★★★★★★★★★★★★

Another night passed without the Dark River Dream. Despite my new-found courage and confidence, I still fear that the dream might emerge again in my subconscious although, in truth, I am convinced that it will not. I believe that Many Tongues and I have completed our Joining and I am now another—a new Old young One and have hopefully purged the evil of Norval from controlling my mind.

Although I know that our joining has been completed and that I am the new Old Young One, I am not certain what that means or portends. Many Tongues had told me on several occasions that as the Old Young One, he had been living throughout the entire history of humankind. He explained that he had been called by the names of dozens of gods and goddesses throughout history. He said it had been his charge to attend to humans and keep them from extinction. But what of me? Am I now the same spirit that he has been? Is it now my task to guide humankind through its trials and travails? Am I to live, and wander, and be as wistful as he has been? I am still weak and too easily tempted by the inane. I do not possess the strength that Many Tongues does. How can I—a miserable, pitiful, childish human—begin to guide humankind throughout our future? How can I even begin to protect us from our own extinction? I shudder at such possibilities. I don't know what I am supposed to do. I don't understand what all of this means. Will the answers come simply because I have learned to believe? Am I suddenly to become enlightened?

And what becomes of Many Tongues, the "old, Old Young One" as he once called himself. Will he continue? Will he live as he has? Is he soon to die and escape the prison of his human form?

So many questions—so many that I am overwhelmed. These are questions I cannot answer. Questions that plague my thoughts. Questions that keep me bound as human in body but spirit in thought.

I do not know what I am supposed to do next—there isn't an owner's manual for this sort of thing. So many events have happened that have comforted me. So many happenings have taken place that have enlightened me. And, yet, I am more confused than ever. Perhaps I have scuttled the childish apprehensions of my twisted life and settled the disorder that followed me from my youth through my young adulthood in Toronto, to my chaos in Beardmore, and finally to the revelation here in Winnipeg. But the answers to who I am, what I am supposed to do, and how I am supposed to live with this new reality—evade me.

Many Tongues, I call for you once more to enter my thoughts. I need you now as much as I ever did before. The belief I professed two nights ago is weakening already. Surely I freed myself from the Dark River Dream—or at least so

I hope—but the strength I felt that night has ebbed and I wonder if truly I do believe.

G

****

JOURNAL ENTRY: APRIL 26, 1979 (1:30 AM)

The past two days have been uneventful, our new apartment looks different, but is not different in terms of the habits of its tenants. Norval, Brian, and Wolf continue their drunken, drug induced debauchery, but I have refrained by telling Norval that I have been feeling a bit under the weather and would like to regain my physical senses before indulging in any psychoactive drugs or drink. In truth, I find the overindulgence in drugs and alcohol irrelevant to my rebirth. Norval has reluctantly accepted my contrived excuse, though he scoffs at what weaklings we white boys must be. At this point I could care less about what he thinks about us white boys or me in particular.

Norval has relented and is permitting me out of the apartment without supervision. I imagine he figures I can't make much of an escape without either the car or money but I am not certain that he cannot penetrate my thoughts, which would allow him control over my actions. He must believe he is able to invade my mind or he would not permit me to wander free. Is my freedom to leave the apartment a positive or is that freedom tempered by Norval's mind manipulation? At some point I must find out.

It sickens me that whenever I return from my sojourns away from the apartment, I return to a literal mess of bear and buffalo hides scattered about, Norval crashed naked on the floor, and Brian parading around the place like the Victor of Stalingrad. In fact, to make matters even more bizarre, I once returned and Brian was sporting a three-inch by five-inch Canadian flag from his erect flagpole. How absurd and childish, but he takes special pleasure in knowing that Norval is fucking him, rather than me. So be it. I have no desire to challenge his amorous ways with the Wicked One!

Norval has no idea that I have now stashed away over $3800, and as far as the car is concerned, I would rather not drive his tainted gift, especially since I have to be accompanied by him, Wolf, or Brian. Some gift. Actually, I wouldn't mind taking a spin around town and out into the country with Wolf. He bears me no ill will and is somewhat of a pleasant companion. Over the past few weeks, Wolf and I have come to a strained but accommodating alliance. He keeps his mouth shut, except of course when it is filled with a pipe of weed or a joint, and I know how to entertain him. All one need do is talk about pussy (no, not the kind that meows) and the type of woman I think would be a successful conquest for him. Not that anything of the sort has never happened. I haven't played matchmaker for Wolf and, truthfully, I don't think he gives a rat's ass about scoring with the ladies. He is always going on about all of the women he has bedded in his lifetime, but since I first met him, I am unaware of any women with whom he has been intimate. I am convinced that Wolf is one of those "all talk and no action" kind of men. Certainly, I suppose, on any of his many trips away from the apartment on his own he could have scored with one of the town's more available strumpets, but I doubt very much that he has. First, he is usually on a foray running errands for Norval and most likely wouldn't have the time (although I'm sure he is one of the "fastest guns" in Ontario), and second, what poor damsel—whore or not—would stoop to the dishonor of savoring Wolf's less-than-clean manhood? Ugh, I can't even imagine. She would have to be completely desperate to initiate a physical joining with poor Wolf.

Given the quiet solitude of the last few days, I think it is time for me to pay another in-person visit to my freshly anointed Companion Traveler, Many Tongues, and discover the answers that have plagued me since the night of the culminating Dark River Dream. I have a few schemes worked out that could get me out of the apartment. I can only visit during the daytime, but that is of little concern. I'm sure Many Tongues would welcome my visit at any time of day. I have resolved to see him sometime in the next two days. After all, I feel the time is quickly approaching when I shall make a clean break and exit my prison, leave Winnipeg and return to Toronto. I absolutely have to have the final answers to this mystery of the Old Young One.

If I have freed myself of Norval's ability to Mind-Penetrate I have nothing keeping me here. Not his mind control, not his money (I have saved enough, although not the amount that Jack had initially suggested back in December) and certainly not feelings for Norval any longer—not as artist, not as genius, not as shaman. Put frankly: I detest him.

Although I sill harbor bad feelings about my participation in our foursome art fraud, I am willing to take responsibility for my participation: Be it legal or simply personal.

I shall see Many Tongues soon, explain my necessity for escape, and finally once and for all get the answers I seek concerning what I am supposed to do as the new Old Young One. Then I shall return to Joanne. I intend to initiate my final acts as Norval's Travelling Secretary/Companion before the week's end.

And yet, much to my chagrin, I still feel the pain of Norval's mind penetration every night as I attempt to fall asleep. His manipulation becomes stronger, more powerful, more invasive. I am torn between believing that my Joining with Many Tongues has freed me from Norval's Penetration or has continued my imprisonment.

G

****

Journal Entry: April 26 (4:18 AM)

Something violent shook me awake at an ungodly hour of the morning. It was horribly painful and felt as though a sharpened spike was stabbing deep into my skull. I felt a hot piercing needle rip through my head and settle into the depths of my brain. My entire body reeled as the unseen drill bored through bone. I became nauseous and trembled as sweat poured down my brow, soaking my evening shirt and whetting my terror. At once I heard the commanding sound of an evil voice attempting to penetrate.

"Little Eagle, it is your master. It has taken me longer than I had expected but I am close to success. I have come to claim what is mine," Norval's voice ordered. "Relent and permit me passage. It will be easier. It will be less agonizing. I demand that we join as one."

The discomfort was relentless. I had never before experienced excruciating physical agony as I did on this morning. But even through the distress I sat straight up on the bearskin hide and took immediate notice of the absurdity of Norval's importuning.

"Relent... permit passage...it will be easier...less agonizing"? His words might have been frightening and threatening, but so too were they incongruous. Without understanding the difference between fertility and impotence the great shaman and supposed Companion Traveler had tipped his hand, revealing his weakness. If Norval truly did have control over my mind and could penetrate without trouble or difficulty, why did he have to ask permission? At that instant I realized that I was the one with the power. Norval did not have the spiritual ability to Mind Penetrate. He could not invade my most private recesses without me allowing access. Immediately I seized the opportunity and scuttled him away.

"Get out and don't try your shenanigans again," I ordered. "Begone, you charlatan...you pretender...you vile imposter. The ancient mariner might have mistakenly slayed what he thought was his demon, but I know mine and order that you break from my mind immediately. I do not have time to indulge your pitiful attempt to initiate control. I have no patience for your inadequacy. Be gone. You have been slain!" With those words I summoned all the strength I could gather and cast Norval from my mind once and for all. And it was curiously simple: All I had to do was erect an impenetrable barrier around my mind with life affirming thoughts. I remembered Many Tongues explaining that the Old Young One existed only as the essence of goodness, not as the font of evil. I focused on all that I regarded as good and pictured my brain being surrounded by a wall of virtue. Within a few minutes my thoughts were protected, my mind was secured and Norval's pitiful attempt to control me had been rebuffed.

The shriek of Norval's voice as his thoughts exploded in defeat reverberated through my skull. It was not unlike the sound of a thwarted banshee when sundered from its prey. In an instant he was gone...overpowered. I had not only survived his pathetic attempt at Mind Penetration but realized that he could not control and keep me as his minion, his captive, his companion slave. I was now the conqueror and he my vanquished. I held the power. He had nothing.

The experience of having someone attempt unsolicited Mind Penetration is painful and unnerving, but I had prevailed. I was relieved that I had dispensed with both the unbearable pain and the tormenting fear that Norval could keep me controlled as his prisoner—at least through Mind Penetration. Norval's thoughts had been crushed, never again to disturb my sleep, or my life.

At last I could comfortably and securely fall asleep.

G

✱✱✱✱✱✱✱✱✱✱✱✱

Journal Entry: April 27, 1979

Since two days ago and my early morning experience of casting out Norval from my thoughts, I have noticed that he not only avoids conversation with me, but hurries away whenever we come into close contact. Obviously this new behavior does not bother me, not at all. In fact it has been a relief not to worry about him possessing me as his mind hostage every time I see him. It also keeps his despicable self away from me. Now I am free to focus on my physical escape. And it brings me great joy to watch Norval scurry away from me like a child afraid of his own shadow. Truly, the bogus shaman has been rendered impotent!

I have spent the last two and a half days deciding which of my schemes I should implement to get out of the apartment to visit with Many Tongues. I settled on the one I believe to be perfect.

Norval mentioned early yesterday that he wanted to close out his bank accounts in Winnipeg and head back to Beardmore—again!—but this time venturing nowhere near Tansleyville. How fortunate that ever since my lie about the two men searching for him in Tansleyville, Norval is now frightened to venture outside for longer than five minutes. What a great set-up. With Norval immobilized, who better than me to me initiate the withdrawal of his funds and the closure of his accounts. Given his new fear of being away from the apartment, he arranged the necessary papers for me to be his Financial Power of Attorney which means I can legally execute any banking deposits or withdrawals in his name without suspicion or complication. However, I surmised that my visit with Many Tongues might take longer than the amount of time necessary for closing his bank accounts, so I added to my list of errands supposedly snooping about the immediate area for signs of Volpe's thugs.

"To check things out to make sure our sinister visitors aren't lurking about," I told Norval. That would add the time I needed to make the withdrawal of his funds and to visit Many Tongues. He welcomed my deceit; of course not knowing it was deceit.

I must initiate my scheme as soon as possible. I dare not tease Norval with my newly discovered authority for long. He is a clever man and will undoubtedly think of a way to counter his loss of Mind Penetration. Even though I am convinced that he no longer believes that he can control my thoughts I am a bit surprised that he is allowing me to go about town on my own. I think it is because he has become so intimidated by the possibility of being abducted—or worse—by Volpe's thugs that he is willing to chance me walking off.

After we had finalized the plan to close his accounts and check out the neighborhood for Volpe's men Norval seemed pleased that I had taken it upon myself to complete the tasks for him. "Astute thinking, Little Eagle. You turn out to be more than just a good fuck," he simply said upon approving my scheme. Poor

Norval. He has become so frightened of what might happen to him that he lacks the bullying factor that for so long has been his calling card. He has become a sniveling child-like ghost of himself. I couldn't be more delighted!

Without hesitation I was out the door, down the one flight of stairs, and headed to the first bank before Norval could change his mind as he is often apt to do. I completed the transactions at the bank without hitch although the vice-president of the institution was not necessarily happy with closing an account that had accumulated over $38,000. He reluctantly wrote me a check for the amount; I secured it in my wallet and was off. No huffing, no puffing, no blowing anyone's house down. Of course, I have to admit that for a moment or two I considered pocketing the check, going to the bus station, and heading out of town without guilt or recrimination. But, I did owe allegiance to Many Tongues—my friend and Companion Traveler—and couldn't bring myself to steal away without at least saying goodbye. Besides, I cannot and would not forge Norval's name. Attempting such an act would be nothing more than foolish. Furthermore, I had no intention of adding grand theft to my list of crimes— art fraud is quite enough. Besides, I do have my ethics, though they have been strained throughout the past four months.

I decided to go to Many Tongues' apartment before visiting the other two banks. It was conveniently located on the way to the second bank. Within a half hour, I was at the steps of the building where Many Tongues had been residing. I climbed the steps to his apartment, knocked on the door, but was met with silence. I knocked again, then again, and finally was pounding on the door and calling his name. It was unusual for Many Tongues not to be home since he rarely went out anywhere other than by way of dream travelling, and by this time of day, he would be up and about. Unless...

Several minutes passed with me pounding on his door and calling for him to answer, when a stranger came up the flight of steps, stopped and inquired as to whom I was hoping to find in an empty apartment. It was the landlord who had heard my disturbance and had come up to see what was going on.

I was as polite as possible: "I'm looking for a friend of mine. An older Native gentleman named Many Tongues who has been living here for over a year" (I really didn't know how long Many Tongues had been residing in this particular apartment but took a wild guess).

The landlord looked baffled. "An old Indian guy, huh?" he asked. "Goes by Many Tongues?"

"Yes," I simply replied.

"How old a guy?" he asked.

I'm not sure why that mattered when I had already described my friend as 'an older gentleman,' but answered anyway. "He's in his early seventies but looks older."

"Nope," the landlord responded. "Hasn't been any one of that description living here. In fact, this apartment has been empty for well over six months.

Don't know why, but I can't rent it out on a permanent basis. Whenever I get a sucker to take it, they're gone in a week or two. All of 'em."

Empty for six months! I was dumbfounded. And a number of people had leased the place then had moved out soon after renting it. None of this made any sense.

For a moment the idea flashed through my mind that perhaps Many Tongues had assumed the visage of different people and had come and gone on a regular basis. But I quickly dismissed that because first, Many Tongues had never revealed to me that he had any powers of shape-shifting or taking on the appearance of other people. And second, I had visited him here twice, and his place was obviously well lived in—no signs of simple temporary accommodations. Surely he didn't—couldn't—pack and unpack all his personal belongings so quickly or so often: Clothing, candles, religious artifacts, the rock he held so precious, and the humble furniture that he had told me had been his since he had been a young man. I wasn't sure what to do. I knew I had the right apartment.

"Sir," I asked in my most apologetic manner, "are you certain that no one lives here? I was just visiting my friend just a couple of weeks ago in this building at this apartment."

His patience was wearing thin. "Look kid, I'm not stupid—I'm not an idiot. I've owned this building for seven years now, and I'll tell you again: hasn't been any old Indian man living here in the past six months, not ever for that matter! Now get on out of here and quit bothering me with your dumb questions. You've made a mistake; probably got the buildings mixed up. All these places look the same. Check your address again. Now on with you."

So on with me it was, with my head spinning and wondering again what the heck was going on? Why was it that every time I get a chance to take control, some issue rears its ugly head and slams my plans to the ground? What was going on now? Where was Many Tongues? What about the unlived-in apartment? Was I imagining all of this just in an attempt to free myself from Norval's grip?

Again I considered the check from the bank. Should I dare try and cash it and get the hell out of Dodge? No! As I wrote earlier, I couldn't legally cash the check and even if I could I would undoubtedly end up being caught, arrested, tossed into jail and charged with stealing thirty-eight thousand dollars from the great Norval Morrisseau. Not a good idea. I wouldn't stand a chance of getting by with such an act. Norval would be so furious he wouldn't come to my rescue. Plus, more importantly, such a crime was in complete conflict with my own sense of morality.

I wandered back to our godforsaken place in a depressed haze where, undoubtedly, Norval and Brian would be fucking away and Wolf would be passed out on the floor from over-doping and drinking.

Damn! I cursed to myself. What the fuck is going on? Where was Many Tongues? Why was his apartment empty? Why had he apparently never even lived there? And…

...had there ever truly been an old Native man called Many Tongues?

G

✦✦✦✦✦✦✦✦✦✦✦✦

Several more nights have passed without the Dark River Dream, and for that I am grateful. And yet, I am confused by my complete lack of understanding concerning my Companion Traveler, Many Tongues.

Attempting to visit him at his apartment and finding that no one of his description had ever inhabited the place disturbed me greatly. Even with the experience of our Joining after the final Dark River Dream I now find myself having no more understanding of who Many Tongues is, or if indeed he truly exists. Had everything to do with Many Tongues been little more than creations in my own mind to keep myself sane? The Joining that had begun at his apartment and had been completed during the Dark River Dream seemed so distant and mystifying. That is probably the best word I can come up with to describe my experiences with Many Tongues—mystifying!

Despite my confusion concerning Many Tongues, I was forced to temporarily abandon concerns about my Companion Traveler and turn my attention to the situation with Norval.

I had to implement my plan of escape that would once and for all free me from this counterfeit shaman. It seemed easy enough to simply grab the keys to the car, take my stash of $3800, and split. But Norval kept the keys to the car in the pocket of the filthy jeans he wore day after day. He only changed his clothes once every few weeks and I didn't want to wait for another cycle of grime to be completed. Nor did I have any desire to rummage through Norval's smelly pants while still on his body.

I could try to overpower him and take the keys, but that was absurd. How could I possibly overpower a man considerably larger than me and how would I even begin a scuffle that would result in me being able to flee with the keys anyway? We had little interaction since the incident two nights ago other than when Wolf, Brian, and I were toking up with him. The thought of three against one, even if the three were completely wrecked on drugs, did not portend success. Brian and Wolf certainly wouldn't join my incursion against Norval but rather come to his aid. Brian was pathetically enamored with Norval, and Wolf was like a puppy dog that dared not leave its mama. The idea of physically overpowering Norval made no sense whatsoever, so I quickly abandoned that idiotic scheme.

There was only one possibility for escape: Another lie in order to get the car keys from Norval and go from there! But what deceit could I initiate this time?

Then it came to me. Ingenious! I had already closed Norval's bank accounts and had checked out the immediate area for any sign of Volpe's hoodlums. But there was still the entire town to scour, making certain that none of the hoods were hanging about. I could tell Norval that I would cruise the town looking for any sign of them. I would be virtually unnoticed. Surely, they wouldn't expect to see me driving about in a brand new canary yellow Firebird. I was sure Norval would agree to my plan given that he was incredibly frightened of these men and their head honcho Jacques Volpe.

Ah, but the chink in the plan.

Norval's instructions about me using the car required that either Wolf or Brian be with me whenever I took the auto. But chinks can be straightened. Regardless which of the two would accompany me, I could, with little trouble, dump him off—trick him into leaving the car and then put pedal to the metal and be gone.

If Wolf accompanied me, I would suggest we stop at a local watering hole for a couple of beers and a shot or two of his favorite Tequila, get him drunk, wait until he had to urinate and when he went to the men's room—off I would be. Wolf is a sure thing for alcohol, so tricking him into having a few drinks would be no trouble at all. Wolf would just as soon drink and party as he would breathe.

If it were Brian who would accompany me—no problem either. He was as amenable to seducing a cute young stud as Wolf was to drinking himself into oblivion. I would conveniently drive through the gay section of Winnipeg, innocently drool over a few hot numbers and let him take it from there. Of course it would have to be on the sly, since Brian was so enamored with Norval that any dalliance would have to be a secret. I would have to promise Brian that I would not reveal his debauchery to his honey back at the apartment. Brian was so sexually weak that he would easily fall into my trap.

Feeling quite pleased with myself, I put the plan into motion that evening.

After dinner, I brought up the subject of Jacques Volpe, wondering aloud who this man was and why he was so hot on the tail of Norval.

At first, Norval roared his disapproval of me even mentioning Volpe's name, but when I suggested my idea of cruising about town in search of Volpe's companions to make sure they had left Winnipeg, his interest became keener.

"But," he reminded me, "if they were still in town wouldn't they recognize you and become suspicious if you began asking about my whereabouts?"

"Not at all," I reasoned. "It had been several weeks since they had seen me, so they probably wouldn't even recognize me. Plus, the last thing they would expect to see would be me driving around in a new model Firebird. Besides, I was not the target of their search. If I were recognized, I could elaborate on the lie I had already told them about you ditching me. I was hunting you down because you owed me money." Norval liked the idea and agreed that I would be able to collect as much information about whether or not they were still around town or if they had any nefarious plans ready for action.

"Not bad, Little Eagle," Norval crowed, "not bad at all. I think you have come up with the perfect plan. You see this is why I hired you as my secretary in the fist place. You are cunning, intelligent, and filled with just enough trickery. I have trained you well."

How ironic, I thought to myself. Indeed, I am filled with trickery and you, great Thunderbird, shall experience it tomorrow. Believe me, you have taught me better than you think. But do not credit yourself too much since my trickery has evolved more from my own experiences than it has your tutelage. Like the fly and the spider, soon you shall be ensnared in my web.

"Remember, Little Eagle, Wolf or Brian must go with you. You might be as smart as a whip, but I can't trust you alone with the car."

"I am well aware of your rules, Norval," I responded with a fair amount of faked disgust. "Just pick the one that pleases you. I have nothing up my sleeves— see," I said, rolling up the sleeves on my shirt and smiling with the grin that on the first night we met had melted Norval's heart.

"Brian shall accompany you. Wolf has to run an errand for me tomorrow. We're just about out of both weed and coke, and he has already made arrangements with his connection."

"Then Brian it is," I cooed. I glanced at Brian who looked dejected, knowing that our trips out together were generally marred with me lecturing him about being careful with Norval. But tomorrow would be different. I would be jovial and light and easily manipulate him into a fucking frenzy with one of the hot cuties in Fag Town, Winnipeg.

G

PART FIVE

Escape, Freedom, and Beyond

(April 30 – May 17)

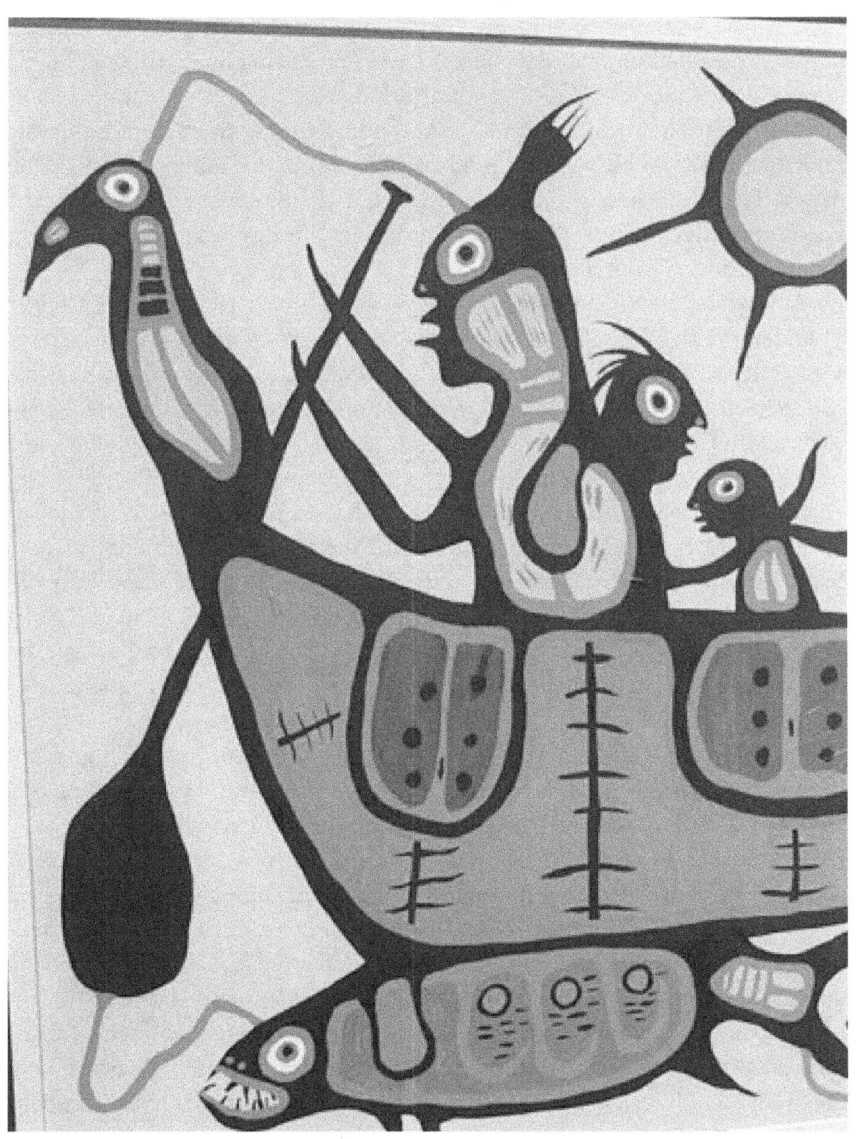

I am free!

It is just after sunrise as I write. I awoke quite early this morning and for the first time in months arose with a sense of hope. Spring seems to have finally chased the snow from the fields as it initiates the anticipated re-awakening of the landscape. A splay of crocus spread their radiant hue across the valley and sleeping dandelions begin appearing everywhere, readying to launch a complementary display of color. It is a cool morning. The sky is blue with only a hint of cumulus clouds dotting the horizon. A playful breeze teases my at my flesh as I sit beneath a towering White Pine and scribble in my journal. I listen to the soothing sounds of Purple Martins and Pine Warblers as a pair of Broad-winged Hawks circle ever closer to the Earth in search of an early morning meal. Everything reminds me of those cherished summer days back at our cabin during my childhood. I don't know if it's the promise of resurgent warmth that encourages my enthusiasm or the new reality into which I am eager to settle. Regardless, I embrace this day remembering the Bible verse my mother had taught me so long ago: "This is the day the Lord has made; rejoice and be glad in it." I am rejoicing, I am glad...but I can't say with certainty whether the Lord made this day or whether my recent experiences have culminated in this glory.

At long last, the shadow of Norval Morrisseau—international artist, Copper Thunderbird, shaman, and fraud—has passed into recent memory. I enacted my plan yesterday morning and took to the road, speeding as fast as I could, while still remaining legal, and fled four months of mind-numbing decadence. I traveled as far as a half tank of gas would take me and took refuge in a godforsaken fleabag motel some two hundred miles from Winnipeg and from Norval!

My plan played out far more easily than I had expected. After Wolf had left on his drug-buying mission, Norval handed me the keys to the Pontiac, gave Brian last-minute instructions not to let me out of his sight, and we were off, ostensibly, to drive about town searching for any sign of Volpe's men.

At first Brian was his normally whiny self. He complained about having to be with me and bitched for ten minutes about how Norval was not as passionate or as interested in him as he had once been. He droned on and on about how horny he was, how he couldn't even pass a few hours without springing a boner and having to masturbate, and how desperate he was to get laid. He was falling into my trap without a hitch and without any prompting from me. Perfect!

Rather than heading directly into the downtown area to begin our pretend game of I spy, I drove to a restaurant that led us through the section of Winnipeg commonly referred to as Fag Town. When Brian questioned the detour, I pretended ignorance about the route and casually diverted his attention by talking up the idea of sex and getting laid. I piled it on heavy, using sex-laden terms that I knew would bring him to excitement—and desperation. I commented that I was just as horny as he was and that the idea of a hot young stud always brought me to elation. Of course I also added that I dared not engaged in such lascivious activity because I had had a slight bout of stomach upset that morning and didn't want to spread any possible virus among the unsuspecting. I feigned sympathy for him and suggested there just might be a younger guy looking to give a quick head job or take it up the ass, so why not take advantage of the opportunity. It was just the two of us, and I reminded him that Norval had lost complete interest in me as well. I told him that I felt for him and knew how uncomfortable it could be to be as randy as a fox but have no where to deposit one's essence. For a moment or two he stared at me like I had lost my mind: what was I doing, suggesting that he pick up one of the hungry twinks in Fag Town? I play-acted being horny by rubbing my crotch and smiling wickedly (knowing he wouldn't even consider me as an option). My god, he was pathetic. He grabbed his package, winked and smiled at me, and howled with delight.

Brian was worse than a ten-year-old at an amusement park. All he could utter as we headed up the main drag of Fag Town was, "I'm getting laid…I'm getting laid…I'm getting laid." He squealed like a piglet in a mud bath and wondered aloud how long it might take to find a treasure to satiate his desire. Then his childish abandon turned to complete seriousness and he cried, "You'd better not say anything to Norval, or I'll make you so sorry that you'll beg for mercy as I whoop your ass!"

"Nothing to worry about," I answered. "Why would I tell Norval when he'd bash me for letting you out of the car and taking leave of me?" He agreed my point was valid and accepted my prompting by returning to his chant of "I'm getting laid."

I didn't even have to enact the part of my plan wherein I would point out possible conquests. When we stopped at a red light before we had even traversed a third of Fag Town, Brian spotted a potential victim and flagged down the boy. The kid couldn't have been any older than sixteen or seventeen, and Brian was ready for the assault. His engorged penis was already protruding from his jeans fly, and he ordered me to pull over.

After a short exchange between the two men (Men? That hardly described those two hungry jacks!) and the boy eyeing Brian's hard-on with anticipation, Brian told me to give him a half hour or so, park in the empty lot we had just passed, and wait. He'd be done and ready to go on with the rest of our tour before I knew it, but before he left the car, he asked if we could come back this way for another go-around on our way home.

"Damn, you are a hungry little fucker," I joked. "Two tricks in one day? Sure, why not? We can drive back this way. Norval will never be the wiser."

With my assurance of both waiting for his first conquest and a return engagement on the way back to the apartment, Brain was out of the car and disappeared into an alley between two buildings. How romantic, I thought, such a beautiful spot for making love. But then, Brian was getting his rocks off, not making love, and I could have cared less, anyway. I was about to drive away a liberated man.

And it worked. Brain got his long overdue piece of ass, and I ended up in a shit-hole motel room—crummy as it might be—freed from the agony of my 'winter of discontent.'

As for my concern that Norval might yet have control over my mind through Penetration, I have dismissed my worry knowing that the power I had exerted in expelling him from my mind was all consuming. At least to the point of frightening him away in the physical which would likely keep him away in the spiritual.

The only fly in the ointment was Many Tongues. I hadn't had the opportunity to see him again before I enacted my escape. His disappearance, or rather the possibility that he was nothing more than an escape fantasy in my four months of hell with Norval, bothered me. But I was at a loss concerning what to do about the unnerving situation. I had tried to visit but he had vanished into thin air. I couldn't help but continue wondering whether there had actually ever been a Many Tongues—or was he and everything that had taken place involving him nothing more than fantasy?

I am so elated with my newfound freedom that I have dismissed Norval's invasion of my mind with what I hope is not childish caprice. And I have written off Many Tongues' existence as little more than a way to retain sanity amidst chaos. I hope that someday I will know the truth about the dream I called Many Tongues but resolved to not let his mystery conflict my escape—and my freedom.

G

★★★★★★★★★★★★

APRIL 30, 1979
Joanne:

Just a brief note, my friend. I am on my way home! I am finally free of Norval's insanity; however, I have decided to meander about this part of Canada before returning to Toronto. Don't worry, I am taking this time simply to decompress from the past several months and to regain my sense of humanity. This time spent with Norval Morrisseau has taken its toll, and I want to become myself again—rather, make that I want to regain the better self that has evolved since last I was in Toronto. I have already become twice the person I was when I left several months ago.

I will try and keep you informed about my whereabouts and what is going on, but I do want to be alone—there hasn't been much of that in the past couple of months. I must regain an understanding of what I want to do once I return to Toronto and whether or not I want to remain there. At this point I am fed up with the art world and want nothing to do with it any longer. I need serious change in my life. It is time I escaped the tumult that has shadowed me since I first left home as a young man. I must now go forward as Gilbert Petén, not the sniveling man-child I was in Toronto. I am confident. I am secure. I am a new person.

Again, do not worry. I am fine. I am physically healthy. And I know that my mental health will bury the horror of these past several months once I am completely free of Morrisseau.

Gilbert

❋❋❋❋❋❋❋❋❋❋❋

JOURNAL ENTRY: MAY 3, 1979

I have done little but drive through the wilderness of Canada, taking in the beauty of this wonderful country, meditating, and taking refuge in a couple of less than desirable motels. I have been trying to contact Many Tongues through Thought Projection but so far to no avail. I wonder about him, who he truly was (or is!), why he came to me the way he did, why he did not project to others as he did to me, and why there was no evidence of him living in the apartment in Winnipeg.

I wonder too about Norval, Wolf, and Brian. What happened when Brian finished his Fag Town fuck, what happened when he returned home to Norval without me? What did he tell Norval? How did Norval react? Did Wolf achieve his drug-finding goal when he left that morning? And what is happening with those three losers now? Not that I really care, but after having been in their presence, sharing so many nasty experiences, I cannot help but be a bit curious. And yet, I couldn't care less about Brian. He exemplified everything unfavorable about a gay man and did nothing more than perpetuate the negative images most people have about us queers. I could care less about Norval, except hoping that he gets his due one of these days for his art forgery and fraud, his deceitful shamanism, and his shameful insistence that he is the reincarnation of the Thunderbird Spirit. I hope I never see that man again, unless it is at his funeral! OK, I don't wish him dead. That's a bit much—a spurious desire that I would not wish upon anyone—not even the man who tried to screw me up more than I already was.

Actually, the only one of the three for whom I have any feelings is Wolf. Even though he was little more than a drunkard and drugged-out stereotype of a Native, he at least had a sense of humility and a modicum of humanity that far exceeded anything displayed by Norval or Brian. There were times when Wolf and I actually got along fairly well, although there were many more when he simply existed as Wolf, the younger brother of Norval Morrisseau—without opinion, without his own thoughts, without his own sense of identity. Still, of the three, I wish the best for him. Perhaps someday he can shake himself free of Norval and begin living a life of his own. I hope that for him.

I still have to figure out what to do with the car. I did abscond with it, but I have no intention of keeping it. I think I will drop it off at a police station in one the small towns around this way—late at night when no one might see me doing as much. I will leave a note on the driver's seat concerning who it belongs to and where he is. Then I'll bus back to Toronto and be done with anything having to do with Norval Morrisseau. I don't know if that will release me from criminal intent but I seriously doubt that Norval would press any charges given his current situation.

I intend to take another week of simply driving about this part of Canada before returning to Toronto. I still have to figure out what I want to do when I return home—if I can call Toronto my home—and I have to try at least once more to contact Many Tongues. That is essential. But, it is growing late and I tire more easily than I have in quite a while, probably because I am finally relaxed and liberated.

G

✦✦✦✦✦✦✦✦✦✦✦

Journal Entry: May 5, 1979

At breakfast this morning, in a greasy spoon dive somewhere in the middle of the Canadian wilderness, I picked up a local newspaper and was drawn to the headline half way down the front page:

MORRISSEAU MISSING, AGAIN

Shenanigans Suspected

I stared at the headline with interest as a number of possible reasons for his disappearance raced through my mind. Had he been approached by Volpe's hoodlums again, then fled? Had they kidnapped him? Was this just another one of his pranks to draw attention to himself? Was he going back home to attend to family matters? Was this a stunt to sell more "original" Morrisseau paintings—after all, he claimed to need money (despite having bundles of it stashed in various banks all around Canada). And why had this disappearance made the media? Unfortunately, the article revealed nothing more than what I already knew about Norval.

According to the article Norval Morrisseau, famous Canadian Ojibway artist, had disappeared on May 1, 1979 as reported to the police by a man named Wolf, who claimed to be his brother, and by a young unnamed companion (Brian?). The article went on to report that there had been rumors of art forgery involving Morrisseau and several of his students in Winnipeg, and that he was believed to be heavily in debt to the Canadian mob (Jacques Volpe?). Other than those simple speculations there was little of consequence or information other than the comment that it had been well documented that Morrisseau frequently went missing after drifting across the county, periodically returning to Northern Ontario.

The article did mention Norval being known as a shaman who played his position for all it was worth. It continued that he often sold his paintings for alcohol or drugs but was, nevertheless, regarded as a mythic figure in the Canadian art world. All in all, the article didn't seem to take the disappearance seriously and evidently reported it only because Norval was so well known. It was written by the 'white' media, so I had to filter the article and read only for the facts.

The part of the article that attracted my interest was the passage that explained that Norval had been reported to the police as going missing by a man named Wolf and by the young unnamed companion. I wondered: Could they have reported his disappearance because he was kidnapped? Could they have reported it because they had been threatened? Could they have reported it because Norval had disappeared only after Volpe's thugs had come looking for him again? Or, could they have reported it thinking it had something to do with my disappearance? I quickly dismissed that possibility because there was no mention in the article about another person who had been in their company and who had also gone missing, nor was there any mention of me by name, appearance, or anything that might identify me as part of their foursome! Still, other than the fact that Norval's disappearance warranted coverage in a local small town newspaper, I chalked up his going missing to simply being—Norval. He had done this before while I was in his employ and nothing about the article seemed new, unusual, or surprising to me.

How convenient, I thought. *Dropping off the car at a police station would just add more intrigue to Norval going missing. That seals it: The car is just as good as on its way to a cop house.*

I finished my coffee and headed for the door ready to continue on my journey but ready, also, to put an end to my several months with Norval. I couldn't help but think about the Copper Thunderbird throughout the rest of the day, however. And my thoughts kept returning to having no concern about his disappearance. No sympathy for his situation. No empathy for him whatsoever. All I could ingest about Norval Morrisseau without gagging or vomiting was thinking: "So, the Copper Thunderbird, mystic shaman, and famous Ojibway artist was missing yet again. Honestly, I couldn't care less."

G

＊＊＊＊＊＊＊＊＊＊＊

JOURNAL ENTRY: MAY 5, 1979

I think I've lost my mind.

I am tired of it all. I am sick and tired of everything. In my recent letter to Joanne, I made it sound like I had finally gotten 'it' all together, but evidently I have not. I've been driving around central Canada for several days now and I just want to go home. I'm not even sure what 'it' means anymore. Is 'it' my immediate circumstances? My future? My mental health? My life-way?

I am tired of central Canada—in fact I am tired of Canada in general. I am tired of thinking about Norval Morrisseau. I am tired of thinking about Wolf. I am tired of thinking about Brian. And I am completely tired of thinking about Norval going missing. I am tired of these past few months. I am tired of the art fraud and hoodlums chasing after us. I am tired of the inconsistencies with Many Tongues. I am tired of Norval's fake shamanism. I am tired of intrigue and mystery. I am tired of it all.

I've been rereading a number of my journal entries and realize that they sound so absurd, but more than absurd they sound pathetic, childish, and... well...crazy. I write as though I have had control over everything that has happened in my life—and yet I have not. I write as though I can slough off the unexplainable—and yet I cannot. I write with a certainty of confusion. I write with abandon. I write with train-of-consciousness thinking. I write with a tenor that suggests insanity.

I feel like Dorothy from the *Wizard of Oz*: I just want to go home.

But where is home anymore?

G

✦✦✦✦✦✦✦✦✦✦✦

JOURNAL ENTRY: MAY 6, 1979 (3:32 AM)

It's the same night as when I started this entry or rather it's the next day—quite early. We tend to think of a day to early morning continuum as the same night rolled up into one singular passage of time, and in a way, it is the same night because it is the continuation of whatever one was involved with at the beginning of that passage of time, but not actually. If I were out partying I would consider 11:59 PM and 12:01 AM all part of the same night. Were I to be home alone watching the TV or listening to music the same would apply. However, ending one day at 10:49 PM and returning to what seems as the same period of time after jolting awake at 2:53 AM, is in actuality beginning a new day, a new quantifiable passage of time—not the same night. We humans are so hung up on time. I am as connected, confounded, and contemptuous of time as philosophers have been. The only difference between the great philosophers and me is that they have education, a degree, and experience to legitimize their musings. I have only my ignorance with which to defend my rambling.

Good god, my words are not quite the catalyst for intellectual thought but it's how I'm thinking right now. I am tired of it all. And that hasn't changed since I made my first entry last night at 10:35 PM. Now, after rereading my entry I suddenly realize how many times I used the word "night." I should know better than to be so repetitious with language. If I remember anything from the one creative writing class I took in school, it is from Mr. Borrows 9:30 AM composition and language class.

"Don't repeat yourself," he would bellow. "Whether it be in thought or action or language—don't repeat yourself. There is little worse in literature than a writer who is repetitive; it is banal and tedious. One who repeats himself is a languid fool with an embarrassing lack of command of the language—SO DO

NOT DO IT! When I read your next free writing assignment, anyone with one single repetition will receive a failing grade."

I got an 'A' on the assignment and, obviously, I didn't repeat one word throughout the entire writing (with the natural exception of conjunctions and articles, which I think is forgivable!).

I hated Mr. Borrows, even though he was a great teacher and an excellent writing mentor. I hated him because he was a queer—like me—and was too frightened to come out of the closet. He was the physical realization of what I was and I didn't like seeing myself in a mirror of disgust. Of course, in retrospect I can't blame him for not jumping head over feet out of the closet. Back then he would have lost his job instantly and wouldn't be hired at any other educational institution, anywhere, ever. I didn't give his situation that much credence or thought back then—when I was only sixteen and desperately wanting to share my sin of homosexuality with someone who would understand. I urgently needed someone to look up to—a role model, a hero. But it couldn't be Mr. Borrows since he was a closet case and since his reflection revealed the hidden truth about myself that I hated so much.

Every kid in school knew he was effeminate and overly dramatic about even the smallest of irritations. Every kid in school knew he trekked off to other cities to find a quick blowjob or a cumbersome lay. Every kid in school knew he constantly checked out the hottest seventeen-year-old studs. Every kid in school knew he was queer. How was it that the entire student population at Saint Francis had figured out Mr. Borrows' little secret, but the powers that be apparently were ignorant to the fact? How could the administration be so lame? How could they not know? Or was there some sort of shared silence about anyone who hid behind a different façade. Perhaps it was a type of "I'll keep quiet about you if you do the same about me." After all, the physical education coach was a drunk and took several shots of Hot Damn between every class. Our French teacher was thrice divorced and was fucking a girl twenty-five years younger than he was. Our math teacher had once been caught trying to shoplift a candy bar from the drug store—one inconsequential candy bar! What a boorish idiot. And yet, even though we all knew about our teachers' idiosyncrasies, no one in administration ever paid the slightest attention to the teachers' transgressions or exerted any type of punishment—let alone enacted any morals charges, thankfully.

In truth, I hated Mr. Borrows because he was me.

I suppose in retrospect it wasn't a very good reason to hate the man. After all, he hadn't done anything to offend or irritate me; it was simply because I suffered at the hands of all the boys in school and had been tagged the 'fairy boy,' 'queer Petén,' and 'homo-suck-em off' (that last one was at least a bit clever). I was alone and had no one to whom to turn. So, given that we all knew Mr. Borrows was homosexual (the word gay wasn't used much back then), he became my target of disgust and hatred. And making fun of him was the one thing I could do that made me part of the group—I could be the same as the other boys. Interestingly, many of the boys at school participated in some form of queering around, and the loudest of those who condemned Mr. Borrows were the ones who partook in the most numerous liaisons with other boys. It seems that reality can often swirl too close to home. "Me thinks thou dost protest too much."

What made me hate myself as much as being queer was the fact that I laughed at and told nasty jokes about Mr. Borrows just to be part of the group that detested me. The more I repeated the vicious rumors about him I realized that I was secretly telling them about myself. Every condemnation aimed at Mr. Borrows was bouncing off him and hitting me. Every time I spoke ill of the man, I was in truth speaking ill of myself. The self-hatred that I kept hidden deep inside spilled out onto Mr. Borrows but ultimately flooded over onto me.

Back then, I was convinced that Mr. Borrows hated me as much as I did him because he would always take a fancy to the cute sexy boys who took no shame in displaying their jeans-protected erections as they paraded up and down the aisles of his classroom. He didn't seem to realize that they were purposefully taunting him and making fun of his sexuality. Or maybe he did understand their jaundiced humor; he just didn't care since he was witness to the teasing treats that welled beneath their trousers. After all, he got to enjoy the display for which he longed.

Mr. Borrows favored them with shorter assignments, better grades, and extra point totals at the end of each grading period. They weren't stupid. They knew on which side to butter their bread. But, he totally ignored me, and it wasn't like I was a wretched hunchback! I don't know why he had such a disliking for me. Perhaps it was because I was his reflection just as he had been mine! Regardless, our mutual disrespect for one another continued throughout my years at Saint Francis and on the evening of my escape from that hated school our stand-off relationship came to a head (pardon the bad pun). My drunken parents hosted a graduation party for me at our house to which several of my teachers had been invited, including Mr. Borrows. It was then that he acquiesced and showed me favor. He propositioned me in a clumsy but provocative manner.

I was outside on the patio finishing a glass of wine when he came up from behind me, placed his hands on my butt, slowly ran them around to my crotch and gave a hard squeeze to my penis.

"And so your journey at Saint Francis has come to an end and you have graduated into the world of grown-ups and adult passion," he awkwardly slurred as he downed his fourth Vodka Sour. "You are looking well tonight, young man," he moaned. My god he sounded like a female bitch in heat. "Indeed, you are looking more than well—I would venture to say that you are looking quite pluckable."

"Pluckable?" I thought, how old fashioned and weird, but all I heard was "fuckable" and whirled around, grabbed his crotch, and naively, embarrassingly, and with all abandon replied:

"And you look tempting as well, Mr. Borrows. Take me. Fuck me. Fuck me with all you've got. I've waited for this all year." I couldn't believe what I was saying, but several glasses of Shiraz and a growing erection emboldened my response and desire.

I don't think he expected such a quick and definite reply to his importuning but accepted my positive rejoinder to his comment with a big smile and what turned out to be a bigger dick.

He yielded. I yielded. We both yielded. And for the next month of that summer we continued our illicit, secretive affair—I was still only seventeen and illegal. It didn't matter where we did it (well, of course it mattered. We tried to maintain some sense of decorum about our boffing). We did it in my room when my mom was away or passed out. We did it at his apartment. We did it in the woods behind the school. We did it on the football field early one morning—just to spite Saint Francis Academy. We did it in the backseat of his car. We did it beneath the falls in Flowing Creek. We did it beside the dumpsters at the burger stop, and we did it several other places that now I can't remember. We did it right up until he resigned from Saint Francis Academy and moved to Quebec City without a word to me about his plans. My heart was broken even though our relationship had been nothing but physical. Well, my heart wasn't broken as much as my need for sex had been disrupted! My libidinous needs came to a crashing halt.

The one thing that really pissed me off about him resigning and leaving town so quickly was that he didn't say goodbye. I heard the news from a friend during a casual conversation. That jerk? He didn't even allow me a final fuck!

But, he took absence and I was left alone again, with our secret in my memory and only my right hand to comfort me for the rest of the summer.

I don't know what got me off on this tangent, other than the fact that I am sick of everything—especially thinking back upon the humiliating sex with Norval—and being sick of everything made me remember the last time I had had a sexual encounter that was spontaneous, somewhat equal and—fun! I sometimes wonder what ever became of Mr. Borrows. Did he finally come out? Did he find love? Did he partner or marry? Or did he merely repeat his clumsy advances to boys twenty-some years his junior? Unless we should run into one another at a high school reunion, which is highly unlikely since I have no desire go back or to relive those terrible times, I shall never know.

But now it is late again, and I should get some sleep since tomorrow I head back to Toronto. I have decided to abandon the Pontiac at the local police station with a note indicating ownership and bus my way back home. I don't know what to expect when I get there. I don't know what I'll do to shake these past few months from my mind. I don't know what kind of employment for which to search in order to support myself. I don't know how long I intend to remain in Toronto. And when I do leave that city, I don't know to where I will go.

What I do know is that I am sick and tired of everything and want to go home.

G

✸✸✸✸✸✸✸✸✸✸✸✸

JOURNAL ENTRY: MAY 6, 1979 (5:20 AM)

I generally don't awaken this early but something, another dream?—shook me into consciousness. This wasn't a continuation of the kitchen dream. I had dispensed with that a while ago. And this wasn't a reprisal or sequel to the Dark Waters Dream. Many Tongues had secured an end to that fiasco. No, this was a dream that answered the questions I have been mulling over in my head about my Companion Traveler—the Old Young One—my friend Many Tongues.

He came to me as though we were sitting across from one another in his apartment or at least what I thought was his apartment. Since he evidently had never lived there, I'm not sure where we truly were in this dream. And I'm not sure it was even a dream, although it was most definitely Many Tongues.

"Mandamin," I heard him whisper, "it is your friend and Companion, Many Tongues. You are lost and in need of direction."

I was dumbfounded and hesitant. "Who?" I asked. "Many Tongues, is that really you? But where have you been? I have been calling to you and Thought Penetrating for several days now. I went to your apartment but was told you had never lived there. I have conjured you in my dreams to no avail. Why do you come to me now? Why when I am leaving for Toronto—for home—this morning?"

"That is why I come to you now," he answered. "I come because you are leaving and returning to your home, far away from who and what and why you are. I am coming to implore you to stay with me, so we can travel eternity together. I am coming to you to save your spirit from forever ruin."

"Stop," I shouted in the dream. "You deserted me when I was at my most vulnerable. You left me alone to wander in the wilderness—alone, filled with doubt, fearful of being exposed by Norval or Wolf or Brian. When I became certain that I had lost my mind, you still did not come to save me and help me from my own insanity," I cried.

"But I am here now," Many Tongues shot back. "I am here in the darkest hour of your need. I am here to save your spirit and to answer your questions. Be calm, Mandamin: Still your fears. Quiet your doubts. Embrace my return. I am here."

At that point I had no choice but to accept that Many Tongues had returned and was with me, where ever we were. I will ask the questions for which I want answers and he will provide them, or I shall divorce him from my life and never think of him again.

"All right, Many Tongues, let's get on with it. I do have a number of questions to ask."

"Then do so, my child, ask them."

My child! I railed to myself. Many Tongues had never referred to me as a 'child' before. My anger at his absence for so long was now being compounded by his apparent disrespect for me.

"I am not a child," I shouted. "I am a grown man who has suffered the most humiliating, frightening, and embarrassing several months of his life. Do not call me child."

"Forgive me, Gilbert" (He called me by my Christian name for only the second time during our friendship). "Forgive me, but you are a child and have yet to enter the manhood of your existence. You have experienced humiliation from Norval. You have been rightfully frightened by the men who have followed you since your first encounter at the cabin near Beardmore. You have become embarrassed by the fraud, the deception, and the depravity of not only Norval but also Wolf and from Brian—though Brian's part in this tragedy is miniscule. And yet, you are still a child. Do not question my authority in this matter. Accede to my will and question only those matters over which I have control. I do not control your life-way. I do not control your whims or your pleasures. I only control that over which we both are participants—that of being Old Young Ones and Companion Travelers. Indeed, you are still a child; otherwise why would you have so many questions to ask? If you are not still a child why could you not answer the questions for yourself? Why have you anxiously awaited my return if you have entered your manhood?"

"Fine," I responded. "I acquiesce to your authority and will accept, for your benefit, that I am still a child. And, yes, I do have questions for which I want answers."

"Then ask," Many Tongues quietly whispered.

I took several minutes to collect my thoughts and decide which of the many questions I wanted answered first. My hesitation obviously provoked Many Tongues as he suddenly blurted out, "Enough time, Companion Traveler. If you have not considered the questions you want answered by now, you never will."

Good point, I thought to myself. *OK, Many Tongues, be prepared to answer these questions I have decided upon.* The first being: "What is your true name?"

Many Tongues sighed as though perturbed by my impertinence. "If you don't know the answer to that question by now, then you have not been hearing our many conversations over the past few months. I am The Old Young One. I am the Spirit of Companion Travelers. I am both of the two together and of the one alone. I have carried the name Many Tongues since I was born to my parents as a human, but I do not know why they chose that name. I do not know why I am know as Many Tongues other than because I am able to speak in every language known to humans: English, French, Spanish, Russian, Greek, Germanic, Arabic, Chinese, and Hebrew among many others, as well as every indigenous language known to hundreds of tribes throughout the Earth—even the Aboriginals of the Australian Outback and the Inuit of the Great White North. But of course my parents would not have known of my language ability when I was born. Perhaps my human mother and father were given information through dream or from a spiritual message of which they were unaware. I am sure they believed they had thought of the name of their own harmony. I do not know. You have called me by the names Many Tongues, the Old Young One, and Companion Traveler throughout different stages of our friendship, so why do you ask again?"

"I'm not sure why I asked that," I responded, "It just seemed like a good jumping off point. All right then," I continued, "tell me, how old are you?"

"Again, new Old Young One, you know the answer to that question as well. My human form is seventy-one, but as spirit I am as old as the Earth itself. I came into existence long before any humans roamed the world on their travels from the continent of Africa to where they live today. Depending upon the accuracy of science, I am well over four and a half billion years old. I have lived through every epoch known to humans. I have witnessed the emergence of every race and group of humans. I have beheld the births of the Christian Savior, the Muslim prophet the Hindu gods of the Far East, the Lord of the Israelites, and every other prophet or god that is known to humans.

"I have observed the letting of blood in wars that crippled the nations of Earth. I have labored over the plagues that claimed millions of human lives. I have wept with humans throughout devastation and despair. I have watched the innocent be swallowed by the waters. I have cried with the shaking of the Earth and the explosions of the mountains. I have wailed when the storms and winds took life from the children. And I have walked with the giants of human science, art, politics, philosophy, and theology. I have existed since the beginning and shall be forever."

"In other words, your claim is the same as that of all the gods of human kind—that you are eternal!" I spoke with near incredulity.

"I claim nothing, Mandamin. Be as skeptical as you please. I tell you what I know. You asked a simple question and I responded with a simple answer. I am who I tell you I am." Many Tongues appeared to be growing tired of my simplistic questions and had adopted an air of insolence and irritation with my skepticism.

"I apologize for my disrespect, Many Tongues, but throughout our relationship, you have given me only bits and pieces of your history. I am trying my best to understand fully who and what you are," I offered.

"I understand," Many Tongues replied, but I didn't get the idea that he actually did. "Please continue with your examination of my history, Mandamin."

"An easy question now," I offered. "Are you human or spirit?"

With this question, Many Tongues burst into laughter—an emotion he infrequently displayed. "Indeed," he continued, "Consider my age, Gilbert" (there was the condensation to my Christian name again). "If I were only human, could I possibly be over four billion years old? Not likely. Even Methuselah of the Bible's Old Testament lived only nine hundred years, and that is of great debate among scholars. The only time I become human is when I Join with another mortal during the ritual of bonding, such as with the young boy from the greatly suffering Ojibwa, or most recently when I joined with you. My becoming human is but for a moment in time. When I Join with another I absord the other into my essence, not me into the other, and it becomes spirit with me. When I Joined with you, Mandamin, I did not become human as you would define, but could be seen as human for your convenience. You were joined into me—from human into spirit. All humans with whom I have Joined have become a part of me. Many years ago I began this journey as Many Tongues—a human—but have been transformed into the Old Young One, the Companion Traveler. Until we Joined you saw me and interacted with me as Many Tongues, the human man. After our Joining you have known me as absolute Spirit. I have never become part of another human. They become subsumed by me. I have, and always will be, Old Young One the spirit."

Many Tongues had a swift and seemingly coherent answer for each of my questions although there was something about his quickness with responses that bothered me. I'm not sure what it was, but even though the answers were believable, I just couldn't wrap my mind around them. Since I had escaped Norval's clutches, things were returning to normal—my normal that is whatever that might be—and I was becoming more and more hesitant to rely on Native mysticism and spiritualism as an answer to the concerns about my life. Nevertheless, I continued.

"What about the apartment, Many Tongues?" I asked. "When I went to see you several days ago, without your invitation, it was empty and the landlord of the property told me there had never been an older Indian man living there."

"Mandamin," he continued, "we were never in that physical setting nor ever in an apartment. When I summoned you to come visit, I did not bring you to the address to where you believed you were going." Many Tongues' voice began to fade a bit, like a radio transmission that was fluctuating because of distance or weather.

Still he went on: "When we visited, we did so through Mind Penetration. Much the same way Norval tried unsuccessfully to control you, but he does not have the power as you discovered. I created the appearance of an apartment to make you more comfortable with your surroundings. You would not have accepted our meetings or discussions had you believed they were because of Mind Penetration. It was yet early in our knowledge of one another and you were not ready. The time was not right. I entered your thoughts while you slept and allowed you to penetrate mine. It is a simple procedure for an Old Young One."

"Wait," I interrupted. "What do you mean 'an Old Young One?' You speak as though there are more than just you?"

At that point Many Tongues roared back, "There is also you, Mandamin. I am one, you are another, and there have been others as I explained many days ago and have repeated in our current exchange. Every Old Young One passes throughout its Earthly existence as human so others with whom it comes in contact will not become frightened by that which cannot be explained by science. With the demise of one Old Young One—the human form it maintains—another arises. One in the Same. One Eternal. Soon after the Joining, the older Old Young One fades and the new Old Young One continues with the same memories, the same experiences, and the same Unity of All. Do not parse my words. You are becoming belligerent with your questions and present a demeanor that apparently does not believe my words but suspects me of treachery."

I was shaken. "No, Many Tongues, no. I apologize. I do not mean to sound as though I do not believe you or that I think you are somehow tricking me. Please continue."

"I accept your apology. I realize this is yet so very new, and I expect more from you than you are currently able to provide. In time, you will understand and not present yourself as doubtful or churlish.

"As I indicated, I penetrated your mind and allowed you to penetrate mine without your knowledge. That is not how an Old Young One should conduct himself, but it was necessary. We could not physically meet while you were under Norval's influence, and so I did what was necessary. I apologize for my insolence in assuming that I had your permission to do as I did." At that point Many Tongues chuckled, "Although I really don't need your permission, now do I?"

"No, I guess you don't," I answered. "And you need not apologize since your intentions were honest and honorable. I have trusted you, Many Tongues, from the very first time we met. I didn't understand at that time why I trusted you, but I can see now that it was because of who and what you are. I am honored that from among all the humans you have met in your long life, that you have selected me as your apprentice."

"I did not select you, Mandamin. The universe made the choosing, we have discussed that previously." Many Tongues began fading in and out again, his voice ebbing, but he continued chuckling to himself. Our Penetration seemed to becoming weak. I grew concerned.

"Many Tongues, what's happening? I can barely hear you and your words sound distant."

"Not my words, Gilbert" (there it was again, Gilbert!), "but your Penetration. You are becoming fragile. You are allowing yourself to doubt me and in doing, so you are putting strain on the link we have established through Mind Penetration. You chance losing me altogether."

"No," I shouted. "Do not leave me. I have waited so long for this discussion. I will strengthen my resolve. I do trust you. I do believe you. I do not want you to leave me forever."

"Then continue with your questions," a much stronger and resolute voice continued. Ask what you will, but bring this to an end as soon as possible. There is much work to be done and I cannot labor here for long."

I only had a few more questions to ask although there were still several issues yet unresolved.

I hesitated but finally blurted out another question: "Why on Earth did you befriend Norval Morrisseau? Why a scoundrel like him? He is so beneath the dignity of a Companion Traveler. How can you pretend to be, on the one hand the Old Young One—a spirit billions of years in age—and on the other a friend of a fraud, a cheat, and a drunken, drugged-out loser?"

Many Tongues took a long, deep breath before continuing. I could feel his mind within mine searching for the right words, looking for some manner by which to explain his incomprehensible relationship with Norval. It seemed like hours before he finally began the account of his relationship with Morrisseau although only seconds had passed. At last he thought:

"I do not pretend anything," he roared. "Do not be so impertinent, or I shall end this mind-sharing immediately!" I nearly cowered at his commanding voice, but fortunately, he did not end our mind sharing and continued:

"I did not seek Norval. He found me many years ago when he was young and still clean. He had only then realized the spirituality within himself and was experimenting with the power he believed he possessed. Quite by accident, in his attempt to practice Mind Penetration, his thoughts projected to mine, and he was suddenly a part of my thoughts. We were close in physical proximity which allowed the Penetration to occur and which can be dangerous. An Old Young One must move with care among the people of the Earth. As it was with Norval it is possible, although infrequent, that unintended Mind Penetration can occur. Mind Penetration that is not initiated with purpose can cause damage to the unsuspecting. Norval was my only inaccuracy, and as I am sure you have determined, that misstep came with consequences. Norval and I did not experience a Joining such as have you and I, still the reality that I can penetrate his mind at any time has been a burden I must bear. He cannot penetrate my thoughts. He was able only to do so on that initial experience and quite by mistake. Norval is barren. He is sterile. He is without significant spirit. He is able to provide counsel and dream interpretation because he had been touched by the Thunderbird Spirit early in his life. But he cannot see the future. He cannot prophesize what is to come. He cannot rejoin the living with the dead."

Many Tongues words were becoming nearly inaudible, but he regained his comportment and continued, "Returning to your question, Mandamin: You must understand that Norval has not always been a coarse man given to drink, drugs, and dishonesty. In reality, Norval Morrisseau is a great man. A hero to his people, a champion to his homeland of Canada, and a gift to the Earth's creative world. He is truly a man of many talents whose life-path led him astray, and he ended up where he is today: Lost, alone, lonely, and pitiful. Norval carries a great weight upon his shoulders. He paints images of his people's history and religion and for that he was severely criticized by many of the elders of the Ojibwa, especially when he first began selling his paintings for the white man's money. His images translate the history of the Ojibwa for all humans to view. His brush strokes are those of storyteller and genius. His subject is life. His canvas is the Earth itself. And for those beautiful elements the Elders condemned him, because it had always been spoken that no human other than the Ojibwa should know of their history, their religion, their gods, and their tales. It was spoken that no depiction of their ways should be displayed for other humans to see.

"Initially, he was scoffed at by white critics who regarded themselves as the guardians of true art and considered his paintings childish and simplistic. His family ostracized him for betraying the ways of the Ojibwa, and his friends condemned him as pompous and radical. At that time in his life, he lived only to paint with his heart and his soul.

"Norval is a loving, caring, and giving man. He has always helped those who were in need be it for food, shelter, health, or love. And for that, too, he was rebuked.

"He has supported his family through all these years, through all his tribulations, through all his wickedness and wrongdoing. He has given money to his wife and children. He has provided them with safety and security. Although his critics claim he has abandoned his family—he has not. He has loved and lost, accomplished and transgressed, succeeded and failed. And he has fallen to the bottom of the dark abyss and still has survived.

"When he penetrated my mind with his thoughts at our first meeting, he did not know into what he had tapped. He believed me to be but another shaman, like him, who was a bit more practiced, a bit more accomplished, and quite a bit older. But he did not know that Many Tongues was and is the Old Young One—Gitchi Manitou that is spoken of in Ojibwa mythology. And to this day he does not know who I truly am. He does not know that I am One and Everything. His ignorance is not a fault but one of inexperience and ignorance. I have let him believe what he does because he is Norval Morrisseau: hero, champion, artist, and shaman.

"Falling into debauchery and wickedness is but is not Norval's fault nor flaw. It is his fault because he allowed the purge to happen. It is his flaw because he is human. But, when one carries the weight of his people upon his shoulders, that one does not sense when he is slipping into depravity. Christians believe they carry the weight of the cross upon their shoulders, and they must profess the divinity of Jesus Christ to be saved from eternal punishment. Jews believe their purpose is to carry out what it holds to be the only Covenant between God and their people. Muslims believe that there is no God but Allah and Muhammad, His messenger; they must believe or perish on judgment day. Every religion on Earth professes similar tenets be that religion popular or be it followed by very few.

"Aboriginal people around the world hold beliefs that share great similarity, but their values have been misrepresented by Christians for the purpose of separating those creeds from what has been regarded as 'truth'—the way of Jesus Christ, Son of God.

"Norval was raised Roman Catholic by his grandmother but taught the ways and traditions of the Ojibwa by his grandfather. He became confused at a young age and ultimately rejected the way of Christianity and adopted the path of the

Ojibwa. But he did not truly follow the ways of the Ojibwa either. Unfortunately, for Norval, it was his confusion that led to his demise as an honest practitioner of any pious belief and he found himself falling deeper into secular temptation. He tried to salvage his spiritual void by adopting the practices of shamanism, but he did so poorly and has yet to recover.

"As the man Norval emerged, he began to drink alcohol. He began to indulge in the use of drugs. He began to put reality to his sexual fantasy and took every young man he could entice into becoming his physical partner. Norval could not accept that he was a Two Spirit human—a homosexual. But it is too easy to call Norval a Two Spirit because the term, itself, has many different meanings and is complicated and regarded differently by various tribes of people throughout the Earth. Still, accepting that he was—by his definition—a Two Spirit, he allowed himself to practice the act of loving both man and woman. Unfortunately, Norval remained hidden to himself and manifested his desire for younger men in a manner that is controlling, blasphemous, and pitiful. He used the younger men to satisfy his hunger for sexual fulfillment as well as his yearning for power. He ignored the needs of these young men and satiated only himself. He defiled the very nature of the Two Spirit for it is not a wicked temptation but is a beautiful life-way.

"Eventually, he became little more than a shell of the man he had been when he began his life journey. He devolved into what you know him to be: Lewd, angry, coarse, filthy, greedy, controlling, and humorless. As his money mounted, it did not take long for Norval to follow the easier route to success—fraud. That was when he began signing his name to paintings that his students had rendered. When he enticed you and Wolf and Brian to aid in his deceit it was not the first time he had done so. You three were only the most recent among many of his attempts to deceive. And it did not take long for him to amass tremendous debt to those who sold him the drugs and covered his scam with their connections. Now he is in constant fear that these wicked men will hunt him down and take what is theirs—his money and his life.

"That is all you need to know. Understand that I will always call Norval my friend."

Many Tongues sighed deeply in my mind and fell into silence. I was stunned at what he had revealed but not necessarily surprised. I had suspected for quite some time that Norval was being hounded by drug-lords of some type. I had believed that he was a sham and a fraud. I had accepted that he was little more than a leach who took benefit from those with whom he came into contact. But, I did not know that he had been as generous to his family, to his friends, and to strangers as Many Tongues had explained.

I felt weary. I felt the contact of Mind Penetration beginning to wane. I sensed that we neared the end of our conversation—not only on this night but perhaps forever. But I had one more question to pose before our link broke.

"Why me, Many Tongues—why me?" I asked.

Many Tongues drew a long breath, sighed, and spoke, "I cannot answer that question, Mandamin. As I have told you previously, the universe chose you. It chose both you and me and the others who have joined as Companion Travelers throughout time. I cannot tell you why any of us were chosen. It is one of the great mysteries that no human can answer. You must discover your own life-was as an Old Young One. I cannot give you reason or purpose."

The old spirit fell silent for several minutes, which at first, I thought was him ending our conversation. Then he stirred again and continued, "When I first came to you at the cabin near Beardmore, I came because your spirit had entered my thoughts. Not by your doing, nor by mine, but by something that is greater than either of us and greater than all humans who ever have lived. It is the essence of everything that exists. It is all that is in our world and all that it beyond our planet. Some call it God, others name it the Great Spirit, and still others say only that it is the Universal Mind. I do not know. I cannot pretend to understand the expanse of all that exists in this world and everywhere beyond. I am too insignificant to attempt to label that which is. I cannot call it by name. I only know that it the totality of that which we experience through our physical being as well as our spiritual. After I first met you, my duty was to remain with you and encourage our joining. But, why you…I do not know.

"Long before any humans existed on this world or on worlds beyond the millions of stars that we see at night, there was the greatness of everything that we perceive and all that exists in form and spirit. Eventually that greatness gave rise to us humans. Only then did we try to list, and to name, and to put meaning to all that surrounds us. We tried to understand, but we cannot. We fail miserably. But we trick ourselves into thinking that we comprehend. And with our arrogance in thinking that we can understand the depth of the universe and its entirety of meaning, our world fell into darkness—a darkness created by our ignorance and pride. The existence of the stars and planets and all that subsists between is not for us to define, or to understand. We are but diminutive forms of life that inhabit this world for a brief time, then pass into the universe and rejoin with that from which we came. Perhaps then we might know.

"Until the time that we pass from this world to whatever comes next we must live as best we can. Neither harming or condemning that of which we are a part. We are an insignificant fragment of all that we can see, feel, hear, taste, and smell. We are so irrelevant that it frightens us, so we attempt to make sense out of chaos. We try to put meaning to that which we cannot fathom. We try desperately to explain who we are, from where we came, why we are here, and to where we go when we exit this life. We live, we breathe, we suffer, we die. But when we die, we pass only from this world, not from this universe or from others that exist beyond ours. Ashes to ashes and dust to dust. We are star stuff, Mandamin, we are star stuff.

"I know not why you penetrated my thoughts. I dare not assume nor become haughty with conceit. I am simply Many Tongues, the Old Young One and

Companion Traveler with whom you are now joined. That is how you came to be here, now, with me—you are the new Old Young One."

With his explanation, Many Tongues fell back into silence. I did not speak immediately but echoed his quietude. Then, as a result of his last response to my question, a final desperate sequence of questions spilled from my mouth:

"If we cannot know anything about the spiritual depth of the universe and assuming that we cannot define who we are, what then is our purpose as Old Young Ones? Why have we joined? Why have you existed for millennia? Why have you made it seem so important that I continue as a uniquely spiritual being? What am I supposed to do now that we have Joined?"

I heard a sigh slip from his lips, and Many Tongues seemed to wilt with my question. Even though I could only hear him and not see him, I could picture my friend slumped in his recliner saddened and defeated.

"I discussed our—your—purpose on the first night we began the Joining many weeks ago," he whispered. "I will not repeat myself regarding something you should have ingested and kept. I will only remind you that you and I, as Companion Travelers, are but two in a long line of spirits that have gone before us and more that will continue after we are gone. I am the Old Young One, and now you are the Old Young One. You will know when another spirit emerges and must Join with you as the new Old Young One. All that we have discussed, all that has passed between us in spirit and in mind is with you still. You must think upon all that we have thought throughout these past weeks. You will know the answer to your questions when you remember. You will answer it for yourself. I need not respond for you.

"Soon I shall pass, Gilbert," Many Tongues whispered. "I will go to where my heart longs—into the spirit world but not unlike the land upon which I played as a child. When I pass, Mandamin, you must rise like the Phoenix from ancient legend and live.

"Mandamin," he mused, "do not take lightly your burden. Truly it is great and demands constant attention. The honor of becoming the new Old Young One is not one to dismiss with indifference. There are great accomplishments yet to be done and many lives yet to embrace. Your journey will be long and lonely. But as you travel the path that awaits you, you will find refuge among other members of the tribe. Do not pass them by but enfold them and walk with them."

His simple words continued: "We have discussed whether you selected me or I selected you to enter into the Joining but I fear that I have not been honest with you for concern that I might frighten you away from your destiny. Hear me now: It was neither of us that arranged our meeting and our Joining. As I have spoken, it was the universe! That which came before us and that which will endure beyond us. It is not I who choose you. It was not you who found me. We walked separate paths until we stumbled upon one another without plan by either of us. Do not betray that which has come to you. Do not risk us fading into oblivion.

"As I have told you many times I have been called Many Tongues, The Old Young One, and a thousand others names throughout time and history. But I am only one of many who came before me. A hundred and more Travelers preceded me and many will follow me, and you. It is the way of the universe. It is the way of life. Do not cower, do not fear. Accept who you are. Welcome your purpose."

And finally Many Tongues prophesized an ominous warning with words that made me shiver and tremble like a child alone in the dark. "Only one Companion Traveler did not Join with its progeny; he was rejected by the one who would become the new Old Young One. That one lonely Companion Traveler was thus doomed to wander the universe until its human body decayed and its spirit slowly, painfully, pitifully faded and dispersed into nothing. Only by the will of the universe was another selected to take the place of the lost Companion. But the years that passed after the Companion Traveler had been rejected were grim and wearisome. Do not let your hesitation condemn either of us to the shadows. Do not let your reluctance doom time and space."

With those final words, Many Tongues slipped into complete silence despite my attempt to call him back. Within minutes, I too began to tire and was suddenly, unexpectedly in a deep sleep.

G

✦✦✦✦✦✦✦✦✦✦✦✦

Journal Entry: May 8, 1979

I slept for an entire day. My Mind Sharing with Many Tongues evidently took more out of me than I expected that it would. I had never been as weary as I had been after the Sharing of two nights ago. And I awoke with the same gnawing feeling that our most recent Mind Sharing would be the last I ever shared with Many Tongues. But I cannot explain why I had that uncomfortable feeling. It was just an impression and if I have learned anything over the past several months, it is not to trust my feelings.

Now that my last task is complete—meeting with Many Tongues—I am ready to leave this part of Canada and make my way back home if, indeed, Toronto is my home! I have no desire to tarry here any longer. I will think upon our Mind Sharing, as Many Tongues commanded, but not now, not at this moment. Later will be soon enough. 'When the time is right.' I have accomplished that which I set out to do when I first hatched my plan to escape Norval and my destination is clear: Toronto and Joanne. I'm sure she will be surprised when she hears a knock upon her door, opens it and finds a weary, thinner, gruffer, but worldlier Gilbert on her stoop.

G

****

JOURNAL ENTRY: MAY 8, 1979 (a few minutes later)

I imagine that because I am so wrapped up in getting completely away from Norval and getting back to the civilization of Toronto, that I forgot to mention in my last entry: Norval Morrisseau is still missing!

So be it. I could care less.

G

****

JOURNAL ENTRY: MAY 10, 1979

I returned to Joanne's late yesterday, much to her surprise and joy. She gave me a long once over, made comment on now much I had physically changed, did not mention my emotional and spiritual changes (which obviously she could not see) and prepared a regular feast—at least a feast compared to what I had become accustomed to in the company of Norval Morrisseau.

We dined on my favorite dinner—beef roast with red potatoes, carrots, and onions stewing in the meat's juice, au jus gravy, and a fine red wine. I ate until I thought I would burst. We spent the rest of the evening with me regaling her with the stories and tales of my adventure with the great Ojibwa-Canadian artist. For some reason, I purposefully left out the sexual aspects of my experience. In the past, Joanne and I giggled like school children when I entertained her with the whory details of my various sexual conquests. I don't know if I was ashamed, disgusted, embarrassed, or had simply matured but the details of my experiences with Norval seemed best kept silent.

Joanne listened intently, then at the end of my blabbering added that an exhibition of Norval's most recent paintings was currently on display at a local gallery. Did I want to go, she asked? "No," I answered without hesitation. Although I did not say as much to her, I had seen enough of Norval's paintings over the past few months to last the rest of my life and had no desire to see any more, let alone decipher whether or not individual paintings were actually his or forgeries. So, we continued catching up with one another's lives and drinking wine until early the next morning.

Now here I am writing in this tattered journal that has recorded history: Not only my own history of self-discovery but also a brief snippet of Norval's history. I'm sure that no one—at any time in the near or distant future will be the least bit interested or amused by my incoherent ramblings. And yet they serve me well and, honestly, I could care less if anyone ever reads these sad pitiful entries. Curiously I even saved copies of the letters I sent to Joanne during my sojourn. I used old-fashioned carbon paper to copy the letters I as wrote them. Why I copied the letters I do not know. I had no intention of sharing them with anyone; perhaps I did so simply for my own pleasure and a history of my trip to where ever and back.

But enough. I grow weary of writing.

✴✴✴✴✴✴✴✴✴✴✴✴

JOURNAL ENTRY: MAY 24, 1979

I have been at Joanne's for nearly two weeks now, and it is time I made decisions about my life. Shall I stay in Toronto and re-engage in the art scene? Shall I search out a job and get a place of my own? With my experience as Norval Morrisseau's secretary and travelling companion and my past history with Toronto's galleries, my skills would be in great demand. Should I simply pick up where I had left off prior to taking to the road with Norval?

None of the options appealed to me or to my better sense of what would be best for my future.

I laid awake this morning feeling the sun creep in through my eastward facing window and wallowed in its warmth and protection. I felt much like the child I was twenty years ago when I would awaken in my bed back home hoping that the new day would bring happiness and peace in my life.

How could I be happy or expect peace in my life when each day offers little more than the same old, same old? How could I face each new day with the knowledge that Norval Morrisseau had been a part of my life? How could I walk the streets of Toronto searching for a job with what has become an albatross around my neck—the art world itself! I have grown tired of art, artists, gallery owners, and critics. I think that when I do find a place of my own—where ever that might be—I will have bare walls: no paintings by any one shall adorn my home.

So, as I laid in my bed on that warm spring day in May of 1979, I made my decision.

I can no longer remain in Toronto. It harbors too many unpleasant memories of my former life as little more than a whore. It reminds me too much of everything I now hate about the art world. It allows me nothing more than ugly thoughts and disagreeable memories. I can no longer be fulfilled here.

Joanne has moved on with her life and although she had been over-joyed at seeing me in one piece, I cannot become a burden. She has generously told me I can stay at her place as long as I need, but I cannot engage that offer. She has moved beyond me, and we can't begin to recapture the excitement and intimate friendship we once shared.

I have no wish to find a job in an art gallery.

I have no desire to reconnect with my living family members.

I have absolutely no longing to return to anywhere in central Canada.

In fact, I have no want to relocate to any place in Canada—I have already seen as much as I care to see of my beautiful homeland.

And so, that leaves me with few options other than the one I have been mulling over in my mind since long before I hooked up with Norval Morrisseau and began a journey that took me to the depths of anguish and the heights of elation:

Get the hell out of Canada.

G

PART SIX

The Present

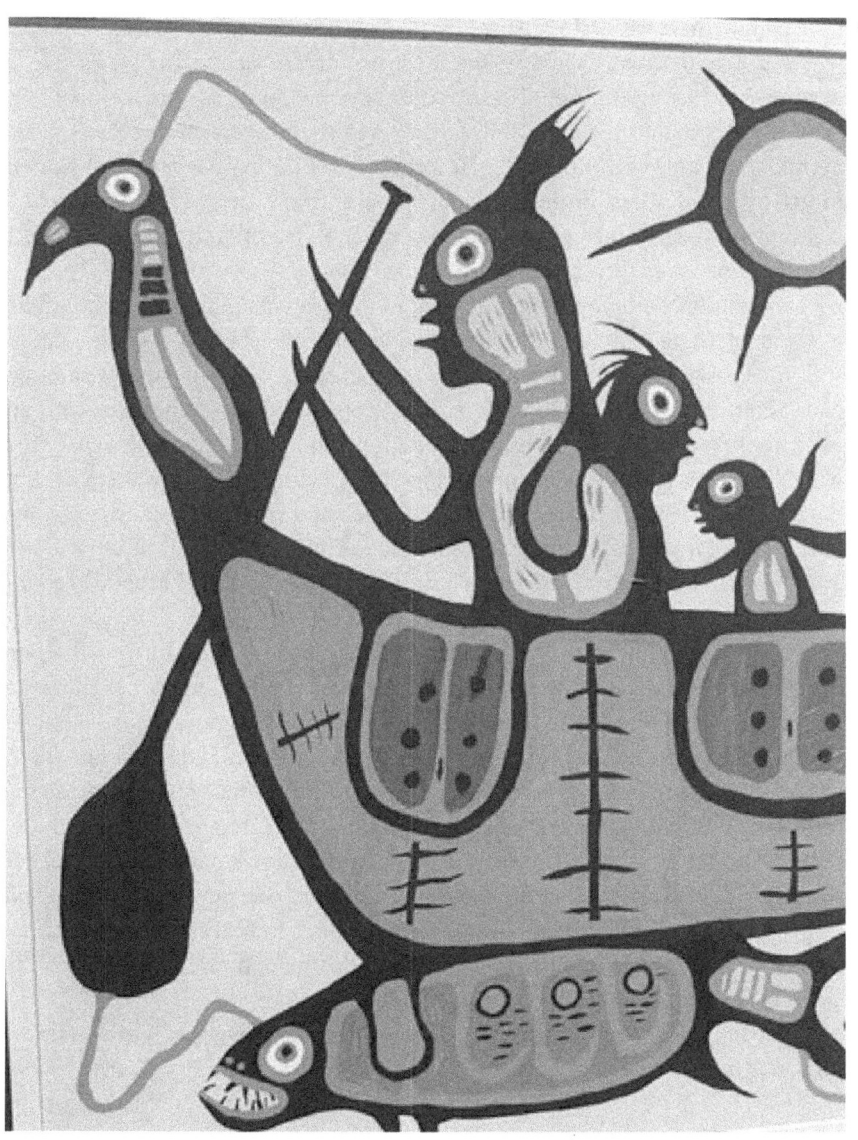

My god, has it really been twenty-eight years since I made an entry in this old tattered journal. I haven't even read through it for over twenty of those years, but I thought this entry was appropriate—even necessary to bring an end to my four-month life on the road with Norval Morrisseau.

First, just for clarification, I have been living outside San Diego in southern California for almost twenty-seven years now. After realizing that there was nothing keeping me in Canada, I wanted to move to a warmer climate where I didn't have to deal with cold weather and snow from October through mid-May. I don't recall what made me choose San Diego in particular, but I'm sure it had to do with an agreeable climate, beautiful blue skies, being on the coast, and hearing that there was a somewhat vibrant gay community in the area.

I am now married to Jeffery, the most wonderful man in the world. He is not only my best friend but also my confidant, my lover, and my companion. We've been together for over twelve years, and they have been the most wonderful, productive years of my life. He knows about my experiences with Norval Morrisseau and about my early history of whoring around in an attempt to legitimize myself—and he understands and accepts without condemnation. I couldn't have asked for a better more loving husband.

I am gainfully employed in the financial investments industry and continue to avoid anything to do with the art world as much as possible. My eagle tattoo still shines brightly on my upper thigh and often reminds me of the first painting Norval did of me—the beautifully colored depiction of a young man with an enormous erection, arms outstretched, reaching for the sun. As much as my time with Norval has become a distant memory, it is still unpleasant to remember, but the eagle tattoo makes me recall who I was then and why I allowed myself to be pulled into Norval's tapestry of manipulation. Thus, I am proud to wear it and even prouder to show it to anyone who cares to look although I seldom recount the story that surrounds the etching.

I do visit with my brother and sisters from time to time. All three still reside in Canada. We have become closer as we have grown older. I suppose such is true with any siblings who weren't necessarily close as children but who develop patience, understanding, and wisdom as they age. My mother and father have both passed. Father a number of years ago from a particularly nasty flu that made the rounds, and mother just a few years ago. Unlike father's, mother's was not unexpected. Of course, mother had been a heavy drinker and smoker all her life, but she didn't die of cancer or an alcohol related disease. She developed ALS—Lou Gehrig's Disease—in her early 70s and passed after four years of deteriorating health. I'm sure the drinking and smoking didn't help; both habits most likely aided in the quick regression of her well-being.

But back to my reason for writing this journal entry twenty-eight years after I escaped both Norval and Canada.

As is my regular morning custom, I awoke this morning with great anticipation for the day, poured a cup of coffee, and snatched a pastry that Jeffry had purchased the prior evening (he surely knows the path to my heart—right through my sweets-demanding stomach). I picked up a copy of the New York Times and began scanning as I sipped and snacked.

I read through the national and world events section, then casually opened the Culture and Arts section. That is where I saw it, and the reason for reopening this journal and that painful chapter of my life.

I read with awe and interest but not so much shock. The headline grabbed me immediately, and I was forced to read the entire obituary:

WORLD FAMOUS ARTIST DEAD AT 75

By Randy Kennedy

December 8, 2007

Norval Morrisseau, also known as Copper Thunderbird, one of Canada's most celebrated painters and an important influence in the development of North American indigenous art, died Tuesday in Toronto. He was thought to be 75, though his birth year has been listed as both 1931 and 1932.

The cause was complications of Parkinson's disease, said the Assembly of First Nations, which represents Canadian Native tribes.

Mr. Morrisseau, an Ojibwa (also called Anishnaabe or Chippewa) shaman, was one of the first Native painters to adopt modernist styles to convey traditional aboriginal imagery and to have a crossover career in contemporary art. His style, which became known as Woodland or Legend painting, evoked ancient etchings from birch-bark scrolls and often used X-ray-like motifs: skeletal elements and internal organs visible within the forms of animals and people, and black spirit lines emanating from them.

"Saturated with startling, often contrasting colors, such paintings appear to vibrate under the viewer's gaze," said the National Gallery of Canada, which organized a retrospective of Mr. Morrisseau's work in 2006, the first solo show for a Native artist in the institution's history. It is now on view in Lower Manhattan, New York, through January 20 at the George Gustav Heye Center, part of the Smithsonian's National Museum of the American Indian.

Of a 2001 New York show at the Drawing Center of Mr. Morrisseau's drawings, made on sheets of paper towels while he was in jail in Canada in the late 1960s, Holland Cotter of The New York Times wrote: "The results aren't ingratiating or beautiful. Like visionary work in many cultures, they're aggressive, sometimes violent, as much about fearfulness as about transcendence."

Born Jean-Baptiste Norman Henry Morrisseau in northern Ontario, he was the eldest son in a family of seven and was raised, according to tradition, by his maternal grandparents. His grandmother was Catholic, and his grandfather, whom he described as his most important influence, was a shaman. Their discordant views formed the background for much of his early life and his development as a self-taught artist working between two worlds.

He was believed to have been given his Native name in his teens when he became seriously ill. He said his life was saved by a medicine woman who renamed him, calling him Copper Thunderbird; a thunderbird is a powerful symbol in Ojibwa folklore.

Mr. Morrisseau, who dropped out of school at a young age and lived much of his life in poverty even after becoming established, was known as a charismatic, often unpredictable figure in the art world. He frustrated dealers, sometimes calculating his paintings' worth not by their quality but by the square inch ($3.55 at one point, according to a gallery owner). He battled alcoholism his whole life, and at a low ebb in the 1980s, living on Vancouver's streets, was known to trade his work for liquor money.

But after the tremendous success of his first exhibition in Toronto in 1962, he was also often prolific and showed his work around the world. Marc Chagall, who met him in Paris when both artists were having exhibitions there, compared him to Picasso.

He is survived by numerous children and grandchildren. In his later years, as accolades piled up, his life became more orderly, and he continued to paint until 2002, when Parkinson's left him unable to do so. In 2005 he was elected to the Royal Society of Canada. He was also awarded honorary doctorates from McGill and McMaster universities and received the highest honor awarded by the Assembly of First Nations, the eagle feather.

"Why am I alive?" he said in a 1991 interview with The Toronto Star. "To heal you guys who're more screwed up than I am. How can I heal you? With color. These are the colors you dreamt about one night."

I put the article down and immediately became flooded with memories of my time with Norval. I was overcome with the accolades that punctuated the obituary. I had not heard anything about Norval since our last encounter in Winnipeg, my escape, and his subsequent disappearance. How long he had been missing, I will never know. Had he been able to escape the clutches of the drug-lords that hounded him, I will never know. Were the drug lords even behind his vanishing? Again, I will never know. Perhaps his disappearance was just another one of Norval's stunts to get attention. Or, maybe he was off attending to family as Many Tongues had explained during our last Mind Sharing many years ago. Had he been able to put down the bottle and the drugs? Evidently he had become sober, at least according to the obituary—but not until later in his life.

So many mysteries still surround Norval Morrisseau, but he has been acclaimed by the art-world, the National Museum of the American Indians, and the government of Canada as an artistic genius (which he was) and a national and Indian hero (which in my estimation is debatable). I read nothing about the art fraud, his lechery, his lawlessness, or his vile temper and despicable demeanor. But, of course, obituaries generally present only the best of one's life and ignore the more unpleasant aspects. Still, I felt a pang of regret that only I, those closely associated with Norval, and the few other young men he had hired as a traveling companion and secretary knew the truth. He was a cad! Or was that simply my interpretation of the truth?

Certainly, I was saddened by the fact that he had become incapacitated with Parkinson's disease, and although I have few pleasant memories of the man, I would wish no ill upon anyone—not even Norval. I am glad that he was able to put his affairs in order later in his life and accept the honors that were bestowed upon him. I am pleased that at long last the elders of his tribe had forgiven him for depicting Ojibwa legends for the entire world to see. Despite his many shortcomings, Norval Morrisseau was truly a genius. His art will live forever, and I am thankful that my role in his life—though insignificant—might have helped direct him towards world recognition.

But now the man is dead. Too early at only 75, but too late for the dozens of people he had negatively impacted during his turbulent time of drugs, alcohol, debauchery, and chaos.

And then my mind drifted back to Many Tongues, The Old Young One and the spirit that claimed to be my Companion Traveller.

As I suspected on our last night of Mind Sharing, I never had contact with Many Tongues again. He had warned me that night, that leaving for Toronto and abandoning him and our spiritual connection would be the end of our relationship and my experience as the new Old Young One and Companion Traveler. But that night I was confused, frightened, and lost. I did not fully understand his warning at the time. Obviously, I did not head his caution.

Given that I had been raised a Roman Catholic but had rejected the mythological teachings of Christianity, I was quick to dismiss Many Tongues' conversations and philosophical ramblings as soon as I had returned to Toronto way back then. It was easy to set aside our connection because Toronto re-engulfed me in a world from which I had wanted to escape, just as much as I had wanted to free myself from Norval's clutches. I do remember Many Tongues referring to the Old Young Ones as the 'One' and the 'Eternal.' Although, I didn't give it much thought at the time, in retrospect, his claim is not unlike the same spoken by the followers of God, Allah, Jehovah, or any one of the hundreds of other gods worshiped throughout the world. Why should I have accepted Many Tongues, or any other with whom he had joined, as the One and the Eternal when I summarily dismiss the Christian God with whom I grew up? Thus, I figuratively (and literally, I suppose) figuratively divorced myself from Many Tongues and made no attempt to contact him ever again.

Even now I can only surmise that I made the right decision. After all, my life is good. It is beautiful. And it is filled with love. But, sometimes, late at night when I am alone with just myself and my deepest darkest thoughts, I wonder—what if?

What would have happened if I hadn't left Canada but had remained with Many Tongues and his ancient mysticism and spiritual way? What would have taken place had I returned with him and acquiesced to being the new Old Young One? What would have become of me had I endured? Would Many Tongues have eventually passed into nothingness? He warned me that his time was short. Would I have assumed his power and strength? He insisted that I would. Would I now be the Old Young One who carries the weight of the world on his shoulders—in his mind? Would I have eventually learned what my place was in this universe? Would I have accepted my responsibilities as an Old Young One?

No, I reject all explanations to my questions. Many Tongues was merely a manifestation of my desire for order and logic in my life. He was nothing more than a substitute for the God of Christianity that I had rejected. He was, in truth, a non-existent entity. He never did, he never had, and he never will be real. He is not the One and the Eternal any more than is God, Allah, Jehovah, or any other god-creature created by humankind. I was taught that God created us in His image, but I believe the reverse to be more accurate: We humans created God in our image!

But as I reject the idea of Many Tongues being anything more than what he was on this earthly plane—a man, not a spirit—I can't help but remember his final counsel about denying what he considered my responsibility of becoming the new Old Young One. I can almost hear his commanding voice though now it is nearly three decades later:

"Only one Companion Traveler did not Join with its progeny; he was rejected by the one who would become the new Old Young One and was doomed to wander the universe until its spirit slowly, painfully, pitifully faded and dispersed into nothing. Only by the will of the universe was another selected to take the lost Companion's place. But the years that passed after the Companion Traveler had been rejected

were grim and wearisome. Do not let your hesitation condemn either of us to the shadows. Do not let your reluctance doom time and space."

I wrote earlier in this entry that my life has been good. Bountiful. Happy. But I wonder—has it truly been as I protest? I am employed in a career that has been financially beneficial. I am loved—or at least accepted—by a dear husband and friend. I have enjoyed the time that has passed since I left Canada for good. I have many friends. I am successful. I am…

…or am I?

I suppose if I were to be brutally honest, I would be forced to report that life could have been better. My career choice could have been more in the direction of doing for others more than just for myself. I have grown weary of investing other people's money. I have grown tired of the monotony of repetition and shallow relationships. I could have helped those who suffer more than I do by focusing on more than simply amassing riches for myself. I probably could have loved more deeply and with more passion than simply settling for a dutiful husband, a fancy house, a new car every few years, and that quintessential white picket fence that surrounds my yard. I have enjoyed the time that has passed since I left Canada, but I sense that life might have been more challenging, more bountiful, more satisfying had I accepted the calling from my long-ago Companion Traveler.

And as I consider what is and what could have been I begin to slip back into the indecision and depression that haunted my youth and young adulthood. I waffle. I wilt. I seethe with distress.

I have to admit that every time I think of the man Many Tongues or whisper his name to myself I suffer in quiet desperation. If only…

…if only.

But now it is over. Norval Morrisseau is gone. I'm sure that his brother Wolf has passed (given his age and tendency to drink and do drugs). Brian is probably sill alive and living a life of desperation and loneliness. And Many Tongues has drifted away into the distant past of childish lore.

And yet, sometimes, though I am hesitant to admit this, when I hear the wind blowing gently through the trees on a calm and warm summer night, I can almost hear a faint voice calling…

"Mandamin, I am here."

Epilogue

THE LIGHT OF THE MOON floods a lonely lake in northern Canada. A heavy mist encourages the heat, strangling a rain forest deep in Brazil. A blistering simoom smothers the shifting dunes of the African Sahara. Fear threatens, then attacks the desperate streets of Los Angeles. London suffocates beneath a smothering cloud of human ambivalence. A morning fog quiets a sleepy hollow in the Smokey Mountains. Swelling tides assault the banks of the raging Yellow River in central China. A saltwater crocodile pulls an unsuspecting wallaby to its death in Australia. Everywhere, lonely men and women and children weep and cry and wail. Evening and morning have exchanged their countenance and pass into day and night as they have for eons, and as they should for millennia yet to come; but, they will not. With each passage of twenty-four hours hope dims for continuity and continuance. All around the forsaken planet humans endure life and death, without remembering what has come from the past nor considering what is destined for the future. The unsuspecting are like children alone in the wilderness: Isolated and threatened by that which they cannot, nor dare not, know.

As each moment passes and as the universe pauses, a single ghostly figure limps haltingly along a path that leads into nowhere. It tries to sing but can only moan. It attempts to laugh but can only weep. It longs to join but persists desperately alone. It can no longer contain the winds. It can no longer halt the rains. The cold, the snow, the heat, and the waters change, alter what had been for thousands of years, and swallow the land that gave life and home and charity to people who were born, who lived, and who passed. Science cannot impede change. The physical world shifts. The human world will soon come to a close. Only time and space occupy dream. All is empty. All is desolate. All is at an end.

The shadowy figure can do nothing to avert what is to be. It is saddened by the reality that portends death and destruction. But it is powerless, helpless, barren.

Many Tongues gathers himself as he has for tens of thousands years and wanders into the distance. Slowly, as he fades from the dark, his whisper disperses into the void. His human temple wearies and dissolves.

The Old Young One came into this world—this universe—as a young boy who grew as would any. Who lived as have few. And who will perish as only he must. He evolved from man into spirit and now passes unnoticed into forever. His destiny has not been met. His reason is incomplete. His purpose is unfulfilled. His adventure has come to its end.

But as he fades his voice whispers with one last attempt at rapture: "Mandamin, I await."

About the Author

John Arthur Maddux is an Associate Professor Emeritus at the University of Cincinnati. Professor Maddux is a life-long social activist and has been a leader in the GLBTQ civil rights movement since the 1980s, as well as participating in anti-war protests, and African American, Native American, and women's equality movements. Professor Maddux has been arrested multiple times for civil disobedience—all in the name of social justice and human equality.

Professor Maddux's publications include one volume of poetry, a collection of essays, a Star Trek trivia book, and numerous articles for scholarly and popular publication.

Dr. Maddux is single and lives in southwestern Ohio with his dog Jacques. He is an avid coin collector, a camping enthusiast, and thrives on Cincinnati Reds baseball and University of Cincinnati Bearcat sports.